MURDER AT SPIRIT FALLS

MURDER AT SPIRIT FALLS

A No Ordinary Women Mystery

to Susan

by
Barbara Deese
and
Dorothy Olson

Enjoy!
Barbara Deese
Dorothy Olson

North Star Press of St. Cloud, Inc.
St. Cloud, Minnesota

Dedication

To the many women in our lives who are anything but ordinary. . .
. . .and in memory of Molly, a dog of boundless energy and curiosity.

ISBN: 978-0-87839-614-6

Copyright © 2012 Barbara Deese and Dorothy Olson

cover art by Schwartzrock Graphic Arts
author photo by Karen Beltz

First Edition, September 2012

Printed in the United States of America

Published by
North Star Press of St. Cloud, Inc.
P.O. Box 451
St. Cloud, Minnesota 56302

www.northstarpress.com

ACKNOWLEDGEMENTS

Heartfelt thanks to our book club friends who were with us on that dark and stormy night when the idea for this novel was hatched: Pat Almsted, Jane Anderson, Mary Ellen Hennen, Mary Pat Ladner, Kay Livingston, Mary Murphy, Mary Ross, Linnea Stromberg-Wise, and Laura Utley. You have been a source of inspiration and support.

Many thanks to our husbands, Bob and Dick, for putting up with the hours and weeks and years that went into this book.

Thanks also to Carolyn Pittman, Andrea Deese, Daisy Merritt, and Diana Lukich, who never stopped believing in us.

We're most grateful to Neil Ross, who immediately saw the possibilities of this mystery series and shared his wealth of knowledge about the book world.

And to Wally Roers, Karen Beltz, and Sherry Janes, your critiques were always kind and always helpful.

To Corinne and Seal at North Star Press: thank you for taking a chance on us in a tough publishing market and making the whole process of publication as painless as possible.

To all the rest of you who encouraged us, inspired us and shared in our enthusiasm.

PROLOGUE

Perhaps we had tempted fate by calling ourselves *No Ordinary Women*, as if the five of us were a fleet of Superwomen, able to leap tall buildings in a single bound.

Arriving at the cabin, our expectations were simple: camaraderie, laughter and good food—requirements for any slumber party—and because of our love of books, we knew we were in for many lively discussions about what we'd been reading.

The almost century-old hunting lodge sat on 150 acres of lush Wisconsin woodland, half a mile in from a gravel road, and remote enough for us to shed the restraints of city living, hike in the woods, take moonlight walks and ditch our bathing suits to sit under the waterfall.

For our last three retreats we'd chosen a thematic book—*A Walk in the Woods*, *Woodswoman*, and *In the Lake of the Woods*. This year Foxy tried to sneak in a grisly murder mystery, Appalachian-style, but we vetoed it in favor of Thoreau's *Walden* and declared a yearlong moratorium on mysteries. That's what gave it such irony, because by Monday morning we had a pretty good inkling we were up to our bifocals in a mystery. For real.

Forty-two wooden steps up from the creek near Spirit Falls, the Bentley cabin stood in the idyllic vacation setting of tall swaying white pines and tamarcks. A few tendrils of smoke curled from the top of the chimney to join with the smoky plumes escaping from between the chimney stones.

Inside the cabin, eyes streaming, Robin Bentley dashed about the spacious room throwing open the windows and waving her hands to help evacuate the smoke. Twice, she halted and bent at the waist, bracing herself with splayed hands on thighs to cough convulsively. Catherine Running Wolf knelt in the relatively smoke-free zone near the floor, trying to mop up the dirty mix of ashes, water and foam from the fire extinguisher with a beach towel.

Soon, the breeze wafted through the house, starting to clear the air. Robin gulped in the fresh air and wiped her eyes on her sleeve before offering her friend a hand. Catherine's knees made audible popping sounds as she eased herself off the floor. She rubbed the aching joints, grimacing.

"Oh, Cate," Robin moaned, "How could I have forgotten to fix the crack in the chimney?"

Catherine grabbed the poker from the stand that held the fireplace tools and began separating the smoldering logs in the fireplace.

Robin coughed and flapped her hands at the airborne ashes. "It was the first thing on my list—the list I made the last time we were here and . . . left at home." Creases bracketing her large blue-green eyes and full mouth gave her a look of suppressed merriment.

"How could you have known it would start a fire?"

"Oh, I knew, all right. I had to stuff that old towel up into the flue before we left last time so bats didn't come in through the cracks in the chimney. Why do you think it was on the list?" Her eyes traced the black streak where flames had licked out of the chink in the mortar to burn the adornment over the stone mantel. She bit her lower lip.

"It's not fair," Catherine said, replacing the fireplace screen. "Everyone forgets things, but now that we're fifty, they start blaming it on our age and our hormones."

"*Lack* of hormones, you mean."

Cate snorted.

Robin Bentley and Catherine Running Wolf surveyed the spacious living room of the Bentley's cabin. This room had been the center of the original lodge, built in the early 1900s exclusively of peeled-pine. During the Truman administration, someone had cobbled together a screened porch and a patio. Thirty years later, the owner shored up the sagging porch, expanded the kitchen and added a sleeping porch, indoor bathrooms—a huge benefit in mosquito season—and a new roof. The furniture, gleaned over the years by various cabin owners, had been a motley assortment of unmatched discards until Robin had painted wicker and wood the same buff color and sewed slipcovers with stripes of burgundy, moss green, and buttery yellow. Gone were the old hunting-motif curtains that had reeked of tobacco smoke and the mustiness of disuse. When Robin had grabbed hold of them to pull them down, they had disintegrated in her hands.

Over a century of heat and smoke had darkened the pine around the massive fieldstone fireplace, now frosted with fire extinguisher foam, over which hung a huge, dusty moose head, glaring down at them balefully with an undignified puff of foam on its nose. The stench of its singed hairs still hung in the air.

Looking up at this relic of the cabin's past, Robin sighed. "Brad's going to think I burned it on purpose."

"That's a possibility."

"I've made it pretty clear how I feel about hanging dead animal parts on my walls."

"I did my part." Though Cate had given her best arguments to Robin's husband, even put him on the mailing list for PETA, the decades-old hunting trophies remained.

Cate and Robin gazed up at the dust- and soot-covered glass eyes.

"Look at that expression." Catherine said. "What do you suppose Malcolm would say if he could talk?" She had named the dead moose after the erstwhile University of Minnesota president, Malcolm Moos.

"I think it's a *she*, and *she* would be asking, 'Is it hot in here, or is it just me?'" Robin wiped the back of her hand across her forehead.

Catherine burst into laughter. "You too?"

In answer, Robin pulled off her sweaty baseball cap the color of bubble gum, revealing graying blond hair cut pixie-style. Her usually pale complexion was flushed and her mascara, the only makeup she wore, was smudged. "I couldn't tell if I was having a hot flash or had caught on fire!"

They laughed about that until the reality of the cleanup they faced sobered them.

Catherine slid her turquoise amulet back and forth on its chain as she often did while she thought. Though it represented only a fraction of her heritage, she had the long thin nose, high cheekbones and dark complexion of her Cherokee ancestors. "Where do you keep your scissors?"

A grin crinkled Robin's eyes as she followed her friend's upward gaze. In their thirty-one-year friendship, Cate and Robin often communicated with minimal verbiage, especially when they were getting into mischief. Going to the oversized pine cupboard in the corner of the living room, Robin pulled open a drawer, withdrew a hefty pair of sewing shears, and handed them to Cate.

Dragging a sturdy oak chair to the fireplace, Catherine stood on it and carefully snipped off the charred ends of the moose's beard. A rain of hair fell to the hearth. Finally satisfied, she hopped down.

"Oh, that's really bright, Cate—jumping with scissors. Didn't your mother ever tell you not to—"

"Run, yes," Catherine interrupted, "but she never said a word about jumping."

Robin just shook her head. Looking at her watch, she sighed. "It's almost one o'clock. I suppose we should talk to George before the others get here."

"Certainly before we build another fire."

With the hems of their jeans tucked into their socks to keep wood ticks from latching onto their flesh, they started down the long driveway on foot toward the home of George Wellman, the local handyman, who lived at the edge of the Bentley property. Robin walked faster than Cate, whose stride, though long, could best be described as ambling.

"As I remember, it was warmer last year, and not nearly so wet," Catherine said. "What a difference a year makes."

"For me, that weekend's just a blur," Robin said, thinking about the last time the No Ordinary Women book club had stayed at Spirit Falls. Only ten days later she'd had her surgery. She felt Catherine's eyes on her and knew her friend was gauging how chemotherapy had aged her.

Catherine's floppy straw hat snagged on an overhanging branch and she stopped to retrieve it. "Wait up."

Robin waited.

Cate caught up to her and said, "I like your hair short. It's easier, isn't it—short like that?"

"Easier, yes." Robin eyed Cate's thick dark hair with envy. "You know, even though I'm adjusting to everything else, I just don't recognize me with this hair. I catch my reflection in a mirror and think, 'Who's that hedgehog?'"

She chuckled. "But hedgehogs are adorable!" After walking several yards, Catherine said, "I don't know if I should be saying this, but I've been getting strange vibes ever since I turned off the paved road yesterday. It's just—" She spoke haltingly. "Well, when I—"

Robin grinned. "Cate, you have to finish your—"

"—sentences, I know."

Although the teasing was both familiar and affectionate, Catherine frowned and hugged herself tightly. "I just wish you weren't all by yourself so much."

Robin did her best to appear unconcerned, but she knew from experience that it would be unwise to disregard Catherine's premonitions. If it hadn't been for Cate's dream, she would never have demanded a CT scan.

Glancing over her shoulder, Catherine said, "I know I've said it before, but I still wish you'd take one of the dogs from the shelter. At least you wouldn't be alone so much, and it would give you some measure of protection."

"You know how Brad feels about more pets." It was easier to blame her husband than to say no to her old friend. This wasn't the first time Catherine had tried to talk her into a canine companion. Or feline or avian or porcine. *So far, she hasn't suggested I adopt a Holstein or a wild mustang*, Robin thought, though it was probably just a matter of time. In Catherine's years of volunteering at the local no-kill shelter, she had given new meaning to the term *matchmaker*.

Robin stopped suddenly and pointed to a dark amorphous shape in a red pine tree. "See the porcupine? I shot him just before you came yesterday."

Catherine blinked hard before slapping herself on the forehead. "No matter how many times I hear that phrase, I get this image of you aiming a shotgun instead of your Nikon."

On either side of them, the pines gave way to oaks and maples. They stepped off the main path and soon came to a little clearing.

Catherine smiled broadly. "It's a little slice of heaven, isn't it? You'd never know we're anywhere near civilization. All I hear is the breeze blowing and birds chirping." She cocked her head to one side. "I even have to listen hard to hear the waterfall."

Robin nodded. They crossed the clearing, and the brush closed in again. "You start listening differently after you're here awhile. What I notice is when a sound doesn't seem to belong to this place."

Barely visible through the trees stood George's one-bedroom trailer, propped up on blocks. Evidence of his pastime, collecting roadside treasures, lay about everywhere. Within view under the deck, black garbage bags spilled their contents of cans and bottles that George would eventually turn in for a refund. An assortment of hubcaps and deer antlers leaned against the uprights of the cedar deck's railing, as well as several unrelated sneakers, a Frisbee, plastic Happy Meal toys and a yellow foam Cheesehead. Robin's eyes drifted to the lawn chair, faded to a sickly green by age. Beneath it in the grass sat a naked Barbie doll, legs splayed.

"Hello there, Mrs. B." George's greeting preceded him out the door. Cleaning his glasses on his shirttail, he broke into a dimpled grin and stepped off the deck. "A couple minutes earlier and you would've caught me in the shower."

Catherine tried to push the image out of her mind.

George Wellman was about Robin's height, just short of five-foot-five, and wiry. His graying hair, showing pink scalp on top, curled wetly over his collar in back. "I thought I saw activity at your place."

Robin smiled. "You remember my friend, Catherine Running Wolf, don't you?"

"Sure do. Good to see you again, Miss Wolf." He stepped forward to greet her.

Catherine reluctantly extended her hand.

Robin said, "I'm having my reading group up here this weekend."

"The Wonder Women? I remember them."

"The No Ordinary Women," she corrected.

Running the tip of his tongue over his upper lip, George nodded. "Well, it looks like it's shaping up to be an interesting weekend. *He's* having another wing-ding at his place, too." He inclined his head in the direction of Ross Johnson's cabin and sneered. "He thinks he's such a hot-shot with his big important friends driving up in their big fancy cars. But like I always say, you can dress a pit bull up in a suit and tie, but if you cross him he'll still go for the throat."

Robin had no idea how to respond. Catherine looked dubious.

"Anyhoo, what can I do for you, ladies?"

As Robin told him about the chimney fire, he chewed on the inside of his cheek. "I guess for now you can pack the chinks with steel wool," he suggested. "You can get by with that until your lady friends leave, but then I'll fix it up proper. That cabin's mighty old. Wouldn't take much for the whole thing to go up in flames."

Once they were among the trees and out of George's hearing, Catherine grabbed Robin's arm and rasped, "What was that business about seeing activity at your place? We're half a mile from the road, and his place isn't even visible from the driveway."

Robin frowned. "Hmm."

THEY SEARCHED THE STORAGE shed for steel wool and found nothing, but in the cabin Cate found the solution under the kitchen sink—an old box of S.O.S. pads. Standing again on the chair, she tried to shove the pre-soaped steel wool pads into the chinks in the chimney. "It's like trying to force a hockey puck through a keyhole."

Robin looked at her over the top of her bifocals. "I suppose you've tried that," she said. "with a hockey puck."

"Okay, Miss Smarty Pants, you know the rule," Cate said, stepping down from the chair.

"That's only for husbands!"

"Uh-uh. You criticize, you get the job."

Robin took the S.O.S. pad from her and wet it under the kitchen faucet to make it more malleable. It worked.

They heated a can of tomato soup and took their steaming mugs onto the front porch. They didn't have to wait long before the first vehicle appeared through the trees.

The black Saturn came to a halt. The driver's door opened and a small black-and-white ball of fur sprang out. Molly Pat, Foxy's dog of questionable parentage, made mad dashes from one side of the cabin's yard to the other, bounding over the log parking barriers as though they were hurdles in her own personal track.

"Looks like Molly Pat's glad to be back." Catherine hugged Foxy and grabbed a bag from the trunk. "I know you said she's a Border collie and terrier mix, but I swear she's part greyhound."

Foxy's face broke into a proud parent's grin. "You should've seen her, sound asleep until we turned into the driveway, and suddenly she was ricocheting off the windows. She obviously remembers the place." Robin and Foxy muscled the cooler into the kitchen and went back for another load.

Although Foxy Tripp was Robin and Cate's senior by three years, she could have passed for half her age if you didn't look too closely at the inevitable wrinkles around her eyes. Her hair was lush and curly, and its color so resembled that of a fox's that almost everybody knew her by her nickname instead of her given name, Frances. "Absolutely glorious," Foxy pronounced, stretching her arms as if she were trying to touch the trees.

Again, tires crunched along the driveway, and Louise Trenton pulled up. Though she was a large-boned woman, Louise's movements were fluid and graceful and decidedly feminine as she stepped out to engulf them in hugs. Her style of loose-fitting slacks and silky blouses was anachronistic, reminiscent of a young Katherine Hepburn.

"Dear Gawd!" Louise exclaimed in a southern drawl barely affected by her years in Minnesota. "I always forget how *remote* this place is. I mean, I love Spirit Falls, you know that, but don't you ever get the willies staying here all by yourself?"

"Not if I don't think about it," Robin said a bit too enthusiastically. "Besides, I have a phone, and if it really gets to me, I sleep with all the lights on."

Catherine arched one eyebrow, a talent she'd tried unsuccessfully to teach Robin when they'd been college roommates years ago.

Robin met her gaze. "Besides, I'm not alone, not if you count the resident bats."

"Oh, Lord, don't remind me!" Louise shuddered.

Robin flicked her hand dismissively. "They keep the mosquitoes down. Given the choice, I prefer bats."

Coming out of the cabin, Foxy set a water dish down for the dog.

"I thought Grace was riding with you." Catherine peered into the backseat.

Louise laughed. "Yeah, well, by the time I got everything stuffed into my car, there was no room. Besides, Grace wasn't sure when she'd be ready, so we just scrapped the whole carpooling thing."

They all turned when Molly Pat, barking sharply and running in tight circles, alerted them to the last arrival. It was minutes before Grace Samuel's station wagon emerged from the tunnel of trees that defined the driveway. As soon as her car door opened, the dog leapt onto Grace's lap and wet her face with kisses. "Ooh, you're just so sweet," Grace cooed. Molly Pat accepted the adulation until the antics of a pair of red squirrels got her attention and she was gone.

Catherine opened the car's back door and a paper bag tumbled out, spilling its contents. Falling to her knees she reached under the car to retrieve the can of Deep Woods Off and two rolls of toilet paper, brushing the dust off before sticking them back in the bag. Composing her face as if nothing had happened, she asked, "So, what's new, Gracie?"

Grace snorted. "New? We're talking about my life."

Lately, Grace had begun grousing about her ordinariness, from her average height and shapeless shape to her lank hair (a non-descript brown) and smallish eyes (hazel), now hidden behind prescription sunglasses. She had a predictable workday wardrobe of suits (black, navy, beige, or taupe) and another wardrobe for the weekend—today it was jeans, tennies and a plain white sweatshirt.

Grace jabbed a thumb over her shoulder. "Hey, what's going on across the street? I saw a catering truck heading down the drive."

"Oh, that's Ross's place." Robin wrinkled her nose. "I guess he's having a party."

Louise called in her throaty voice from the doorway. "Did someone say party?"

That speeded up the unpacking. In a few minutes the five women had gathered in the kitchen for their traditional champagne toast, accompanied by strawberries.

Raising her fluted glass, Foxy flipped her auburn hair over her shoulders, sniffed the air and, instead of toasting Spirit Falls and its gracious hostess, she said, "Why do I keep smelling burned hair?"

"That," Robin pronounced, "would be Moose flambé."

As Robin and Catherine recounted the story of the cracked chimney and singed moose, they all trooped in to see the damage.

"Thank God y'all were here when it happened," Louise said with a hand to her chest.

The others laughed as they moved to the screened porch at the front of the cabin where they kicked off shoes and socks and made themselves comfy on cushioned deck chairs before laying waste to Louise's Brie quesadillas and a second glass of champagne, observing their first and only commandment: Thou shalt not utter the word diet.

Foxy flung her shapely legs over the arm of her chair. Even in simple movements, her dancer's discipline showed. "How can an hour and a half make such a difference?"

The others murmured assent. It was the smell of pine, the sound of bullfrogs, and the tranquilizing effect of the waterfall, they agreed. It was not having a schedule. It was not having to meet anyone else's demands. All that, and more.

Louise stretched her arms over her head and shook her curls. "I can't wait to spend some time down on the beach," she exclaimed.

"And sit behind the waterfall." Grace shut her eyes and smiled broadly, remembering their last retreat here.

Thoughts of the previous year's adventure momentarily silenced the women. Scrambling over the slippery rocks below the waterfall, they had cringed as cold water tumbled over them. Blindly, they'd felt for the hidden crevice to sit behind the watery curtain with their feet sticking out to catch the sun's warmth. They'd sat like this, chattering like a tree full of sparrows.

"I hate to tell you," Robin said, ending the rare moment of silence, "the last two steps to the creek are underwater. If we sat under the waterfall this year, it would be the last breath we'd take. In fact, the water's running so fast, we won't even be able to swim below the falls this time." She took a sip of champagne.

Grace groaned. "And I forgot my bathing suit, just in case we wanted to go skinny dipping again."

"Whatever we do, we'll have fun," Foxy didn't need to remind them. "Even with clothes on."

"True." Grace turned to Robin. "So, tell me more about this neighbor—Ross, was it? I don't remember him from before."

Robin settled back in her chair. "Ross Johnson and his wife built that cabin right after we bought this one, and for years we used to get together as couples. I always liked him and Sandy, but then three or four years ago they got divorced, and since then his entertaining has been . . . well, let's just say it's the kind men don't want their wives to find out about. The women are young, the men mostly paunchy and middle-aged."

"Our age." Louise's tone was lugubrious.

"Thanks, I needed that reminder," Foxy said.

Sprawled on her owner's lap, Molly Pat watched the women intently, her eyes following the route of each morsel of food.

Robin continued. "Last night when Cate and I made a run to the liquor store, there was a gorgeous young man there, not the type Ross usually entertains—Latino, I think—who was buying a bunch of high-end stuff—Chivas, Courvoisier, Stoly—enough for a real bash. Cate, of course, was hovering right over him and heard when he told the clerk to put it on Ross Johnson's account. The guy was charming, but something about him was just off. Cate and I both felt it."

"True," Catherine chimed in. "Something about his eyes."

"Besides the fact that they were gorgeous and a startling blue," Robin hastened to add.

Grace eyed them both. "That's the second time you said *gorgeous*."

"Well, he was. Not to mention, half our age," Catherine said. "But there was definitely something about his eyes that made us think he was high on something."

"Maybe they're growing pot over there," Grace said. "It'd be a good place to hide an operation like that. Or even a meth lab."

Catherine twisted her mouth to one side. "I think Robin would have noticed a marijuana farm. She's probably photographed every square foot of these woods."

"How's the book coming, anyway?" Foxy asked.

Robin's contract promised delivery of approximately 125 photos with accompanying text. Her publisher hoped the coffee-table book, *Seasons in the Woods*, would come out in time for Christmas. "I have all the photos, captions, and most of the writing done for summer, fall and winter. Yesterday I got some great shots of a pileated woodpecker, a porcupine, and some wild turkeys near the falls."

Glancing in the direction of the falls, Louise said, "You *are* going to write up the legend, aren't you?"

"Of Spirit Falls?" Robin shrugged. "I'm not sure. As far as I'm concerned, it's bad enough having the local kids scrambling along the cliff at night hoping to catch a glimpse of the poor woman's ghost wandering along the creek."

"I thought it was the ghost of a baby," Louise said. "Wasn't it a baby that drowned?"

Grace shook her head. "No, it was the mother, wasn't it?"

Clasping her turquoise amulet, Cate turned to Robin. "You'd better tell it again."

Robin nodded, folding her legs as if sitting around a campfire. "Just before the Civil War broke out, a young family was picnicking upstream, a mother, father, and their son. The toddler was playing at the water's edge and fell in before the mother could stop him, and the father drowned trying to save him."

"So whose ghost is it?" Foxy asked.

Robin splayed her hands. "Supposedly the mother's. The legend goes that she went mad with grief and guilt after losing both her husband and son, gone in an instant, and so she spent the rest of her short life wandering up and down the banks of the creek, dressed in the puffy-sleeved blouse and long skirt she was wearing for their picnic. They say she can still sometimes be seen along the creek near the falls, a figure in white."

Grace leaned forward. "Have you ever seen her?"

Robin grinned. "You mean, do I see dead people?"

"I think it should be in your book," Louise drawled. "Like it or not, tragic stories have romantic appeal."

"True," Robin agreed, "but this is basically a book of nature photography, and so far I haven't managed to get a picture of the ghost."

They looked, not speaking, out into the trees. Shadows lengthened on the picnic table. Several squirrels darted from branch to branch, down the trunk of the largest white pine and back to the safety of its greenery. Molly Pat took it all in, her ears twitching. The peacefulness was pervasive and unshakable. Or so they thought.

Across the road at the nearest cabin, Ross Johnson stepped onto the deck. He was tall and well-built, projecting a ruggedness that, despite his urbane wardrobe, looked more at home in the out of doors—the Marlboro man in Brooks Brothers.

It was not quite dusk, and the air was still and humid. His shirt clung to him, the charcoal gray silk blackening in growing patches on his chest and back. He sucked in his gut and eased the fabric away from his skin. As soon as Melissa was out of the shower, he'd ask her if she had talcum powder. His date for the weekend, Candi-with-an-*i*, had nothing but baby powder, not exactly the image he was going for.

He slapped his arm, then his bare ankle. His palm came up bloody. Swearing under his breath, he slid the door back and ran his hands under the kitchen faucet. "Do you remember where I stuck those torchieres, the ones that keep these fucking bugs away?" he called to José. He squashed another blood-filled mosquito on the back of his neck, then washed and dried his hands a second time and stuck his head into the living room. "Did you hear me?"

José looked up from the sandwich he was assembling at the bar. He said, "Sorry, boss, I can't hear you over the music." After rearranging the meat on the deli tray, he returned it to the refrigerator behind the bar. "Okay, whatchew need?" He grinned, showing even white teeth.

"Torchieres," Ross said. "Those outdoor candlesticks. I want them on the deck."

Wiping mayonnaise from the corner of his mouth, José finished chewing and swallowing before answering. "I think maybe they're in the firewood bin on the deck."

Exasperated, Ross turned to leave the room. "Well, then, put them out in the holders and light them."

"Sí, boss." José flashed a smile before adding under his breath in perfect Oxford English, "When I'm good and ready, you pretentious git."

Ross checked his Cancun-tanned image in the hall mirror, tilting his cleft chin up to make sure he was cleanly shaven. He squared his shoulders, which retained the powerful look of his bricklaying days, even though, as owner of the fastest growing construction company in Minnesota, he did precious little manual labor any more. "And get me another Rob Roy—not with that cheap shit either," he called out.

An olive slipped from José's fingers and bounced along the floor in time to the Caribbean beat. Retrieving it, he dropped it into Ross's glass. "I don' give you no sheep shit, boss," he said, sliding back into his Hispanic persona. "Maybe I get those bug candles now." As he handed the drink to a scowling Ross, they both turned at the sound of a door opening.

Emerging from a steam cloud, Melissa exited the bathroom with wet hair and a towel that didn't quite meet in the back. She strode purposefully down the hall, oblivious to the two men who watched the pink triangle of her right buttock winking at them until she disappeared into the bedroom she shared with Ross's old friend Martin.

"She's a looker, that one," José said. "She keeps checking me out. You think your friend would mind—?"

Ross inspected his nails. "Yes, Martin would mind very much if you messed with Melissa. Your role tonight is bartender," he said close to José's ear, "not gigolo."

"I'm—whatchew say—ambidextrous. I can do both, no?" José grinned again.

There was no warmth in Ross's smile. "No."

As José sauntered from the room, he said, "I think maybe I'll check on Candi. See if she needs something, you know?"

"My guests will be here in less than an hour," Ross called lamely after him. He clenched his jaws. It wasn't so much the idea that José might attend to Candi's needs, but it was his damned insolence. By providing Candi for Ross's weekend entertainment, José was merely letting Ross know that in some matters he had the upper hand. It galled him! He walked into the kitchen, bumping over a stack of boxes the caterers had left in the corner.

A door slammed downstairs. "Damn mosquitoes!" Martin yelled, as he stomped up the stairs.

Ross laughed. "Well, it is almost dusk. Isn't this your second walk today, buddy?"

Martin lifted his nylon windbreaker and checked his pedometer. "Eight point two miles." He took his baseball cap off and pushed thin, sweaty hair to one side.

Ross had never known Martin to be particularly conscientious about exercising. He looked leaner than he had in years, but had gone from pudgy to skinny without ever passing through fit. His cheeks bore deep vertical creases Ross had never noticed before, and purplish smudges under his eyes bespoke the insomnia he'd been complaining about of late. Martin, thought his friend, looked all of his fifty-four years and then some. "When did you start wearing pink?" Ross teased him.

Martin looked down at his windbreaker. "It's coral."

"Oh, yeah, that sounds much more masculine."

Ignoring the jibe, Martin looked over his shoulder. "What are the girls up to?"

With a theatrical eye roll, Ross said, "I hope you don't call them *girls* at the college?"

Martin snorted, poured a half tumbler of Courvoisier and ran it quickly under the faucet. "You think I'm an idiot? It's a good way to get your ass sued for sexual harassment. Just this spring I had to suspend one of my professors for referring to his teaching assistant as Miss T and A."

Ross's expression was pained. Before he could respond, Candi came in, wearing a black dress that hugged her curves, sleek as a seal's skin. "José said to tell you he went to the gazebo until everyone gets here."

"I see."

She smoothed her short bob and licked her lips. "I wondered if you could give me a hand with my zipper."

Christ, she's insatiable! Ross thought, touching her waist as he zipped up her dress.

She slipped out of his reach, smiling coquettishly over her shoulder as she walked back toward the bedrooms.

"Let's go out on the deck," he said to Martin. "It's stifling in here."

Some time later, José and Melissa came up the back steps onto the wraparound deck.

Ross heard the wheedling tone in Melissa's voice "But I don't understand," she was saying to José. "Why all the secrecy?"

José laughed mirthlessly. "Trust me, chica, there'll be no photography once the guests arrive. I think you just took your last picture.

THE INSIDE OF THE CABIN, unlike its rustic exterior, had the appearance of a gentlemen's club, complete with oak paneling, wainscoting, and massive leather furniture. Here a successful man, and Ross was certainly that, could bring his girlfriend, smoke a Cuban cigar, indulge in the finest French brandy and not have to answer to anyone. Here he felt validated for his years of hard work.

Sometimes he could almost convince himself it was nobility of character that led him to share this refuge with other carefully selected guests, those who knew how and why to be discreet. Ross took a quick visual inventory of his guests gathered near the stone fireplace, knowing he had chosen well.

Tonight the cigar smoke mingled with the sweeter smell of marijuana. The room currently held an octet of guests, most of them well into inebriation. The men were conversing—and *per*versing, as Ross liked to say—with obliging and attractive younger women.

He made his way over to a man who sported well-defined biceps and the striking woman with him. "Hey, Johnson!" the man began.

Ross held up his hand. "No last names tonight."

"Right, like nobody's gonna recognize me," the professional athlete said, showing his famous lopsided grin.

His girlfriend laughed, letting out the smoke she'd been holding in her lungs.

"It's a house rule we all respect." Ross watched as the man digested his meaning, then he resumed a casual air. "Did José take care of you?"

"Oh, yeah." He gestured to the hand-rolled joint his companion was sucking on. "He took care of us real good."

Ross clapped him on the back and moved about the room. His eyes rested on Martin and his girlfriend. Yesterday, when Martin and Melissa had arrived, they'd been all over each other, holding hands and gazing into each other's eyes—obviously more than a dalliance.

It had made Ross downright queasy to watch his old-enough-to-know-better friend's mind turn to mush, and so, shortly after they'd arrived, he'd asked Martin to help him chop firewood. After a few minutes, as Ross had hoped, Melissa had gotten bored and announced she was going to walk down by the creek. For a couple of hours, Martin had been his old self, and then Melissa had come back from her walk, her nose pink from the sun.

But looking at them tonight, Ross saw the lovebirds were showing signs of discord. In the last few minutes, Melissa's giggles had given way to a strident insistence that Martin had been ogling Candi, who now rested her fingers on José's arm as they talked.

Ross stepped closer to his friend, noticing the sweat beading on Martin's upper lip and forehead. Martin's normally intelligent dark eyes had a fevered look, and his movements were quick and agitated.

Melissa's eyes flared. "I know what I saw!" She spat the words at Martin. "You think I'm stupid?" She inched forward on the sofa, her crimson silk dress hiking up to show slim, freckled thighs.

Ross's lips tightened. He circled around behind the sofa, clutching Martin's shoulder, leaving a damp palm print on his shirt. "Maybe you'd have more privacy outside."

Martin jumped at the touch, his eyes wary.

Nervously Melissa slid her bracelet around her wrist, her long pale nails clicking against the metal. "Maybe I'll just leave," she said, oblivious to the heads now turned in her direction. She swiped the back of her hand under her nose.

Martin's eyes darted about the room. He touched her thigh. "Aw, can't we just—"

Like a pouting child she thrust his hand away. A tear rolled down her cheek and she slumped forward, covering her mouth with shaking hands.

"C'mon, babe," he said, more gently. "You're in no condition to drive."

This time she didn't push him away. She turned her face to his. Martin ran a finger along her jaw line and kissed her forehead. Her features softened into the homegrown Minnesota wholesomeness that had first caught Martin's attention. She twirled a strand of hair around her finger.

From a discreet distance, Ross watched them. *She really is delicious,* he thought, tilting his head to view the full length of her legs. He knew her to be around thirty, give or take a year, with a body she obviously worked on and eyes that evoked childlike wonder. Her long auburn hair tumbled over her face as she sagged against Martin's shoulder.

Ross pulled his eyes away from Melissa's dress, now hiked up to show the black lacy edge of her panties. He crossed the room and when he looked up, it was into José's eyes.

The corners of José's mouth were upturned in something that bordered on contempt. "Are you keeping *me* away from her for *his* sake?" he said, gesturing with his chin toward Melissa and Martin, "or could it be you want her for yourself?"

"What happened to your slimy Latin Lover accent?" Ross said.

José clicked his tongue, flipping an imaginary switch. "Whachew mean, boss?"

"Just keep it zipped. The mouth, too."

"Man, you're so tight, you're gonna snap. Maybe you need something, you know?"

Yeah, maybe he did.

Though the weather had been ideal earlier in the day, by Friday evening Robin felt the wind shift and stepped onto the back porch to look at a sky that held nothing more sinister than a few scattered clouds. Nevertheless, she set several mismatched candles, unlit, about the living room and porch.

In the kitchen, Catherine chilled stem glasses with ice while Grace juiced a couple lemons into the gin and olive juice. Louise slid a tray of pistachio puffs into the oven. She had attended cooking schools in France, Japan, and Italy, and her creations were always delicious and beautifully presented.

Robin walked in saying, "As soon as I smelled the olives, my mouth started watering."

Catherine opened her mouth to say something, then frowned. "What is it?"

"I can't think of the guy's name—that Russian scientist who trained dogs to salivate."

"Does the name Pavlov ring a bell?" Robin prompted.

Grace and Catherine rolled their eyes at each other before going to the the screen door to tell Louise and Foxy that it was "time to move inside for the next feeding." The sun was low on the horizon and hidden behind trees.

With a sharp bang, Louise returned, slamming the outside door shut. "Those mosquitoes are positively vicious," she said waving her hands over her head. The odor of her last cigarette of the evening accompanied her into the room.

Foxy strode through the living room, glancing up cautiously, sure that at any moment the bats would swoop down on any insects that had followed them indoors. Molly Pat cocked an ear and sat, suddenly fascinated by the ceiling. As if on cue, a squeak came from the rafters.

Leaving the dog to her vigil, the women retreated to the back porch for dirty martinis and smoked oysters. The first drink disappeared quickly. When Robin poured a second round, she noticed how much condensation had pooled beneath the pitcher.

"You're awfully quiet tonight, Gracie," Cate said. "How's everything in the investment consultant business?"

Grace shrugged. "Fine."

"Fred and the boys okay?"

"They're fine." The lower part of Grace's heart-shaped face crinkled in a smile that did not extend to her eyes, and a sort of wistfulness settled on her features briefly.

Conversation cascaded from one topic to another. The five women munched away at hors d'oeuvres, with the waterfall shimmering in the moonlight only a hundred yards away. In the middle of one of Louise's stories, Robin's head snapped to one side. "Did you hear that?"

Nobody had, including Molly Pat, who lay in an overfed stupor at Foxy's side.

Robin rose and walked through the living room, slipping down the hallway and out the door on the other side of the cabin. She ducked her head around, trying to penetrate the darkness. "Hello," she called out to the trees. "George?" There was no answer.

Rejoining her friends, Robin said, "I guess I'm just imagining things." But she was sure she'd heard it—feet pivoting on gravel just outside the front porch.

"Surely George wouldn't come at this hour to fix the fireplace, would he?" Catherine asked.

Louise gave an involuntary shriek when a flutter of wings overhead reminded her there were bats in residence. "Which one was that?" she asked, flapping a hand in front of her face.

In fact Robin couldn't tell them apart, but she pretended to recognize each by name. "I didn't get a good look. Either Bat Masterson or Batsy Cline, I think." The bat flew a little higher on its return trip and settled again in the rafters. "Nope," Robin amended, "Definitely Belfry Lugosi."

Wind gusted through the screen, scattering napkins across the porch. The moonlight on the water blinked out.

"It's only 8:05. Can that be right?" Foxy squinted at her wristwatch. "Look how dark it is!"

Nobody else wore a watch.

"Who's ready for dessert?" Robin asked.

Louise reached for the last oyster. "Hors d'ouevres and dessert! What a perfectly delightful way to live!"

Robin headed for the kitchen, but instead of getting the praline cheesecake, she grabbed a flashlight and stepped outside. From the doorstep, she shone a thin stream of light on the ground by the screened porch. There were footprints, plenty of them, none distinguishable except for the dog's. She turned the light off and peered at the nearest trees.

But then, before her eyes could adjust to the dark, a series of sounds immobilized her, a car on the gravel road, traveling east, if she had to guess, then a thud. She held her breath. Her heart thumped in the silence. What exactly had she heard? She waited, hearing only the crackle of heat lightning in the distance.

Cursing to herself, she hurried back inside. "Did you hear that?" she called.

Heads shook. "Hear what?"

"Don't tell me we've discovered a new symptom of menopause!" Grace wailed. "Hearing things! Good Lord, they'll have us put away."

"It sounded like . . . I don't know . . . maybe a car hitting something out on the road."

"Oh, not another deer." Catherine's hand flew to her chest.

"You've got some hearing," Louise said. "The road's pretty far away."

Molly Pat roused, and Foxy stroked her ears. "I'm sure it's nothing. Just the wind. Maybe a tree fell in the—"

"If a tree falls in the forest and only one person hears it . . . Shoot, I know there's a punch line in there somewhere," Grace said as she sneaked another cracker to the dog.

"And maybe it was a car, like Robin said." Catherine folded her arms around herself, suddenly chilled. "I say we go check it out."

As soon as Catherine and Foxy stirred, Molly Pat ran to the door, barking.

"Grace and I will hold down the fort," Louise announced. "Want the cell phone?"

"Won't work here, especially in a thunderstorm," Robin called on her way out.

They traipsed down the driveway—Robin, Catherine, Foxy, and the dog.

Catherine grabbed an arm on either side of her. "We're off to see the wizard," she sang.

"No heart, no brain, no courage. That pretty well sums us up," Robin intoned.

"And Toto leading the way," Foxy added. "Now all we need is a tornado."

They'd gone only a few more steps when lightning flashed across the sky to their left and wind whipped the trees into a frenzy. "Now you did it," Robin said. Her flashlight flickered and she shook it back to an insipid glow.

"Look!" Foxy said in a stage whisper. She pointed, and they saw headlights through the trees and heard a car engine purr as it came to life. The lights moved slowly at first, then gathered speed and disappeared down the road. "You were right, Robin."

"If they hit a deer, shouldn't we see if it's hurt?" Catherine's question was answered by big, fat drops of rain angling down through the trees. Thunder and lightning now came ominously close together.

"Molly Pat!" Foxy yelled as they turned back. "Where is that fool?" They had the cabin's lights in view when the dog finally pelted towards them from the direction of the road, then past them, heading for the door where Grace stood waiting to welcome the soggy bunch. In the shelter of the overhang, Molly Pat plunked herself down, whimpering as she waited for the bipeds to catch up.

Grace handed out towels, stooping to dry Molly Pat, who whined and shuddered through the pampering. "It's all right, girl, it's just a storm," she said, toweling the dog's fur. "Hold still, Molly Pat. What have you done?"

"What's wrong?" Foxy bent to look.

"There's blood on the towel. Look." Grace held out the white towel with its faint, reddish smudge.

Foxy lifted up the frightened dog and carried her inside. She held her in the light of the bare hallway bulb as Catherine put on her reading glasses to check each paw. Finding no wound, she and Foxy ran their hands methodically through the dog's fur, coming up with wet but unbloodied hands.

"Not a single cut," Catherine said. "But look at her. She's terrified."

"Thank God she's not hurt." Robin reached for the phone. "I think you're right about the deer, Cate. I'd better report it to the sheriff." She poked at the buttons, frowned, and set the phone back in its cradle. "It's dead."

They all jumped at the crash of thunder, turning to see the sky light up again.

Robin draped her towel over her shoulders and watched nature's fireworks. "Sorry, ladies, but I've got to get some shots of that lightning." She took off, her leather sandals squishing as she strode down the hall to the storage room where she kept her backup camera loaded with black-and-white film. Lightning crackled all around them now, and she shook trying to get the right filter on the lens. Then, with one spectacular *crack-boom*, the lights went out.

Robin grabbed a shelf for support, tried to catch her breath. Cursing her stupidity, she remembered leaving the flashlight by the door. The darkness was almost total. "Oh, God," she said, slumping to the floor and pulling her knees to her chest. From the other end of the cabin, she heard Cate calling her name. She tried to answer, but what came out was the whimper of a frightened child.

4

Ross Johnson sat on a leather-upholstered barstool, smoking a contraband cigar. He and his guests were unaware of the approaching storm.

At the first crack of thunder, Ross clutched his chest, and for a very brief moment thought he'd had a heart attack. He knew it was possible, knew that even younger men in prime physical condition suffered sudden coronaries when they messed with the stuff, sometimes even the first time. It could happen one day, his heart could just up and quit: *You've fucked with me once too often,* it would tell him. But he'd loved it from the very first sniff. Loved the warmth creeping, sometimes galloping through his body, loved the potency the magic powder delivered.

When his wife—ex-wife, now—had found out about the cocaine, she'd pounced on it to explain all that had gone wrong in their marriage. Oddly, she wasn't particularly angry at him, but at the drug, to which she ascribed a human willfulness to enchant her husband.

It had taken her some time to figure out his connection to José, a fact he found endlessly amusing. "Why would you want to hang around with him?" she'd ask in that prosecutor's way she had. "And what does he have in common with you? You're old enough to be his father, for God's sake!" She poked and probed, sure he'd taken the beautiful young man as his lover—a simple matter of transference, of course. She'd never understood until after the divorce that José was Ross's link to the world of drugs.

He looked over at the young man leaning against the doorframe, his pale blue eyes a startling contradiction to his dark complexion and ebony hair that hung to his shoulders. He remembered the lustful way his wife had gazed at José Churchill, like some freaking teenager.

Ross walked across the living room, retrieved his date from a flirtatious encounter with the blond jock, and pulled her down onto the pillows by the fireplace, where he began idly stroking her hip. Candi-with-an-*i* stroked him back.

As lightning strobed outside, he wondered what had become of Martin and Melissa. If she'd been telling the truth, Melissa had never tried cocaine before, a hell of a spot for Martin to have put them all in. Under its influence she'd obviously become belligerent, and then she'd demanded to be taken home. Maybe by now the high would be wearing off and they'd be back.

Pretty girl. Smart, too. He just hoped Martin was being careful. All it took was one whistle-blower and the party would be over, and not just for tonight. It was always risky with an employee, he'd warned Martin from the beginning.

Not to mention that Martin was a married man who, when it came right down to it, did not want to risk losing Brenda, his wife of almost three decades.

But risk, Ross knew, could be a powerful aphrodisiac.

Candi's playful fingers failed to arouse him. Ross's eyes wandered about the room. When he didn't see José, he pulled himself away from Candi and began working the crowd himself, ensuring that his guests were well supplied with food, drinks, and cigars. As for the nose candy, there was still an adequate supply on the mantel, complete with the necessary paraphernalia.

It was an impressive assemblage: a realty company executive, a high-powered attorney, an oral surgeon, a pro ball player and his old friend Martin, now a college president. The girls weren't your run-of-the-mill bimbi either, except for Candi, maybe. Melissa had graduated from one of the Seven Sisters, either Wellesley or Bryn Mawr, he thought, and had come to Martin's notice at Bradford College when she'd developed a program credited with almost doubling alumni giving in its first three years.

Ross wandered into the kitchen. Damn that José, he thought. Where was he?

Turning at a scraping sound, he looked out into the dark. Flickers of lightning showed a human form at the deck's edge. Ross slid the door open. "José?" he called softly.

There was no answer.

"Martin?" It was difficult to see clearly, but he thought the figure beckoned to him. "George, is that you?" he asked, stepping into the dark.

IT HAD BEEN SEVERAL MINUTES since the lightning, with one brilliant white flash, had knocked out the electricity. Guided by the cabin windows, dimly lit from within by the fireplace's glow and by the frequent flashes of lightning, Ross found his way back across the gravel driveway and fumbled his way up the outside stairs, his hand slipping along the slick wet deck rail. Once inside, he abandoned his soggy loafers just inside the kitchen door and stepped barefoot into the room. Snatching a dishtowel, he swiped it across his face and began blotting his hair. Outside the lightning continued to crackle.

With a prickly feeling, he sensed someone watching him. Raising his eyes, he uttered a strangled cry and clutched the counter. The woman had flames emanating from her body and electricity springing from her head. Vertigo seized him. He lowered his head and gulped air, blinked and looked again. She was still there, silhouetted in the doorway, the fire casting kaleidoscopic shadows in the living room behind her—not a flaming woman or a hallucination after all, but a trick of the light.

She covered her mouth, not quite suppressing a giggle. "Sorry, I didn't mean to startle you."

He recognized her as the oral surgeon's girlfriend. Finding his voice, Ross croaked, "No problem."

"Oh, you poor thing, you're sopping wet!"

He stared past her, flicking his tongue over his lower lip. "I closed everyone's car windows," he said, adding unnecessarily, "It's really coming down out there."

She turned to look out at the pouring rain.

"It's all taken care of," he assured her and steered her back toward the living room. "Go back to the party. I need to change into dry clothes."

EVEN IN DRY SLACKS and a heavy cotton sweater, Ross shivered. The temperature must have dropped twenty degrees since the storm front moved in, and yet his guests, gathered around the fireplace as they were, drinking and partaking in their drugs of choice, seemed unaware of anything going on outside. They probably wouldn't notice unless the roof blew off, he thought, leaning heavily against the end of the bar.

He heard Martin trudge up the basement stairs, saw him turn toward the bedroom he and Melissa shared. When he came out again, Martin was twitching at the collar of his fresh dry shirt to flatten it. "What now?" he said, sliding a look to Ross.

Ross appraised him. "You're fine. Come on." As he shepherded him into the living room, Martin sniffed and wiped his nose with his wrist.

"Hey, check that out." Ross motioned with his chin to where the ballplayer sat in the middle of the cordovan leather sofa, his left arm draped over the shoulder of his girlfriend, the right over Candi's shoulder.

Martin followed Ross, who slipped behind the sofa to hover over the trio. They were just in time to hear Candi say, in a breathless tone, "Sure, why not?"

The man's eyes were closed as his oversized hands moved over the women's breasts.. "Sure, why not?" he echoed. "That is, if I read you correctly,"

"Must read Braille," Ross said under his breath. "They say he's good with his hands."

Martin jerked his head, as if coming out of a trance. "How can you be so cavalier?"

"About Candi?" Ross spoke inches from Martin's ear. "We have no relationship. It doesn't matter to me who services her."

Martin turned to look at his friend whose features morphed in the shifting firelight. They had been friends for over twenty years and yet here he stood looking at a stranger. "Jesus! You're a cold son of a bitch!"

"Get a grip." Ross's hand was heavy on Martin's shoulder.

Martin involuntarily pulled away.

In a voice meant for a larger audience, Ross said, "Excuse me."

The ballplayer opened heavy-lidded eyes, hands abruptly motionless. His girlfriend sat up.

"Oh, hi, we were just talking." Candi said, disentangling herself.

"Yeah, we noticed."

Ross's head swung in an arc, encompassing his roomful of guests. Placing thumb and index finger between his lips, he whistled.

All heads turned his way.

"Hey! Listen up!" Ross called out, "Seems one of our guests decided to go home, even though we tried to persuade her to stay."

Martin sucked in his breath sharply at the derisive snort from a corner of the room, where José materialized from the shadows.

Ross continued. "These things happen. No big deal, really, unless she gets stopped by the highway patrol." He paused, waiting for the implications to sink in. "Well, when they find that the car's registration isn't in her name . . . No need to panic, just a little heads up, in case the authorities come calling." The brief silence ended with scuffling and grumbling and a few choice expletives. Candi, giggling nervously, extracted a small plastic bag from her purse and poked it into her bra. "Jeez, I hope Melissa's okay. She's really nice. Smart too."

Ross saw José slip into the kitchen and out of sight. He thought of following him, but was stopped by a woman's voice from the bathroom, saying that the toilet wouldn't flush. One of the men, in paternalistic tones explained to her that with the power out, the pump couldn't refill the tank.

"What are we supposed to do now?" the woman wailed.

The stout attorney who Ross knew to have political aspirations snatched a bottle of Chivas in one beefy hand and Stoly in the other, wended his way through the crowd and disappeared into the bathroom. The sound of bottles glugging their contents into the flush tank was followed by a loud groan from the ball player. "—the fuck you doin' in there, man?" he said as the lawyer walked past him to grab two more bottles of premium liquor and the ice bucket, which he emptied into the tank.

Too late, Ross realized what he was doing, and mentally tallied what he'd spent on the booze that was now being swept into the septic tank.

"I think we're going to hit the road," said the oral surgeon uneasily, scratching his bald head and taking his protesting companion by the hand.

Ross stepped forward, gesturing with an open hand. "People, people! Let's not overreact. Nobody's going anywhere. That's what put us in this predicament in the first place."

"But what if the police come?"

Ross gave a reasonable facsimile of a chuckle. "We'll cross that bridge when we come to it." He shot a look at Martin, whose mouth hung slack. "Besides, we're just a bunch of friends getting together for a few drinks. Right? Nothing illegal about that."

The realtor's girlfriend bobbed her head eagerly. "He's right." The multiple gold and gemstone rings on her fingers picked up the firelight as she gestured with her hands. "And because we're law-abiding adults, we made the responsible decision to stay the night rather than drive under the influence, right?"

There was a murmur of assent.

As he spoke, Ross fingered his shirt pocket. *Enough left for one line, anyway,* he thought as he looked around for José.

One of the women, the leggy one who'd come with the ball-player, offered to make coffee.

The ballplayer scratched his jaw and grunted. "Coach always told us coffee wouldn't sober us up, just turn us into wide-awake drunks."

Ross looked from one guest to the other, "I think everyone should stay here 'til morning. By that time I hope the young lady will have gotten home without any trouble, and will, with any luck, be sleeping it off."

Martin snuffled loudly against the back of his hand.

Within minutes, the partiers were back to drinking the contents of the remaining bottles as if they'd lost precious time. "By the way," Ross said in an affable tone, though his words were anything *but*, "if anyone should ask, for any reason, I will deny any of you were here. I expect you'll do the same."

That prompted raised eyebrows, a few hastily whispered words. Then, slowly they began to nod.

Ross nodded back, then sought out Martin. "What do you suppose that prick José is up to?" he said through clenched teeth. "I'm beginning to think he's more trouble than he's worth."

5

Morning sun filtered through the trees and onto the bed where Robin woke slowly, seeing the sunlight through closed lids, a golden glow that turned, wavelike, to scarlet and back to gold. Snug under her puffy comforter, she listened to a cacophony of bird sounds outside the screened sleeping porch, and wondered what part of her memory of last night's storm was real. It all had a nightmare quality, especially that embarrassing scene in the storage closet after deluding herself into thinking she'd conquered her fear of the dark.

As she had each morning since her surgery, Robin woke to find her hand covering the flat spot where her left breast had been. The mastectomy itself left a curved line, roughly the shape and position of a bra's underwire. Connecting to it was a pink vertical line that ended where her nipple used to be. There was a small indentation just to the right of that from the biopsy, a larger one under her arm where seven lymph nodes had been removed, and below that, the incision that had caused the most pain, the one for a drainage tube that had stayed in place for almost two weeks after she'd left the hospital. The still-pink scar tissue was numb and yet somehow tender. To her, it felt alien, as if sculpted out of Silly Putty.

Although her oncologist was confident he'd "gotten it all," he'd insisted on chemotherapy. The prognosis was hopeful. Still, she knew that cancer cells had escaped the affected duct to infiltrate breast tissue and one lymph node. For all she knew, there were still marauding cancer cells moving silently through her body, looking for a new site to plunder. Reflexively her hand moved over to her healthy breast.

Breathing deeply through her nose as she'd been taught, she visualized toxins and worry leaving her body with each exhalation. In her mind, the toxins were lime green blobs, the worry, tangled gray corkscrews. Inhale, exhale, inhale. She inhaled the aroma of freshly brewed coffee. Opening her eyes, she saw that all the beds except Foxy's had been vacated. After a quick detour to the bathroom, she grabbed a mug of coffee and followed the voices to the front porch where Louise and Grace sat wrapped in quilts, discussing the difficulties of owning a small business.

Grace patted the sofa next to her. "I'll even share your afghan with you. Did you sleep okay?"

Robin nodded and nestled next to her. "Keep talking. I'll just listen until the caffeine kicks in."

Prompted by Grace, Louise continued. "It's not that we're not getting along. Charlie's a real love," she said with a shake of the head that made her curls bounce. "But we eat and sleep together, run the shop together, go on buying junkets together to get more antiques for the shop, then come home and start the cycle all over again. I mean, sometimes, it gets a little close."

"Hmmm." Grace tilted her head. "I guess I don't understand, then. What would change if you and Charlie got married?"

Louise laughed. "Would it sound crazy if I said there's something romantic about our arrangement that I don't want to ruin by being, well, respectable?"

"Respectability isn't everything," Grace erupted. "Some people our age with good careers, living in picture-perfect homes with nice, respectable husbands and kids that can fend for themselves, suddenly find themselves thinking more and more about what it would be like to risk it all for a little excitement, one crazy adventure, a walk on the wild side." She cleared her throat and looked away. "You know what I mean."

Louise and Robin raised eyebrows at each other. The silence became uncomfortable. Robin carefully sipped the steaming brew before asking, "Where's Cate? I suppose she was up at the crack of dawn looking for the wounded deer."

"No, we told her she had to wait for the rest of us," Grace answered. "I said if it was wounded, it would be long gone by now, and if it's dead, it'll still be dead when we get there."

"She's outside with Molly Pat," Grace answered. Hearing her name, Molly charged across the clearing to scratch on the screen door.

Robin let her in and wiped her muddy paws on a towel before the dog settled on Grace's feet.

"Breakfast will be ready in about twenty minutes," Louise said. "Should I wake up Foxy?"

"She's up," Foxy groaned, padding her way over to the rocking chair opposite Grace and Robin. "Not awake, but up." Scratching her mass of auburn curls and yawning, she flopped into the chair.

Molly Pat leapt onto Foxy's lap and slid a wet tongue the length of her owner's neck.

"Okay, okay, Mol, I'll get your breakfast."

"Oh, good," Catherine chirped from the doorway. "They insisted I wait until you were all up." She shifted her weight from one foot to the other. "I'd really like to check on that deer."

Enough about the damn deer already, Robin wanted to say, but she held the thought.

"I'd really like to eat first," Louise said, coming up behind her.

"Me too," Grace and Foxy said.

Outvoted, Catherine gave in.

When there was nothing left of the salmon and spinach quiche but a few morsels reserved for Molly Pat, Catherine said, "I'll clean up while you get dressed. Who wants to walk out to the road with me?"

"Me," Foxy said, and headed for the dressing room.

"Me too, but I think y'all are just plain lucky you didn't get struck by lightning last night," said Louise, sitting back in her chair and lacing her fingers behind her head. "Besides, I'm not convinced anything happened last night, other than that gully-washer."

While they changed out of their pajamas, they talked about the storm, but none of them, Robin noticed with relief, made mention of her panic attack last night.

Grace held up a sodden jacket. "I left this on the bench outside last night, so I guess I'll just wait here."

"No problem." Robin directed her to where she and Brad hung spare jackets and sweaters on pegs in the storeroom.

In a few minutes, all five women proceeded carefully down the driveway, sidestepping tire ruts now filled with muddy water. Molly Pat uncharacteristically trotted beside them, head down. More than once she nuzzled Foxy's hand. Other than the occasional birdcall the woods were unusually still.

Reaching the road first, Louise looked in both directions, adjusting her prescription sunglasses on her nose. "Except for where the gravel's washed over the road at the bottom of that little ol' hill, I don't see a thing," she declared.

"Everything seems quiet enough," agreed Foxy.

At first they stood in a cluster to look around them at the flattened grasses in the ditch, with the residual rain still dripping off the trees, then they began to disperse. Foxy watched Molly Pat wander down the road, intently inspecting each square inch of the gravel shoulder. Within seconds, Foxy lost view of her entirely as the dog moved into the underbrush. When she called the dog's name, Molly Pat emerged to bark three sharp barks before disappearing again.

"You heard me, Molly. Get back here," Foxy commanded.

This time the dog didn't respond. In exasperation Foxy started after her, Catherine following close behind. Carefully, Foxy stepped down the slight decline into the ditch and up the other side to where Molly Pat enthusiastically sniffed the ground at the base of an old oak.

"What did you find, girl?"

Molly looked up, cocked her head and barked peremptorily.

What is it?" Robin came up behind them, her breathing labored.

"There was an accident, all right." Foxy pointed to a gouge on the tree trunk.

Robin ran her fingers across the gash and sniffed the exposed wood. "It had to be last night."

"Paint," Foxy mused, pointing to a yellowish smear on the bark.

Slipping a camera from her jacket pocket, Robin started clicking.

They looked at the tree, and then wordlessly cast their eyes to the ground, pointing out marks in the soil, tire marks leading to and away from the damaged tree. Despite the heavy rain, there seemed to be several indentations—no continuous lines, but enough to surmise where a car had left the road, then reentered it.

Robin squatted to inspect the grasses in the shallow ditch. In several places, they were not only matted by rain, but crushed, presumably by car tires. She took more pictures. Molly Pat flew past her, stopped, spun, backtracked. In the ditch a couple yards from Robin she sniffed avidly.

"That's just a rock, you nitwit," Foxy said, when she saw the focus of Molly's attention.

Catherine stood peering into the woods.

"What are you thinking?" Robin asked.

"If the car crashed there," she said, more to herself, "and it left the road here, assuming it was driving on the right side of the street, then the deer . . ." her voice trailed off.

Robin asked, "Do you think we should call the police?"

"What for?" Foxy asked. "I doubt they'd come over to investigate a dented tree, and even if a deer did get hit, it's long gone."

"Way I see it, this was some good ol' boy who'd had a few too many," Louise offered, "and when he reached in back for another six-pack he just swerved right off the road."

"What about the blood on Molly Pat?" Grace asked.

Foxy said, "There's no blood on the road."

"The rain would have taken care of that," Grace responded.

"Okay, here's what happened," Louise announced. "The guy gets out to see what he's done to his big old gas guzzler, and he stands there weaving around saying, 'Oh, Lord, why me?' and all the time he's bleeding like a stuck pig from this head wound that looks a lot worse than it actually is." To dramatize her narrative, Louise held her head and stumbled a few steps, then gasped and looked down the road. "And suddenly he hears thunder, but he thinks it's the cops who followed him from the tavern, so he jumps in and guns the engine. Wonder of wonders, the sucker still works. So he just backs it up onto the road again and heads home, wondering if he should stop and have a quick one while he figures out what he's going to tell his momma about her car."

Though Louise hadn't taken the stage in decades, her theater major had not been wasted. She still had the knack for turning a mundane occurrence into a howlingly good story.

Catherine chuckled along with the others, but her attention was drawn to Molly Pat, whose barking had turned to a persistent, high-pitched whine. She sidled over to her, and the dog let Catherine collect her in her arms.

"What's the matter, Mol? Tell me what the problem is," she murmured to the trembling animal. She closed her eyes to sense what the dog was trying to communicate, but no picture came. Only a flutter of fear.

"It's the Dog Whisperer at work," Grace said, not quietly enough and with a touch of derision.

Catherine tried to ignore the jibe, but her concentration was broken.

"What did Molly say?" asked the others when Catherine rejoined them.

She looked at their bemused faces. "She didn't say anything."

"Nothing at all?" Grace asked, ruffling the dog's fur. "What's the matter, cat got your tongue?" She was rewarded by a couple of grins. "C'mon, what did she tell you?"

Catherine shrugged. "Actually," she said, lowering her voice conspiratorially, "she did tell me something, but I didn't think you believed in such things."

With a glance at the others, Grace persisted. "Well, are you going to tell us, or is it some kind of doctor-patient confidentiality thing?"

Robin, guessing what was coming, gave Catherine *the look*.

But Catherine, said, "Okay, if you really want to know, Molly Pat asked me to give you a message." She looked to see she had their attention. Grace leaned forward. "She says, 'Arf, arf, arf, arf!'"

The rest of them laughed, but Grace looked abashed. "I guess we—I deserved that," she said, more to herself than to the others.

When the group started back toward the cabin Grace hung back, her eyes downcast as she shuffled along, falling further and further behind her friends. Something in the road caught her eye and she squatted to pick up an ornate metal button, a Celtic knot forged in silver.

"Look what I found," Grace said, but either no one heard her, or, she suspected, they were ignoring her to let her know they disapproved of her mockery. With a shrug, she dropped the button into her sweater pocket.

"Good morning, my beautiful beasts," Robin said to the cats lying at the foot of her bed. Samson and Delilah stood, stiffening first their front legs then their back in a stretch, arching with a ripple that went from nose to tail.

Brad was long gone. In the three days since she'd returned to their house overlooking Lake Harriet, she'd seen very little of him, which was not unusual, nor was it unusual lately for them to converse with words that just skimmed the surface. He'd asked the proper questions—how the cabin looked, if she'd taken a lot of pictures, how high the creek was. She'd asked about his week—had he played racquetball, did he meet Catherine's husband, Erik, for lunch as planned, or had he once more been called away to deliver a baby— all which once would have stimulated animated conversation, but had lately become no more than mechanical pleasantries.

While she showered, Samson and Delilah took turns drinking from the faucet she'd left dripping into the vanity sink. They waited at the top of the stairs while she toweled off, and purred loudly as she slipped into leggings and a sweatshirt. Like synchronized swimmers, the smoke-gray cats pushed off the top step and arced down ahead of her, hitting the landing at the same instant, rounded the corner and skidded to a stop in front of the refrigerator. Samson, the one with longer hair, crowded in to supervise every movement of Robin's hands as she operated the can opener. Delilah sat motionless, squeezing her eyes together in pleasure.

"You really are luscious creatures," Robin cooed as she scooped fishy-smelling mush out of the can. They chirruped a response and dipped their faces into their hand-painted dishes. She continued to eulogize them as they ate, and when they were done, they stretched out on a sunny spot on the kitchen floor to have their lithe bodies brushed and stroked, ending with a gentle tug on the two tails.

Brad's breakfast dishes were still in the sink, so she rinsed them and put them in the dishwasher. The coffee carafe was cold to her touch though it was not yet seven o'clock. She poured herself a mug and slid it into the microwave.

With reheated coffee, her reading glasses and the *Star Tribune* in hand, she settled in her favorite spot in the sunroom, an extra-wide, high-backed chair with an oversized ottoman. Samson plopped himself on the stack of newspapers next to her like a furry animated paperweight, and began to perform his ablutions. Robin eased the front section out from under him, glancing at the headlines and the highlights from other sections of the paper.

"West Saint Paul Woman Missing. See page 1C," was the front-page teaser. She sighed and pushed her glasses up to rub the spot between her eyes. Despite the spring sunshine she felt a chill. No one forced her to read it, of course, but when Samson went tearing maniacally after dust gremlins, Robin's eyes were drawn to the missing woman's face, smiling at her from the stack of papers.

She was an attractive young woman with shoulder-length dark hair and an endearing smattering of freckles across the bridge of her nose. *Somebody's daughter*, thought Robin. *Her family must be half-mad with worry.* She hurled the Metro section across the room.

It had been forty years since Robin's school picture had graced the pages of the *Star* and the *Tribune* and the *Pioneer Press*, but it wasn't the kind of thing one ever forgot. After losing Robin in a custody battle, her father had taken her on a not-so-scenic tour of the United States that had lasted the better part of a year, a trip that had cost him his freedom and her mother her laughter. Instead of skipping rope and roller-skating and having slumber parties with her classmates, Robin had spent what should have been her fourth grade year being hustled from one tacky bungalow or motel room to another, crammed into a closet whenever someone came to the door, with instructions not to make a peep.

Delilah's low yowl brought Robin back to the moment. She lifted the cat to her face, nuzzling the silky fur against her cheek to restore her own inner warmth. She brushed a tear off the top of the cat's head, and Delilah turned adoring eyes to her.

"Oh, you precious girl. Thank you for loving me," Robin said, and Delilah did her squint-eyed version of a cat smile before curling into a ball next to her owner.

One hand stroked the cat while the other turned pages of the newspaper in her lap. Robin tried to read the international news, but found that while her eyes scanned one story, her mind was on another.

The photo that had already imprinted itself on her brain was that of a grown woman—not much older than Cass or Maya. Robin thought about her two daughters, far away in their small liberal arts colleges, one on either coast where they didn't have to endure at close range their mother's constant fretting over their safety, or witness just such scenes as this, when the mere photo of a stranger could elicit not only anguish, but a seemingly endless list of cautions, and many sleepless nights.

She left the crumpled newspaper where it lay, put on her shoes and grabbed a handful of tissues before heading down the hill for her daily walk around Lake Harriet.

Lake Harriet was just one of twenty-two lakes within the Minneapolis city limits. Four, along with their parks, formed the Chain of Lakes, beginning with Cedar Lake, connecting to Lake of the Isles made famous by the Mary Tyler Moore show, then Lake

Calhoun, the largest and most urban, and finally Lake Harriet, one of Robin's favorite places to be, long before she and Brad purchased the newly-remodeled 1930's home. It was, they were certain, the ideal location to raise their daughters, and only minutes from downtown and from both hospitals where Brad had privileges.

Robin was always uplifted by her three-mile walk. Sometimes she wore headphones to listen to a book on tape, but today she wanted to hear the birds and let her thoughts coalesce as they did sometimes when her body was in motion.

The path she shared with roller-bladers and dog-walkers took her past two beaches, the rose garden, the resurrected Como-Harriet streetcar line and the fairytale-like band shell, popular with music lovers, picnickers, and artists. Bicyclists swished past her on their designated path. Today there were two small sailboats on the water, but all the rental canoes remained in their racks.

The temperature hadn't quite reached the promised high of sixty-eight degrees, but with the sun on her back, she was grateful for the breeze. When she became overheated, she held her sweatshirt away from her midriff, wishing she'd layered her clothing for the inevitable hot flashes. By the time she got home, she was ready for another shower.

WITH A CLAMMY HAND, Martin wiped his mouth and stepped in front of the college monument. It was one of those spring days when the campus just begged to be photographed. New grass blanketed the grounds in soft green velvet, and clusters of apple trees in full bloom looked like white and pink cotton candy. A pair of students flung a Frisbee back and forth, several others sat along a brick wall talking or reading, but most were in classrooms, yearning to be outside.

Martin cleared his throat and drew the corners of his mouth into his public smile. He watched the anchorwoman—wearing jeans and black blazer, her idea of collegiate wear—prepare for her segment. Her hair was sunny blond, her eyes blue.

She gave the cameraman a few instructions, positioned herself on Martin's left and, on cue, spoke into the microphone. "In this lovely place of higher learning, seemingly sheltered from the rest of the city, police are hoping to learn what's become of one of Bradford College's employees, Melissa Dunn, whose disappearance was first noted Monday when she failed to show up for work. I'm speaking with Bradford College President Dr. Martin Krause. What can you tell us about Melissa Dunn?" she said, thrusting the microphone under his chin.

"Miss Dunn is our director of Development and an important part of our family here at Bradford College. Of course we're—"

"How did you learn of her disappearance, President Krause?"

"The secretary in the alumni office came to me just this morning. Miss Dunn had evidently called in sick last Thursday morning and has not shown up for work since."

"And no one has talked to her since then?"

"Not to my knowledge. One of our staff attempted to contact her several times. Each time her answering machine indicated it was full. She finally contacted Miss Dunn's mother, who, in turn, contacted me."

Speaking into the camera, the newswoman said, "Although her car remains in the underground parking garage of her apartment, Melissa Dunn has not been seen. Police are asking for anyone with knowledge of Miss Dunn's whereabouts to contact . . ."

Martin's face was grim as he, too, looked into the camera. It wasn't until the crew turned off their blasted lights and started packing away equipment that he realized the interview was over. When they piled into the news van and took off, Martin headed to his own car, where he pulled his cell phone out of the pocket of his sports coat, scrolled down his address book and pressed SEND.

Ross answered on the third ring, annoyance evident in his voice.

When Martin finished telling him about his television interview, Ross said, "It sounds like you handled it the way you had to. Is there anything else?"

Still talking, Martin wheeled his car out of the parking lot. "I just can't stop thinking about her. I keep picturing how she was . . . so vulnerable." Tears welled up in his eyes.

There was a long silence before Ross asked, "Why do you keep referring to her in the past tense?"

"I just mean, the last time I saw her. She was so beautiful." He was almost sobbing now. "I just want her back. All day I half expected her to walk into my office and say she just needed some space to cool off. She's done that before, you know, just started beating herself up for being involved with a married man, pressuring me to leave Brenda, and then she doesn't speak to me for days. She always came back, though, Ross. Always."

"I know." Another long pause. "You need to pull yourself together. She'll turn up eventually and you—"

The car ahead of him suddenly slowed in traffic and Martin slammed on his brakes.

Ross, once the squeal of rubber and Martin's swearing subsided, said, "You'd better concentrate on your driving. And unless you want to tip your hand to Brenda, you'd better put Melissa out of your mind. If Brenda gets any hint that there's a connection, well, I don't have to tell you. Martin, listen to me, there's nothing more you can do."

"I was just thinking—"

"There is nothing more you can do," he repeated.

WORKING IN HER DARKROOM, Robin's mind played around the edges of the state of her marriage. Neither of them, she realized, had made much effort to please each other lately. For some reason, they had, without even discussing it, settled into a routine of separate mealtimes. Part of it, of course, had to do with Brad's hours. But that was nothing new.

It had been a long time ago, but she remembered very fondly the early years when he would come home late and they'd dine on cheese and pâté, crackers and wine. More often than not, exhausted though he'd usually been, he'd had energy for lovemaking in those days. She smiled sadly remembering those evenings, how they used to finish their bohemian meal, then begin undressing each other in stages, his jacket and belt, her shoes and pantyhose coming off in the living room, his shirt at the top of the stairs, her blouse and bra at the bedroom door.

When had it changed? When the babies had come, when she'd had to choose between Brad's unpredictable schedule and regular mealtimes for the children, she had begun eating with the girls. Brad's meal was set aside to reheat whenever he got home. But then the girls left home, first Cass and then Maya, and she and Brad had distanced themselves even more, like those pitiful couples who, once the children are grown, find the only thing they had in common was their offspring. Had it really come to that?

Having lost her concentration, Robin set aside her equipment and left her photographs for another day. Climbing the stairs from the basement, it struck her that perhaps it wasn't Maya leaving home that had brought about the most recent changes, but Robin's almost concurrent diagnosis of cancer. First the surgery, then the chemotherapy, when certain food smells caused her to throw up whatever she had been able to eat. Brad had taken to stocking the refrigerator and pantry with bland food for her—Jell-O and chicken soup and crackers—then eating his own dinners, usually fast food, on the way home, so as not to fill the house with offensive cooking smells.

"Well," she said to herself in the hallway mirror, "You can be a victim or you can get off your butt and do something about it. What's it gonna be?" Her image nodded back at her.

Tonight, Brad expected to be home at a reasonable hour. Surely it would set a new tone if she fixed him one of his favorites for dinner, maybe stuffed pork chops with braised apples. She made a list and set off for the grocery store.

Back home, she unpacked the groceries and unwrapped the cut flowers, iris and daffodils, which she arranged in her grandmother's cut-glass vase. When the girls were young, this time before dinner had been Robin's favorite part of the day, when Cass and Maya would sit at the kitchen counter to do their homework. Invariably, they would stop now and then to talk about their day at school, rewarding her with little glimpses into their lives away from home.

She'd always had something for them to snack on—homemade cookies, still warm from the oven, clusters of grapes, pretzels to dip in cream cheese. She used to tune the kitchen radio to a classical station, in the belief that it would aid their studies and calm them after a busy day. Usually they would leave their studies after a while to give her a hand with dinner. They were both proficient and inventive cooks by the time they were in junior high. At least, she told herself, the girls would not be living on Cheetos and candy bars at college.

Chopping an onion, Robin's eyes watered. She wound up wiping her mascara off on the back of her hand. After sautéing the onion in butter, she added it to the bread and corn stuffing, which she packed into the slit pork chops. Humming as she worked, she wrapped the chops with twine, browned them and slid them into the oven. There were so many dinners she had eaten alone in recent years, a fork in one hand, a good book in the other, and although she had come to enjoy her alone time, there was something immensely satisfying about cooking for someone else.

Tonight, she set the table with cloth napkins, blue pottery dishes, the flowers and a vanilla-scented candle. Even if Brad didn't comment on her efforts, his mood would be mellow. She ducked upstairs to reapply makeup and slip into a black sundress that Brad particularly liked. Once she slid her prosthesis into the built-in bra, she checked herself in the mirror and liked what she saw.

The house was filling with the aroma of good food. Robin snapped off the kitchen radio, the classical station having gone to its scheduled talk format, and absent-mindedly turned on the small television near the breakfast counter to watch the six o'clock news while she prepared the rest of the dinner. She had so completely pushed aside her earlier distress that she was ambushed by the lead story. Salad tongs poised over wooden bowl, she looked at the screen, averted her head, looked back.

"I know that man," Robin said out loud. She wiped her hands and dialed Cate's number. "Turn on Channel 4," she said.

The cream Porsche crawled up the long driveway, slowing as it passed the Johnson cabin and nearby gazebo. Seeing no other cars, the driver proceeded to the far side of the property where two neglected outbuildings stood. The paint, once traditional red, had been subjected to sub-zero winters and hot humid summers so that now only patches of pinkish brown remained on the weathered wood. The Porsche stopped within fifteen feet of the larger shed, the one that had once housed farm animals but was now used for storage.

The driver sat motionless for a moment after turning off the engine and with it, the muffled bass of the stereo. Retrieving a small cylinder from the glove box, he pocketed it.

José emerged from behind the wheel, alert as he scanned his surroundings, silent but for the poplar leaves fluttering in the breeze. He strode almost noiselessly to the shed and, grasping the door's wooden handle, threw his weight into it. The warped door groaned open.

Dusty motes of moldy hay attacked his nostrils. After sneezing violently in the shadowy interior, he pulled out a fresh handkerchief and blew his nose. Setting his sunglasses atop his head, he paused to let his eyes adjust to the darkness, but no matter how long he stared at the space beneath the loft, there was no ladder where it had been only days earlier. Nor was there anything, he decided, looking around, that he could use to improvise. Cursing in two languages, José kicked the wall, setting off a new dust shower. He groped his way to the outside where his sneezes, though they echoed loudly, failed to clear his sinuses.

He considered his options. Undoubtedly, his presence had already been noted by the nosy little handyman, he reasoned, so he set off on foot in search of the man's trailer. After twice finding himself following a dead-end path, he turned and spied George's green trailer through the trees.

Someone was singing, if that atonal and nasal sound could be called singing. "*His clothes are dirty but his hands are clean. And you're the best thing that he's ever seen.*" The words were vaguely familiar. José shook his head and almost stumbled over George, who knelt behind his humble dwelling, apparently sorting his roadside treasures for recycling.

George jerked his head around and, losing his balance in the process, rolled with a clatter onto a mound of aluminum cans.

"Maybe you should just pick one key and stick with it," José said, offering a hand and a broad smile.

"Key?" George's puzzled expression softened into a lopsided grin. "Oh, the singing." He laughed in little bursts. "Heh, heh. Pretty bad, was it?" He stood, wiped his hands on his jeans and looked back at the pile of crumpled metal. "Well, at least I put my can in the right pile. Heh, heh."

José snorted. "I guess you did."

"What can I do for you?"

"I was wondering if you know where Johnson's ladder is. He wanted me to do some jobs." His fingers closed around the canister in his right pants pocket.

"Sure, it's up at the Bentley place." He hooked a dirty thumb in the direction of Robin's cabin. "The chimney needed—wait. What jobs? Far as I know, I'm the one who takes care of the Johnson place." George eased his glasses off and began polishing them on his shirttail. "Besides, I know you. You're the bartender."

"Hmmph." José shifted his weight. "Johnson's business associate, actually."

"Oh, a contractor, huh?" George settled his glasses back on his nose and adjusted the wire bows over the tops of his protruding ears. "I don't think so." He squinted up at the sun and shook his head. "Nope, not a contractor. You don't work with those hands."

José made a show of inspecting his hands. "I guess it depends on what you mean by *work*. I never had complaints from the ladies about my handwork."

George tipped back on his heels and did his *Heh, heh* of a laugh.

After sharing the laugh with him, José reminded him of the reason for his visit. "So, is it okay if I use the ladder?"

George grunted and bent to straighten up the pile of cans. "Never did say what you're doing up here."

"Ross wants some papers from the storage shed. See, I do his international business."

"Oh, yeah?" Again, he squinted into the sun. "Only a moron would keep papers in that shed. Can't even leave my work gloves there without mice eating the fingers right off 'em."

José rolled his head around, as if loosening a kink in his neck. When he looked at George again, he grinned sheepishly. "Okay, you're right, it's not papers." He laid a conspiratorial hand on George's shoulder. "Truth is, Johnson's girlfriend was coming on to me pretty strong the other night, and we had a little, whatchew say, tryst, in the hayloft. You know how it is."

George nodded, his tongue playing at the corner of his mouth.

"It was wild," he said letting George imagine it. "Anyway, when, uh, when we were finally done, she couldn't find her bra, a lacy little number."

George's head bobbed faster.

"I thought I'd better find it, you know, before our friend Ross Johnson does. He's got quite the temper. Besides," he said, leaning closer and cupping his hands in front of his chest, "Those babies shouldn't go unsupported."

George rubbed sweaty palms together, picturing it.

In LESS THAN AN HOUR, José was back, this time in the Porsche. He parked near the trailer and walked to the far edge of the clearing where George knelt to pat soil down on a newly spaded flowerbed. "*Lay across my big brass bed*," George sang, still searching, evidently, for a key he could stick with.

"I left the ladder by the shed like you asked," José said.

"Find what you were looking for?" George craned his neck toward the car.

"I did," he said, slipping a folded bill into George's shirt pocket. "I hope this'll stay between us."

"Mr. Johnson and I rarely discuss women's, um, underthings," George said peering up at him, and they both grinned.

José prodded a clump of dirt with the side of his shoe. "You didn't dig all that up just this morning, did you? It must be thirty square feet."

"Naw, it's an old bed. I had tomatoes there last year, but the darn squirrels and woodchucks and deer ate 'em, so I thought I'd try something with thorns this year. I just had to turn over the soil and put in a special fertilizer is all."

José pulled his sunglasses down to inspect the newly planted rosebushes, neatly lined up in the rectangle of soil. Then he turned on his heel and got into his car.

As soon as the Porsche was on its way, George reached into his pocket. He stared at the hundred-dollar bill.

After SPENDING PART of the morning on site with one of his foremen and an HVAC engineer, Ross Johnson took sanctuary in his cherry-paneled, plush-carpeted office with a view of the Mississippi River. From behind his desk he could see three of his downtown buildings— one still under construction—as well as a couple of warehouses he'd converted into posh offices and condos.

His secretary was a bony woman a couple years his senior with a tubercular-sounding cough. She walked soundlessly across the carpeted floor and plunked a stack of papers on his desk, giving him instructions about where he needed to sign the various documents, as if he couldn't figure it out from all the little yellow Post-It notes sticking out from the stack.

"Oh," she said as she turned to leave, "your last appointment for the day called to cancel."

Ross checked his watch, considering how to spend the unexpected free time.

They were startled by the sound of someone clearing his throat in the outer office. José strolled into the office, his long hair tucked behind his ears.

"It's okay, Maisy," Ross said to his secretary, "I think I can spare you for a bit while you run those spec sheets over to the architect." He motioned José inside.

She left with a surreptitious glance at the man's exotic face and tight black pants.

José fingered the Remington sculpture of a horse as he passed it, taking his time, forcing Ross to ask, "What are you doing here?"

"Well, boss, it's like this." He slouched in the leather wingback and stretched his legs in front of him. "See, I'm just going about my business, keeping a low profile. You know me, the soul of discretion. I see only what I need to see, you know, just concentrate on keeping my customers satisfied."

Ross gripped the edge of his desk. "Get to the point."

"Do I tell you how to tell a story?"

"Just say it!"

José tented his fingers, nodded slowly and continued. "So here I am, minding my own business, and I stop to get a few groceries, you know, bread, milk, a couple of man-goes . . ." He stretched out the syllables, enjoying Ross's irritation.

Ross jammed his pen into its holder. "You didn't come to tell me your grocery list."

"You know, I'd get through this a lot faster if you'd quit interrupting."

Johnson glared at him.

José examined the crease of his trousers before continuing, "I just happened to glance up at the rack where they display newspapers, and who do you think's on the front page?"

Ross turned to look out the window and scowled. "Yes. The young lady has been reported missing. So?"

His eyes were unblinking. "So I thought maybe we should talk about it. I mean, there are people who know she was at your place. People who have something to tell." He shrugged. "You know—if anybody asks."

Despite his urge to throw the man through his eighth-story window, Ross leaned forward, pressing himself into his desk. "Why would they do that?"

"Do what? Ask or tell?"

"Either. What's the connection?"

"You tell me."

"Okay, my friend is the missing woman's boss. So what?"

"She's got a name, you know. Melissa Dunn."

Ross glowered at him. "Yes, most people do have names. And employers. The fact that Miss Dunn works for the college hardly sets the bloodhounds on Martin's trail." He clasped his hands in front of him and smiled thinly. "And certainly not on mine."

"So what do you suppose happened to Melissa?" José asked in a conversational tone. "I mean, if she was too wasted to drive home, you'd think somebody would've found the car crashed somewhere along the way."

Ross restrained himself from massaging the throbbing vein in his right temple. "What are you saying?"

"I'm saying maybe other people who were there are asking themselves the same question. What could have happened to her? No crashed car, no body . . . Thing is, they all know Melissa was there," he said, accentuating her name.

"And they will all deny it," Ross growled. "You, for instance. As the man who supplied her with illegal drugs, I'm sure you're just itching to call the authorities."

José shrugged. "I'm not the only one who knows Melissa was at your place. I think you know what I'm saying."

Ross stared at him.

José stared back. "I think the phrase the police used is, 'Foul play is suspected,' and I think you know that's what we're talking about."

"Is that a confession?"

José snorted. "Gee, I thought it sounded more like an accusation."

Ross's fingers played over his top drawer where he kept the amber prescription bottle. It still had a little of the magic powder left in it. He wanted to reach in and snag a fingernail full to calm his nerves. "You're accusing me? Oh, that's rich." He tipped back in his chair, stared at the ceiling and shook his head. When he sensed José shifting in his chair, he lowered his eyes in a challenge. "Perhaps the authorities would be interested to know where you were when the young lady took off. As I recall, you were missing for a rather lengthy time yourself that night."

José stood. His teeth flashed whitely. "Just off satisfying my sweet tooth, boss—having some Candi, if you know what I mean."

Ross knew he was being baited. He just couldn't figure out why. "If there was foul play," he said, clipping his words, "you obviously know more about it than I do. Did you do something to her?"

"Did you?"

"You bastard."

"Oh, sure, I'm a bastard until you need a little fix. He pulled a glassine envelope from his shirt pocket and dangled it in the air, noticing how Ross's eyes fixed on it. "Which I'm thinking you need right about . . ." He laughed and flicked it across the desk to him. "Now."

Holy Redeemer Lutheran Church, flanked on three sides by small single-family homes, shared a city block with the neighborhood library that provided the growing church with overflow parking on Sundays. Robin had always loved the steeple, towering above mature oaks and maples like a beacon of safety. When, as a child, she had finally been reunited with her mother, she was humbled to discover that the congregation had prayed ceaselessly for her safe return.

Like so many of its members of Germanic and Scandinavian descent, the church building was tall and white. The essentialist artwork kept the interior from being downright austere, but it was the people who provided real warmth.

Even though it was still more than half an hour before the service started, a few parishioners had already staked out their territory in the sanctuary, making sure nobody else took the choice back pews that offered an inconspicuous haven for the terminally reserved.

Robin and two other choir members set up music stands in the choir loft for the special musicians—trumpet and French horn players and a flutist—then slipped back downstairs for a last-minute rehearsal. This day's service was to be a celebration of music, a highlight of the choir's musical calendar before their summer break.

A flurry of activity created its own percussive music in the carpeted church basement. Mrs. Gilbertson, the five-foot, silver-haired dynamo of the Martha Circle, yipped orders to the Luther Leaguers, who were fixing trays of refreshments for the social time that would follow the service. They clicked silverware onto laminated tabletops, snapped coffee decanters open and banged cupboard doors. Two girls slathered circles of date bread with cream cheese, garnishing each piece with a slice of pimento-stuffed olive. When the trays were finished, Mrs. Gilbertson carried them to the serving table. With a wary glance at one lanky boy with glasses, she held the plate close and said, "These are for *after* the service. God is watching."

As soon as she left, the boy slid back the plastic wrap from a plate of bars. Robin cleared her throat and he looked up guiltily.

"Go ahead," she whispered to him. "God's watching the date bread." Guilt turned to glee and he snagged himself a frosted brownie.

In the kitchen, Mrs. Gilbertson, whose first name may have been known to some but never used, measured coffee into a large commercial coffeepot, grumbling as she had for years about the Health Department's edict against making egg coffee.

In the far corner of the basement, the brass players began warming up and the flutist went through a set of scales and trills.

Robin, already gowned, took her place among the sopranos for their own warm-up exercise—singing the tongue twister, *aluminum, linoleum, aluminum,* in descending chromatic scales. She kept shifting her attention from the choir director to glance at the exterior door, willing Grace to appear.

The director looked at the wall clock and asked, "Robin, if Grace doesn't show up, are you prepared to do her solo?"

A muffled *aluminum, linoleum, aluminum* came from the doorway and Grace rushed in, grabbed a gown from the rack and slipped into line beside Robin.

"Thank God!" Robin breathed. "Where have you been?"

"Sorry. Overslept. Oops, we're going up." They turned to follow the rest of the choir. "Your shoes!" Grace hissed at Robin as they ascended the stairs.

Robin looked down at her white and red Reeboks. "Yeah, my feet hurt."

"Did Millie see them?" Grace asked, referring to their choir director, whose interdiction against tennis shoes and dangle earrings had caused at least two members to drop out of choir.

"She's not happy, but she said she'll overlook it this time."

"Oooh, Robin's on probation," Grace teased just before they entered the sanctuary, giggling.

The program was the best Robin could remember. Their music selection was diverse and carefully picked to showcase a variety of talents. The choir really got into the gospel songs, shedding, for a time, their natural reserve, to sway and clap and shout out their lines responsively. Two of the numbers were accompanied by bongo drums. Grace's solo, the second verse of "Beautiful Savior," was flawless, and the flute descant gave Robin goose bumps. The children of the Cherub Choir sang audibly and not one of them cried. Millie was beaming.

With the last notes of a trumpet fanfare reverberating in the sanctuary, the choir sang a benediction as they recessed down the center aisle, through the narthex and down the stairs.

In the basement, Robin and Grace hung up their robes before settling at a table with coffee—decaffeinated, the only choice—and some goodies.

Many parishioners left immediately after the service, most likely to glory in the spring weather. The faithful came to worship, but they sure as heck didn't want to be stuck within the painted concrete walls of the church basement when the weather turned nice. They might just miss spring all together.

"So how'd you wind up oversleeping today of all days?" Robin asked Grace.

"Just another night of tossing and turning. That is, until about 4:30 when I slept like a rock. I thought I had set the alarm, but maybe I turned it off in my sleep. Thank goodness Buffy woke me up," Grace said referring to her aging cockapoo.

"Where was Fred?"

"Fishing. Unwinding at the end of the school year. I didn't see Brad today. Or your mom. I thought they'd both be here." She glanced around the room.

"Brad had a middle-of-the-night baby. He just got home when I was getting up. And then Mom called to say she just remembered she'd signed up for a senior bus trip to the casino, of all places."

"Really!"

In past years, Grace and Robin had brought their mothers to church, where they would all sit together, and then go out to brunch afterwards. But two years ago, following a broken hip, Grace's mom had gone into assisted living and began a slow decline, mentally as well as physically.

Watching Grace's face, Robin figured she must be missing her mother. "Everything okay, Gracie?" she asked softly.

Grace appeared to be concentrating on nibbling a piece of bread. She stared at the last bite and sighed heavily. "I'm sick of it! Really sick of it!"

Robin was taken aback by her friend's vehemence. With visions of Grace upending the serving tray, she said, "But the date bread's traditional."

Grace stopped mid-rant and laughed dryly. "Not the date bread. My life! I'm sick of always being nice, boring Gracie."

Robin stifled her laugh with a napkin as one of the Luther Leaguers, a tow-headed teen with a pierced eyebrow, offered more coffee, brownies and date bread.

Grace held out her cup for a refill.

"Sorry," Robin said as she rolled her cup in her palms. "I really do want to hear what's on your mind. I thought things were good."

"They are. I have a great husband and two wonderful sons and a great job."

Robin nodded and waited. "Did something happen?" she asked at last.

"No, nothing happened. That's the point. I feel unexciting. Invisible."

Robin sobered as she considered the comment. "I suppose that's true for all of us. I sure haven't turned any heads since I turned forty. But we're not exactly chopped liver, more like vintage wine—"

"Where'd you get that? In your book of tired platitudes?" She winced as soon as the words left her lips. "I'm sorry, Robin, it's just that I'm so goddammed—" Immediately she covered her mouth and looked around to see if she'd been heard swearing in God's house. "I'm sorry. I don't know what's gotten into me lately. You know I love you like a sister." She put her hand on Robin's. "Maybe all I need is a makeover, you know, new hairdo, tummy tuck, facelift, liposuction, laser eye surgery, husband transplant."

Robin laughed. "Okay, you've made your point."

When Grace didn't respond, Robin let her eyes rest on the wall hanging, the quilting group's contribution to the church decades ago. At first glance, it was a simple tree, its wide-spreading branches reaching to the quilt's borders. Closer examination of the tiny fabric squares revealed a menagerie of animals, cleverly incorporated into the leaves and trunk, the ground and sky. As a child, she'd been told it meant that there was life in all things. But couldn't it also illustrate how we can be deceived by appearances? Or had there simply been a sale on animal-print cotton?

"Isn't it terrible about that missing girl from Bradford College?" Grace said, breaking an uncomfortable pause.

Robin sighed. "Those poor parents, not knowing what's become of her."

Grace wadded up her napkin and shoved it into her empty cup. "I don't understand it. Minneapolis used to be so squeaky clean."

Robin blinked. "Bad things happened in the good old days, too."

Grimacing at her faux pas, Grace said, "Of course they did."

"Makes you worry about your kids, doesn't it?" Robin asked. "I thought by the time they left home, we could stop worrying about them."

"Stop worrying? Yeah, fat chance." Grace gave a dry laugh. "How are Cass and Maya?"

Robin lifted her shoulders and eyebrows to indicate she didn't know.

"Aren't they done with classes?"

"Cass is, but she got a summer internship in the lab that includes room and board on campus, even a small stipend. Maya's done with her finals, but, being Maya, she got an extension on her Brit. Lit. paper and decided to room with a friend in the city while she finishes it. I'll see her later this summer. She hasn't bought a ticket to come home yet, so God knows when that'll be, and it looks like we'll have to make a trip to Portland if we're going to see Cass."

It was clear to Grace that Robin struggled with the separation. "These are weird years, aren't they? I don't know which is harder, having them too far away to check up on, or having them at home but without rules. Either way, they make sure you know only what they want you to know."

Robin laughed appreciatively. "I promised myself I wouldn't bug them, but after reading about that missing woman, I couldn't stop myself. I tried calling them both this morning but wound up leaving voice mail at both places."

"Maybe they were at church."

That made Robin giggle. "Yeah, like that's how we spent our Sunday mornings in college."

"Well, I did."

Pausing only a second, Robin said, "Okay, I guess Cass sometimes goes to church, but it was only six o'clock her time when I left the house. And what about Maya?"

"Either one could've turned off the ringer. Or slept at a friend's," Grace offered.

Robin smiled weakly and tilted her head in assent.

One of the Luther Leaguers came by with a fresh tray.

"Ooh, nut bars," Grace said. "You want one too?"

Robin declined, but Grace dropped a bar in front of her anyway.

"By the way," Robin said, picking a peanut from the goo and sticking it in her mouth. "Did you see them interview the Bradford College president the other night?"

"Martin Krause? Yeah, Fred was shaking his head at the obvious PR blather reassuring the public that his pristine campus is the safest place on earth." Grace understood the politics of academia better than most. As school superintendent, her husband, Fred, had employed those techniques on several occasions.

Robin nodded. "He looked familiar to me, but I can't figure out where I've seen him."

Grace said, "Fred and I met him and his wife at a literacy fundraiser a couple years ago. I can't remember her name, but we recognized each other from the Lakeside Health Club, back when I had a membership there." She patted her belly. "Maybe I should start going again." She looked at Robin. "And why are you wearing that scheming look?"

"I was just thinking that maybe you could, you know, accidentally run into what's-her-name, the president's wife. I bet she has some inside skinny on the police investigation." Robin wiggled her eyebrows.

Grace smiled wryly. "Yeah, and I'm sure she's going to volunteer all this classified information to a relative stranger."

"Of course she will. People always tell you things, Gracie. There's just something about you that inspires trust." She patted her friend's hand.

"Really?"

Robin saw something in Grace's eyes that hadn't been there for a while. Excitement, maybe. "Really," she said. "If a stranger walked in that door and sat next to you, he'd wind up telling you more about his life than he ever intended. I've always found it remarkable. It's your calling, Grace."

As Grace contemplated this, she began to grin. "So you're sending me on a mission?"

"If you choose to accept it."

The receptionist smiled and handed a membership folder to Grace. "Welcome back to the Lakeside Health Club."

Grace took the papers from the woman's tanned hand and tucked them into the side pocket of her gym bag.

"Have a fun workout," the health club worker chirruped.

"Fun workout," Grace grumbled as she headed down the hall. "Not everyone would put those two words in the same sentence."

Seeing the industrial-strength scale in the women's locker room made her shudder even before she stepped on it. The LED glowed her weight redly. At five-foot-seven she carried her 174 pounds well, but somehow it had settled more around her middle in the last half decade. Self-consciously she turned to see a petite woman nearby. "Who'd think a pair of earrings could weigh that much?" Grace quipped, but the woman's frosty smile told her that middle-age spread was no laughing matter here.

Casting her eyes about the communal dressing area, Grace hoped to see the college president's wife among the hard bodies in miniscule underwear. She hung her tailored navy suit and jade silk blouse in a locker and wiggled into her new black leotard. "They should put a warning on these," she muttered to a plump young woman who was attempting to put on her bra without removing her towel. "Spandex may be injurious to your sense of humor," she said, and the woman grinned without making eye contact.

Her black stretch pants hugged curves and exposed winter-white flesh from mid-thigh to ankle socks. Grace rolled her eyes, slammed the locker door and strode purposefully toward the exercise area. She did the two stretches she could remember, then tried merging into traffic on the oval running track. She jogged about halfway around, then slowed to a walk to complete the lap before moving on to the Nautilus equipment where she took her time and kept the weights light. No point injuring herself right off the bat. Although she kept scanning the room for President Krause's wife—what was her name, anyway?— it was almost an hour into her workout before she saw a tiny woman mounting an elliptical machine. Brenda—the name came to Grace as soon as she saw her. In skimpy yellow shorts and yellow-and-black striped tank top, Brenda Krause looked like an anorexic bumblebee.

Grace rolled her eyes again and sighed. Taking a huge swig from her water bottle, she stepped onto the adjacent machine.

Brenda looked up, smiled her recognition. "Haven't seen you in a while," she said, skewing her headphones to expose one ear.

"Oh, hi," Grace said, faking a double take. "Yeah, it feels good to be back." She slid her eyes sideways, and, seeing the little wattle under Brenda's chin, relaxed a little. "You've obviously kept up your regimen."

Brenda gave a little laugh. "Yes, but it gets harder and harder to see any results." She inclined her head in the direction of a curvy jogger who was attracting the notice of several males and a few females as she effortlessly circled the track, the whale tail of a thong showing above her workout pants. "No amount of exercise can compete with that."

Contemplating all that youthful exuberance made Grace weary. "I don't think I could survive being young again."

Brenda looked at her as if she'd committed blasphemy.

"Besides," Grace said, "would you really want to wear a thong? I mean, I've had underpants that aspired to being thongs. I never found the sensation pleasurable."

Brenda blinked and smiled crookedly. "Nor I."

They sweated together in the companionable silence of fellow sufferers until Brenda's machine blinked the end of her thirty minutes. "Have you done the Nautilus yet?" she asked as she wiped down her machine. Her cheeks were red and her breathing audible.

"Not yet. I'm not sure I remember how." Grace's hair clung wetly to her temples and forehead.

"Just follow me on the machines. It'll come back to you."

Grace inwardly groaned and massaged her aching glutes. If she was going to make it as a sleuth, she'd need to be a better liar, she thought. "Practice makes perfect," she said aloud.

"*Perfect* is no longer a realistic goal." Brenda swung a leg over the bench of the lateral pull machine and produced a thin smile. "We'll have to be happy with *Good Enough*."

Grace watched her pull the bar down to chest level, slowly letting it return to the top. She knew better than to make comparisons, but if she had Brenda's toned and taut body, she was pretty sure she'd consider herself good enough.

Or would she? Hadn't she always found fault, even thirty years younger and forty pounds lighter? It seemed the only way she'd ever liked her body was in retrospect. How often had she looked at an old photo of herself and thought she'd love to have that body back. Of course, at the time, she'd loathed the way she'd looked in a bathing suit, inspected the silvery stretch marks on her hips and pinched her flesh around her middle. She was pleasant-looking, comfortably married, her life predictable, but she longed to hear the word *beautiful*. Sometimes she thought herself a fraud being the only ordinary woman in a book club dubbed *No Ordinary Women*.

"Do you suppose you could take your nap someplace else?" a voice said behind her. "Some of us came here to work out."

Startled, Grace looked up to see a twenty-something man, his hairy shoulders glistening with sweat, lips turned down in derision. She hopped off the machine, seething at his condescension.

"What gives him the right?" she hissed at Brenda as she settled into the ab machine next to her.

"It's what I was saying. He's young. That's what gives him the right, whereas we are of an age to be disregarded." She took a swig from her water bottle. "Look."

Grace followed her gaze and saw the man suck in his gut when a scantily clad beauty stepped into the exercise pit.

"One consolation about our age," Grace said to Brenda, "is that we'll never be asked out by that arrogant prick."

Brenda covered her mouth to keep from spitting water all over the rowing machine.

IN THE DRESSING ROOM, Grace, feeling like her junior high self facing gang showers for the first time, changed in a private stall. As she applied makeup at the overlit, wall-length mirror, Brenda joined her, spreading out an array of cosmetics on the ledge. The bottles and compacts and tubes were an advertiser's triumph, the kind of overpriced snake oil women bought because on a subliminal level the packaging made them feel pampered, feminine . . . works of art, even. Despite her cynicism, Grace eyed the pretty packages, resisting the urge to say something like *Why don't you come over and we'll fix each other's hair and do makeup and nails.* She flushed hotly when Brenda seemingly read her mind.

"I got these when I had a makeover," Brenda said. "You should try it some time, but if you're going to do hair too, you should ask for my stylist. She's the only one I'd let touch my hair."

Grace wondered if she'd been insulted, but watched as Brenda pulled a salon's business card and pen from her planner and carefully wrote the name "Sonya" in fuchsia ink on the back.

"It couldn't hurt," Grace said to herself in the mirror. She tweaked a stray tress.

"That's not how I meant it." Brenda's mouth twisted in embarrassment. She took a gold chain and earrings from a drawstring pouch and put them on. "I thought I'd treat myself to lunch next door. Want to join me?"

GRACE WATCHED HER LUNCH companion tear unbuttered sourdough bread into delicate nibbles. Grace buttered and salted hers. They talked about the beautiful weather and laughed about the average Minnesotan's obsession with humidity readings in the summer and wind chill readings in the winter.

Brenda said, "We usually go someplace warm during semester break. It kind of breaks up the long winter, following the college calendar like that."

Grace didn't waste the opportunity. "Speaking of the college, I saw your husband on television talking about that missing girl. It must be so awful."

Brenda picked at her bread and frowned.

"For the girl's family, of course," Grace prompted, "but it's got to be a nightmare for the college too. I know how it is for my husband when there's bad press about any of his schools."

"Uh hum," Brenda said as she chewed.

"I suppose everyone's got a theory."

Brenda sighed. "Martin really can't say much. I know you understand."

"I'm going to order an iced tea. How about you?" Grace signaled the waiter and they placed their order. "They say it's usually a husband or a family member," she persisted.

"She's single."

"Then it's got to be a boyfriend. I'm sure they're checking that angle."

"You're a regular Nancy Drew, aren't you?"

Grace stopped, grinned. "I own the entire set. When I was a kid, I wanted to be Nancy Drew more than anything. She was so brave, and even when she was scared, she just went right ahead with the investigation and went into the dark basement with nothing but a flashlight."

"And she had that boyfriend. What was his name?"

"Ned. I used to picture kissing Ned." Grace stopped, embarrassed at the schoolgirl tone to her voice. "Do you know if Melissa Dunn has a boyfriend?"

Brenda took a gulp of water. "Rumor has it there were several. Not that I'd give much credence to campus rumor, but I do know she was a college employee dating students, which strikes me as inappropriate even if they weren't a decade younger. And I do think it will come out that she liked them younger."

"More power to her," Grace said.

The waiter set steaming bowls in front of them, and Grace dug into the tomato basil soup.

"WELL, I TALKED TO HER," Grace reported to Robin by phone that night. "Her name's Brenda, and she's intelligent and poised and actually quite nice. She filled Robin in on the conversation, as much as she could remember, and said, "I'm putting my money on one of the students. Some young guy, a college student who's attracted to older women."

Robin considered that. "If he's dating an older woman, would he be more likely to brag about it, or would it put him outside of the mainstream and force him to be secretive?"

"Hmm."

"It's possible she made it clear to him that it's against school policy and if they were going to continue dating, he'd have to keep his mouth shut."

"Right. He couldn't take her out in public."

"There's been nothing in the news about her dating students."

"Which is a good thing."

"Absolutely. I hate the way they always blame the victim's lifestyle, dredging up every boy they ever dated, every petty fight with a roommate, journal entries when they were angry or depressed. And college is such a time for experimentation," Robin said.

"Did you ever get hold of the girls?" Grace asked, mentally kicking herself for the lousy segue.

"Yeah, Cass pretty much shut me down. She said something like, 'Do you think one more story about a missing, kidnapped, murdered girl is going to keep me any safer? All you're doing is giving me enough nightmares to last five lifetimes.'"

"She never did mince words."

"And Maya got all sarcastic and said not to worry, that she's decided to avoid boys altogether."

Grace laughed. "I would never have talked to my mother the way kids talk today. But you know I've thought about my boys too. What if one of them was dating a girl who went missing. He'd be the number one suspect."

Robin shuddered. "So, what's next?"

"I guess if we're going to get the inside story, I'll have to keep close to Brenda. Maybe you want to meet her. You could go to the club with us Tuesday."

"Thanks, but I'm headed back to Spirit Falls. I know this was partly my idea, pumping Brenda for information, but do you mind?"

"Are you kidding? This is the most fun I've had in a long time."

When her car, seemingly of its own accord, turned onto the dirt road, Robin was surprised to find herself at the cabin already. Had Brad been with her, he would be chastising her for inattentive driving. Cass would be laughing about her "out of body" experience, ignoring the danger of driving on autopilot.

From the time she'd gotten onto I-94, her mind had been probing dark places. That damn missing person report had pushed her maternal button. She'd worked so hard to separate her experience from theirs, but she'd called them anyway, warned them, knowing as she did so that every time she tightened her grip on them, they pulled away a little bit more.

Her musings accompanied her to the cabin. Parking next to George's truck, she saw a ladder leaning against the southwest wall.

"Morning, Mrs. B.," George called from the roof. "Hey, I just finished checking your chimney—dug out an old squirrel nest and put a new screen in there too. It should work just fine now."

He clambered down and stuck out a sooty hand, then withdrew it. A black streak covered his forehead. "I'd help you with your stuff, but as you can see—"

"That's okay, George. I didn't bring much." She slung her camera bag over her shoulder and got groceries from the back seat.

He watched her, shifting from one foot to the other.

"Can I make you some iced tea?" She beckoned him inside, but he shook his head.

"Too grubby," he said, making no move to leave.

She reached into the grocery bag, fished out two lukewarm bottles of spring water and handed one to him. "Is everything okay?" She sat on the picnic bench.

He stood, uncomfortably, in front of her. "Don't know if I should mention it, but I heard something last night. Probably nothing, but I figure it came from around here. By the falls, kind of." He scratched his neck, didn't meet her gaze.

Robin waited. After all these years he was still an enigma to her, charming and laid-back one minute, edgy and awkward the next.

He made an odd grimace, as if preparing for the sting of a hypodermic needle. "It was kind of a scream, like. Just raised the hair on the back of my neck, I can tell you."

Robin's mouth had gone dry, but she smiled. "Don't tell me you believe in the ghost of Spirit Falls," she said in a teasing voice.

He rubbed at the soot on his hands.

"Was it like a woman screaming?"

He shook his head slowly. "Nope, not human, I think."

"A bobcat? Sometimes when somebody's cleaned fish at the creek, they carry on like that, screaming and yowling." She stopped, seeing him shake his head even more determinedly.

"That was no bobcat. I'm sure of it. It was like a real loud hissing, but as soon as I say that word, I know that's not it. Sorry, Mrs. B. I've been trying to come up with the right words, but I just can't. Thing is, if I say what I first thought, you'll really think I'm bonkers, but I thought it was the devil himself talking."

Robin wrapped her arms around her and stared at him. Was he trying to scare her? Maybe she should have paid more attention to Cate's reaction to him. Was there some reason he didn't want her here?

"Aw, dang it all," he said, thumping himself on the side of the head. "When am I ever going to learn to keep my big mouth shut?

Just forget I said all that." He gulped down the last of his water and carried the ladder to his truck.

WHEN HE'D LEFT, ROBIN sat on the back porch overlooking the falls and plugged her laptop computer into the outlet. After a couple hours, a warning message informed her that the computer was low on batteries and should be shut down immediately. She checked the cord. It was still plugged in. She turned the knob on the floor lamp. Nothing happened. Grabbing a flashlight, she headed to the back room to check the fuse box.

Her hand was on the master switch when she noticed two fuses were missing. A search of the tool drawer turned up no replacements.

That's odd, she thought as she hopped in the car and drove down to George's trailer. Though his truck was there, nobody was home. Through the screen, she saw a small brown bag with the blue lettering of the hardware store on the counter.

Opening the door, she went inside. The bag contained, as she'd expected, her replacement fuses. Of course in his telling her about the "devil's voice" he'd forgotten all about the blown fuses. She put the bag in the pocket of her denim shirt and looked around for a pen. In the second kitchen drawer was a pencil and as she snatched it out, she noticed a bracelet peeking out from a stack of papers on the counter. She eased it out. It was lovely, a broad and irregularly shaped band of gold and silver. It looked oddly familiar. One of George's roadside finds, no doubt.

She wrote him a note on a paper towel, thanking him for buying the fuses and telling him she would replace them herself.

ALTHOUGH THE MOON was bright that night, Robin left lights on. It was after midnight when she finally fell asleep with a Janet Evanovich book in her hands, but two hours later she was awake again. She kicked off her covers, read a few more pages, slept again, only to wake, her mind buzzing with ideas. She padded into the living room and turned on her computer, trying to capture the phrasing that had struck her as so profound when she'd thought it in her waking moments.

Several minutes later, nothing had come to her. She felt the sweat on her upper lip, felt the warmth rush into her chest and start her heart beating harder. A classic hot flash, according to her gynecologist. She closed her laptop and, stepping out onto the back porch, she let the slight breeze blow through her thin cotton pajamas.

When she heard it, she knew instantly it was the sound George had tried to describe and it took her breath away. It came from high up, either on the bank across the creek or in the trees overhead.

The writer in her tried to put it into words. "I froze at the sound, a horrific rasping scream," she wrote in her mental journal, "like a lion with laryngitis."

The next series of shrieks came, and she stared into the nearby trees, silver-edged by the moonlight. Again she tried to capture it in words. "It had an eerie, rasping quality, like a banshee being strangled."

Maybe George's description was the best.

She guessed it was a bird of prey—something big. As she stood in the pale light, her hot flash subsided, and she shivered in her sweat-dampened pajamas for a few more minutes before ducking back inside to wrap herself in an afghan.

Back on the computer, she plugged in the phone jack and logged onto the Internet. After typing the words "eagle, hawk, owl," she pressed the SEARCH button and followed the links. Before long, she found the culprit when she clicked on the picture of a barn owl, and a now familiar sound screeched from her computer.

She began clicking on more links, intrigued by this bird with its white, almost human face, and found that she and George were not the first to be unnerved by its ghastly sound.

"More than one culture believes that the barn owl's call invites Death," she read, "and the mere sight of a barn owl means somebody is about to die or some Evil is nearby."

The idea excited her. It would be a great addition to the book—the text drawing on folklore and superstitions. The photos, moonlit, would suggest the mystical quality of the woods. She grabbed her hooded sweatshirt and slid into a pair of scuffs in order to set up her camera on a tripod outside, then went back inside to do more research.

When the owl called again, she slipped out and shot a full roll, fairly certain she'd gotten a couple keepers of the ghostly creature perched in a pine, and several more of it gliding in silent flight. She reloaded and waited, letting her eyes adjust to the darkness. A pine bough bobbed, but before she took a shot, something else caught her eye, somebody slipping through the trees away from her cabin. And toward George's trailer.

IT WAS DAWN WHEN ROBIN fell asleep again. Her dreams were chaotic and troubled—wandering the streets of a strange city, alone and afraid of shadows. Or having the sole responsibility of several impossibly small babies that kept getting into a filled bathtub, one after the other so that while she was saving one, another would fall in. Or her cat Delilah running away and her other cat Samson barking at her.

She woke slowly, her eyelids too heavy to lift until she recognized Molly Pat's bark, accompanied by another, a bellow, actually. Groaning, she hoisted herself to look out the window just in time to see Catherine with what appeared to be a dirty white yak on a leash, the terrier leaping around it, yapping. And there was Foxy trying to get her little dog under control, but the yak circled Cate twice, three times, the leash binding her legs.

"Oh, Lord, now what?" Robin muttered. She quickly threw the sweatshirt over her pajamas and rushed outside. Cate, now untangled, but far from free, was being dragged toward the open cabin door at an astonishing speed. Foxy, weak from laughing, leaned against a tree.

The yak was making straight for Robin and would have toppled her if Cate hadn't jerked on the leash.

"What on earth is that?" Robin asked.

"We think he's a sheepdog/Great Pyrenees mix." Cate didn't look directly at Robin when she answered. "I got to thinking how much safer you'd feel up here with a dog."

"Dog?" She had the feeling this was still her dream.

"He's a sweetie, really. He's housebroken and neutered and really smart. You can't help but fall in love with him. Just look at those eyes."

Robin winced. "Cate, you can't keep doing this."

Just then, the dog bunched his shoulders, gave a mighty tug and was off, the leash bouncing behind him. Molly Pat raced after him and they disappeared behind the cabin.

"Grover! " Cate yelled, breaking into a run.

Robin turned to Foxy. "You're in on this, too?"

Foxy, holding her sides, nodded, tears of laughter in her eyes.

Grover reappeared, bounding and tugging as if pulling a sled. Cate had the reins again and wasn't about to let go.

Closing her eyes, Robin slumped onto a canvas chair by the side door. "Good Lord, Catherine, what were you thinking?" she asked, and dissolved into laughter.

Cate and Foxy sat too. Grover whined and rolled his eyes.

"He's just excited," Cate said lamely. "He'll settle down after he's checked the place out." She cupped the dog's huge jowly face in her hand and said, "Won't you, baby boy?"

"You mean he's not full grown?"

In non-answer, Cate turned to Foxy to ask if Molly Pat was okay off on her own and Foxy assured her that the smaller dog could be trusted to obey.

"Doesn't he just have the most luscious coat?" Cate asked, finger-combing Grover's fur. "And those eyes! Can you believe his owners just dropped him off at the shelter like he has no feelings?" Cate continued. "He'd do anything for you. You can see it in those eyes." She scratched his domed head and he flumped to the ground, rolled over to expose his belly, and moaned in ecstasy when Cate scratched it.

"What time is it, anyway?" Robin asked. "You must have gotten an early start."

Foxy looked surprised. "We woke you up, didn't we? It's a little after noon."

Cate looked at Robin with obvious concern. "What's with the dark circles?" She hardly missed a beat before adding, "See? If you had a dog here to protect you, you'd sleep. What time did you get to bed?"

"Which time?" Robin asked, then told them about George and the owl. She went in and got her spiral notebook and read to them some of her more interesting finds:

"The barn owl has been called ghost owl, death owl, hissing owl, hobgoblin owl, demon owl. Because of its human face, it has been thought to be a witch's familiar."

Catherine broke in. "Oh, nonsense. In Indian lore, owls embody wisdom and prophecy. They're considered helpful."

"Right, it says that, too. Owls have always been associated with magic and shamanism." She read from her notebook, "Egyptians and Mayans and Aborigines used owls in their art to be deities of death or wisdom. Athena, Goddess of Wisdom, has an owl on her shoulder, and in one of Michelangelo's sculptures, a barn owl stands at the feet of a naked, sleeping woman to guard against the darkness."

With a groan, Grover flopped over on his other side so that his big head came to rest wetly on Robin's foot.

"You slimed me," she said, easing her foot out from under the weight.

"Here comes Molly Pat," Cate said. "Come here, girl."

Grover sat up, suddenly alert.

Molly Pat, far less energetic after her romp, approached them, her tail swishing proudly as she dropped something at Foxy's feet.

Foxy patted her dog's head. "Where have you been? You're all wet."

Molly Pat sat and smiled her terrier smile.

"What did you bring me, girl?"

Molly Pat kept her eyes on her owner's face as Foxy bent, picked up the dog's gift, and began to inspect it.

Robin and Cate saw Foxy's expression change suddenly from one of curiosity to revulsion. With a strangled scream, she flung the object to the ground.

Perched against the top of the picnic table, Catherine angled her long legs down, her heels digging into soft dirt, her fingers fidgeting with the cord of her windbreaker. Robin, slumped on the bench, stared into the trees as if in a trance.

A few feet away, Foxy did a strange dance, her head and feet shifting to get a better vantage point to look up the cabin's driveway. "What time is it now?" she demanded.

Glancing at her watch, Cate answered, "One seventeen. Two minutes since the last time I checked."

"Foxy, come sit with us." Robin tried to keep the panic out of her own voice. "It's going to take the sheriff at least fifteen minutes to get here."

"I can't. Not when there's a dead body down there. Shouldn't we be doing something?" Her voice had gone up several notes.

"We did. We got the dogs away. At least they won't do any more damage." Cate looked back at the two dogs whining and pawing to be let out of the cabin.

"And we called the sheriff. What more can we do?" Robin asked. "Wait, that might be them now."

A siren wailed and the dogs started barking wildly. A few minutes later a sheriff's blue and white came into view, the siren dying to silence. A man hoisted his bulk out of the driver's door. He smoothed sparse, blondish hair back before putting on his hat, tugging it slightly to secure it. Giving the vehicle's door a shove, he made a futile attempt to hike up his pants under his protruding belly, then glanced quickly at the dogs, who were still causing a commotion. Out of habit, his right hand rested lightly on his revolver's handle as he walked toward the anxious women.

"This the Bentwood residence?" he asked laconically.

"Bentley. I'm Robin Bentley." She stuck out her hand.

"And I'm Sheriff Harley. Now what's this about a body?"

Just as Robin opened her mouth to respond, the canine chorus began a new refrain to announce the appearance of a second official vehicle skidding to a stop behind Sheriff Harley's car. A small but muscular woman in uniform emerged and purposefully strode toward them. Robin couldn't help noticing her wide-shouldered bearing, as if by affecting an exaggerated man's walk, she would exude confidence.

"Sheriff," the woman said, ginger curls bouncing as she nodded to Harley, "I caught the call and thought you might need some assistance."

"Ladies, this is Deputy Brill."

Deputy Brill's expression remained unchanged as the women nodded acknowledgement. Extracting a notebook and pen from her pocket, she flipped several pages and stood poised to record.

Harley put one foot on the picnic bench and rested his forearm on his thigh. "Why don't you start from the beginning. What are you all doing here?"

This is my property," Robin said.

"And your name again?"

"Robin Bentley."

The deputy looked over the top of her sunglasses. "Robin, like the bird?"

"Yes, and Bentley, like the car."

"Middle name?" the deputy paused, pen ready to jot down the answer.

Robin shifted uncomfortably. "Hood," she said, her voice barely audible.

All eyes but Cate's turned to her. Foxy's eyes were wide and full of mirth.

"My mother's maiden name," Robin muttered.

Sheriff Harley stuck a piece of gum in his mouth. "Okay, let's move on. Now who discovered the body?"

"Molly Pat did," Foxy answered.

"And which one of you is Molly Pat?"

"Oh, that's her. The smaller one." Foxy pointed to the now silent Molly who stood with her front paws resting against the screen door.

"The dog?" The sheriff glanced in Molly's direction.

"Uh-huh," Foxy answered.

"And you are—?"

"Foxy Tripp."

Brill slid her sunglasses up, headband-like. "So the dog's name is Molly Pat and your name is Foxy?"

"Frances M. Tripp, actually, with two Ps."

"Okay, Frances," Harley continued. "Did you actually see a body?"

She grimaced. "Well, at first it was just the finger. Molly had it in her mouth. We thought it was just a twig or something, but when she dropped it at my feet, literally, we could see that it was a finger . . . well, part of one—mostly just the bone."

"Are you sure it isn't just a chicken bone?" Brill began to close her notebook.

"It's not!" Cate almost yelled. "Look for yourself." She gingerly held out the Ziploc bag.

Brill took a quick look and handed it to the sheriff. "And your name would be?" She turned to Cate, who spelled her name for the deputy.

"Catherine Running Wolf," Brill mumbled as she wrote. "So, all of you have animal names?"

Cate's eyelids lowered a notch.

"And who owns the dog—the one with the person's name?"

"I do," Foxy said, and the deputy scribbled again in her notebook.

Sheriff Harley, apparently done with his cursory examination of the finger, hoisted himself upright and handed the plastic bag to his deputy. "Record this as evidence," he instructed.

While his deputy put the plastic bag in a cooler, Harley asked, "So where's the body now?"

Cate pointed toward the creek. "We asked Molly to show us where she found the finger and she led us through the woods to the edge of the creek, down where it makes a bend."

"We could see an arm through the brush," said Foxy, looking uneasily toward the creek.

Robin massaged the space between her eyebrows. "I suppose you want us to show you."

"Yup." Harley nodded. "Let's take a look."

Brill rushed to join them, pushing her way through the undergrowth as they clambered down the bank. "Yow!" she yelled as her curls caught on a bramble. She extricated herself and caught up with the others.

By the time they reached the bend in the creek, the sheriff's face was flushed.

"Over there." Foxy pointed.

Brill grunted and moved toward the pale arm, now partially visible in the underbrush. "Here's the rest of her."

Inching closer, they could now see legs, from the knee down, dangling off the slight embankment, bare feet in the water.

"You better stay back while Deputy Brill and I take a look," the sheriff instructed.

Robin, Cate, and Foxy watched from a respectable distance as the deputy bent over the body, which lay as if stretching out in this improbable area to take a nap.

Kneeling, Deputy Brill moved the weeds aside.

Looking over her shoulder, the sheriff's breathing became audible. "She must have been in the water a while. Probably got hung up on these." He gestured at the gnarled tree roots now exposed on the eroding bank.

Deputy Brill used her pen to move aside the dark hair that had fallen over the bloated face like a veil. "Nasty head wound."

Harley expelled a mouthful of air. "Looks like another canoeist went over the falls."

"In a dress?" Brill said, without looking up.

"Isn't that one of those things women wear over swimsuits?"

Deputy Brill shrugged her answer.

"Where's the canoe? I haven't heard of any showing up downstream."

"Mighta gotten hung up somewhere, or maybe someone found it and just figured they got lucky." He shouted up to Robin, "Seen anyone canoeing this spring, Mrs. Bentley?

"Not with the water this high."

"That could expl—"

"Sheriff, I don't think it's a canoeist," the deputy interrupted.

"What then?"

"Don't know. Maybe a fall from higher up."

They all looked at the rocky cliff, their eyes following a possible descent.

"Mrs. Bentley, I hate to ask you to do this, but could you come here and see if you recognize this woman? I have to warn you she's in rough shape."

Robin looked hesitantly at Foxy and Catherine before slowly making her way to where the sheriff and deputy stood. Her hand flew to her mouth. For an agonizing second, the dark hair and the body's position made her think of Cass, her firstborn, who in sleep always looked like a rag doll tossed carelessly on the bed. She shook her head. "No," she said hoarsely. "I don't think so."

"Sorry, I had to ask," he said as Robin, blinded with tears, stumbled back to Cate and Foxy. He barked at the deputy to call for the coroner.

"Don't you think bringing a boat from further down river would be faster?"

"Fine. Call Steve and tell him to get a boat here. Pronto. Then stay with the body until he gets here. I don't want any more critters grabbing a free lunch here." He turned and motioned for Robin, Cate, and Foxy to go back to the cabin, oblivious to the fact that Foxy was getting rid of her lunch in the bushes.

ROBIN OFFERED A STEAMING MUG to Foxy. "Ginger tea to settle your stomach," she said.

Molly Pat and Grover, eager not to miss any event that might involve food, trotted behind Robin to the living room where they sat expectantly in front of Foxy, watching as she sipped the herbal brew.

"I don't understand it," Cate objected. "A woman is found dead and the sheriff acts like it's no big deal."

"I know. He wants me to stop by his office tomorrow to sign a statement, and I'm just not convinced it's an accidental drowning." Robin paused, and added, "Although we do seem to have a drowning every few years."

"She didn't look like any canoeist," said Foxy.

"And that business about her dress. Robin, you were closer, did it look like a swimsuit cover-up to you?" Cate asked.

"I didn't really look at it." Robin shuddered involuntarily. "But someone slipping on the rocks, that makes sense. The other side of the creek is awfully steep."

"I'd like to know where George was during all of this," Cate said.

Robin sagged into the couch. "Why?"

"The guy seems to see everything. Why hasn't he come around to see what the sheriff was doing here?"

Robin squeezed her eyes shut and started to massage her temples, "I'm sure that if the sheriff hasn't talked to him already, he will. After all, George's place is the next cabin upstream."

"Cabin? You're calling that trashy little trailer a cabin?" Cate draped an afghan across her legs.

"What about that creep you were talking about, the party animal up the road," Foxy asked.

"Ross? He isn't up here any more often than I am, and just on weekends."

"Got a headache?" Cate asked Robin.

"Yeah, a real doozy."

"Why don't you go lie down and I'll wake you up in an hour and then we'll decide what to do about dinner."

Robin stood and headed off down the hall. "I'll try to get some sleep, but the thought of food—Ugh!"

"I FEEL GUILTY HAVING to get back to the Cities," Foxy said.

"It's okay," Catherine reassured her.

"I wish I didn't have that massage in the morning. I'd cancel, but it's one of my physical therapy clients." Foxy looked in her appointment book again. "You and Robin will be back in time for dinner at the Lexington, won't you?"

Cate looked blank.

"Dinner before the lecture," Foxy reminded her. "Tomorrow night."

Cate made a sucking sound through her teeth. "Yeah, we'll be back. If we don't make it in time for dinner, we'll just meet you in the auditorium."

"Are you sure you want me to take your car, Cate?"

Cate glanced toward the bedroom before answering. "There's no way I'm leaving her here by herself tonight."

"I can hear you," Robin yelled from the sleeping porch. "You don't need to babysit me."

"Like I'm going to leave you here in the middle of the woods after we discover a dead body. I don't think so," Cate yelled back. "We're roomies tonight, just like old times."

There was a crash and a clatter and the three women dashed to the kitchen. Robin, barefooted, stepped in something damp before she noticed the overturned garbage can. She grabbed a paper towel and wiped coffee grounds off her foot.

Kneeling next to Grover, Cate stroked his head and said, "We're going to have to have better manners than this, my friend. We're guests of Auntie Robin's tonight." Looking up at Robin, Cate gave her a don't-be-mad-at-him grin. "Go back to bed. I'll clean this up," she said.

Robin sighed. "Cate, you don't really expect me to keep this doofus."

"Hey, you'll give poor Grover a complex with those derogatory terms."

At the sound of his name, Grover wagged his tail, splattering the refrigerator with wet coffee grounds.

LATER, AFTER A DINNER OF SOUP and toast, Robin was curled up in the overstuffed chair while Cate stretched out on the couch under an afghan. They stared into the flickering flames in the fireplace.

"Doesn't today seem surreal?" Cate asked.

"To think she may have been lying down there the whole time I've been here," Robin said with a shudder. "It's just so . . . *ishy*"

"You know *ishy* isn't a word, don't you?"

"It is in Minnesota." After several minutes, Robin said, "Cate, thanks for not leaving me tonight."

"What are friends for?"

After closing up the cabin the next morning, Robin drove with Cate and Grover to the new brick county courthouse. Parking in the shade, Robin hopped out and entered the building while Cate stayed behind to get Grover settled. The dog finally groaned and lay down on the back seat with head resting on paws. She scratched his muzzle and said, "Don't worry, boy, I won't be gone long."

Grover tilted his huge head to one side as if he understood.

She rolled the car windows down several inches and got out, apologizing to Grover about the inconvenience and promising a swift return. She entered the building, ignoring the dog's pitiful whining, and walked down the hall to where Robin waited, none too comfortably, on a metal chair in Harley's office, staring out the large window that framed, like a Wisconsin tourism ad, a forest glade surrounded by rolling hills.

Sheriff Harley sat a few feet away at his cluttered desk, his fingers clicking haphazardly on the computer keyboard. "Just about done," he said, sensing Catherine's arrival.

Robin pointed wordlessly and Catherine looked out the window. About twenty yards away, a doe and her fawn stepped to the wooden box in the clearing and began daintily nibbling at the corn. Another deer, mostly concealed by prairie grasses, drank at the pond's edge.

Harley pushed his chair back with a clatter and waited for the printer to spit out its pages so he could snatch them up. He handed the affidavit to Robin. "They don't scare too easy," he said, with a nod to the deer. The doe looked through the window at them, twitched her ears, and kept chewing.

Robin read the statement carefully, handing each page to Catherine as she finished.

"Well?" Harley rubbed the back of his neck. "Did I get it right this time?"

Robin saw that he'd nicked himself shaving—twice, right under his nose—"Pretty much," she answered, "but Catherine is spelled with a *C*, and Grover is *not* my dog."

He looked at Cate. "Yours?"

"Not for long," Catherine answered, shooting her friend a grin. "I brought him here figuring he could keep Robin company when she's at the cabin."

"What about when she's *not?*" Robin muttered under her breath.

Catherine sighed. "Will this take much longer? I left the dog in the car."

"Just about done. Any more corrections to the statement?"

Robin and Cate exchanged a look before Cate said, "You refer to the woman as the 'drowning victim.'"

"And you think it should be . . . ?" He made it a question.

"I thought this was a 'Just the facts, ma'am' kind of statement."

The sheriff turned his full attention to Catherine. "Okay?" Again, a question.

"Well, it sounds like opinion to me. We don't know she died from drowning, do we?" Despite Cate's soft voice, Robin could tell she'd dug in for a battle.

His bemused expression didn't wane. "We could say 'her *water*logged body, found in the *water* below the *water*fall.'"

"That would be more factual."

"Anything else?"

Catherine's jaw had hardened. "You're treating this as an accidental death, aren't you?"

"For now."

"What about the dress?" Robin asked.

"That's in there," he said, poking at the statement.

Cate read, "'The body was clad in a red dress, slip, or bathing suit cover-up.'"

"Yes?"

"It was a dress."

Unperturbed, the sheriff tilted his head and smiled. "That's your assumption."

"Well, what was she wearing underneath, a bathing suit or underwear?"

Harley scribbled something on a notepad.

Robin cleared her throat and asked, "How long do you think she was in the water?"

"The coroner thinks a week or two."

Robin blinked and slowly turned her eyes to meet Cate's.

"Oh!" Cate exclaimed.

"That's—" Robin cut herself off abruptly.

"That's what?" he prompted after an uncomfortable silence.

"That might have been when we were here. There, I mean, at my cabin," Robin said at last. "Almost two weeks ago. Five of us."

Catherine nodded. "The last weekend in May."

There was a commotion in the outer office and Harley's face registered annoyance. Deputy Brill appeared in the doorway. "Oh good, you're still here," she said to Harley, completely ignoring Robin and Catherine. "I had a 10-33 on Overlook."

He grunted.

"Is this their statement?" Brill asked. Still not addressing the women in question, she took a copy and began to read.

"I've got it covered, Brillo." There was a growl in Harley's voice.

From the way the deputy's cheeks flushed, Robin guessed it was not a favorite nickname. "I'll just take a quick look."

"I'm still revising it." Harley rearranged the chairs by his desk and motioned for Catherine and Robin to sit. "The last weekend in May," he said. "Is that beginning Friday the twenty-fifth?"

"The two of us came up Thursday, but the others, three more, came after work on Friday."

"They were at the falls at the end of May?" Brill made a point of searching the affidavit. "I didn't see that here."

"I said I wasn't finished." Harley tapped on the keyboard, asked questions, tapped some more. "So, there were five of you that weekend—so, besides the three of you, who was there, then?"

When they explained that it had been an all-women book club, Brill cut in. "You all drove from Minneapolis to discuss books? Nothing else?"

"We did other things," Cate answered hotly.

"Tell me." Deputy Brill planted her feet wide and folded her arms over her chest.

Catherine's eyes narrowed. "We ate, talked, laughed, went for walks. And yes, we did talk about books. And tonight the five of us are getting together again for dinner and to hear a Minnesota author read from his new book."

"Nothing wrong with that," Harley interjected.

The deputy continued, asking what kind of books they liked.

"This month it was a nonfiction, but we talk about all kinds of books," Robin answered. "Historical fiction, biographies, mysteries, classics, fantasy."

Brill sniffed. "I read books, too. I just never knew you had to be in a club to do it. What's the point of that?" When she shook her head, her Orphan Annie curls didn't budge.

Catherine, smiling as she sometimes did to disguise anger, said, "It's a common bond, that's all. And it forces us to read a variety, so we don't just do all murder mysteries, for instance."

"Ah! Murder mysteries, for instance," Brill echoed. "I see the problem there. You sit around reading murder mysteries until every dead person has to be a murder victim."

"Deputy, why don't you go check on their dog while I finish this. Maybe take him some water," the sheriff suggested.

When she'd gone, Harley resumed the questioning in a less irritating manner. They told about the storm and about hearing a thud, then finding paint on a tree the following morning. Harley took it all down. "Have you seen anything strange on this visit?"

Robin began to tell about the eerie sound she'd heard—was it last night or two nights ago? "It was like nothing I'd ever heard, and when I stepped outside to check it out, I saw something moving in the trees."

From the doorway came Brill's voice. "Let me guess. It was a woman—a beautiful young woman walking along the riverbank in a flowing white dress—kind of transparent, like you can see the trees through her."

Catherine jumped up. "No!" she shouted before bolting for the door.

Robin found her friend's reaction inexplicable until she looked where Cate had been looking.

On the other side of the window, Grover bounded across the clearing, looking more yakkish than ever, in hot pursuit of the deer. Then came Catherine, rounding the corner at a dead run. Though Robin and Harley and Brill could see she was yelling, no sound came through the reinforced glass, and so they watched it like an old silent movie. All that was missing was a little chase music. And like moviegoers, none of them made a move to help.

The deer melted into distant trees. Grover came to a halt only after he found himself slogging through a muddy marsh. Dejectedly, he turned back, reaching solid ground at about the same time Catherine caught up to him. Seeing her chance, she made a grab for him, missed and fell forward with a splash in the mud. Grover, reinvigorated by this new sport, leaped on her, knocking her back down whenever she tried to stand up.

CATHERINE SHOWERED in the jail intake area and changed into fresh clothes from her suitcase. Brill hosed the dog down, penance for opening the window "just a little bit more so he could get his head out."

Harley finished typing the statement and handed it to Robin to read. "It's a damn shame. Must've been a pretty girl before . . ."

Robin's reaction was immediate. "Based on what? And will it be less tragic if it turns out she wasn't pretty?"

He rolled his lower lip between thumb and forefinger. "You're right."

She handed him the signed affidavit, saying, "It is a damn shame. But you've got to wonder, where is her mother in all this?"

"What about her father?"

Robin looked up, surprised. "I guess I always thought a mother would know if something happened to her daughter."

"Hmm. Like a test of love? If she doesn't have a continuous psychic connection with them she must not love them enough?" His eyes passed over her face.

How could he have known? She felt herself flush. *All those years of therapy,* she thought, *and we're right back to that same childish assumption that a loving mother should be able to protect her children from all harm.* "What are you doing to find the woman's identity?" she asked.

"I sent something around to the surrounding counties. Not too effective without the coroner's report."

"What about that missing Minneapolis woman?"

"Which one?"

"The one from Bradford College."

"She's not the only missing person," he said with a weariness. "Going missing isn't all that unusual in the big city. No, I'm betting she's a local girl."

She started to protest, but he held up his hand. "Now don't be obsessing over it. Better you leave it to the professionals."

Cate returned, toweling her hair with Robin's beach towel. She shut the door behind her and stood next to the filing cabinet.

A dripping wet Deputy Brill tapped lightly on the door and poked her head in. "The dog's drying off out front. Don't worry, he's on a leash." She had the grace to look chagrined.

"Thanks, Brillo."

The deputy nodded without a smile. "By the way," she said, turning to Robin, "does your reading club have a name?"

"We, uh, we call ourselves the No Ordinary Women."

Brill snorted. "Figures." She turned, leaving wet footprints as she walked from the room.

THE LEXINGTON, WITH ITS DARK paneling and heavily gilded frames, had the clubby smell of old wood and old money. Martini lunches and cigars had left an indelible aura in Saint Paul's historic restaurant on the corner of Lexington and Grand.

"We're meeting friends," Robin informed the hostess before spotting them under the chandelier.

"You must be the detectives," the hostess said in a low voice. She grabbed a pair of menus.

Cate and Robin exchanged quizzical looks. As she led them to the table, the hostess, now in a conspiratorial whisper, said, "Don't worry. I won't blow your cover."

"Okay, who told her we were detectives?" Cate demanded.

Foxy faked innocence. Louise laughed.

It didn't take a detective to figure out that Foxy had already told the others about their gruesome discovery at Spirit Falls. Though their words conveyed a sense of horror, the women showed open curiosity when they asked about the dead body. As they leaned forward, pressing her for details, Robin wanted to recoil. The word that came to her mind was *Schadenfreude*, one of those uniquely German compounds to describe the secret pleasure some people derive from another's misfortune, but she soon realized this was the way they'd chosen to deal with it, like whistling in graveyards. By allowing themselves to be caught up in the plot, treating it as just another murder novel to discuss, they were distancing themselves from the ugly reality of a decomposing corpse and a family caught in a nightmare from which they would never wake.

Like a tag team, Robin and Cate picked up where Foxy's account left off, describing their own reactions and their interactions with a kindly, if somewhat condescending, sheriff and his well-named deputy, the abrasive Brillo.

"Did you get a good look at the body?" Louise asked indelicately.

Foxy set her fork down and covered her mouth with her napkin. Robin shot Louise a warning look.

"I'm sorry," Louise said. "I didn't want to hear the gory details or anything. I just wondered if the hair color and age of the woman matched that missing woman from the college."

Cate glanced quickly at Robin and nodded. "It's impossible to tell. The body was so . . . yes, we think it could be her."

Robin finished her sentence. "But the sheriff is stuck on the idea that she's from Wisconsin, so he's just focusing on the counties around there."

"And basically told us not to worry our pretty little heads about it." Cate tossed her hair over her shoulder. "It just pisses me off."

Equally incensed, Grace said, "Well, *some*body's got to be worrying their heads off over her."

Robin threw her hands up. "Oh, no. Apparently missing people are a dime a dozen in the Twin Cities. At least that's how the sheriff talked."

"I guess we just have to expect that kind of thing in the Big City," Cate added bitterly.

Louise drummed her nails on the table. "So he won't even send out a description to Minnesota? What's a dead girl got to do to get attention?"

There was some nervous laughter.

She stopped talking when she noticed the waitress was lingering at the next table, getting an earful as she poured coffee from what looked like an Acme bomb straight out of a Roadrunner cartoon.

"Didn't you say he was going to wait for the autopsy report?" Foxy asked when the eavesdropper left.

"How long can that take? Surely they can tell the sex, age, height and weight without cutting her open and—"

"Louise!" Cate and Foxy said together. Several diners turned their heads.

"Okay, topic change," Grace suggested.

"That was insensitive of me," Louise admitted.

TWENTY MINUTES BEFORE 8:00, the five women were seated in the auditorium at Macalester College, waiting for the author to read from his latest bestseller. They passed the time talking about books, and Grace brought up a mystery, written by another Macalester alum, that had prompted one of their best discussions.

"That story still gives me the creeps," Foxy said. "Did we ever decide if the woman died by the end of the book?"

"He left it up in the air," Cate answered. "You kind of make up your own ending."

Grace said, "That's what drove me crazy about that book."

"That's what I loved about it," Louise countered.

Robin jumped in. "Can you imagine just settling for a 'presumed dead' pronouncement?"

Foxy looked at her intently. "We're not talking about fiction now, are we?"

Robin looked away, her eyes brimming with tears. "I saw the sheriff's report, referring to her as 'Jane Doe.'"

Foxy blew air out of her cheeks and shook her head.

"They'll find out who it is." Cate took Robin's hand and squeezed it. "And if they don't, maybe the No Ordinary Women will have to."

"We won't let it go unsolved," Grace said for them all before adding, "In fact, I found a great trench coat at T.J. Maxx this morning. I'm all ready to go undercover."

I t took Robin a long time to fall into a fitful sleep. Soon she woke to Brad shaking her shoulder. "What's wrong, hon?" he asked in a froggy voice.

"I finally fall asleep and you wake me up to ask me what's wrong?" she snapped. Whatever she'd been dreaming was lost in her irritation.

"You were chasing cars in your sleep again."

What did he expect from someone who'd just discovered a dead body? "Very funny," she said, grabbing up her pillow to take to the spare bedroom so at least one of them could sleep.

"Stay here. I'll move." He looked all rumpled and bleary, and she knew he needed his sleep.

"No, but thanks. I'm not sleeping so well, anyway." She tousled his hair and left the room.

The sun was well above the horizon when she woke to the sound of her doorbell. Snatching her terrycloth robe from the bedroom, she rushed down the stairs, all the while pawing inside the robe for the sleeve opening. Samson and Delilah, having been awakened from their mid-morning nap, thundered past her down the steps, a favorite game of theirs. Delilah had already reached the bottom of the stairs when the doorbell rang again, but Samson abruptly stopped on the third step up to look back up at his mistress.

Trying to sidestep him, Robin stumbled and grabbed the railing, wrenching her shoulder.

Samson blinked, apparently astounded by her clumsiness.

Through the sidelight, Robin saw Cate preparing to push the bell again.

"I'm coming," she yelled, wondering, as she often did lately, about short-term memory loss. She flung the door open. "Cate, did we—?"

"Yeah, I know we were supposed to meet Grace at her office later." She slid a large purple shawl from her shoulders and slipped through the open door and into the kitchen. Setting her batiked tote on the table, she extracted a folded newspaper. "Here, read this."

Robin stopped mid-yawn to take the *St. Paul Pioneer Press* from her outstretched hand. Sitting at the kitchen table, she scanned the front page, her eyes widening.

Cate, hovering over her shoulder, instructed, "The full story's in the local section. Here."

Robin turned to a photo of Melissa Dunn flanked by two smiling parents.

"There are more photos on the next page." Pausing for breath, Cate added, "Her folks live in Highland Park. They still have no idea where she is."

Robin directed Cate to make coffee, hoping the diversion would end her friend's chatter so she could absorb every word of the article.

Without hesitation, Cate opened the proper cupboard, pulled out a filter and the coffee canister and soon had a fresh pot brewing. "The reason I came here is that Grace called," she explained. "She isn't going to join us for lunch. She says she made other plans and when I asked a question she acted all mysterious." She filled two china cups and set one in front of Robin.

"Hmm." Robin skewed her mouth to one side, thinking about Grace.

"Well, keep reading." Cate flapped a wrist toward the newspaper. "It says the police have talked to some of Melissa's friends, including her boyfriend who's a grad student." She raised one eyebrow.

Robin read from the article. "Authorities are looking into the possible connection with a body found in Wisconsin. Pending the coroner's report . . ." She turned to Cate. "It's our body, isn't it? It's got to be."

SHERIFF HARLEY GRABBED THE PHONE on the first ring and barked his title, then leaned back in his chair, swiveling to face the windows. "Whatcha got?" Looking out into the trees, he listened in silence. "When do you expect you'll have the final report?" He nodded at the reply, turned to replace the phone, and saw his deputy standing in the doorway, arms akimbo.

"Was that the coroner?" she asked.

Harley sighed. "Yes, Brillo. What do you need?"

"What did he say?"

He slapped his thigh. "Inconclusive. He won't commit to anything before the results come back from the main lab, but he's got nothing yet that proves she drowned. The tox screens should be back by the end of the week, and her prints have been sent off to Madison."

"So basically, we know nothing."

Sheriff Harley grimaced as he shuffled through some papers. "Blast it, where did it go? I think we need to talk to that Wellman fella again." He pounced on an official document and flipped through it. "I know there's something here . . ." His voice trailed off, and Deputy Brill backed out of the room, leaving him to his musings.

§ • ∞

MANEUVERING HIS WAY DOWN the gravel driveway, Harley's chapped fists gripped the steering wheel. Just before his car pulled to a stop beside George's old pick-up, a pair of pheasants whirred past the open passenger window, causing Brill to gasp. Embarrassed, she turned it into an elaborate throat clearing.

"Looks like he's home." Harley heaved himself out of the prowler, pausing to adjust his holster.

An overturned bag of aluminum cans covered the path.

"What a dump! What does he do with all this junk?" the deputy asked.

"He's what you call a 'committed recycler.'"

"Yeah, well maybe he should be committed," muttered Brill.

As soon as Harley knocked, the inner door opened and a disheveled and unshaven George came into view. "H'lo, sheriff." Bobbing his head toward the deputy, he addressed her as, "Ma'am."

"Sorry to disturb you again, Mr. Wellman, but I need you to take a look at something. Can we come in?" Sheriff Harley reached for the screen door.

"I guess." George smoothed the front of his shirt as he backed up to allow them entrance. "Wasn't expecting anyone." He snatched a dishtowel and tossed it over the magazines on his coffee table.

Deputy Brill stopped just inside the door, pulling notebook and pen out of her pocket while she scoped out the kitchen, with its small gas stove and Formica table.

Harley paused to scan titles of books filling three shelves of the narrow bookcase in the living room. "I see you're quite the history buff," he said to George.

"Yeah, you might say that."

"Second World War, Civil War, Vietnam," Harley said, touching some of the book spines. "Were you in the service?" he asked casually.

"Yeah, I went into the army after high school. Did a tour in 'Nam."

"Army?"

"Marines."

Harley nodded. "Well, let's get this over with." He motioned to the well-worn couch. "Just a couple questions."

"I already told you," George said, clearly nervous. "I didn't see any canoes on the creek. The water's been too dang high."

"Yeah." Sliding a photo from his shirt pocket, Sheriff Harley flipped it for George to see. "Ever seen her before?"

His Adam's apple bobbed up and down. "Oh, Lord, that's her, isn't it—the dead girl they found?"

"You know her?"

George shook his head.

"Seen her around town?"

No response.

"Maybe you ran into her at a bar. You like the Bear's Den, don't you?"

George was trying to remain calm but he could feel the color rising along his neck. Suddenly he stood and jerked open the refrigerator door. "Can I get you two something to drink?" George asked.

"No thanks," they both answered.

"Well, I'll have one." George cracked open a can of beer and shoved things around on the counter, his back to his uninvited guests. He took a long swallow before turning to them.

The sheriff scratched the top of his head and said, almost to himself, "Attractive girl. Hard to forget if you saw her."

George leaned against the counter and crossed his arms. His lips were pressed together.

"I hear rumors, you know." Harley frowned as if it pained him to say it. "People say there's not much around here you don't know about, that you keep a real good eye on your neighbors."

After another gulp of beer, George said, "I pretty much mind my own business."

"Hunh!"

George readjusted his glasses.

"But you do like to know what other people are up to."

No answer.

"Thing is, George, I need your help. An innocent girl is dead and I think you can help us find out who she is and how she came to be dead."

"I don't know!"

"What the sheriff is pussy-footing around about is that we know you're a window peeper," Brill burst out. When she saw the anger in her boss's eyes, she added, defensively, "Well, it's true. He's just lucky no one's filed a complaint yet." She slipped the towel off the table, revealing a *Hustler* magazine beneath. "Well, well, well."

George snatched at it. "That's mine!"

"Sit down, George," the sheriff said tiredly.

Reluctantly, he sat.

Brill fanned herself with the magazine. "Are you saying you don't like to look at naked women?" she taunted.

"Oh, hell, who doesn't?" Harley snarled. Turning to George, he assumed an avuncular expression. "I know how it is, George. It's hard to meet pretty girls around here, right?"

"Yeah," George conceded.

"So this girl—" He held up the photo again. "Any normal guy's gonna look at her."

George nodded slowly.

"So what happened? Did she catch you looking at her? Things get out of hand?"

A dark look settled on George's face and he leaped to his feet. "If you don't have a warrant, you can just get out of my place."

As the screen door slammed behind him, Sheriff Harley turned and said, "If you suddenly remember something, you be sure to call us."

AFTER A LEISURELY WALK around Lake Harriet, Robin and Cate decided to forage in the large Bentley refrigerator for lunch. They put out last night's asparagus, al dente, with a sauce of stone ground mustard mixed with lemon and mayonnaise, a chunk of whole grain bread with olive oil, and some smoked whitefish. When the coffee pot was empty, they switched to ginger iced tea.

"Great necklace, by the way," Robin said, reaching across the table to touch the polished pink stone hanging slightly above Cate's turquoise pendant.

Cate stroked both pieces. "Thanks, it's rhodocrosite. As soon as I finish the matching earrings and bracelet, they're going to a shop in Door County."

Robin shook her head and laughed. "So you can write off your Wisconsin trip this fall, right?"

Cate wiggled her eyebrows. "Growing up poor, I guess you never stop looking for bargains. But speaking of jewelry, I have to drop off my booth fee with the art fair people this afternoon. They're scaling back the number of artists this year and inviting only those who made two-thousand dollars in sales last year. The cut off is—Yikes!" she said, looking at her watch. "In one hour. Got to go."

Robin slid her bifocals to the end of her nose in her best rendition of their old English professor, and said in Professor Godfrey's quavering voice, "I accept no late work. In my class, it's Bettah Nevah than Late."

Cate shut her eyes, covered her ears and squealed in protest. "Don't!" Then, facing Robin in all earnestness, she said, "You know, I still have nightmares about him. Do you realize he's still head of the English Department?"

"Oh, my Lord, he's got to be ancient!"

"Let's not do the math. I don't want to think how long ago college was."

ONCE CATE HAD GONE, Robin tried to occupy her mind, but it kept returning to the photo of the missing woman's parents, so much like snapshots of her own mother all those years ago—the same brave hope, the same hollow-eyed sadness that had never quite gone away. There was only one thing to do.

In the Saint Paul directory, she found the name, the only Dunn in Highland Park, and jotted their address on an index card. Then, opening her overfull desk, she dug through the second drawer where she kept an assortment of greeting cards and stationery. Inside a note card with an English garden scene, she penned a note to Melissa's parents, dropped it in the mailbox and watched as their mailman— actually a pony-tailed woman in shorts—picked it up a few minutes later.

14

avenous from an extended workout with Brenda, Grace nevertheless agreed to split a salad with her at the Malt Shop. With each mouthful of healthy greens, she felt her deprivation more acutely, her eyes following each sumptuous-looking order of sandwiches and french fries and thick malts, none of which was destined for their table.

Brenda rubbed her eyelid with her fingertips and sighed. "I was hoping the gym would revitalize me. I just feel so tired lately."

"This whole thing with the Dunn woman must be wearing for both of you," Grace said softly. "I mean your husband must feel responsible in some way."

Brenda's fork paused midair. "What do you mean?"

Grace squeezed her eyes shut and let out an exasperated sigh. "That came out wrong. I just meant if he's anything like my husband, he agonizes over every little thing that goes wrong at school, no matter who caused the problem. And being the good wives we are, when we see them taking the weight of the world on their shoulders, we try to fix it. Right? I know what that's like."

Brenda averted her eyes.

"I suppose you've been following the story of the body they found in Wisconsin."

Brenda dabbed the corners of her mouth with a napkin and slowly nodded.

"Do you think it's her?"

She looked thoughtful. "If it is, at least it distances her a bit from Bradford. That's some small compensation."

"Yeah. I heard they've been talking to someone in Wisconsin— a handyman, I think they said." Grace refilled their water glasses from the pitcher. "But I don't think he did it."

"No?"

"Nope. I'm a firm believer in the theory that you shouldn't be looking for outlaws when it's almost always the in-laws, the husband or the boyfriend, usually. Wasn't she dating a grad student at Bradford?"

Brenda nodded. "Tom Hill. Or maybe it was Todd. I met him not too long ago at a faculty social. Melissa bringing him was a rather daring choice, and I'm afraid some of the faculty wives let their disapproval be known."

Grace leaned forward. "Really! Because of his age?"

"Actually he's not much younger than she, but it was the whole faculty-student thing, and, oh, I know I sound hopelessly outdated, but I just can't get used to ponytails and earrings on men."

"That describes one of my sons," Grace said with a sigh. "Fred bugs him about it, but I defend his right to look any way he wants, just as long as his attitude is good."

Brenda traced a water circle on the tablecloth with a short red fingernail.

"Besides the ponytail, what's he like?"

Brenda frowned as though weighing her answer. "It's not really fair, based on one meeting."

Grace waited.

"It struck me as peculiar the way he watched people, as if he was mentally recording everything they said. I found it unnerving. So did some of my friends. In fact, I heard he hangs out at the coffee shops in Dinkytown all day long and eavesdrops on people's conversations," Brenda said, referring to the small city within a city that had grown up around the University of Minnesota's East Bank campus.

"That's odd."

"I should clarify. He's there only when he's not in class."

"What's he studying?"

"Psychology."

"Maybe it's research for his thesis."

"Maybe. You know, I don't like to repeat gossip, but under the circumstances, it seems foreboding that several of us thought he was overly possessive of Miss Dunn." She gave a little shudder.

"Do you think he killed her?"

Brenda pursed her lips. "It makes sense in one way, maybe as a crime of passion, perhaps if she told him she was breaking up with him or something like that. Sometimes even a gentle person can just snap."

"True," Grace said, thinking about a couple she'd worked for as a nanny the summer before her senior year in college. Long after Grace had lost touch with them, they'd shown up in the news when he was arrested for murder. After admitting to stalking and killing his wife's lover, he'd turned the gun on himself. Everyone who'd known him was shocked. They remembered him, as Grace did, as a quiet, kind soul, always smiling, always deferring to his wife's more powerful personality.

Brenda's eyes were unfocussed as her fingers slid up and down the stem of her water glass. "Somehow the idea of him committing cold-blooded murder seems unlikely."

LATE THE FOLLOWING MORNING, Robin got a call from Melissa's mother, thanking her for the beautiful note. "When someone offers to pray for my daughter, I take it seriously," Mrs. Dunn said. "Do you know I can actually feel it?"

"I know what you mean. I really do."

"I think I've heard from every psychic in Minnesota," she said, her voice tight. "She's alive, some tell me, other say she's . . . not . . . that she's trying to contact me from the other side. The police warned me that the newspaper article would bring all the crackpots out, but there are good people too. I'm overwhelmed with all the cards we've gotten, all the prayers . . ." Her voice faded. Then, as if waking from sleep, she said, "You've been there. You know. I was hoping to take you up on your offer to meet with me, but you'd have to come to my house. I don't want to leave, you know, in case—"

"Of course."

ROBIN DROVE SLOWLY down the fourteen hundred block of Pinecrest Place and pulled to the curb in front of an unremarkable white two-story with blue-gray shutters. Everything looked so benign on this tree-lined boulevard. Taking a deep breath, she got out of the car and rang the doorbell.

"Mrs. Dunn?"

Framed by glasses, the petite woman's bloodshot eyes looked huge. "You must be Robin Bentley. Come in," she said warmly. "Bless you for coming. And please call me Carol."

As Robin followed her to the living room, she noticed how loose fitting the woman's slacks were, as if she'd lost quite a bit of weight. Both the couch on which Robin sat, and Carol's adjacent chair were upholstered in blue velour with a tiny floral pattern in cream and yellow.

"It's been hard on us, me and my husband." When she spoke of him, she tilted her head toward the empty recliner. "We had her later in life, in fact we'd come to accept that we'd never have children . . ." Her voiced drifted off. "And now—"

Robin clenched her jaws and managed to hold her tears back. "It must be terrible not knowing. Years ago my mother worried about me too."

Carol Dunn clutched her hand. "That's what you said in your card. Tell me."

Robin took a deep breath and told her story. "It was when I was ten. My parents were going through a divorce, and my father decided to get custody . . . his own way. He picked me up from school one day and said we were going on a trip, just the two of us. He said it was okay with Mom and promised me we'd call her. Of course it was a lie. I didn't see her or talk to her for almost a year." Her voice cracked. No matter how many times she spoke about her abduction, she could never tell when the emotions of long ago would blindside her.

Carol's hand gravitated to the filigreed cross she wore around her neck. "Dear Lord. A year!" she wailed. "How horrible! Why did it—?"

"Take so long?" Robin sighed heavily. "For starters, I was young and I loved my father, so when he told me people were trying to take me away from him, I was terrified. Then there were all these bad people that we had to elude. We made a game of it. He cut my hair short, and every time we moved I got to pick out my new name."

Mrs. Dunn simply stared, tears leaking out with each blink.

Robin looked around the room. Lace curtains framed the windows. Built-in shelves held hardcover books, figurines and a framed photo of a dark haired girl, laughing into the camera.

Carol followed her gaze. "That's our Missy."

"She's beautiful."

She beamed. "Just as beautiful on the inside, too." She smiled at the photograph as if having a telepathic conversation with it. Suddenly, the smile collapsed and her eyes got watery again. "I know what some people are saying, but Missy would never go off without telling me. She always called me, at least a couple times a week, even when she was on one of those fund-raising trips for the college." She pressed a wad of Kleenex to her puffy eyes. "The police told us they found a body in Wisconsin." She squared her jaw and stated, "It's not her."

Robin's hope welled up, but it was fleeting.

"It can't be her. She has to be alive. I keep praying to God to bring her home." The sob sounded like a hiccup. "God would never let that happen."

"I have two daughters myself," Robin answered softly. Unable to look her in the eyes, she stared at the porcelain Madonna figurine on the coffee table while she wondered how to respond. She could not, in all conscience, encourage false hope, and she was sickeningly certain that the body they'd found was this woman's daughter. But she didn't have to say a word, because Melissa's mother suddenly shifted gears.

With a hopeful smile that broke Robin's heart, Carol Dunn set the picture back on the shelf. "Would you like some tea, dear? I put the water on the minute you said you were coming."

"That would be nice."

A few minutes later Carol reappeared carrying a flowered china tea set on a tray.

Robin let the hot liquid soothe away the lump in her throat.

"Would you like to see some other photos of Missy?"

"I'd love to."

Picking up the faux leather album from the coffee table, Carol opened it, angling it on her knees for Robin to see. "These were taken at a family reunion. My brother Bill had just gotten one of those new digital cameras. Too fancy for me. I'll just keep using my point-and-shoot."

Most of the photos were posed group shots that included a smiling Melissa. Robin turned the page to a candid close-up. Melissa's chin rested on her loosely fisted hand, her smile as enigmatic as the Mona Lisa. "Looks like her mind was a million miles away in this one," she commented.

"Yes, she did seem to do a lot of daydreaming lately."

Robin leaned closer. "What an unusual bracelet," she said.

Carol lookedand nodded. "I think she wore it every day since her birthday. Her boyfriend gave it to her."

"Oh? Who was her boyfriend?"

"Todd's the only boyfriend I ever knew about."

"Todd?"

"Yes, Todd Hill."

They sat in silence as Robin turned a few more pages.

Carol leaned back, closed her eyes. "I can't imagine your poor mother going a whole year never knowing if you were alive." The anxiety was back in her voice.

"But that was a long time ago, before Amber Alerts and the Missing Children's Network and the Internet."

"My husband wants me to put her picture on the Internet. He says the more people see it, the better chance we have of getting Missy back."

Robin said, "I volunteer with a group for missing children. They might know a web site for missing adults. Would you like their e-mail?"

"We don't even own a computer." She sighed heavily and stared at her lap.

"If I find a group that will get her picture out there, I'd be happy to set it up for you," Robin offered.

Carol brightened. "Oh, you'll need some pictures, then." She pointed to the album. "These are the most recent." Her hands fluttered over the pages. Carefully removing two photographs, including the Mona Lisa, she handed them to Robin, saying, "Please be careful. Until we get Missy back, this is all that we have."

Robin took them by the edges. "I'll do what I can. I'll bring them back to you as soon as I've made copies."

At the front door, they hugged. Carol Dunn said in a near whisper, "Thank you. You have renewed my hope."

As she hurried down the steps to her car, Robin remembered why she had, for her own sanity, cut back on volunteering to talk to families of missing children.

But once in her car, she was already rehearsing what she would tell Sheriff Harley about the bracelet.

He sat, just as Brenda had described him, three tables away with his back to the window, a diamond stud glistening in his ear, his dark hair pulled into a ponytail. He scratched notes on a legal pad, listing to his left side to get a better view of the three coeds talking animatedly at a nearby table. When they left, he turned his attention to a geriatric hippie in a black beret, flipped a page, and wrote, sipped his tea and wrote some more. He had yet to turn his beautiful blue eyes, exactly the color of his denim shirt, in Grace's direction.

Typical, she thought. Good old Grace—nice, dependable, maternal. Invisible.

Just then, he looked at her—a quick but thorough look that almost convinced her he'd read her mind. When he looked up again, they smiled at each other, though something in his quick glance had unnerved her. All right, this is it, she said to herself. Grace the Boring has left the building. Grace the Sleuth is now in charge. She stood, refilled her coffee cup and water glass at the counter and approached his table.

"If you're hitting on me," she said, setting her beverages on the table and lowering herself into the chair opposite him, "I just thought you should know I have sons your age."

"Oh." He averted his eyes. "Oh, no. I, uh, I wasn't, I mean," he stammered.

"I'm kidding." She stuck out her hand and said, "I'm Grace."

Taking her hand, he said, "Todd. That's a big *T* and a little *odd.*"

She laughed a bit too loudly and covered her mouth. "That's a great line. Sounds like you've used it before."

He broke into a modest grin and shrugged. "I guess I call it the way others see it."

Grace took a sip of water before asking, "You think others make that judgment about you?"

"You must admit, you found it a little odd the way I was watching people, didn't you?"

"Well—"

"Sorry, I didn't mean to put you on the spot. It's for a study I'm conducting—just field notes of my observations." He shook his head. "I'm always worried someone's going to think I'm stalking them or something."

"Oh, I'm interrupting your work. I'm so sorry." She braced her hands as if to push her chair back, but he stopped her, just as she'd hoped.

"No, stay, please. My concentration just isn't there today. I'd welcome the company."

She settled back. Being matronly had its advantages, and she was determined to make it work for her. "You must get girls all the time who think you're making a pass at them."

His smile faded and he fingered the pages of his notebook. "Yeah, it can be awkward."

She chuckled. "A great gimmick to meet girls, though. Stare all you want and then tell them it's just research. I wish I'd thought of it when I was in college."

He shifted uncomfortably. "Actually, it's not like that." He stared at his hand on the table.

"Ah, you already have a girlfriend, right?"

His jaw muscles tensed, and he began drumming his fingers on the tabletop. "Okay, which is it, reporter or detective?" he asked in a flat tone.

"What?"

He flushed. "Which are you, news reporter or detective?"

"Neither. Why do you think that?"

"It's not like everyone isn't looking at me—wondering, you know."

Grace shook her head. She made her face blank. "I'm afraid I don't follow."

"Because of my girlfriend."

She produced a befuddled look and he continued.

"Melissa Dunn, the missing woman from Bradford. You must have heard about her. It's been on the news every night."

Grace paused a few beats, let understanding seep into her expression. "She was your girlfriend?"

His shoulders sagged. "I'm not ready to say 'was.' We weren't exclusive, but I'd say it was fairly serious, at least on my—why am I telling you all this?"

She placed a motherly hand on his arm. "I'm so sorry," she said softly. "How awful for you. I had no idea."

His eyes welled with tears. "Oh, God, this thing is turning me totally paranoid."

"I can't imagine what you're going through."

"Hell," he said simply, "I'm going through hell. No matter who I talk to, I feel like I have to weigh every word. The psych major becomes subject of the study. The Watcher watched."

"It must be very difficult." Even though she was playing a role, she didn't have to fake her sympathy. Obviously this young man, with the dark smears of sleepless nights under his eyes, was suffering.

By the time Grace left, she'd found out where Todd Hill lived, how he and Melissa had met in this very coffee shop, and about his growing suspicions that Melissa had been suffering from depression, as evidenced by detachment, evasiveness, and a certain caginess.

What went unanswered was her own growing suspicion about Todd Hill. Her pulse raced, not with fear, but with—she had to call it what it was—Excitement.

Grace needed to tell someone what had transpired. She decided to swing by Robin's house on the chance she was home.

Robin, wearing khaki shorts and a white tank top, stood on tiptoe watering the purple petunias, yellow pansies, and white bacopia cascading from her window boxes. She saw Grace's car and broke into a wide smile. "Good timing," she called out as Grace stepped onto the pavement. "I just made a pitcher of lemonade."

"Great." Suddenly aware of all the ice water and coffee she'd consumed, Grace added, "But I need to use your bathroom first."

A few minutes later, Grace and Robin were comfortably settled on the porch chairs. "I just have to tell you. You're not going to believe this," Grace began. "I just—well, let me begin at the beginning."

The weather was glorious, the afternoon sun was warm and the wind wafted the sweet scent of lilacs through the screen. Robin stretched out her bare legs and settled back for a long story.

Grace was particularly animated as she related her encounter with Todd. "He was taking notes on everyone in the coffee shop, everyone but me." She shook her head. "Really! Sometimes I'm unthreatening to the point of invisibility."

Robin pulled her mouth to one side in thought. "Invisibility's good. Like Harry Potter's cloak."

A grin grew on Grace's face. "I like that. Well, I could certainly use a cloak of invisibility for what I want to do next."

"Which is—?"

"Follow Todd Hill, see if he does anything suspicious. Trouble is he's seen me."

Robin nodded, conceding the problem.

"And, " Grace leaned forward dramatically. "It's just possible he's seen you too."

"Me? When?"

"See if this sounds familiar: a long dark ponytail, beautiful blue eyes. I don't want to get carried away, but I really think he could be that hunky guy you and Cate were raving about, you know, the one buying liquor for Ross Johnson the very weekend Melissa Dunn went missing."

Robin was stunned as she pondered the possibility that Grace had just spent most of an hour conversing with a murderer.

"So you see?" Grace pleaded. "We need to follow him so we know one way or another."

Robin sat in thought before peering back at the grandfather clock in the entryway. "Oh, Gracie," she moaned, putting her head in her hands. "What are you getting us into?"

Thrill of a quest lit Grace's eyes. "It's got to be tonight. Fred's got a school board meeting and won't be home 'til late." She waited until she saw Robin's look of resignation.

Then, with a lopsided grin, Robin said, "Come with me. I just might have a magic cloak or two upstairs."

From the linen closet, Robin hauled out a zippered bag and dumped the contents on her bed. Grace pawed through the assortment of hair clips, makeup, wigs, and false eyelashes. "I've never seen you in this," she said, holding up an auburn wig.

"I wore it only once." Robin tugged at her own short locks. "To a hospital dinner. I was having fun flipping my long, dark hair around, when that old goat Crippen, the guy Brad bought the practice from, sidled over and leered at me and asked Brad, and I quote, 'Who's the dish?' Before Brad could answer, Crippen leaned over and said to Brad in a stage whisper, "Sorry to hear about your wife's cancer, but I'm glad to see you're getting over it. When did she pass away?"

Grace's hand flew to her mouth. "Oh, God, what did you do?"

"Went in the bathroom and threw up. Here, try it on."

Grace looked dubious.

"Don't worry, I washed it."

Robin helped Grace pin up her own hair before slipping the wig over it. After tucking in stray strands, she said, "Now, take a look."

Grace peered at herself in the full-length mirror. The transformation was remarkable. Pirouetting, she sang, "I feel pretty, oh, so pretty."

Robin laughed. "Hold still. You need to darken your eyebrows." Robin reached into the pile and selected a pencil slightly darker than the chin-length curls. "And a different lipstick." She began rummaging in her walk-in closet. "Try this," she said, tossing an orange linen jacket at Grace.

"Who wears orange to go undercover?" She looked at the label and handed the jacket back. "Besides, I haven't worn a size ten in decades—in case you haven't noticed." She cocked her head at her own reflection. The wig did make her look younger. She covered her belly bulge with both hands and stood a little straighter.

Robin studied the new Grace. "Okay, wear your own clothes, but definitely lose the glasses."

Grace took them off. "I guess I don't have to actually see what I'm doing." She squinted at the mirror and smiled broadly. "I feel positively clandestine." Suddenly she turned to Robin. "But what about you? He may have seen you too."

In answer, Robin disappeared into the closet and returned wearing black leggings, a black turtleneck and an oversized denim jacket. "Do I look like a middle-aged punk?" she asked as she opened a tube of gel and slicked her hair back, combing two strands into long curves that came out, flapper-like onto her cheeks.

Grace stared at her. "You don't even look like you," she said, her voice conveying awe. "Of course, I'm not wearing my glasses."

They stood side by side in front of the mirror.

"You sure you want to do this?" Grace asked, biting her lip.

"Oh, yeah," Robin answered. "I'm sure."

AS DUSK SETTLED, ROBIN would have felt invisible even without a magic cloak. Alone in her car, she tuned her radio to KOOL 108, laughing out loud when she heard the serendipitous lyrics, *The night has a thousand eyes.* Soon she was singing along, her fingers tapping out the beat on the steering wheel as she continued to watch the lighted entrance of the coffee shop.

The door swung open and Grace emerged. She strode across the street in an unintentionally comical imitation of a runway model.

Robin lowered the window and took the plastic cup of iced cappuccino Grace handed her.

"He's still in there." Grace said breathlessly as she opened the passenger door and got in.

"Does it look like he'll be heading out anytime soon?"

"Yeah, I think he's getting ready to leave."

"I just hope it's soon. All that lemonade." Robin squirmed.

"You'd better use the bathroom here. Hurry."

Two songs later, Grace suddenly sat forward and squinted to see Todd stepping into the circle of light at the coffee shop's front door, Robin right behind him.

Todd turned toward the parking lot and Robin veered toward her car. Sliding behind the steering wheel, she let out a pent up breath. "It's not him."

Grace's face fell. "Are you sure?"

"He's nice looking, but very midwestern. Our Hunk was exotic."

"Rats."

Their eyes were fixed on him until the young man vanished into the darkness of the unlit parking lot.

Robin turned the ignition switch and Grace cocked her head in the direction of the parking lot. "There." She pointed at an old

Honda Civic hatchback easing onto the street. "Follow him!" she commanded. "But not too close, we don't want him to make us."

"Make us? Geez, put you into a wig and your whole vocabulary changes." Robin allowed one car to pass before pulling out into traffic.

"What's his address again?" Robin followed him when he turned east onto University.

"His address? Ahh . . . something to do with a president." Grace's brow furrowed. "Drat, I can't remember. It was in North Minneapolis, though."

"Nordeast? If he's going home, he's taking the scenic route, because we're going in the opposite direction."

"Gun it. The light's changing."

With a look of determination, Robin stepped on the gas, and her car flew through the intersection just as the light turned red. She was grinning like a maniac.

They followed the Honda into Roseville where it turned into the parking lot of a three-story brick apartment building. Slowing the car as they passed the driveway, Robin continued to the corner where she made a U-turn.

"What do you think? Do we dare go into the parking lot?"

"Why not?" Robin turned her wheel. The expression on her face was unruffled, as if it was perfectly natural to drive all over creation at night, wearing disguises and following strangers.

Grace's pulse was racing. "There. He's still in the car. Park over there where we can watch him." With impatience, Grace wiggled her fingers, urging Robin on.

"How's this?"

"Perfect."

Robin stopped near the back of the lot and cut the lights. The anemic security lighting of the apartment complex rendered cars, pavement, Dumpster, and bushes various shades of gray. They were fairly invisible, but, then, so was pretty much everything else.

"I don't get it," Grace said several minutes later. "He's just sitting there looking at the building." His presence was scarcely discernable, and Grace hoped that gave her and Robin cover as well.

"It looks like he's waiting for someone. Why doesn't he just go up to the door?"

After a long pause, Grace said, "One of us has to walk by him to see what he's up to."

Another silence was broken by Robin's heavy sigh. "Fine, I'll go."

"Okay, just pretend you're walking up to the building and then double back."

Robin got out and, with a casual stride, circled behind the other parked cars. Grace's eyes widened when she saw Robin stop when she was even with the Honda.

"What are you doing? Keep walking," Grace said under her breath.

As if by telepathy, Robin moved on and then was out of sight.

Alone, Grace fidgeted. Then, without warning, Robin appeared at her open window and Grace yelped.

"He's just sitting there," Robin whispered. "He's resting with his head on the steering wheel and his shoulders were shaking, like he was sobbing."

"He was crying?

Robin nodded.

"I wonder who lives here."

They looked at each other and said, simultaneously, "Melissa."

Looking up, they were distressed to see Todd slipping through the building's rear entrance. A few moments later, the lights in a corner apartment on the second floor came on.

Grace jumped from the car and raced toward the building. Robin almost collided with her when they reached the door. It was locked.

"Now what?"

Robin took in the scene. "If I could just get—Wait!" She sprinted back across the lot to the double Dumpster. "Come help me," she called hoarsely. "If we stand on this, I bet we can see right into the apartment."

One hand on her hip, Grace looked incredulous. "How about if *you* get up there and *I'll* stand guard." She shifted her weight from one foot to the other. "And exactly how are you going to get on top of the Dumpster?"

"Shhh! We don't want to attract attention." Robin tried to look stern, but she felt on the verge of a giggle fit. Grabbing a recycling bin, she placed it upside down, mounted it and threw herself at the covered half of the Dumpster, landing with a belly flop, half on, half off the lid. Her fingers barely grasped the inner edge of the lid. "Oh, gross!" she wailed.

Rushing to her, Grace snorted loudly and clapped both hands over her mouth.

"Help me." Robin's feet flailed in the air.

"Well then, stop kicking." Grace braced her hands against Robin's rear and pushed, moving her all of two inches.

"Hey!" Robin rasped. "Thrilling as that was, I'm still draped over a garbage can and it smells like—oh, God, I don't even want to think about what's in here."

Grace stepped back. "Great view."

"Wanna trade places?" Robin felt Grace grab her feet.

"Okay, let me give you a push."

Robin, unprepared for the shove, felt her knees buckle.

"Oh, for crying out loud! Work with me!" Grace still gripped her feet. "Make your legs stiff. Good. Now, on the count of three, pull yourself forward. One, twooo, ooomph."

With the combined effort, Robin slid . . . and kept sliding—head first into the open half of the Dumpster.

"Oh, my God!" Grace's concern turned to a screech of laughter as Robin righted herself, sputtering and swearing with only her head visible over the top of the Dumpster.

Grace, borrowed wig askew, gawked at her helplessly. "Oops! Now how are you going to get out?"

"Now you think of it." Robin saw, in the dim light, that her fall had exploded several plastic bags, now gaping to reveal potato peelings, mushy lettuce, coffee grounds, and other sordid goo.

"You weren't supposed to do a nosedive into the garbage."

"Are you suggesting I did it on purpose?" With an audible shudder, she brushed at her clothing. Then she ducked down and began to pile the more substantial bags of garbage against the Dumpster's side.

All the while, Grace kept hopping up, trying to get a better look.

"Stop bouncing and give me a hand." Like an aging ballerina, Robin stuck one leg in the air, managing to hook a heel over the edge, working it forward to a position she'd last achieved on the monkey bars in grade school.

"Hold on, the lights just went out."

They held their breath as the door swung open and a silhouette appeared in the wedge of light.

"Don't move a muscle." With those words, Grace ducked for cover, leaving her friend in a position that guaranteed a trip to the chiropractor.

Robin shut her eyes when Todd came heart-stoppingly close to where she perched in the garbage bin. When she heard his car engine start, she opened her eyes and saw the Honda leave.

Only then did Grace reemerge from shadow. "Stick your hands out," she instructed.

"I can't," came a groan from the Dumpster.

"Come on, work with me."

"Where have I heard that before?" Robin clung to the Dumpster's edge, her legs shaking uncontrollably. "You'll have to get a forklift."

"You're coming out." Seizing Robin's arms, she again counted "One . . . two . . . threeee."

Accompanied by grunts and groans, they maneuvered Robin to straddle the edge, where she balanced briefly and precariously, emitting a raspy squawk. Suddenly she pitched forward, and together they tumbled to the ground.

"Ow!" Grace yelped, rolling Robin to one side and standing. "Now let's get out of here."

Robin came to her feet painfully. "Wait, my shoes."

"Forget the freakin' shoes." Grace tugged her arm and they bolted for the car, where she immediately rolled her windows down. "What is that god-awful smell?"

Slowly, with exaggerated pronunciation, Robin answered her. "Eau de Fish."

And suddenly, all the tension dissolved in uproarious laughter.

ACROSS TOWN FROM WHERE Robin took a lengthy shower with perfumed soap, Martin raised his garage door and wheeled the garbage bin through the gates and to the street.

"What the hell took so long?"

"Jesus, you scared me!" Martin clutched his shirt as he spun around, giving a sigh of relief when he recognized Ross stepping out of the shadows. "You trying to give me a coronary?"

"I've been waiting in your bushes for fifteen fucking minutes." Ross lit a cigarette and inhaled deeply before letting the smoke out in a long stream. "What kept you?"

"I had to wait until Brenda went upstairs." Martin glanced up at the darkened second-floor window.

"To take the trash out?"

Martin shrugged and continued down the drive, positioning the bin at the curb before returning.

Pulling something from the pocket of his jeans, Ross handed it to Martin. "That's the last of it, at least until that asshole José returns my calls. I don't know what his game is, but I don't trust that slimeball." He took another drag and flicked the butt onto the driveway. "Have the police talked to you any more about Melissa?"

At the sound of her name, Martin's eyes stung. "Just that they've identified her, um, her body."

"Any theories?"

Martin shook his head. "They said the Wisconsin authorities think she may have fallen on the rocks."

Ross grunted and lit another cigarette. "I got a call from George. Seems the sheriff hauled him in for more questioning."

"That handyman? What'd he tell them?"

"Nothing."

"Why'd he call you?"

Ross flicked his cigarette butt into the bushes. "He wanted advice, and then he asked if I'd find him a good lawyer."

"Why do you even mess with that nonentity?"

"I owe him. He saved my ass."

Martin blinked, remembering the story. "But that was way back in high school."

Ross sighed heavily and raised his shoulders in a shrug. Yes, it was way back in high school—it had just been a kid's prank. After downing a couple of six-packs, the two eighteen-year-olds, Ross and his buddy Al, had set out to paint their school colors on the water tower just before Homecoming. But Al had slipped coming down the ladder and fallen the last thirty feet to the concrete below. Ross had panicked and run. From the two cans of paint and two brushes, the police surmised Al had not been alone when he'd fallen to his death.

But just when Ross had thought he was screwed for good, a miraculous thing happened. Lurking outside the locker room after football practice one day was George Wellman, a dorky hanger-on who seemed to think Ross was his friend. "I know it was you," Wellman had whispered. "I saw the whole thing, but don't worry, I won't tell." After that, Wellman had begun cozying up to him, slapping him on the shoulder when they passed in the hall, hanging around his locker, and inserting himself into his social life. Hell, they'd even double-dated, with Ross, of course, providing the girl.

What Ross hadn't expected was that when George had been questioned, he'd told a half-truth, saying he'd seen it all, telling in detail how Al had gone up—by himself—and had slipped to his death. The school board concluded that George Wellman must have been the second painter and voted to expel him, and in those days, being eighteen and not in school put a guy in a uniform. In George's case, that uniform accompanied him to Vietnam.

"What the hell did they want from Wellman?" Martin's question jerked Ross back to the current predicament.

"Seems they found Melissa's bracelet in his trailer."

"What?"

"They had him dead to rights. George says it was some fancy custom-made job."

"Silver and gold?"

Ross held up his hands to indicate he didn't know.

"Crap! Sounds like the one I gave her." Martin's voice cracked. "How the hell did he wind up with it?"

"He claims he found it along the road and, judging from the fact he wasn't calling from jail, they must've believed him."

"Oh, Jesus."

"Get a grip."

"She was so young, so beautiful." Martin paused. "I never even told her I loved her."

"There's nothing you can do about it now. "

They stared at each other in the dim light before Martin's head swung in the direction of the upstairs window. "I'd better get back inside before Brenda gets suspicious." Pain on his face was evident. "You know, despite all I've done to the contrary, I don't want to hurt my wife. She's a good woman."

16

José had barely worked up a sweat on the tennis court, just enough to give his muscles definition and attract the attention of two girls in plaid, parochial school uniforms who whispered and giggled on the other side of the fence. José, seemingly oblivious to them, moved effortlessly, popping the ball just over the net on the right, then deep into the left court.

Ross, breathing audibly, let the ball go. "Your game," he gasped, bracing his hands against his knees. He took the water bottle José handed him and sucked it dry before asking again, "Did you bring it?"

"Of course." José grinned lazily, tossing a towel over his shoulder. "But due to circumstances beyond my control, the price has gone up."

Ross scowled, shifting his eyes to the next court. "What circumstances?"

"Let's hit the showers first," José suggested, tilting his head toward the arriving players. "I'll catch you in the juice bar."

ROSS FIDGETED WITH HIS GYM bag strap while José order a smoothie with protein powder and spirulina. "I ask again, what circumstances?" Ross fairly growled when José joined him at the table.

Maddeningly, José pulled on his straw for a while before answering, "It's like this. I go up to your little hideaway in the woods with some prime stuff, and one of your brilliant friends decides to hide my entire supply in case the place gets raided."

"So?"

"So he walked off with it."

"It was paid for, you dirtbag."

"Yeah, but it means now I have to make another run sooner than I'd planned."

"You poor bastard, having to fly to the tropics, suck down Goombay smashes on the beach and watch the girls jiggle past wearing nothing but dental floss." Despite his shower, Ross felt flushed.

José leaned back, a derisive grin on his face. "It's not like that, man. You rich white boys all think you can do a few lines any time the mood strikes you, no matter the cost to anyone else, and the thing that's funnier than shit is you think you can do it without ever getting your hands dirty." His voice took on a sinister tone. "I can assure you, it's not all that easy or that safe on my end of the deal. I think that's worth something to you, am I right?"

Ross tried to match his nonchalance. "Seems to me, it's just a hazard of the business."

"Seems to me," José said, mocking his tone, "doing business with you got more hazardous since your party." He stood and crumpled his empty paper cup. "Anyway, the cost of insurance has just gone up."

Ross swiped a hand across his upper lip. "She wasn't the only one who left the party. Where'd you go, anyway?"

José stood up. "I saw you, man."

"You saw nothing. Nada."

José's lazy smile mocked him. "I saw you go out in that storm."

Ross assessed him, his eyes narrowing. "Speaking of insurance, I hope you're paid up on your life insurance."

José circled the table and leaned close to Ross, pinching the nerve running along the top of his shoulder. Ross felt the instant, disabling pain. "And you," José said close to his ear, "You better make sure your medical insurance is paid up. You start shopping for bargains, it could affect your health, if you know what I mean."

ARMED WITH A FOLDER filled with her best Internet research, Robin went to see Dr. Kellner. The waiting room was cozy, done in rich maple and brocade furniture. End tables held large vases of cut flowers and a lighted stand in the corner displayed a blown-glass sculpture that resembled a multi-colored jellyfish encased in a cylinder of water.

Once in the examining room, she tied a pink paper gown about herself, grateful that the sleeves covered most of the bruises. It had been less than twenty-four hours since she'd gone Dumpster diving, and her upper arms bore red scrapes and magenta bruises. Her inner thighs were worse. The back of her right knee sported a purple bulge.

She studied Dr. Kellner's family vacation photos on his desk while she waited: husband and wife, son and daughters, posed on a ski slope or in front of the Moulin Rouge or atop a catamaran. The parents looked like older siblings of the teenagers, and Robin wondered how much plastic surgery they'd had.

Rudy Kellner swept in, proffered a hand, and settled on the stool, his legs stretched out in front of him. "So, you want to talk about reconstruction," he prompted.

"I've been reading about TRAM flaps," she said, referring to a procedure in which a section of the transverse rectus abdominus muscle is cut out, along with the overlying tissue, and used to form a breast. According to testimonials, the new breast was very natural in appearance. Besides—something that appealed to Robin—the procedure would effectively give her a tummy tuck as well.

She noticed his frown.

"I'm not sure that's your best course," he said. "The surgery is a long one, about five hours, and the recovery takes about six months. You'd be unable to stand up straight while the belly muscles healed."

"But," she said with an attempt at humor, "as you can see, I've been growing belly fat for just this reason." She was chagrined not to have considered another plan.

He referred to her chart. "You had your babies by caesarean, right?"

There was hope, then. "Right, so I already have a scar."

"And that's the problem." He described to her how, because the scarring went all the way through her abdominal wall, there was a chance of the transplanted tissue dying from lack of circulation.

"Okay." She held up her hand. "I can see I need to shift mental gears. What do you recommend?"

Robin stared at the wall. Dr. Kellner eased open the front of her gown and began probing her mastectomy scar with his fingertips. Her skin had no feeling, the nerves having been severed during surgery. "You didn't have radiation, did you?"

She shook her head.

"Well," he said, scooting his stool back and placing his hands on his thighs. "You have good, resilient skin, and I think I can make a breast you'll be happy with, although it's never a perfect match to the other."

"Okay?" She looked at him quizzically.

His smile was boyish. "Some women get offended when I say this." He rolled himself forward once more, reached into her gown and cupped her good breast in his hand. "But the simple fact is that this is a fifty-year old breast. Many women opt for a lift on the unaffected side just to achieve better symmetry. Others choose to keep what sensation they have."

Robin's eyes welled with tears. What did any of it matter? When had Brad last touched her anyway?

He patted her knee. "Why don't you get dressed and we'll talk some more. Do you want to wait for Brad?"

She waved away the suggestion. "He's obviously tied up."

Dr. Kellner gave her a wry smile. "I usually like to include the husband in these discussions, but as a gynecologist, he already knows the options."

Robin nodded. Tempted as she was to voice her disappointment over Brad's no-show, she couldn't very well complain to a colleague of his. She said, "This whole thing has been hard on Brad. I mean, he examines women all day long, but when it comes to his wife . . ." She shrugged.

His look held so much compassion, she could barely meet his gaze. "Yeah, sometimes we doctors are the worst about it. Now, I'll let you get dressed. You can meet me in my office next door and we can talk about your options," he said, and left the room.

The very act of getting dressed brought on a hot flash, and by the time she entered his office, Robin's face was red and shiny and she wanted nothing more than to dump the contents of the water cooler over her head.

Seated across the desk from her, Dr. Kellner opened a drawer and took out two breast prostheses, handing one to her. "This is filled with a saline solution, basically a bag of salt water. It's fairly natural, but tends to wrinkle under the skin. And this," he said, handing her another sack of fluid, "is silicone, about a B-cup. Silicone got a bad rap a few years ago, but the most extensive study to date has shown no increased risk with it. It feels much more like the natural breast."

Robin felt it and set it back on the desk.

"They come in different sizes." He opened the drawer again and produced a larger sample, his hand resting on it as he spoke. To Robin's consternation and amusement, he unwittingly groped it, kneaded it, even rolled the center of it into a pseudo-nipple as he talked.

"You wouldn't be putting that exact implant into me, would you?" she asked.

It was his turn to redden. "Professional hazard," he said with an embarrassed grin, and put it back in the drawer.

WHEN ROBIN GOT HOME, she put in a call to her oncologist, asking for his advice on reconstruction.

Dr. Khan, when he called back, piggybacked on Dr. Kellner's advice. "My issue with the TRAM flap," he said after she outlined her options to him, "is that it covers the area we want to watch, and that's a problem if your cancer ever came back. You see, your tumor was very close to the chest wall, and that would be the likely site—"

"But it's not going to," she interrupted.

"Keep that attitude."

His cautionary words stuck with her the rest of the afternoon.

Brad was home in time for dinner, looking, as he frequently did these days, harried. Robin stabbed at her shrimp scampi. "I'm sorry you couldn't make it today."

Brad looked perplexed, then wary.

"I saw Rudy Kellner today."

His face said, *Oh. Shit.* His mouth said, "Oh, God, Robin, I'm sorry. I had a prolapsed uterus with some of the worst endometriosis I've seen. She needed two units of blood." He pushed his hands through his hair and avoided looking at her.

"Do you want to know what he had to say?"

"Sure, if you want." He dabbed his mouth with a napkin. "Can it wait until after dinner?"

But after dinner, Brad kicked off his shoes and retired to the sunroom with a magazine, one of his professional journals.

After loading the dishwasher, Robin sat next to him on the loveseat. She cleared her throat, wanting desperately to get through this without disintegrating into tears. Brad never responded well to tears. "We have to talk," she said softly.

He sighed at the dreaded words and stared at the magazine a little longer before closing it. "I have a pretty good idea what Rudy said. So what have you decided?"

"I'm still thinking about it, but I don't want to do the recon-struction right now."

"It's your decision." He sighed heavily. "Frankly, I'm relieved. I don't like the idea of you having more surgery."

A tear slid down her cheek. "Actually, that's what I wanted to talk to you about."

He tilted his head to look at her. "Didn't you just say—?"

"I'm not talking about reconstruction. I'm wondering if I should have the other one removed—preventively, I mean."

He tilted his head back, eyes closed. "A prophylactic mastectomy, Robin? Why, in God's name?"

"Because every time I hear about someone's cancer coming back, I think I haven't done all I can. Because I wake up every morning with my fingers on my good breast, feeling for lumps."

When he turned to face her, his eyes were wet. "Haven't they done enough cutting? Do you really want to go through all that just when things are getting back to normal?"

"Normal?"

"I mean, you had a problem. You took care of it. Why can't you just put it behind you?"

Flicking tears off her cheek, she said, "The truth is, things aren't ever going to be just like they were. Never again. Can't you support me in this?"

He pressed his lips together and slowly shook his head. "Does my medical expertise count for nothing?"

"It's not about you!" Robin said and rushed from the room.

By the time her bag was packed, she was done crying. Brad appeared in the door of her darkroom, watching silently as she unclipped her dry photos from the wire and threw them into her plastic transport box.

"What are you doing?"

She tossed a few rolls of film into the box. "I have work to do at the cabin. You knew I was heading back."

"Right now? I thought you were going tomorrow."

"Actually, if you remember, I was going to leave after my appointment today. I stuck around to report to you how it went."

He leaned wearily against the doorframe. "I'm sorry, Robin. Please don't be this way. I know I screwed up, but it doesn't solve anything if you run off?"

She looked him in the eyes and shook her head sadly. "I'm not running off, Brad. Really. I just need time to think."

BY THE TIME SHE REACHED the cabin, the mosquitoes were in a feeding frenzy and she almost cranked up the engine to head home again. But if she went back now, she was afraid Brad would, oh, so graciously, be willing to forgive her little outburst and discount the very real emotions behind it. She hauled her belongings into the living room and poured herself a glass of Chablis.

On the large trestle table in the main room, she spread out the newly developed photos and set up her laptop computer. After a few moments she was humming to herself. A tap on the screen door made her yelp.

George grinned disarmingly under the porch light and let himself in. Immediately he began flailing at the flying insects that came in with him. "Heard your car. I wanted to make sure it was somebody who belonged here."

Unable to find her voice, Robin, with one hand clutching her throat, simply blinked at him.

"Oh, gosh, I scared you now, didn't I?" George dipped his head in embarrassment. "And after all that ruckus last night."

She continued to stare at him as if she hadn't known him for years.

"Yeah, the whole thing was bogus. The sheriff and that woman cop came and asked me about something I found by the side of the road, and that bi—oops, sorry, Mrs. B. She wanted him to arrest me but I guess the sheriff finally figured the whole bracelet thing made more sense my way."

"Bracelet?" She felt the hair on her neck rise.

"Yeah, I found it near the bridge a while back. The sheriff took it last night as evidence. Anybody that knows me knows I pick up junk."

"Was it junk?"

"Actually, it was kind of pretty."

"What were you going to do with it?"

He shrugged. "Doesn't matter now. They took it."

Robin nodded. Her breathing became easier as she remembered all the roadside finds he'd shown her over the years.

He moved closer, and, without waiting for an invitation, sat down and started thumbing through her pictures. "How come that husband of yours never comes here anymore?" he asked casually, not making eye contact.

The question didn't feel harmless. She felt herself flush. "Ob/Gyns keep horrible hours."

"Yeah, I can see how he'd really get into his work." He laughed his little *heh, heh* laugh.

The misconception wasn't new to her. Most men couldn't comprehend how Brad could come home from a long day and complain about having to "look at bottoms all day." She always reacted with some unease to this particular idiocy, but from George, it was downright creepy.

Oblivious to her reaction, George switched his attention back to the photos. "Here's that old pin oak." He jabbed a finger at one. "There's that owl that always sits up there where he can watch for little critters."

Robin breathed a sigh of relief and slid another picture to him.

"Yeah, that's him, all right." The ghostly face of a barn owl peered from the foliage. He picked up another photo, adjusted his glasses on his nose and looked more closely.

"Which photo is that?" Robin asked.

He ignored her outstretched hand and stood, holding it up to the light.

Robin eased the photo from his grip. "Oh, yes, the deer," she said. "Aren't they beautiful?"

He looked at her oddly. "Yup. Well, I guess I'll leave you be." He stuck his hands in his pockets. "I just thought I'd come by and let you know you're not out here all by your lonesome." The screen door banged behind him.

You're not alone. Robin said the words to herself. Was it a reassurance or a threat, she wondered?

IT WAS HER SUBCONSCIOUS MIND that woke her the following morning, urging her to look again at the photograph George had been studying. She made herself some herbal tea and a bowl of granola, yogurt and red raspberries, all organic, and sat on the porch to eat. The sunlight made a dappled pattern on her bare feet as she sat, listening to a symphony of birdcalls. It was just the kind of setting that always brought about serenity, no matter what chaos existed elsewhere. Her previous worries now seemed laughable.

But today she had to force herself to finish breakfast before she took her magnifying glass from her camera bag and sat once more at the trestle table. The deer were still beautiful, the scenery still idyllic. The high, rocky banks of the stream formed a fascinating study of light and shadow. She moved the glass back to a particularly interesting outcropping. There, above the waterfall, she now saw, lay the figure of a female stretched out on the flat limestone ledge, an arm flung over her face, and on her wrist, a glint of light.

Robin sat back, frowning. She pulled out her photo log to make sure of the date. She'd shot several rolls that day, the day of the storm.

Feeling a hot flash coming on, she fanned herself with her notebook. Her eyes fell again on the photo. She brushed at some white flecks with the side of her hand, but they remained. Again she picked up the magnifying glass, pulling back with an intake of breath when she figured out what she was seeing. At the edge of the woods, just behind the woman, were two elliptical bright spots, just the size and shape and position to suggest the sun was glinting off a pair of glasses. Someone had been watching—she might as well say it— someone had been spying on Melissa Dunn.

She was on her way to the kitchen phone when it rang, startling her into momentary immobility.

It was Cate. "Brad told me you were at the cabin. What's up? He sounded worried."

"He's being irrational," Robin said, using their code for "We had a fight and when I've calmed down, I'll admit we were both wrong."

"Men!" Cate said, their code for "Tell me whatever you want to and I'll take your side and still like Brad when it's all over."

"I don't want to talk about Brad at the moment. I need to think this through by myself."

"Okay." Cate took that to mean a change of topic and launched into the reason she'd called. "I took a look at the photo you dropped off. You were right. It was one of my bracelets that I sold at the Uptown Art Fair last summer."

Robin sucked in her breath. "Do you remember who bought it?"

"I checked my records. I sold six of a similar style that weekend. My notes say the guy who bought that one paid in cash."

"A guy?"

"If memory serves me correctly."

"What did he look like?"

"That's the part I can't remember." She snorted. "Well, one of the many, actually. Maybe if I think about something else, it'll come back to me."

"Okay, here's something to think about," Robin offered. "George came to check on me last night."

"I thought he was in jail."

"Nope, they never arrested him. Cate, I swear the man is harmless, but it was a peculiar little visit."

"He's a peculiar little man," she said icily.

"Granted, but the thing with the bracelet—I'm sure he found it just like he said, by the side of the road. That's what he does. It makes sense."

"Hmmm."

"But listen, Cate, there's more."

"I knew it."

"Not about George. It's a photo he was looking at." She told Cate about the reclining figure and the twin spots of light at the edge of the woods. "I just have to believe it was Melissa Dunn, and, please don't laugh at me, but I think someone was watching her—someone wearing glasses."

But Cate didn't laugh. "George wears glasses," she said simply.

Robin couldn't think of a response.

"Are you there?"

"Hold on a sec. I thought I heard something." Robin put the phone down and walked into the living room, her heart pounding audibly as she scattered the prints on the table. Her mouth went dry. After a quick scan of the room, she grabbed the phone. "It's gone, Cate. The picture I was telling you about."

C ate could hear Erik downstairs, the television turned up loud enough to be heard over the treadmill. Usually, she found the noise aggravating, but today it felt reassuring and in stark contrast to Robin's solitary life at the cabin. Her big orange tabby, Oscar, purred next to her on the mission-style couch, as if he'd never lived on the streets where he'd frozen his ears to rounded nubbins. Carlton, an aging black lab, and Mitsy, a patchwork dog that looked like she'd been built by an ill-advised committee, were curled together on the cool tile of the adjacent foyer. Grover, sprawled at her feet, snored loudly.

On the phone, Robin was telling her that, as far as she could determine, that creep George had come into her cabin and stolen a photo that almost certainly implicated him in a murder. Cate was in no frame of mind to argue about his alleged harmlessness. Speaking calmly but with authority into the phone, she told Robin, "I want you to grab your purse and your keys and get the hell out of there."

"That's ridiculous."

Cate made an exasperated face at the phone. "Ridiculous? What's ridiculous is you staying there after what you just told me. Robin, listen to me, you have to come home."

"I can't do that."

God, she could be so stubborn! She isn't ready to talk to her husband, so she runs away from home—right into the hands of a murderer. "Fine," she said, trying to stay calm. "If that's the way you're going to be, I'm leaving right now."

"No! I'm fine, really."

"I'm leaving. Meet me at the truck stop. You know the one." Cate hung up the phone before Robin could protest further.

Robin knew the one, but didn't appreciate that Cate was leaving her no choice. She began punching buttons on the phone, but stopped, knowing Cate would not answer. As she put the receiver back, she realized that, outwitted and just plain pissed though she was, she supposed she was comforted that Cate was on her way.

When Cate told Erik her plans, he stopped the treadmill and mopped sweat off his face with a hand towel. He was only slightly losing the battle with middle-age spread, but was diligent in his exercise. His olive complexion was almost unmarred by age, except for the crow's feet around his eyes, which were now squinting at Cate in consternation. "If you really believe she's in trouble, why don't you call the authorities? In fact, why hasn't she called the authorities?"

"She'd never do that. She's working on personal empowerment."

Erik rolled his brown eyes. "Is this a real threat or not?"

Cate slid her amulet back and forth on the chain. "Who knows?"

"You're upset enough to go check on her."

"The deputy already thinks we're all suffering from menopausal madness or middle-aged boredom or some such crap."

When he rubbed his chin, it sounded like sandpaper. "Well, honey, sometimes you do let your imagination run away with you."

Cate glowered at him.

Erik shook his head and laughed. "You're really something, you two. Fine, jump on your white horse and save the damsel in distress. Just promise me you'll be careful."

"Here comes my white horse now," she said, as Grover galumphed after her.

CATE PULLED UP UNDER the awning of the truck stop, relieved to see Robin sitting at a table, waving back at her.

"Good Lord!" Robin breathed when she saw that the entire passenger's side of the Land Rover was filled with dog.

Leaving the car windows, now translucent with nose prints and slobber, partially open, Cate patted Grover's massive head and told him to be a good dog. Inside, she shed her heavy fringed sweater and slid into the seat across from Robin. "Are you pissed at me?" she asked.

"Glirked."

Cate looked over the top of her glasses, one eyebrow raised in question.

"Half glad, half irked," came the answer.

Cate laughed.

Looking as if she'd slept poorly, if at all, Robin said, "Honestly, Cate, having you come up here, well, it all seems a little silly at the moment."

Cate cocked her head. "You did the right thing, trusting your gut."

"My gut is telling me I'm overreacting." Robin laughed. "It's *your* gut that's spooking me."

Unamused, Cate pressed her case. "Why take the risk? If I'm wrong, then I'm the one who'll feel foolish, but if you're wrong, well, damn it, there's such a thing as being embarrassed to death." Cate put a hand up to stop any dissent. "You have two options," Cate continued. "Either you follow me back to the Cities or I follow you back to the cabin."

"With the mighty Wonderdog for protection?"

They glanced out to see Grover, drool flying as he snapped at real or imagined bugs. Cate looked at him with the fatuous expression of a new mother.

Robin grimaced. "The thing is, I don't feel great at home, either. Brad's been pulling away from me."

"But you're the one who left yesterday, right?"

Not always receptive to Cate's directness, she pictured telling her to go home and leave her in peace. At the thought, her eyes welled with tears.

"Okay," Cate said folding her arms. "I'll shut up and listen."

She took a few breaths before saying, "Brad doesn't even touch me anymore. I think he sees me as damaged goods." She blotted the corners of her eyes with a napkin.

Cate nodded, remembering six years ago when her own marriage had been threatened. "Okay." She drummed her fingers on the table, choosing her words. "I have to say I don't understand why an otherwise intelligent, loving husband can't see how he's hurting you."

Robin blew her nose. "Maybe we shouldn't assume the *loving* part."

The waitress came to the table.

"The cheeseburger and malt special? Mocha?" Cate asked, wiggling her eyebrows at Robin, who nodded, glad not to have to make a decision.

By the time their lunch arrived, Robin had filled Cate in, as accurately as possible, on her last discussion with Brad.

Cate said, "at least Brad shows passion when he fights—shows he cares."

"If that's the only way he can show passion, I don't need it." Angry tears sprang to her eyes. "He treats me like a leper."

Cate recoiled in mock horror. "He'd better *not* be mistreating leopards!"

Robin wasn't ready to be kidded out of her funk.

"Okay, seriously, has this been mostly since your surgery?"

Robin shook her head. "He's always been consumed with his work, coming home tired, getting up early to visit patients before office hours. But, yeah, it's been worse since then."

"Do you think he's afraid he'll hurt you?"

Robin looked away. "I don't know. There's just this coldness. The other night I fixed his favorite dinner, bought flowers and wine and lit candles, and I don't think he looked at me once. I might as well not have even been there. It's almost like he expects me to die, and showing affection would be . . . well, a poor investment."

Cate swallowed hard. "That just doesn't sound like the Brad I know."

CATE FOLLOWED ROBIN in her Land Rover, mentally berating Brad during the thirty-minute drive.

Once released, Grover flung himself out the door and watered flowers and bushes all along the fieldstone path leading to the cabin.

Robin and Cate sat on the back porch while Grover paced and sniffed, his toenails clicking in and out of the kitchen.

Robin looked into the distance. "The way I see it, I could spend the rest of my life trying to figure out why Brad is the way he is, but at some point the *why* doesn't matter. If he can't be my friend when I most need him, then what's the point?"

Then, before Cate could answer, Robin hastened to abort the conversation by saying, "Let's not waste any more time on him. The next move is his."

Slowly Cate nodded. "Change of subject?"

"Please."

"Can we talk about Curious George? I really think we should do something. How do you feel about calling the sheriff?"

THE SHERIFF SHOWED UP less than an hour later—alone, they were glad to see. Grover jumped up with his paws on Harley's shoulders. "I'm glad to see you, too, little fella," the man said, "but around me you're gonna stand on all fours."

The dog dropped to the floor, awaiting his next order.

Cate stood, open-mouthed.

Harley stroked the dog's silky ears. "So." He turned to the women. "You think George Wellman stole an incriminating photo. Can you make another one?"

"Sure, but the negatives are back in Minneapolis," Robin explained.

"Can you describe it?"

Robin sighed, shutting her eyes to see the photo in her mind. "I was focused on the deer below," Robin began, "but just behind and above them, I inadvertently also captured that natural ledge on the other side of the creek. And Melissa was lying on it."

"Melissa?" Harley tilted his head.

Cate chewed on her lower lip as she and Robin exchanged a look. "The woman you think drowned," Cate answered.

"How do you know her name? We just had it confirmed and nothing's been made public."

Robin puffed up her cheeks and blew the air out. "Just call it women's intuition. You still think she drowned?"

Way to go, Cate thought. *Put him on the defensive.*

"As a matter of fact, the official report from the M.E. is inconclusive, so we're also entertaining the notion that she was dead before she hit the water. What do you say we go outside? Maybe you can point out to me what you're describing."

Grover barked and flew at the screen door. The others followed him out, and as Robin pointed out various elements of the absent photo, Harley asked, "What time of day was this?"

"Mid-afternoon. Two or three o'clock."

He consulted his watch. "Tell you what . . ."

Several minutes later, they were all in position, Robin on the cabin side of the creek, crouching as she had when she took the picture, Harley at the edge of the woods on the opposite side of the creek. Cate lay on her back on the rocky outcropping, looking like some femme fatale on a fainting couch with one arm shielding her eyes from the sun, the other, with her own large bracelet showing, dangling down. When Robin saw the bright spots of Harley's glasses, she gave him a thumbs up, lifted her camera and clicked away until she was startled by a commotion behind her, a crashing sound accompanied by barking and a man's voice, yelling "No! Go away. Get."

She whipped her head around at the noise. Hesitating before she took off in that direction, she turned to see Harley and Cate crashing down the stony path to the bridge. Knowing they were coming to her aid, Robin was emboldened to investigate.

On the pine needles between her and the cabin lay a man. Dancing over him, Grover nudged him with his head and pawed at his arms. His friendly woofing clearly meant he was just playing.

"Grover, get over here," Robin ordered.

Grover wagged his tail.

"Get him off me!" George yelled.

Robin tugged on Grover's collar, to no avail.

Cate, panting from her run, appeared behind Robin. Making no move to help, she folded her arms and watched as George struggled to free himself.

"Stop," said Harley, arriving on the scene, and the dog stopped.

"Sit," he commanded, and Grover came to sit at Harley's side.

Cate looked at the sheriff with awed respect.

Scrambling to his feet, George wiped his shirttail across his face, then stooped to retrieve his glasses from the ground, wiping them on the same shirttail before putting them on.

Harley hoisted his pants up. "What were you doing on Mrs. Bentley's property, George?"

George took off his glasses again and adjusted the frames and the bows, once more wiping them on his dirty shirt. "I heard a car come up here and thought I'd make sure she was all right." He avoided looking at the three pairs of eyes fixed on him. "Besides, I live here." He gestured to the woods.

Harley absent-mindedly stroked Grover's ears.

"If she's alone, I check on any strange car coming up the drive," George explained.

Harley grunted. "So I assume you came to check when this one arrived." He jerked a thumb at Cate.

"Nope." George returned his glasses to his face and looked squarely at the sheriff, his self-confidence returning. "I know their cars by now. I could tell it was Mrs. B. and Mrs. Wolf was following her." His smile faltered almost immediately as he anticipated the response.

"I would've thought you'd recognize *my* car by now, George. It's the only one that has the word 'SHERIFF' painted on it. Both sides." He let George squirm a while before dismissing him. "Well, I'm sure these ladies appreciate your concern, but I've got things under control, so you can get back to whatever you were doing."

They watched George slink off in the direction of his trailer. Harley turned to Robin. "How long will you be here this time?"

She shrugged. "Not sure. A couple days, at least."

Nodding to Cate, he asked, "You too?"

"No, I have to get back tomorrow," she answered with a sigh.

"Is the dog staying?" he asked.

The dog nuzzled against his hand.

"Yes," Cate said emphatically.

Harley tapped the brim of his hat. "Okay, then. I'll make a swing through here tomorrow, but if George Wellman bothers you, you call me, okay?"

BEFORE DINNER, CATE and Robin walked Grover back to the creek, looping around the property and returning by way of the road. No matter what subject came up, talk kept returning to speculations about Melissa and her mother, about George and the photo.

"What do you make of Grover's reaction to George?" Robin ducked under a low-hanging branch. "He certainly doesn't seem to have an aversion to him."

"Hmmph," Cate said, "There's no accounting for taste."

"No, really. Doesn't that comfort you at all?"

"We're talking about Grover here. He likes everybody."

Suddenly the dog shot ahead, disappeared in the tall grasses and resurfaced on the other side of the ditch.

Robin's breathing quickened when she recognized the spot. "What's he doing? Isn't that the place—?"

"Yes, but where's the tree, the one with the paint on it?"

Nose to the ground, Grover moved in a circle around a tree stump. His tail, no longer waving, was rigid.

Robin frowned at the accumulation of sawdust and wood chips. "Do you think he can still smell Molly Pat?"

Cate shook her head. "He's not being territorial. That's anxiety." She strode in his direction.

Grover whined and Cate knelt to pet him while Robin scanned the woods for more newly sawn trunks. She saw none.

There was nothing to do but go back to the cabin, where they made goat-cheese-and-roasted-vegetable sandwiches and played cribbage. They won a game apiece and Robin won the rubber, breaking the tie.

THE NEXT MORNING ROBIN woke reluctantly from a dream in which Brad was kissing her feet, probing the spaces between her toes with his tongue. She let her eyes open a crack, and saw Grover grinning at her, pink tongue lolling. She jerked her feet back and squawked. As she leaped out of bed, she could swear the dog was laughing at her.

Cate was already up. A fire crackled in the newly repaired fireplace.

"Your idiot dog just gave me a footbath and was about to wash my face," Robin croaked.

Cate patted his head. "Good boy!"

With one wag of his tail, Cate's empty coffee mug was airborne.

Muttering, Robin picked up the broken pieces and tossed them into the trash before taking a quick shower and getting dressed. When she returned, Cate stood near the door, purse and tote over her shoulder.

"Last chance," Cate said. "Are you coming back with me or is Grover staying here?"

Robin groaned. "Can't you take him with you to the nursing home? They'd love him."

Grover wagged his tail, basking in the attention.

Cate didn't even have to consider it. The animals she brought to a handful of senior facilities were all friendly, but also mellow and well mannered. "Not an option. You saw what he did to George. Can you picture him knocking down someone with osteoporosis?"

Robin had to give her that.

"Besides, as long as you're here, he's going to protect you."

Almost as soon as she saw Cate drive off in a cloud of dust, Robin found herself reassured by the dog's presence. When he whined and pranced at the door, she put him on a leash, flung open the door, and soon found herself being tugged toward George's trailer.

George, wearing stiff new jeans and a sleeveless undershirt, kept the screen door shut. "Yeah, I cut down one of your trees last week along with some dead ones over on Johnson's property," he told her as soon as she asked. "I didn't think you'd mind. See, Johnson said it was damaged and he was afraid it would fall across the road and hurt somebody. I piled the whole mess at his place like he asked."

18

From George's trailer, Grover led Robin along the road for a bit, then veered off to walk up the long drive to Ross Johnson's cabin. Apparently, she was just along for the ride.

No vehicles were in the driveway and nobody answered her knock, so they descended the stairs, rounded the house and there, as she'd remembered, was Ross's woodpile, covered by a trio of blue tarpaulins. Grover walked along the length of the woodpile, sniffing as he went.

"You lift your leg on that wood, and I'll take you to the pound." Grover whined.

"What is it, boy?" She scratched behind his ears. "Who's protecting who, here? Or *whom*, if you care to be grammatical."

He stuck his nose under the center tarp.

She lifted it and saw immediately what she'd hoped to see. Since her oak tree had been alive when George had cut it down, its logs were clearly distinguishable from more weathered birch and oak. Unfortunately, it comprised the bottom half of a four-foot pile. She sighed and chucked a couple of logs behind her. "You might as well lie down," she said to Grover. "This is going to take a while."

With a huge yawn, he stretched and collapsed, front end first, with his head resting on his paws. His eyes never left her. Robin found him almost endearing.

The sun was hot, but she worked until she had unearthed a log that still bore smears of creamy beige paint, just as she'd remembered.

She tucked it at the side of the garage so she wouldn't accidentally add it to the stack, and then began the arduous task of rebuilding the woodpile.

Overheated as she was, her hands and arms scratched and grimy, she replaced the tarps. When she knelt to take a drink from the outdoor spigot, Grover barked. She scooped water up in her hands and splashed it on her face.

"It's okay, boy, you'll get your turn."

He nudged her with his great head. She sat back on her heels so he could get at the faucet, but instead of taking a drink, he barked again and faced the road. Only then did she hear the car coming up the drive.

A quick glance at the woodpile told her she'd put everything to rights. A glance at her arms told her to stick them under the faucet, where she was able to rub off the dirt. There was nothing she could do about the torn fingernails.

She recognized the Cadillac Escalade. "I think we're busted, Grover." She snapped her fingers and he followed her to the driveway.

Ross stepped out, wearing jeans and work boots and a couple of days' worth of stubble.

Grover rumbled, low in his throat.

"Robin Bentley, what a surprise!" Ross's eyebrows lifted behind his sunglasses. "What," he asked, pointing his chin in Grover's direction, "is that?"

To Robin's surprise, the dog's hackles were raised. "He's just a puppy, not even full-grown yet," she said, with a smile that was downright coy.

He looked as though he believed her. "Since when did you have a dog?"

She instructed Grover to sit and was surprised when he obeyed. "He's just on loan. We were out for a walk and he dragged me up here. You know, I haven't talked to you in ages."

"It has been a while." As Ross began to grin, his eyes came to rest on her chest. "You're looking good. You're all back to normal now?"

What the hell did that mean? "Good as ever," she said, feeling her jaws clench.

"Can I invite you in for a drink or something?" He edged closer and Grover growled again.

"I'll take a rain check. Actually," she said, looking up at him sheepishly, "we just helped ourselves to water from your faucet. I hope you don't mind."

Ross ducked his head in a way she used to find charming. "I've got some good French brandy."

She paused as if considering the offer. "I'd love to," she lied, "but I need to get back and take something out of the oven. Sorry. Maybe another time."

She felt his eyes on her as she walked back down the drive, and realized she was shaking. Turning to give him a parting wave, she saw his arrogant thumbs-in-pocket stance, and hoped her feeble explanation had sufficed.

By the time she reached the road, she let out her breath and bent to pet Grover. "Good boy! Great dog!" she gushed. "You just might come in handy after all."

After a second rejuvenating shower, Robin settled into a lounge chair to file her ragged nails.

The phone rang. It was Lee Ann Almquist, originally a friend of Grace's, and a one-time member of the book club. Her irregular attendance caused her to drop out. They all held out hope she would return. As a longtime flight attendant for Northwest, now Delta, she could pretty much bid her schedule to suit her, but much of the time she wasn't in the air, she was involved in a seemingly endless list of charitable activities. If she wasn't organizing a fundraiser or working at a women's shelter, she was helping Louise at an estate sale or packing blankets, computers, medical supplies—the list went on— to be taken by volunteer flight attendants to foreign countries in need of those supplies.

This time, Lee Ann was calling on her cell phone, not from some exotic place, but from a farm in Wisconsin, where she and her on-again, off-again boyfriend were attending his family reunion. "They're really sweet people," she said of John's parents and siblings, "but I think we've talked about weather for ten of the twenty-four hours since we got here, and his father insists on telling jokes in which the flight attendants, uh, stewardesses, to him, are incredibly stupid or nymphomaniacs or both."

When Robin started to commiserate, Lee Ann interrupted to ask, "Listen, I really want an excuse to get out of here. Would it be okay if I came to Spirit Falls for a couple hours? John's offered to give hayrides to all his nieces and nephews and assorted relatives, and his mother won't let me help with the food. She said, and I quote, 'You don't want to spoil your pretty salon nails.' I truly can't imagine they'd miss me."

Robin checked her watch. "Of course. Spend the night if you want."

"I'm on my way," she said without hesitation.

ROBIN HEARD A CAR COME up the driveway, sooner than she'd expected. With a chuckle, she thought how desperate Lee Ann must have been to escape the family reunion.

As Robin went to the door, Grover appeared at her side, a low rumble announcing not Lee Ann's, but Ross Johnson's arrival.

He sauntered toward her, a bottle dangling from one hand, and with the other he peeled off his sunglasses in a motion that made her think of runway models.

Robin, her heart beating hard, grabbed Grover's collar. "Stay with me, okay, Grove?"

Ross had shaved and changed into linen slacks and a golf shirt. The smell of antiseptic mouthwash mingled with the stench of cigar. "Aren't you going to invite me in?" he asked.

Still holding onto the dog's collar, she opened the door.

"I didn't interrupt anything, did I?"

Before she could answer, he pushed past her into the kitchen and threw open a cupboard door. "I don't suppose Brad is with you." He opened another cupboard and removed two wine goblets. "I guess these will do." He poured out two brandies, and as he stepped toward her, Grover put his bulk between them.

Ross's gaze was intense. She couldn't read his expression.

Had he figured out the real reason she was at his cabin, she wondered. And why in God's name had she gone to his place, anyway?

She took a deep breath. *First I suspect George and now Ross. Get a grip!*

She and Brad had known Ross and his wife, Sandy—make that *ex*-wife—for years. They'd always been on friendly terms. Early on—Robin was embarrassed to admit, even to herself—she'd been flattered by his attentions. Heck, she may as well admit it, she'd flirted back until Brad had suggested, rather unkindly, that she was embarrassing him and making a fool of herself.

Truth was, they'd all changed over the years, and no one more than Ross, whose roguish appeal had become something more reckless. She swirled the brandy around in her glass, feeling queasy. How many mysteries had she read in which the murderer puts sedative or poison in a glass of wine? She set it down, untouched, hoping her smile would disarm him. "It's too early to drink, but thanks."

Ross shrugged and threw his head back for a large gulp, coughed, and wiped his nose against the back of his hand. "I've been wondering when you might come by. When the four of us used to get together, I always thought you and I hit it off. I mean, there I was stuck with the poster girl from the Reach Out and Nag Someone campaign, and frankly, I just never saw any sizzle between you and Brad. Good guy, but bo-o-oring." He sang the last word like a schoolyard taunt, and swayed closer.

Grover stood, rumbling deep in his chest. Then he yipped once, turning his attention to the door. They all looked.

Walking along the paving stones to the front door was Lee Ann, wearing a spaghetti-strapped silk top, white capris and strappy sandals, not exactly the attire for a hayride. Her broad smile faltered when she saw Ross.

Introductions were made, and though his annoyance was palpable, Ross assumed the part of host, offering Lee Ann a drink.

Once they were all seated on the front porch, Grover never left Robin's side. In fact he lay with his head on her feet.

For her part, Lee Ann seemed fascinated by Ross, hardly taking her eyes off him as he downed Robin's rejected drink. "Have I met you before?" she asked innocently, dipping her finger in the brandy and licking it off.

He followed the motion with his eyes. "I don't think so. I think I'd remember." The palm he ran across his forehead came away wet.

It was clear from the brief look Lee Ann gave Robin that she was trying to communicate something of import.

What? Robin's look asked.

Lee Ann tilted her eyes toward the door.

Ross talked, his words clipped and rapid, not slurred the way a person who'd drunk half a bottle of brandy would be expected to talk. "So, you never did tell me why you came up to see me today." He reached for Robin's hand.

She quickly withdrew it.

Lee Ann's eyes widened.

Ross, way too comfortable in the wicker chair, stretched his arms out, addressing both women. "But here I am, ready, willing and, from what I hear, able."

Robin ran through her mental list of responses. They all seemed improbable now. Stifling a gag reflex, she said, "I guess I've just been nervous being up here alone ever since they found that poor woman. You know they brought George in for questioning?"

He nodded.

"You don't think he had anything to do with her death, do you?"

Ross frowned. "From what I heard, it sounds more like an accident. That's what everybody's saying, anyway. I think they're just rattling George's cage for sport. He's a harmless little bugger."

"I hope so."

He turned his attention again to Lee Ann. "So, what brings you out this way?"

She gave Robin a furtive, pleading look. "I have a problem I need to discuss with my friend. A personal problem." She tipped her glass, drained it and said, "Thank you for the drink. It was nice meeting you." To Robin, she said, "Don't get up. I'll see Ross to the door."

With a look of irritation, Ross set down his glass, snatched up his bottle of brandy and left.

"Damn, you're smooth," Robin said when Lee Ann returned.

"Thank God! I thought I'd lost it. It's been a while since I had to fend off a man." Her smile was pure sugar. "Now, I know it's none of my business, but what on earth was he doing here?"

After Robin's abbreviated account of her afternoon's activities, Lee Ann said, "Remember when I told you about that jerk on my flight a couple weeks ago?"

Robin had a vague recollection. "You'll have to refresh my memory. I always love a good jerk story."

"Okay, on my last New York turnaround, I had to fly with Captain Innuendo again, a walking jerk story if there ever was one. I don't know what he'd do if someone took him up on his endless suggestions."

Robin made a face. "All yack and no shack, as Louise would say."

Lee Ann laughed. "I like that," she said. "But he wasn't the problem that day, if you remember."

This was obviously a memory test Robin was not going to pass. "Keep talking. I'm sure it'll come back to me."

"Well, the trouble began shortly before we started our descent into Chicago. One of my first-class passengers started buzzing me and pulling at his shirt, saying he was having chest pains, so I asked him all the right questions while I took his pulse, which was racing. But then he started to calm down. I followed procedure and reported it to the second officer, and he called it in."

Now it was beginning to come back to her.

"So I went back and told the guy he'd be met at the gate and he said forget it, false alarm. By then we were on the ground, and the captain says he wants the airport doc to check him over anyway."

"Can they do that against his will?"

"I don't know, Robin, but that's what they said." Lee Ann fingered her beaded necklace like a rosary. "Anyway, the captain said since there were only about forty people deplaning at O'Hare, they could get off while we waited for the emergency medical people. We told the guy to just stay put, but when I turned around, he'd disappeared. Poof! Gone." She gestured with her hands.

"Why would he leave if he thought he was having a heart attack?" Robin asked. Before Lee Ann could answer, Robin said, "But I guess people are in denial when they're having a heart attack. It's the whole 'embarrassed to death,' thing."

"Or the whole macho thing," countered Lee Ann.

"Or maybe he didn't want to be late for a meeting."

Lee Ann leaned forward. "Or maybe he had something to hide." She shook her head and continued. "We checked the baggage area, but he never responded. He hadn't checked luggage and he'd paid cash."

Robin, who had been caught up in the story, thought she knew where this was headed.

"They even paged him and you'd think even if he wasn't there, there'd be another Johnson in an airport the size of O'Hare. I mean, around here every fourth person is named Johnson," Lee Ann said. "Even the name Ross Johnson wouldn't be that uncommon."

"What are the odds?" Robin muttered.

"One of the gals thought he was high, probably cocaine, she said."

Robin thought about it, slowly moving her head up and down. "It fits," she said. She patted Grover's head, grateful for his presence. Could she ever feel safe here alone again? she wondered. For years Spirit Falls had been her haven, a place to relax and recharge her batteries, and now . . .

"Are you okay?" Lee Ann asked, and Robin realized she'd been talking to her.

"I'm fine. Sorry. What were you saying?"

"I just asked you if you really went to see that man earlier today."

Robin puffed out her cheeks. "Not really." And then she explained about going over there to search his woodpile when he was gone.

"So where's the log with the paint on it, and what does it mean?" Lee Ann asked.

"It's by his garage, and I've no idea how it fits in. Want to go for a little stroll after dark?"

I t was time to get out. José could sense it in the very air around him. He was nothing but a small time player in a game that was no longer his to control. It had started as a favor for a couple friends, but he'd never intended to be a drug smuggler. The life had seduced him—more specifically, Ross Johnson had seduced him into it, offering ever-increasing money and favor in exchange for an ever-increasing habit. And now he found himself not only running a dating service for the stupid cokehead, but in a bizarre game of blackmail, it would seem, with the man who'd become so dependent on him.

He looked around his small, but richly decorated condo. He had a view of the Mississippi. He could see the boats coming through the locks and dams, and from his balcony, he had decent view of the Stone Arch Bridge. Opening the largest of his suitcases, he began emptying his closet. He might as well leave the heavy sweaters and the winter coats—he wouldn't be needing them where he was going. Come to think of it, there was no point in holding onto most of his possessions.

He pictured the simplicity and grace of his mother's island home off the coast of Spain, the place where, as a young girl, she had attracted the attentions of his father, an Oxford student on break. José, their only progeny, grew up in England, but after his father's untimely death, his mother had returned to Ibiza, where she struggled to maintain her beautiful home and beachfront. He had no doubt she would throw open the doors in welcome, never asking why he'd returned.

The picture of bougainvillea and white sand was so vivid in José's mind that when the telephone rang, he had to shake his head to remember where he was.

Candi's voice was high-pitched, agitated. "Can I come over? I really need to talk to you."

"About what?" he asked as he riffled through papers on his rolltop desk. "I'm kind of busy."

"That girl, Melissa, the one who died."

His jaw clenched. "What about her?"

"Well, don't you think they're going to figure out where she was? I mean, somebody's going to talk, and then they'll come to you and me. You know they will."

He squeezed his eyes shut. He couldn't get sucked back into this. He just couldn't.

"Well? What are we going to say?"

"About what? She was there at the party. So what?"

"But we were all doing drugs."

"Actually, I wasn't." He started shoving books into a packing box.

"I really want to talk to you."

"Listen, Candi, if anyone asks," he said, knowing he was being dismissive to someone deserving of more, "you don't know anything about anything. All you have to do is keep your mouth shut."

"But what about Melissa? She was a classy lady and she treated me nice. I don't think she just fell in the water and drowned, do you?"

"Don't be stupid."

"What? I hate trying to talk to you on the phone. How about if I just come over," she wheedled.

"I'm on my way out."

"When will you be back?"

He sighed. "I'm taking a job out of state, so I may not be in touch for a while." Before she could respond, he clicked the off button on the phone and ignored its almost immediate ringing.

IT WAS LATE AFTERNOON by the time Candi turned off the freeway and passed through a couple of towns with populations in the triple digits. Twice she had to backtrack, but her sense of direction was keen, and eventually she recognized the road leading to Ross Johnson's cabin. Pulling in behind his car, she checked herself in the rear-view mirror and applied lip-gloss before exiting her Camaro.

If she'd expected a warm welcome, she was sorely disappointed. Ross glowered at her through the screen door the way her dad always did when the Jehovah's witnesses came, and asked in a growly voice like her dad's, "Do you want something?"

"It's Candi," she said. Her smile faltered. "Remember me?"

He squinted into the sunlight, then nodded and opened the door. In a tone only slightly less hostile, he asked, "What brings you here?"

"You," she answered coyly. "I missed you." She dipped her right shoulder, letting the strap of her camisole slip.

His expression was dubious as he ushered her into the living room and gestured toward the bar. "Help yourself," he said, plunking down in a leather recliner.

She grabbed the nearest bottle and poured herself too much brandy. "Oops." She giggled nervously. "I guess you'll have to help me drink this. I don't want to, y'know, not know what I'm doing."

Ross Johnson stared right through her.

She took a gulp and sat on the arm of his chair, where he laid a hand on her shoulder. He might as well have been comatose for all the feeling he put into it. She tilted her head and her short bob swung forward in a way most men found seductive, but Ross Johnson wasn't most men. He'd blown hot and cold at that weekend party, leaving her wondering if she'd done something really dumb. Her girlfriends at the club said he was probably gay. Who else would pass it up, they'd asked, and for that she had no answer.

She kicked off a sandal and stroked his leg with her bare foot.

He seemed to come out of his stupor a bit and pulled her closer. "So what's the deal?" he asked, his voice harsh. "José wouldn't help you with the rent, so you decided to come here looking for a sugar-daddy?"

It was like he could read her mind or something. Shit! But that was only part of it, and if he already knew what she was thinking, she might as well say it. "I'm scared," she said simply. "I keep thinking about Melissa, and how she was here and then they found her dead, y'know, after she left here." She bit her lip. "I don't know what to do."

His eyes were contemptuous slits. "Why do you have to do anything?"

And then, even though it hadn't gone so well with José, she wound up blurting it out in much the same way to Ross. "I mean, what if they come and ask me if she was with your friend that weekend. I saw him on TV, that Martin guy, the president of Bradford College. He just flat-out lied! So what if they ask me about something that would, y'know, look suspicious since we didn't see her again after that."

As she continued, she felt his tightening grip on her shoulder. She snuffled and looked around for a tissue, slipping off the chair to grab the box from the bathroom.

When she came back, Ross was standing. He kissed her roughly on the mouth and she began to think this might turn out better than she'd feared.

"I was thinking," she said in her little girl voice, "Maybe we could go away, y'know, just the two of us, someplace romantic, and then we wouldn't have to answer any questions or worry about anything at all."

He kissed her again, then guided her, not to the bedroom as she'd anticipated, but to the front door.

"What are we doing?" she asked, her voice cracking.

"*We* are doing nothing. *You* are going home and forgetting about that whole weekend. You shouldn't have trouble forgetting things."

"What are you saying?"

"I'm saying nobody cares what you have to say. Nobody's going to take you seriously or ask your opinions. You're nothing but arm candy."

Her eyes stung. "I know why you're acting like this," she said, unable to keep the shrillness out of her voice. "You're just a stupid prick with a stupider prick, and you're taking it out on me because you can't get it up anymore." She jutted her chin out, almost expecting him to strike her.

Instead, his jaw tightened, then relaxed. He reached into his pocket, pulled out a money clip and peeled off some fifties.

"What's this?"

He laughed and shoved it into her cleavage. "Money. Go home. Pay your rent. Don't bother coming back."

LEE ANN'S DEPARTURE that evening left Robin feeling more alone than she had in a long time. Robin powered up her laptop and tried to write the final chapter, but after filling the screen with awkwardly worded sentences, she typed, "This is all crap. I need to clear my head." As she considered another walk, she shuddered at having another run-in with Ross Johnson.

Grover's eyes followed her path to the kitchen. His ears perked up when the refrigerator door opened, lowered again when the refrigerator closed with no sounds of food preparation.

"No bedtime snack tonight," she said to Grover. "Sorry."

The huge dog sighed and rolled his eyes toward the front door. "You want me to go back, don't you?"

His tail thumped on the floor.

A single tear fell, which she brusquely wiped away. "I suppose we should go home. Staying upset is just too exhausting, isn't it?"

Grover stretched and yawned, the tone rising and falling a full octave, and she couldn't help but laugh. "Okay, we'll go home in the morning."

IN THE MORNING, Robin took the route that passed the sheriff's office. She pulled into the small parking lot. Seeing both squad cars there, she almost didn't get out, but then Deputy Brill swaggered out of the building, touched the brim of her hat and said *ma'am* in greeting before taking off in her vehicle. A couple seconds later, Robin heard the siren wail.

Inside the front door and down the hall, Robin turned left and peered into the sheriff's office.

"Hey, where's that dog of yours?" Harley asked when he recognized Robin in the doorway. "I got him some doggie treats."

"He's not my dog," Robin grumbled. She retrieved Grover from the car and brought him inside where she was forced to watch a ridiculous show of dog training man, even though the man was quite convinced it was the other way around. After several minutes of frolicking, Harley sat to hear the reason for her visit.

He picked up the log and held it in both hands, rolling it as she spoke.

"Doesn't that look like car paint to you?" she asked. "Before it was cut down it was at just the right height for a car fender to have hit it."

He nodded wearily as he set the log on his desk. Turning back to Robin he said, "Maybe you can help me with this, because I just don't see how this log with paint on it connects to the woman we found in the creek."

"Melissa Dunn," she corrected him. "She was a human being long before she became just another case on your desk."

He grimaced and rubbed the back of his neck. "Okay."

She suddenly felt foolish for coming in with so much speculation and so little information. She took in a breath and began anyway. "Okay, in the first place, I heard a crash that night. There was a party going on down the road at Ross Johnson's place, and my first thought was that someone was drunk, got behind the wheel and hit a deer, but there was no dead deer and the tree had a new gouge in it, and Molly Pat—"

"The dog?"

"Yes, the dog. Molly Pat knew something was wrong." She saw the amused pull at the corner of his mouth and said, "Okay, forget about the dog. Just answer this. Why would somebody cut down that particular tree and none other? It was perfectly healthy except for the gouge with paint in it. Somebody was determined to cut it down and then it wound up in my neighbor's woodpile, the same guy who hosted a party that night."

"Correct me if I'm wrong, but didn't you also have a party at your place that same night?" His tone was more playful than confrontational.

Robin couldn't believe he was equating their parties. "I don't think there's any comparison. We don't have orgies. We never drink to excess. We don't even—"

Harley held his hands up. "Okay, okay, I hear you." Then, after some time had passed, he said, "It's just that there's nothing I can do about it."

They both turned at the odd sound, and saw Grover chewing the end of the log. Harley snatched it from his jaws and set it on the filing cabinet.

Robin, seeing her Exhibit A being first damaged, then shelved, said, "Don't you have some way to check out what kind of car it came from? Can't you at least do that?"

He shook his head. "I have to justify how I spend my budget here, and, well, this is just a log with paint on it."

Robin looked at the log, then abruptly took her leave before Harley could see her eyes welling with angry tears.

JUST AS SHERIFF HARLEY WAS READY to lock up the office so he could stop for dinner before going home to watch a rented movie, the phone rang. It was Detective Maki from Roseville, who'd been working on the Melissa Dunn case when it was still a missing persons case. Harley hoped they could keep the investigation local, and, as an accidental drowning, that's where it would stay. And even if it wasn't accidental, the feds wouldn't get involved unless she'd been brought across state lines for the explicit purpose of murdering her.

"Afternoon, Sheriff. I'm sure glad I caught you. Say, we got a call I thought you'd be interested in," the detective said, his hard R's giving away his original home in northern Minnesota's Iron Range. "The caller says she saw the Dunn woman that Friday after she was last seen in Minnesota."

"Uh-huh."

"At a cabin in your jurisdiction. She even gave me the directions and a name. You know someone named Johnson?"

"A few," Harley said, leaning forward in his chair and trying not to get too excited. "-on or -en?"

"Don't know. First name of Ross. Sounds like his cabin is real close to where the body turned up. Fancy place, definitely high buck."

"Yup, I know the one. Ross Johnson, with an O."

"The caller claims Dunn was at a party there, got high and left. And then, she says, the boyfriend took off. We asked her to come in and make a statement. In fact my partner is interviewing her now."

"Taping it?"

"Yeah, we'll make you a copy."

Harley was wired when he got home. He'd handled plenty of deaths in his career—hunting and boating and farm accidents, car crashes, usually involving a drunk driver, domestic arguments that escalated into violence, one or both of them tanked up pretty good. But this was smelling like murder.

He popped in the movie *Dirty Rotten Scoundrels* and sat back with his stockinged feet on the coffee table to watch the opening credits. In a few minutes he was rewarded with another call from Minneapolis.

"She named the vic's boyfriend," the detective said without preamble, "her boss, Martin Krause, the president of Bradford College."

Harley slapped the arm of his chair and whooped.

"You interested in being there when we bring him in?"

"Wouldn't miss it." They made the arrangements before Harley popped the lid of a Hamm's and dialed Deputy Brill, who was pulling night shift at the office. "There's a log sitting on the file cabinet," he told her. "I want you to take it down to the Madison lab tomorrow. See what they can find out about the paint, and make sure they put a rush on it. And call Connie and see who can cover for you."

20

arley woke early and decided to drive to Minneapolis by way
of Mickey's Diner in Saint Paul for good, cheap food and just
enough of an edge to put him in the mood for watching a
murderer confess. He walked into the yellow-and-red enameled
1930s railroad dining car turned restaurant and sat at the counter
next to a man in a business suit. Several stools down sat an old man
who looked like he'd walked out of the pages of a Zane Grey novel,
with his snakeskin boots and rumpled cowboy hat. The cowboy
nodded to Harley and went back to alternately sipping from his
strawberry shake and taking drags off a hand-rolled cigarette.

"What'll you have, hon?" asked the matronly waitress.

Harley ordered up a mess of hash browns, very crispy, and eggs,
still runny, then sat back to watch the banter between cook and
waitress. The food was delicious. He lingered over coffee, his cup
being refilled almost every time he set it down, and felt sure he would
have some answers by day's end.

When he went to the register to pay with his lone credit card,
he noticed the sign instructing patrons that tips were expected in
cash. He pulled out a couple ones and placed them on the counter.

Arriving at the station, Harley parked near the entrance and
sauntered up to the receptionist's desk. The woman was young and
blonde and striking, and Harley found himself stammering when he
asked for Detective Maki. Within minutes, the door to the inner offices

opened and a trim man in a rumpled shirt held out his hand. Although he had a full head of gray hair, his unruly eyebrows were dark brown.

Harley sucked in his gut and pulled his shoulders back.

"Glad you could make it, Sheriff." Detective Maki ushered him into an uncluttered office.

"I think you'll be interested in what we got last night." Detective Maki popped a tape into the VCR. They watched as Candi Damiano gave her name and address, and quickly moved on to describe the last evening anyone admitted to seeing the dead woman, Melissa Dunn.

Just as the tape ended, another detective announced Martin Krause's arrival.

On the other side of the two-way mirror, Harley had a few moments to observe the well-groomed, well-dressed man seated alone at the table. Krause looked every part the college president, unless one caught the occasional wary shift of his eyes or his bobbing Adam's apple.

Detective Maki entered, setting a spiral reporter's notebook and a ballpoint pen between them on the table. They went through a few preliminaries before Maki offered Krause coffee.

"Some water would be fine." When Maki left, Martin scanned the room with its bland off-white walls. He seemed to stare through the mirrored viewing window directly at Sheriff Harley.

Maki returned with a Styrofoam cup of water. "Now where were we? You were telling me about your relationship with Melissa Dunn."

"Relationship? I was her boss. She was Bradford's director of Development. She answered to me." He sat back, opening himself up in the body language of confidence.

"You're telling me your relationship was strictly professional?"

"Of course," Martin snapped.

Maki smiled and waited. Krause shifted. Maki said, "Mr. Krause, do you—"

"It's *Doctor. Doctor* Krause."

"Ah, yes. Well, Dr. Krause, do you know a Ross Johnson, who owns a cabin near where Ms. Dunn's body was found?"

Martin crossed his arms. "I went to college with Ross Johnson. We're still acquaintances."

Maki leaned back and crossed his legs at the ankles. "We know that Melissa Dunn was at Mr. Johnson's cabin the last weekend in May." Watching Martin's face he added, "With you."

Martin slowly took a sip of water and set the cup back down on the table with precision. "Yes, that's true. She was there with me."

"And are you still telling me your relationship was just professional? Would you care to explain?"

"Make this good," muttered Harley behind the mirror.

Krause inhaled deeply through his nose. His eyes shifted briefly to where Harley stood behind the glass. "Yes. She and I were there to get donations for the college."

At this answer, Maki's eyebrows shot up. "Getting donations?"

"Yes, you see, Ross often entertains affluent and influential people. We put together the concept of providing them a relaxed atmosphere in which to offer them an opportunity to participate in the financial health of the college."

Harley hooted but quickly clamped his hand over his mouth.

"Okay, so you threw a party to hit some wealthy stiffs up for money. Exactly what was Ms. Dunn's function?"

It was subtle when Krause's composure began to crumble. He didn't obviously sweat; his posture remained unchanged. But to Harley, it seemed as if Martin Krause was beginning to implode. "As director of Development, Melissa had a knack for fund-raising." Martin drained his cup.

Maki smiled again. He repositioned the notebook squarely in front of him and flipped a page. "Okay, but here's what I find a little odd. Wouldn't this type of fund-raising normally be done on your campus?"

Krause, once more on sure footing, said, "Not at all. It's not at all unusual to sponsor events in homes of loyal alumni, for instance."

"Did Ross Johnson graduate from Bradford?"

"No." He gestured to the notebook. "You probably have that in there. He did not, but he holds Bradford College in high regard. He offered his cabin to host this event as his gift to Bradford."

"Okay, I can see that. But overnight? Isn't that a bit unusual?"

Krause focused on the corner of the room. "Unusual, yes. That was the point. We were thinking out of the box. We wanted to get them out in nature and then explain to them why it was the most natural thing in the world to educate those who—"

"But why overnight?"

"Oh, yes, well, there was also the consideration that we served wine and we didn't want anyone having to drive home." He flipped his hand. "Liability and all."

"What would you say if I told you we know it wasn't just wine? We know about the drugs, Dr. Krause." Maki let that bit of information sink in. "Isn't it true you and Ms. Dunn were using cocaine?"

Martin's face blanched. "Wherever you got that information, it was wrong. We had alcohol, yes. But drugs?" He looked directly into Maki's eyes. "Never!"

"Okay, so tell me, who were these people?"

"The people?"

"Yes, the people at this gathering?"

"I don't recall. They were acquaintances of Ross Johnson's." Martin's fingernails picked at the Styrofoam cup.

"You don't recall their names, and yet you were hitting them up for donations?" Maki asked incredulously.

"Ross hadn't made formal introductions yet."

He let the *yet* slide for now.

"You didn't have conversations with any of them?"

"We, um, it's hard to describe."

Maki tapped his pen on the wooden table as he pondered that answer. "Okay, let's leave that for a minute. How did Ms. Dunn get to this fund-raiser?" His voice was thick with irony.

"She drove."

"You drove separately?"

"No, I guess I picked her up." Martin concentrated on the growing pile of Styrofoam chips.

"Where was that?"

"What?"

"Where did you pick up Melissa Dunn?"

Martin flushed. "At her, uh, apartment. She wanted to change clothes after work and asked—"

"So you picked her up at her apartment and drove her to Johnson's. What day?"

Martin Krause breathed audibly through his mouth. He briefly pressed his eyes shut. "What?"

"Thursday? Friday?"

"Uh, Thursday, as I recall. We wanted to get everything set up. You know, caterers and such."

"Uh huh. So you were there, just you and Melissa Dunn and Ross Johnson, on that Thursday night. Friday was the big party, right?"

"Fund-raiser."

"Yeah, okay. And Melissa Dunn was still there Friday, right?"

"That's correct." Krause splayed his hands on the table, as if bracing himself.

"And then, at some point, she left. When was that?"

Martin shrugged. "I don't know. I never looked at the clock. She just got upset about something and walked out of the room. I had no idea at the time that she'd left the premises."

Maki waited.

Looking down at his hands, Martin took another deep breath. "I don't know what happened. She appeared quite upset about something and said that she was leaving. She could be mercurial."

"Okay, she told you she was leaving. Did she take your car?"

He appeared to consider the question. "I assume she took off on foot."

"Did you try to stop her, reason with her?"

"At first I surmised she'd come back when she was done with her little snit, but then when the storm moved in, I went out to look for her. I never did find her. By the time I returned, I was told a couple people had left, and may have taken her with them."

Maki began clicking his ballpoint pen. "Let's assume that actually happened. What did you think when she didn't report to work?"

"I just figured that she was taking a few days off."

"Is she in the habit of doing that?"

"I really couldn't answer that."

"Didn't your secretary, Amy Nguyen, inform you of Miss Dunn's unexplained absence?"

"I believe so."

"I see. Did you suggest to her that she call Miss Dunn at home?"

"Ms. Nguyen did that on her own. There was no answer, as I recall."

"Right. And after a few tries, she called the emergency contact in Ms. Dunn's file—her mother—did she not?"

"I have no reason to question it if Ms. Nguyen says so."

"At any point, were you yourself concerned enough to call the police?" Maki asked matter-of-factly.

"No."

In the next room, Harley shook his head in disbelief.

"Let me explain to you the Rule of Holes, President Krause. The Rule of Holes," Maki explained. "When you find yourself in one, stop digging!"

T he sheriff blew into his office as if propelled by the wind. At her desk, Brill kept her head down but rolled her eyes up to look at him. "Going for the Paddington Bear look?" She chuckled to herself.

Harley peeled back the hood of his yellow vinyl slicker and stamped his boots.

"They say it's gonna clear out by this evening, but I don't believe it," she said, eying the white paper bags in his hand.

Harley plopped one on her desk, and immediately she plunged her hand in and removed the Double Whopper, squeezed three packets of ketchup on it and took a man-sized bite. A red blob dropped onto her pants. She lifted it off with her finger, put it in her mouth.

"Anything from Madison yet?"

"A fax came in about an hour ago. I put it on your chair." Brill had learned long ago not to place important papers on Harley's desk. He had his own quirky system for putting order to what looked to her like utter chaos.

He motioned to her. She stuffed her mouth with french fries, looked regretfully at her deeply scalloped burger, and followed him into his office.

Harley flung his raincoat in the direction of the wall-mounted coat rack, and it caught.

Grabbing the papers from his chair, Brill placed them in his hand. "The paint comes from a Mercedes, a beige one."

When he sat, she leaned over his shoulder. "See, right here it says—"

"Thanks, I'd like to read it myself."

Ignoring his comment, she continued. "Paint color is weizengelb, number 681, manufactured by Glosser, to be precise. Problem is they discontinued it in 1985. I've already checked with Lois at the DMV. No match in the entire county." She looked pleased with herself.

Harley almost grinned. "Then check the surrounding counties."

"Will do."

When he was done reading the full report, he began tapping out a search on his keyboard.

Brill returned with her own search results. "Nothing in the three-county area."

He hit a new button and waited for his underpowered computer to chug out its answer. "Then call the Minnesota DMV." He glanced at his screen that now informed him he'd committed a "permanent fatal error." Each time he read that stupid, hyperbolic phrase, he pictured himself pulling out his service revolver, pressing it against the side of the monitor and pulling the trigger. "Go ahead. Make my day," he said between clenched teeth.

The phone rang. The caller identified himself as Detective Maki from the Roseville P.D. Harley listened for a moment. "Well, if that don't beat all!" he said. Cradling the phone on his shoulder, he grabbed a notepad and pen, took some notes. "Thanks Detective, I'll fax the affidavit over to you this afternoon."

Hanging up, Harley called out the door, "Guess who owns a 1984 beige Mercedes?"

IT WAS PROPERLY OVERCAST the afternoon of Melissa Dunn's wake. Four of the No Ordinary Women decided to attend, each, in her own way, feeling a sense of responsibility to this young woman whose body had been so carelessly deposited on the shore of Tamarack Creek—the very shore where, more than once, they'd sat on beach chairs and sipped margaritas. Below Spirit Falls, the very falls where, last year, they'd shed about forty years apiece along with their bathing suits.

Robin arrived alone, and saw there were rent-a-cops directing traffic in the parking lot. The death of a young person usually brought out the crowds, and this young person was no exception. Inside, a sign directed her to the largest room of the funeral home, although all she had to do was follow the odor of Stargazer lilies and roses.

Melissa's parents stood by the flower-bedecked casket, their shoulders resolute. He was freckled, like his daughter, with thinning hair. Her hair was freshly colored and matched Melissa's, seen in the numerous photos on a display board nearby. Displaying simple elegance, they greeted the hundreds who had come to pay homage to their only child. They neither cried nor smiled, clearly determined to conduct themselves with decorum, but in their faces it was obvious that gravity pulled more heavily on them than on the other mourners.

Robin, wearing a simple navy dress and flats, went directly to the greeting line, and when it was her turn, she hugged Mrs. Dunn and pressed the borrowed photos into her hands. Her throat closed when she tried to speak.

"I know, dear, I know." Carol Dunn patted her arm. Robin had always found it odd, but she'd noticed before how so often those who grieved the most took it upon themselves to comfort others.

Robin placed her hand over her heart, her eyes moist. "I'm so sorry."

Carol nodded and introduced Robin to her husband.

After muttering her inadequate words to the father, Robin turned to see Foxy at the back of the line, her reddish-brown pantsuit exactly matching the color of her hair. In the foyer, Grace, sporting a flattering new hairdo that framed her face with wisps, was signing the guest book.

Dramatic in an aubergine silk ensemble, Cate entered through another door. She ambled up behind Grace without acknowledging her, signed the book, and followed her into the room. Once surrounded by the crowd, Grace pointed out to Cate the young man with a sleek ponytail who stood far off, talking to no one.

Cate meandered through the crush of people toward him. It was several seconds before he glanced in her direction. She dabbed at her nose with a handkerchief, letting her sleeve fall away to reveal the jewelry on her wrist.

The man Grace had identified as Todd gave her a sad smile and nod. She returned it. Nothing on his face indicated he recognized the bracelet, so similar to the one Melissa had owned. He seemed lost in his own misery.

But even though Melissa's hapless boyfriend paid her little attention, Cate sensed someone else watching her. She looked over her shoulder and saw Sheriff Harley's eyes fixed in her direction. They both looked away. He was not in uniform, of course. Cate had read enough mysteries, watched enough TV, to know that police always go to the funerals of people whose deaths are suspicious. She scanned the crowd, looking for the other plainclothes.

Cate's eyes were drawn to a handsome couple. Martin Krause looked much like his photo on Bradford's website. The skinny, too-tanned woman with streaked blond hair and delicate jewelry next to him fit Grace's description of Brenda Krause. Martin steered his wife through the crowd with a hand on her elbow as if it were a rudder. With the other hand, he pressed a white hanky to the back of his neck. They worked the crowd in that quadrant of the room, looking a bit too much as though they were campaigning. Cate observed two distinct clumps of people she supposed were Bradford employees.

Grace, she saw, had zeroed in on the Krauses. Cate watched as introductions were made. She saw Brenda touch Grace's hair, saw the smile and nod of approval for the new look. Another glance in

Harley's direction told her that he, also, was interested in the threesome. She decided to work her way over to them.

Standing near Grace and the Krauses, Cate heard nothing of import. As she smoothed back her hair, however, Martin's attention was suddenly focused on her exposed wrist, which tingled with the intensity of his stare. *The bracelet.* Her heart began to beat rapidly, a memory picture coming back to her: the man with intense eyes, hastily picking through her jewelry at the Uptown Art Fair, choosing a bracelet, pulling a wad of cash out of his pocket, then quickly, guiltily, stuffing the purchase, wrapped only in tissue, into his breast pocket.

He had that same furtive look now as he leaned over and spoke in his wife's ear. Brenda glanced at him, nodded, then continued her conversation with Grace.

As Martin Krause headed for the exit, a man and woman slipped out the door behind him.

Cate decided to join the parade, which led only to the men's room. The man, a slender Nordic type with tinted glasses, followed Martin in. The woman, tall, fair and hard-bodied, attached herself to the wall of the corridor. Rather than join this woman, whom Cate had pegged as a detective, she used the ladies' room to reapply lipstick.

Robin joined her almost immediately. "What's up?"

Cate bent to glance quickly for feet in the bathroom stalls before saying, "It's him! President Krause was her secret lover. I remember him buying her the bracelet!"

Robin's eyes widened. She bit her lip and nodded, letting the information sink in. It made sense. "We'd better tell the sheriff. Did you see him?"

Cate nodded. "You go out first. I'll try to find him."

Reentering the crowded room, Robin felt the silence. In priest's garb, a youthful yet balding man gestured to the Dunns to take a seat. Those who could find a seat, sat. The others remained standing while the priest intoned, "Hail Mary, full of grace." A strangled groan came from Mr. Dunn. His wife's lips moved, trancelike, with the priest's as she fingered her own rosary beads. In his words of comfort, the priest described Melissa's death as a "homecoming," and reminded them of their responsibility to care for one another. The funeral, he informed them, would be held the next day at two o'clock at Saint Matthew's.

Robin futilely searched the room for Cate and Sheriff Harley. The Krauses stood at the back, hands clasped in front of them, heads bowed. Martin wiped his nose with his handkerchief.

"Amen," the priest said, and Martin, again maneuvering his wife by the elbow, slipped out the door.

Robin stepped out behind them and scanned the parking lot. Grace and Cate had somehow gotten there first. Harley was nowhere in sight, but the man and woman who'd followed Martin to the men's room were now bearing down on him as he approached his Mercedes.

The man called his name and Martin turned. A short conversation ensued and badges were produced.

Brenda's hand flew to her mouth. The detectives paid little notice.

From where she stood under the awning of the funeral home, Robin could hear nothing. She saw Martin nod in submission. Walking between the two officers, he got into the back seat of another car, an unmarked squad, she figured, where he sat with his head in his hands. The female returned to Brenda, putting a comforting hand on her shoulder.

Grace strode over to where they stood. "Is everything okay?"

Clearly shaken, Brenda didn't answer immediately.

"Please step back," the detective said tiredly, as if she were telling her kids to take their feet off the coffee table.

"It's okay," Brenda, composed once more, said to Grace. "They just want to talk to my husband. Standard procedure, I'm sure."

But Grace saw the lie in her eyes.

"Would you like me to drive you home?" the woman asked.

Brenda stared at the pavement, dazed. "That's okay. I can drive."
The policewoman studied her. "Mrs. Krause, we're impounding
your car."

Brenda's eyes snapped up. She opened her mouth, but no words
emerged.

"I'd be happy to take you home," Grace offered, putting an arm
over Brenda's shoulder. Brenda nodded.

Cate and Robin exchanged a look before Robin slipped back
inside, where she found Foxy and gave her directions to a nearby
coffee shop.

OUTSIDE OF THE QUAINT two-story house turned coffee shop, Robin,
Cate, and Foxy sat at an iron patio table. Despite gloomy skies, the
air was warm. A slight breeze kept it from feeling sultry. Robin pulled
a small notebook from her purse and clicked a pen open. "Go ahead,
Cate."

"Martin Krause, Melissa's boss, was also her lover," Cate began.
She told them how her bracelet had evoked divergent reactions from
Melissa's acknowledged boyfriend Todd and from Martin, her boss
and illicit boyfriend. "And Sheriff Harley was there, taking it all in."

Foxy chimed in to say she'd spotted the two detectives
immediately. So much for undercover.

"They took him in the police car," Robin said, "and Grace drove
his wife home."

"Oh, that Grace!" Foxy shook her head. "How does she do it?"
There was more shaking of heads and restrained laughter.

Cate said, "Okay, the police brought Martin Krause in for
questioning, but I'm not quite ready to discount George." She said
his name as if it tasted bad in her mouth.

"You know, I was watching their body language the whole time,
his and his wife's," Robin said. "He was dancing attendance to her,
I mean, he was downright obsequious."

"Ooh, good word," said Cate.

Robin made a face at her and continued. "She was going through the motions, too, just like he was."

Foxy jumped in. "You think she found out about the affair? Or maybe she's known all along, maybe she doesn't like sex, and—"

"Oh, for God's sake, let's not blame the wife every time a husband strays!" Cate interrupted her. "Some men don't need excuses. They just compartmentalize. They don't even consider that the mistress takes anything away from the wife, so long as the wife doesn't know."

"You have a point," Foxy conceded.

"Besides," Robin said, "from what Grace says, Brenda Krause is devoted to her husband."

"True," Cate mused. "So let's say she suspects or finds out about the mistress. Wouldn't it be logical for her to wonder if he had anything to do with her death? Wouldn't that just piss you off to cover up for your cheating husband?"

Robin stopped writing in her notebook. "But why would she stay with him if she thinks he murdered his mistress?"

"Money, status," said Cate.

"Family," Foxy offered. "Or even religion."

The collective words hung in the air.

"Grace will get the scoop, I'm sure," said Foxy. "I wonder if it's too soon to call her."

Robin looked at her watch, made mental calculations. "If I know Grace, she'll call one of us as soon as she drops Brenda off at home." Picking up her cell phone to make sure it was still on, she mused out loud. "I wonder how far the wife would go to cover for him."

Cate chewed at the corner of her lower lip, shrugged.

Foxy drummed her fingers on the table. "Maybe it's not such a good idea for Gracie to be alone with her."

They fell into worried silence. Suddenly Robin exploded in laughter. "Just listen to us! Talk about melodrama!" She shifted her voice into a lower register, held a spoon up to her mouth and intoned, "And now, the next installment of *The Perils of Pauline*."

After a collective moment of chagrin, Robin continued. "We're letting our imaginations run away with us, just like that Deputy Dipwad said."

And that's how they left it, with a good laugh.

B uckled into the passenger seat of Grace's station wagon, Brenda sat motionless except for her manicured fingers twisting and untwisting the tissue in her lap.

There were so many things Grace wanted to ask, but she restrained herself. If the poor woman chose to suffer in silence, she'd just have to let her. She exited the freeway where Brenda indicated, heading toward the Sculpture Garden. Traffic was heavy.

"This has been a very difficult time for my husband." Brenda turned to stare out the window, her fingers still busy with the tissue. "I know you can understand."

Grace nodded. "I'm sure it has been," she said with empathy. They were climbing the hill into the Kenwood area with its large homes and professional landscaping. "But I've heard nothing that reflects badly on Bradford College."

"Not yet." Brenda sucked in her breath, let it out slowly. "But that didn't stop two alumni who've given generously and one of our largest corporate funds from letting Martin know they'd no longer be giving to the college if it, or its president, had any liability in this." She pointed to the house on the right. "Just pull up to the gate." From her purse, she produced a remote control and the iron gates swung inward.

Grace pulled up and put the car in park.

The house, like many in the neighborhood, was large, formal and spoke of old money. Ivy shrouded much of the stucco and brick exterior. Wrought iron boxes under the mullioned windows overflowed with violet petunias, yellow pansies, and sweet potato vines. Sculpted shrubs and gargantuan flowerpots flanked double front doors.

"Thank you so much for the ride," Brenda said mechanically. She put the tissue to her nose and dabbed, staring straight ahead, mute, making no effort to exit the car.

"Would you like me to come in with you?" Grace offered.

"Oh!" Brenda was visibly jolted out of her reverie. "Would you like to come in?"

They entered through the side door into a narrow hallway lined with coat hooks, oak storage cubicles and a modest built-in desk topped with pigeonholes.

Grace marveled at the orderliness. Her own entryway had a narrow table that was usually covered with receipts for items to be returned, a grocery list, coupons, keys, notes she and Fred left each other, library books either coming or going, and unopened mail that sometimes commingled with letters to go out. No attempt at organization had lasted more than a couple weeks. But here, everywhere she looked, Grace saw proof that order was attainable.

They walked through another narrow room that served as storage for crowd-sized serving dishes. Brenda opened the glass door on her left. "We can sit in the greenhouse. It's my favorite room in the afternoon. Just have a seat. I'll be right back."

This room, long and narrow like the others Grace had seen so far, ran the breadth of the house, and was only about eight feet wide. The floor was paved in burnt-umber terrazzo tiles. She sat in a chair that proved less comfortable than it looked.

Shortly Brenda came in and sat on the chaise. She had reapplied lipstick and had exchanged her pumps for ballet slippers. Her suit jacket was gone. "Where were we?" she asked as though they'd been discussing nothing more serious than wallpaper patterns.

Grace swallowed. "You were telling me how people have threatened to pull their financial support from the college."

Brenda nodded. She straightened the fringe of a throw pillow. "They're all so worried about how it will look if it turns out someone at the school did something improper."

Grace noticed she'd downgraded the concern from one of liability. "What do you mean, improper?"

"Oh, you know how it is. Ever since Watergate, everybody's suspicious of a cover-up, sort of a *what-did-you-know-and-when-did-you-know-it* kind of thing. Do they really think we're supposed to call the press every time someone cheats on an exam or an underage student buys beer or a professor flirts with a coed?"

Grace shook her head.

"Of course not." Brenda snorted. "If you say too much, it's bad P.R. Too little, and it's a cover-up. Martin has behaved as any professional would. He's offered condolences to the family and cooperation to the police. He's been more than civil to them. I say the press be damned." Brenda tucked her feet to one side. Despite the vehemence of her words, she looked small and vulnerable in the oversized chair.

"Are you going to be okay?" Grace asked softly. Her mind was sifting through the possibilities. The fact that the police had taken Martin away from the funeral home to question him a second time certainly suggested a cover-up . . . or something more.

"Martin and I never had children," Brenda said, as if that explained everything.

Grace chose to say nothing.

Outside, in the small back yard, a trio of goldfinches clung to a thistle feeder, their efforts littering the brick patio with black seed hulls.

"We were devoted to each other, the way so many childless couples are." She had a faraway look.

Grace did not miss the fact that she'd said *were*. Past tense.

"We got married just before our senior year of college. He's been my whole life." Brenda's voice cracked. "What do you suppose the police want from him?"

Grace shrugged, helpless. "I'm sure it's just routine."

Brenda looked at her, pointedly.

Grace shifted gears. "I'm not sure what's to be gained worrying about it. I'm sure your husband will be home any time now and will fill you in."

"And what if he doesn't come home? What if—"

"As my son would say, 'Let's not burn that bridge until we come to it.'"

The levity didn't work. Brenda's eyes brimmed with tears.

Grace felt helpless. And stupid. In her attempt to ease Brenda's fears, she had cut her off before she finished her sentence, and now she really did want to know how it ended. What if Martin was now under arrest, or what if Martin ran? Was Brenda worried her husband would abandon his entire life along with his career, or was she worried about divorce? She'd certainly thought about losing him, whatever the cause.

"If you don't mind," Brenda said, rising from the chaise, "I think I need to be alone. I'm pretty lousy company right now." She walked through the doorway, expecting Grace to follow.

MARTIN WAS, IN FACT, being detained. They'd left him to cool his heels in the room where they'd been grilling him for the last two hours. He suspected they were now watching him from the other side of the window as he relived the interview in his mind. Undoubtedly that's why they left him in this particular room, where each floor tile, each scratch in the wooden table had been witness to his ignominy.

Too late, he'd realized that hiding, and then admitting, a relationship with Melissa Dunn had moved him to the top of the suspect list. And, interview aside, they'd impounded his goddamn Mercedes. He could no longer delude himself that their interest in him was casual. His attorney charged exorbitant fees, and so far he'd done little more than tell Martin to say nothing. And then that cretin Maki had asked why he hadn't called one of the college's attorneys.

He paled as he remembered his answer. "I didn't want to involve them," he'd said. "It seemed personal." A major blunder. He'd seen it on their faces.

THEIR FACES, MAKI'S and Harley's, were indeed behind the window.

"He's sweating bullets," Maki said with a chuckle. He squinted as he sipped hot coffee.

Harley leaned forward, the cheap folding chair shifting precariously. "Yeah, I wonder if we'll ever have the technology to know what someone else is thinking."

"I can tell you exactly what he's thinking. He's thinking about strip searches and gang showers and public toilets." Maki chuckled again. "Very public toilets."

Harley studied the face on the other side of the glass. "I wonder. I don't think he's quite gotten there yet."

MARTIN SHUT HIS EYES, cringing inwardly as he pictured the rumor mill at Bradford. "*Oh, she was working under him all right.*" Wink, wink. "*Old goat like that, what did she see in him?*" Money, influence, some would suggest. "*If you're in charge, the rules don't apply.*" This from the staff, who'd sat through hour after tedious hour of mandatory ethics training. They'd be full of scorn, and the Political Science prof he'd sidelined for his dalliance with a student would be properly outraged. Of course the board would demand his resignation.

There was no question he and Brenda would have to relocate. Surely there was a college of good reputation somewhere that would overlook a momentary lapse in judgment. They didn't have much in the way of family here, thank God. Of course Brenda had her charity work and her friends, but she really wasn't one to make waves. A few years back, when he'd been courted by a college in Texas, she'd left the decision up to him, hadn't she? With that way she had of looking up at him as if he actually deserved her adoration, she'd simply answered, "Whither thou goest, my love."

Oh, God. Brenda! Who was he kidding, anyway? This wasn't a simple matter of moving anymore. He couldn't imagine how she'd react. They'd never faced anything like this before. If she didn't leave him on the spot, he'd have to look into her eyes for the rest of his life and see his own betrayal.

For over a year now, he'd enjoyed two wonderful lives, one with Brenda, the other with Melissa. He'd been considerate of their feelings. Although Melissa knew he was married, he didn't burden her with talk of his home life, and he certainly didn't say anything to Brenda. No, he'd done all in his power to keep them separate. The way he saw it, it was like the love of a father for his children. More children, more love to go around. If Brenda had been able to sustain her pregnancies, wouldn't they have loved each child equally? Parents didn't feel compelled to justify loving more than one child, did they?

The familiar words of his interior monologue did nothing to comfort him just now. Martin covered his eyes as if he could press the tears back into the ducts. And then he wept, loudly, in front of God and everybody.

A FEW BLOCKS FROM BRENDA Krause's house, Grace pulled over in the shade of a huge, arching elm, one of the few to survive the Dutch elm disease that had denuded much of Minneapolis. She dialed Robin's cell phone.

Robin answered. Foxy had gone home to a full evening schedule of massage appointments. "Cate and I are still on the patio—never mind, we'll wait inside the coffee shop," Robin said. "It's getting a little chilly."

Grace, who was staring at her sweaty brow in the rear-view mirror, clicked the OFF button and headed east.

Twelve minutes later Cate looked up to see Grace striding in. "Geez, Gracie, how did you get here so fast? If I'm over the speed limit by five miles per hour, I get a ticket."

"I'm invisible, remember?" Grace ordered an iced cappuccino and settled into the cushy chair in the corner. After giving them a blow-by-blow account of her discussion with Brenda, she said in summation, "I just don't see him being a murderer. He's too professional and he's too good to his wife."

Robin's eyebrows twitched.

"Not so good that he didn't have a little something on the side," Cate said.

Grace leaned closer. "Oh?"

Launching into her story again, Cate told about Martin's reaction to the bracelet, how it triggered her memory. "He first said it was a birthday present for his daughter, but when I asked how old she was, he got this funny look and I knew he was hiding something."

"He doesn't have a daughter," Grace said.

Cate leaned forward and said, conspiratorially, "At least not with Brenda."

They all paused to look at each other.

Shaking her head, Robin said, "No, Melissa wasn't his love child. He was definitely dating her."

"Hmm. Dating. Is that what we're calling it these days?" The corners of Cate's mouth turned down in disgust. "He's got a beautiful, intelligent wife who's made him the center of her universe, and he's *dating* a women young enough to be his daughter. Freudian slip, if you ask me, to say the bracelet was for his daughter."

The other two nodded.

"And I suppose he's compartmentalizing the whole affair and truly believes it didn't harm his wife." Cate's tone was again angry as she reiterated her views on cheating husbands. Pushing herself out of the chair, she stalked off in the direction of the restroom.

Robin refilled their coffees. She didn't know how much Grace knew about Cate's marriage. Robin was fond of Erik now, but there was a time she hoped Cate would dump him. It had been several years ago that Erik had risked it all—marriage, career and home—to have an affair with a nurse. Through counseling and crisis-induced maturity, Cate and Erik had managed to hold their marriage together. It had not been an easy choice, but they had persevered and managed what few couples did in the midst of betrayal, to forge a stronger union.

Cate returned with a little less mascara. "So, let's list the suspects. We've got Martin Krause and George Wellman. Who else?"

"The other boyfriend, Todd. Is it possible," Robin asked, "that Todd could have killed her in a jealous rage?"

"He's too sweet," Grace said with a vehement shake of the head. "And introspective. He just strikes me as someone who wouldn't hurt a fly."

"I read something one time by a man who was both a lawyer and a psychiatrist," said Robin. "He'd spent years studying the minds of murderers and came to one conclusion: *the only difference between murderers and the rest of us is that we haven't murdered anybody. Yet.*"

Grace faked a shiver. "Do I need to worry about you two?" She giggled.

"Not me," Cate said. She picked up a straw and, with a maniacal gleam in her eyes, she jabbed it up and down in her best reenactment of the *Psycho* shower scene.

23

ushing water was the only sound above Spirit Falls that morning. That and the slight whiffling coming from Sheriff Harley's throat as he slept, slumped over the steering wheel of the patrol car. Sometime in the early hours when sensible people were deep into the REM cycle of sleep, he'd parked behind a thicket of trees to one side of Ross Johnson's gravel driveway, where he'd locked his doors against any surprise visitors and drifted off to sleep.

The first shards of sunlight sliced through the trees, and with the rising sun, the temperature within the vehicle quickly rose. Harley's left hand twitched on the wheel and one eye slowly opened. Lifting his head, he groaned and winced when a loud snap came from his offended neck vertebrae. Probing with thick fingers, he began massaging out the kinks, wondering how much longer his body could take the punishment of a stakeout. Everything hurt—knees, shoulders, and down his right leg, the searing pain of sciatica. In the rearview mirror, he saw neat lines covering his cheek where it had rested on the seamed leather of the steering wheel.

Squinting toward the sun, Harley guessed it was not quite eight o'clock. A glance at his watch confirmed it. Grabbing the car-radio handset, he called his office.

"Did you get it?" he asked when he heard Brill's voice. After arriving home from Krause's interview last night, he had typed up an affidavit and called Judge Kiernan at home, and the judge had promised to get to the courthouse early and, if everything in the fax was as Harley claimed, to sign the warrant.

"Naturally," his deputy said. "And I've got the evidence kit too."

"Good. And coffee?"

"A whole thermos, freshly brewed. I should be there in a few minutes."

Harley pushed open the car door, and prepared to step out when a cramp seized his right leg and all of his attention. He tried to pull his toes upward, a difficult feat considering that he was wearing steel-toed shoes. Once the cramp subsided, he got out and stretched, sniffed under his arms and ended with a full head scratch that left him with Einstein hair.

A quick inspection of the driveway satisfied him that no one had come during the early morning hours. He yawned and scratched and shook himself to wake up, and decided to walk behind the cabin to relieve himself. Afterwards, he made his way down to the creek. The water was still running high and fast. Kneeling on the bank, Harley held onto a sapling with one hand as he cupped water in his other, splashing it onto his face and neck, enjoying the numbing cold.

Another sound broke through that of rushing water—the shriek of a siren—and Harley knew that his trusty but over-exuberant deputy was on her way. He stood and flicked water off his rumpled uniform shirt, brushed off the knees of his khakis and hurried up the hill past the fire pit and around the woodpile to the driveway.

Brill stood at the open door of her vehicle, hands on hips, shoulders thrust back. In full uniform, complete with hat, sunglasses and jacket, she looked downright formidable even before she unbuttoned her jacket to reveal a holstered six-inch Smith and Wesson.

"Thanks for turning off the siren." His tone was heavy with irony.

She leaned into her vehicle and grabbed a red-plaid thermos, waving it in the air at him.

He found himself smiling at her as she poured coffee into the lid. "Aah, you're the best," he exhaled after taking a sip. The minute he saw Brill's reaction, he regretted his choice of words. If she were a dog, he thought uncharitably, she'd be wagging her tail!

Extracting an envelope from her jacket pocket, she handed it to him. "Hot off the press," she said. "Okay, fill me in."

He could hear the excitement in her voice. He swallowed more coffee and wiped his mouth with the back of his hand, letting her wait. "Good," he said to himself as he ripped open the envelope and scanned the search warrant.

"So what happened?"

He folded the paper and tucked it into his pants pocket, enjoying the way she stood at attention.

"Well?"

"Okay, Maki got enough out of Krause to confirm that his girlfriend, Melissa Dunn, was here at Johnson's place before she disappeared. The jerk started out with some cock-and-bull story about bringing her here to raise money for the college." He snorted. "Yeah, right! Like we haven't had our suspicions about Johnson's little den of iniquity."

"Yeah, right." Brill agreed. Her laugh was high and nasal.

Harley thought, not for the first time, that his personal torture chamber would have his deputy's laughter piped in twenty-four/seven. Nevertheless, he was glad Brill was here so they could proceed with their search. Looking now at her youthful enthusiasm, he remembered to thank her for her early morning courier service.

Instead of acknowledging his thanks, his deputy said, "You look like you slept in those clothes." And then she snickered.

Eight in the blasted morning, and she's already getting under my hide, Harley thought. "Cute. Grab the kit."

"So what are we looking for?" Brill walked around the squad car to retrieve a large metal evidence case from the trunk.

"Specifically, the murder weapon, which could be any damn thing, and evidence of foul play—blood, other bodily fluids, signs of a struggle, that kind of thing."

"How about prints?"

"We'll see."

"Drugs?"

"If we see 'em, we seize 'em."

They climbed the four stairs to the front entrance. Pounding on the heavy wooden door, Harley called out, "This is the sheriff." He tried the handle and found it locked. Anything else would have surprised him, since his was the only car there.

Brill removed her hat to scratch the back of her head. Today her wiry hair was tamed into a low ponytail. "What do we do now, break a window or try to break the door down?" she asked with a bit too much eagerness.

His eyes narrowed at her. "Christ almighty! What do you *think* we're going to do?"

She didn't have to answer. A voice behind them said, "Mr. Johnson sure wouldn't like it if you did that."

George Wellman stood below them in the shadow of the tuck-under garage.

Sheriff Harley hadn't expected George to seek him out, but there he was, acting like he owned the place. "You don't happen to have a key, do you George?"

"I might have."

Brill put a hand on her holster. "Well, we've got a search warrant."

"A search warrant?" George paused indecisively. Looking at Harley, he asked, "I don't want to be in trouble with Johnson."

Harley shook his head tiredly. "We've got the warrant and we're going in there one way or the other. It's all on the up and up. Besides, this way you won't have to explain to Johnson why he's got a busted door when you could've let us in."

George's shoulders slumped in resignation. He mounted the steps as if they led to the gallows, and, pulling a circle of keys from his pants pocket, he selected one, inserted it in the lock and clicked it to the right. "You sure I won't get in any trouble?"

"You'll never go wrong cooperating with the authorities." Harley pushed the door open. He and Brill entered.

"Wait," George said as Brill prepared to shut the door behind her.

"You can't come in," said the sheriff.

"But," George wheedled, "I watch out for the place, y'know?"

Harley said, "Go home. You're not in trouble." From inside the cabin, he watched George slouch down the driveway, then shut and locked the door.

Stepping into the posh great room, Deputy Brill let out a whistle. "Holy Moley. This is some little cabin."

Although Harley had been here before, he was still impressed at the expensive furnishings. "And this is his second residence," he said.

"So where do we start?" Brill gave her latex glove a snap that reminded Harley he needed to call to set up his next physical.

"We'll do this together. We'll go through the rooms counter-clockwise." *Don't they learn anything about procedure anymore*, Harley wondered? He rubbed his index finger across his brow as he took in the scene. "He's had it cleaned."

They began their systematic search, unaware that George had turned back to watch them, as best he could, from the shadow of the trees. The pair worked their way around the living room, opening closets, going through drawers, and taking swabs. Each time they found something of interest, they slipped it into a paper evidence bag, identifying the contents on the outside with permanent marker and affixing an official seal to it.

An hour after they'd arrived, the pair had finished with the great room and decided to split up to cover the remaining rooms. As Harley combed the bedspread in the guest bedroom, he heard Brill let out a whoop from somewhere in the back of the cabin.

Harley met her in the hallway outside of the master bedroom. Brill beamed and held a pastel lavender disk out for him to see. "This was wedged behind the nightstand drawer, like it had slipped back there."

Carefully, Harley opened the plastic case.

"Birth control pills," Brill announced. "Only five missing."

He flipped the case over. The prescription label clearly said they belonged to one Melissa Dunn. "Fund-raising, my ass!" Harley snorted.

After bagging the pill case, they returned to their separate searches. When he'd come up with nothing unusual in the meticulously clean powder room, the sheriff proceeded to the storage closet off the kitchen. Reaching into the dark space, he felt around for a light pull and let loose a cascade of fishing gear. An oar fell heavily onto his outstretched arm and he yelped in pain. That brought Deputy Brill on the run.

"Cripes, it sounded like someone was attacking you out here." Brill reholstered her gun. Her boss was grimacing and rubbing his arm. "Let me see that," she said, grabbing for his sleeve.

He jerked away from her. "Don't go all Mother Hen on me."

Red splotches bloomed on her cheeks. "Fine," she said and left him standing there feeling like a jerk.

THE DAY AFTER MELISSA'S WAKE, Grace called Brenda from work and learned that Martin had been released after all, and was, at that moment, attending Melissa Dunn's funeral. Grace was initially surprised that Brenda was not at her husband's side, but she knew the whole mess had to be taking a toll on their marriage.

"How are you doing with all the stress?" Grace asked.

"I'm fine," Brenda answered, her voice tight and controlled. "They kept the Mercedes, though, and it's a real pain having just one car. Martin had to take mine to work, and as soon as he left, I just went completely stir-crazy." Her laugh was brittle.

Grace could understand that. When her boys had started driving, there were times she'd been without a car, and it always prompted her imagination to fixate on everything she could not do without transportation. "Would you like me to give you a ride someplace?"

"You're so kind, really, but actually I thought I might borrow my neighbor's car if I really need to. You're both so gracious to offer."

"Let me know if you feel like talking," Grace said. "Call any time. Really." She hung up and chewed on a pencil while she thought about Brenda's predicament. Maybe her husband wasn't a rat in general, but if Cate was right, he'd certainly exhibited ratlike behavior with Melissa Dunn. Obviously, he was guilty of cheating on his wife. Maybe he was even guilty of sexual harassment, but murder?

What would it do to her, she wondered, if she ever discovered Fred having not just an affair, but one that ended in his mistress's death and the whole sordid mess being discussed on the evening news. It was unthinkable.

She closed her office door and dialed Robin's number. "Did I call at a bad time?" she asked when Robin answered on the first ring.

"I can talk for a few minutes, but I'm waiting for the doctor's office to call back. I've decided to have the surgery," Robin informed her. "Probably in late July or early August."

Shifting mental gears, Grace responded, "You mean on your other breast?"

A single, resolute word. "Yes."

Grace gulped and hastened to say, "Good. You know, I think I'd do the same thing." She felt queasy, but the more Robin explained her decision, the more sense it made. After eliciting the pertinent details, she turned to the reason for her call, a brief retelling of her concern for Brenda. "You know, Brenda never talks about doing things with friends. She's so tightly wrapped, always worrying about how anything she says could reflect badly on her husband, and I just don't think she has any place she can just let her guard down."

Robin thought she knew what was coming.

"Hey, how about inviting her to join No Ordinary Women?" Grace suggested, as if she'd just thought of it. "Call it a mission of mercy."

Robin hesitated before answering. "Hmm. Maybe you'd better run it by the others."

"That's not a ringing endorsement."

Robin hated to step on all that good will. "Don't you think it might be a little awkward? 'Welcome to our little book club, Brenda. I want you to meet my friends Robin and Cate and Foxy. They're the ones who found the body of your husband's mistress.'"

"Well, we wouldn't have to tell her."

"And be sure to save the date. We go to Spirit Falls every spring," Robin continued.

With a groan, Grace acquiesced. "I see your point."

WHILE DEPUTY BRILL SEARCHED the gazebo, Harley checked out the garage, then poked around the ashes of the fire pit in the back. He'd always believed that the best fires started with a thin base of ash from previous fires, and for the life of him, he couldn't figure out why anyone would vacuum their fireplace. Unless . . . He slid his sunglasses down on his nose, pushed his fingers through his sweat-drenched hair and scanned the concrete blocks along the back wall. Directly below the chimney was the telltale metal door, about the size of a breadbox, as his mother would say.

"I'll be in the house," he called in the direction of the gazebo. Pulling a fresh pair of latex gloves from his pocket, he entered through the back door. He looked again at the elaborate shelving and entertainment center that took up the entire back wall of the walkout basement, seeing again the deep shelves and cabinets on either side of a shallow tier of shelves that held video tapes and CDs. They were flush in the front, meaning there was dead space of at least eighteen inches between that shelf and the outside wall. He sprinted up the stairs.

During his earlier inspection, he'd glanced in the fireplace to see if Johnson had built it with an ash dump. Looking in the front for a cast iron door, the usual access, he had found none. Now he grasped the heavy log holder in his gloved hands and set it on the hearth. There in the center of the fireplace floor was, instead of a cast iron door, a removable concrete brick. He used the poker to lift the brick by its embedded steel loop.

"Damn it all!" he swore when it slipped back into the hole. Again, he pried it loose, setting it on the hearth. He shone a flashlight into the opening, his lips stretching into a smug grin.

Back in the squad car, he grabbed a garbage bag, a collapsible shovel and a 3M mask and hobbled down the hill to the exterior ash pit door. It was a dirty job, but he was rewarded after only two shovels full were dumped onto the plastic bag. He slipped on a fresh glove to pick up the half-burnt driver's license buried in soot. The photo was gone, most of the information obliterated, but what Harley could make out as he blew ash off the plastic made his heart beat with excitement. The birth month was August, and the first four letters of the name, *MELI*, were there, along with a partial address. It was enough to know the driver's license had belonged Melissa Dunn.

"Gotcha!" Harley said. Ross Johnson had just earned himself a place on the Persons of Interest list.

24

Robin was having second thoughts, not about her upcoming surgery to remove a healthy breast, but about how to heal the wound it was causing in her marriage. Now that her mind was made up, she and Brad did not discuss it, and that felt as wrong to her as it had when they were arguing openly about it. When Brad had called earlier in the day to say he was making his hospital rounds later than usual, she interpreted it as avoidance.

She stomped down to the laundry room and threw a load in the washer, feeling herself becoming agitated along with the clothes. She checked her watch, and, trudging up to the bedroom, she flung herself onto the chaise and wrapped herself in an afghan to get maximum comfort for the phone call.

"That's a tough one," Cate said when Robin had laid out her worries. "You have to be proactive and do what you think is right about your own health."

"Right," Robin agreed, vindicated.

"And if you have a marriage worth saving," Cate paused, but Robin didn't fill the silence, "then how *he* feels *does* matter."

"You're a big help." Robin jammed her fingers, one at a time, through the lacy holes of the afghan.

"Yeah, I got my counseling license in a Cracker Jack box."

Robin laughed. "Oh, that's what they mean when they say 'with nuts.'"

They giggled about that, then Cate said, "But seriously, you know I don't say it lightly. It's way too easy for a marriage to come apart, and too damn hard to put it back together."

"Yeah."

"I know I say Erik and I are stronger than ever," Cate went on, "and we are, but it left scars. I tell myself I trust him completely, but I have my moments. I mean, if someone as truly good as Erik could deceive me week after week, never once tripping my alarm . . ."

"He wasn't in his right mind. He'd never do that now."

There was a long pause, during which Robin pictured how Erik's attention to detail had enabled him to keep his affair secret until he chose to reveal it. His precise nature was absolutely indispensable in his work as an anesthesiologist, but at home, it sometimes drove the more spontaneous Cate wild. No, Robin considered, people don't really change much—Erik could still be an anal-retentive pain in the butt, and Cate still surrounded herself with creative clutter.

"No, I certainly hope he wouldn't. I'm counting on that." Another pause. "But when Grace was talking about her new friend's situation . . . I mean, Brenda said her cheating husband was her whole stupid, pathetic life, for God's sake!"

Harsh, Robin thought. But in truth, hadn't they all been offended by the betrayal? And didn't they all, on hearing such stories, hold a little tighter to what they had? "You're right, Cate, it could happen in any relationship. And despite vows, no guarantees. But, don't you think, with all you and Erik went through—"

"Oh, I'm not really worried," Cate said, and abruptly changed the subject. During the months Cate and Erik were separated, they'd sought out counseling. One of the more helpful tidbits, as Cate reported, was a way to abort the worry process. "Once you've chewed on something, either swallow it or spit it out." Obviously Cate was spitting it out.

ONLY A FEW MILES AWAY, Ross Johnson, having left the office early to avoid rush hour traffic, was taking the scenic route home, along Minnehaha Creek, one of the more picturesque areas of the Twin Cities. He looped around the north side of Lake Nokomis, slowing to watch a young man throwing a Frisbee to a black lab. In the early years, he and Sandy had come here often and played catch with their own dog, a German short-hair named Klaus. Sandy had been striking back then, with her long legs and tumble of red curls.

He exhaled loudly, trying to clear the memory. It was all part of a life that was no longer his.

Arriving at his two-story, he parked his truck in the three-car tuck-under garage. Overhead, a Boeing 757 roared at full throttle as it gained altitude, a sound he'd long ago tuned out.

After scuffing off his shoes in the mudroom, he headed for the refrigerator to fill a generous highball glass with Jim Beam, enjoying the crackling of fissures in the ice cubes, the clinking of ice against glass as he lifted the drink to his lips. He took one sip at the kitchen counter, another on the way to the loft overlooking his living room. Flipping on the television with the remote, he buzzed through a few channels, threw down the rest of the drink. A convulsive cough made his eyes water. He pulled out his handkerchief, wincing as he dabbed tentatively at the tip of his nose.

His eyes scanned the room, coming to rest again on the television broadcasting some imbecilic talk show. He hit the remote again until he found the five o'clock news, with a perky, dimple-chinned reporter telling about the safe return of a dog. "Sappy" was the word that came to Ross's mind, but he didn't change the channel. Suddenly, over the reporter's shoulder, a photo appeared, the same photo of the dark-haired beauty they showed practically every night now, and the reporter was saying, "Now a new development in the Melissa Dunn case . . ."

His lip curled in contempt. "Christ! Is that all you morons can talk about?"

". . . brought in for questioning for the second time." The picture changed to old footage of Martin Krause being interviewed in front of the sign at Bradford College. "Authorities are calling President Krause a 'person of interest' and say he is cooperating . . ."

Ross pressed himself into the soft pillows of the sofa as a wave of vertigo overtook him. He squeezed his eyes shut, and when he opened them again, a commercial was addressing the seemingly cataclysmic problem of erectile dysfunction.

"Nice transition," he said to the television. He snickered as he thought how Martin's sorry plight was made sorrier by the pharmaceutical sponsor. "Poor old Martin." At first, when Martin had been questioned, he'd felt sorry for him, but the more he thought of it, the more his pity was tinged with disgust.

He tipped his glass back and crunched the remaining ice cube. Martin, he'd long ago realized, was typical of the kind of influential but spineless sort that was always drawn to Ross Johnson's strength. In his pathetic attempt to emulate his old friend, Martin Krause had waded in the pool of risk, but knowing he didn't have the constitution to swim with the real risk takers, he'd blubbered for help as soon as things got a little rough.

Without knowing he was doing it, Ross's hand had slipped into his shirt pocket to grasp the vial inside. He clutched it in his palm, letting it seduce him. Happy dust. In his mind, he lined up the fluffy white contents, stuck the straw in his nostril. His nose throbbed in painful response to the thought.

Holding the vial up to the light, he was surprised at how little was left. He considered the dilemma for only a moment before going to the master bathroom, where he groped under the sink for the white paper bag he'd stashed there only yesterday. His heart raced. Not that he would make it a habit, he told himself. Injecting cocaine was, after all, for hardcore addicts. He ripped open the bag, then carefully, he added water to the vial, drew the mixture into the syringe.

Seated on the closed toilet, he wrapped the plastic tie around his arm at the elbow, made a fist and plunged the needle into the prominent blue vein.

The euphoria hit almost immediately, and it was intense. He moaned with pleasure. The syringe fell to the floor with a double *plink* as plastic bounced on tile.

The first sign of trouble was an involuntary head jerk, a violent clenching of the jaws. The second followed almost immediately, a sharp blow, like a fist striking him in the chest, knocking him back. When his legs jerked out from under him, Ross slumped back and to the left until he was firmly wedged between toilet and wall, his mouth wide as he gasped for breath, his hands twitching helplessly at his throat.

As SOON AS HE AND BRILL left the cabin, Sheriff Harley called the detective in Minnesota. Maki was out, but returned the call within minutes. Harley, who was, at that moment, pulling over a speeder with a broken taillight, said he'd call him from the office.

Back at the office, Brill, bless her soul, had begun the tedious task of making an official report of their morning adventure. Harley whistled to himself as he settled into his chair.

"Isn't that the theme song from *Leave It to Beaver?*" Brill appeared at his side, looking down at him with amusement.

"No," he said gruffly. It was actually from the *Andy Griffith Show*. "I need to make a phone call. Did you need something?"

She shook her head and backed away.

Filling him in briefly on the results of the search, he told Maki, "I told the handyman not to go calling Johnson about the search, but there's no way to stop him."

"We're going to want to talk to Johnson," said Maki. Harley could hear papers being shuffled on the other end. Maki read out loud the Minneapolis address of their latest Person of Interest.

"Maybe we'll get an unmarked out there. We've got one on Krause. We don't want anyone rabbiting on us."

THAT EVENING AFTER A LITTLE meditation in a bubble bath, Robin decided to tackle her worries. She began after Brad had looked at the day's mail and headed upstairs.

"Come sit with me for a minute," she suggested.

With a wary look, he sat next to her on the edge of their king-sized bed.

"Cate and I talked about marriage," she began, trying to ignore how he closed his eyes in resignation, sucked in a breath for the ordeal.

"I'll make this part brief."

"Does that mean I'm going to get it in installments?" He grinned lopsidedly.

"Brad." She took his hand. "I love you. We have a good thing."

"I agree. I love you too." He started to stand up, but she held his hand.

"Cate was talking about the bad times—hers and Erik's—and I just want to say that we can't let it happen to us. We just can't."

"I'm not going anywhere." He looked into her eyes and kissed her with more feeling than he'd shown of late. "I'm not interested in anyone but you." He slid off the bed and went to the sink to wash his face.

Still sitting on the bed, Robin watched her husband as he went through his after work ritual of pulling off his tie and hanging it over the bedside chair, then stripping off his shirt and tossing in onto the bed next to her. She traced the raised pattern of the bedspread with her finger as she took measured breaths.

Most women would describe Brad as handsome. He still had a full head of hair, mostly brown with a few silver strands. His once too-narrow face had fleshed out in recent years. His facial wrinkles, mostly smile lines, only gave him character. She could see why he had more than his share of patients who developed crushes on him.

She took a breath and launched into her next subject. "Brad, I've made a decision."

No response.

"I'm going to have the surgery. It may not make sense to you, but I need to follow my gut on this. Brad? Did you hear me?"

Obviously, as far as he was concerned, their conversation was over.

"So that's the way it's going to be?" She felt tears well up. "You're giving me the silent treatment?"

"You've made it clear it's your decision." He spoke so softly she had to strain to hear him. "I don't see much point in saying something, just so I can be ignored." Stepping into their walk-in closet, he selected a smoky-blue polo shirt, the same color as his eyes. He stood, shirt in hand, seemingly lost in thought.

Robin thought he might say something more, but judging by the thin line of his mouth, she knew she waited in vain. Defensive and frustrated, she saw him with a critical eye. Over the years, Brad often told people that he'd maintained his med school weight. Now Robin noted that some of it had shifted from chest to belly.

She checked out her own reflection in the full-length mirror mounted on the closet door, knowing that her own downward slide had been in progress already when it had been surgically and hormonally accelerated. Having attained her new ideal weight over the course of chemotherapy, she was now annoyed to discover she was regaining the pounds, mostly around her middle—due, in part, to the anti-cancer drugs she would be taking for five years.

What was maddeningly obvious to Robin was that Brad, standing in his boxers, was completely comfortable in his own, well-maintained, middle-aged skin. Aging men simply didn't lose their appeal the way women did, she thought with mounting resentment. She felt the heat in her chest and face simultaneously, felt the sweat pop out on her upper lip, and wished that just once Brad and his ilk could experience a hot flash. She grabbed his cast-off shirt and jammed it into the hamper.

"Tell me," she said, hating the aggressive edge to her words, and knowing she was straying from the topic. "How would you feel if you'd had, say, a radical prostatectomy? Do you think you'd be so comfortable undressing in front of me right now? Do you suppose your self-image would change if you had no testicles, and then, to add insult to injury, you had to take estrogen to keep the cancer away?" She knew she was being confrontational, a stance that never ended well for either of them, but she just couldn't stop herself. Or wouldn't.

He swallowed noticeably and answered without meeting her gaze. "I guess I'd just deal with it."

Her physical self stood completely still while her mental self stuffed him in the hamper and jammed the lid tight over him. Maybe a few turns in the washing machine would get his attention. And then she'd hang him out to dry by his . . . She pulled herself together and said, "That's what I'm doing, Brad. I'm dealing with it. In my own way."

"As you say, in your own way." He shrugged the shirt over his head and left the room.

After staring numbly at the spot where he'd been standing, she desperately wanted to talk to someone without a Y chromosome. She dialed Cate's number, but after getting the answering machine, she tried her cell phone number.

Robin could hear Cate swearing as she fumbled the phone. It clattered and then Cate answered. "Robin, I can't talk right now. I'm on my way to the emergency vet."

Robin wondered which of Cate's many pets or rescued strays was sick this time.

"It's Prickly. I think he's having some type of seizure."

Robin wished her luck and hung up, pondering the disturbing idea of an epileptic hedgehog.

25

He felt the vibration in his bones before he saw the car ahead of him on Interstate 94. Four boys, laughing and gyrating to rap music, waved at him as he passed them in the sheriff's car. He crossed the bridge spanning the St. Croix River that connected Wisconsin to Minnesota.

Harley's mind returned to churn over the evidence they'd found at the Johnson cabin, together with what Maki had told him when they'd talked late last night. Maki thought that with the evidence, his department would be able to execute a search warrant on Johnson's Minneapolis residence today. With any luck, that would end in an arrest. In addition, Martin Krause was supposed to come in for further questioning.

A smile creeping onto his face, Harley knew these two men would have a lot of explaining to do. He looked forward to Krause's next harebrained story to explain the new evidence.

Only minutes across the Minnesota border, traffic slowed to a crawl. Making his way through Saint Paul's rush hour traffic, Harley tapped his fingers on the steering wheel, grateful as ever for his small town life. By the time he merged onto 35E, traffic had eased, but at Highway 36, it was gridlock again.

In Roseville, Harley parked at the far end of the lot adjacent to the police department. Getting out, he clicked the remote's lock button, waiting to hear the lock engage. When he dropped his ring of keys into his pocket, the added weight caused his pants to slip, so he pulled his belt one notch tighter. *I'm becoming damned near svelte,* he thought.

Stepping into the building, he nodded to the receptionist, who gave him a dazzling smile, "Good morning, Sheriff Harley."

Feeling his ears redden, Harley croaked out "Morning."

"Go on back, Sheriff. Detective Maki's expecting you."

"Thanks." Harley grinned self-consciously. He resisted the urge to smooth his hair. As he passed by her desk, Harley caught a whiff of her perfume. Shalimar, he knew that scent, and every time it took him back to the summer when he was twenty-two. That was the year he had met Libby, who was home from a school in New York. He was caught up with her talk of theaters and museums. In the end, their relationship had been just a fling for her, but not for him. *Beautiful and classy,* he thought, pulling his eyes away from the blonde. *Way out of your league, Harley.*

Detective Maki looked up from the stack of papers in front of him. "Come on in, Sheriff. Glad you could make it." Maki stood and they shook hands over his desk. Harley eyed the plain wooden chair, remembering that it wasn't exactly ergonomically designed for his butt. He sat anyway.

"Coffee?" Detective Maki had already turned to fetch a second cup from the Mr. Coffee machine on his credenza. "I decided it was easier to buy my own coffee maker."

"Huh?"

"Sensitivity training."

Harley continued to give him a blank look.

"You know, no asking secretaries to fetch coffee . . ."

"Oh, yeah," Harley said, catching on. "My deputy and secretary did their own sensitivity training. Brill's pretty direct that way."

"The whole idea of having us go through sensitivity training was a good idea, up to a point, but whatever asshole came up with the idea of circulating a list of all the offensive terms we shouldn't use to refer to women . . . Well, let's just say it backfired on them when the men got hold of it. We can't call 'em 'bimbos' anymore, but it doesn't say anything about 'bims.' That kind of thing. And worse."

"I can imagine."

After topping off his own cup, Maki sat back at his desk and absent-mindedly cracked his neck. "After I got your call last night, I sent an unmarked to cover Johnson's house. We're not going to let that SOB skip out on us." Looking at the wall clock, Maki said, "Krause and his attorney should be here any minute."

Maki's phone rang. Grabbing the handset, he listened for a moment. "Thanks, Ginny." He hung up and gathered the papers in front of him, straightening them with a rap on the desk. "Well, our first pigeon has arrived."

Martin Krause appeared to have shrunk in stature. Seated next to him was a haughty middle-aged man in an expensive suit. His hair was poufy and salon-streaked. He gave a nod to Maki and Harley as they entered the room. Harley recognized him as one of Minnesota's most prominent criminal attorneys. *Bringing out the big guns*, he thought. *That'll cost him, unless of course, the college picks up the tab.*

Harley settled across from the attorney.

"My client wants to cooperate in any way possible to clear up this issue." The attorney exuded confidence.

"That would be refreshing." Maki took the seat next to Harley. Though he stared at Martin, his words were to the attorney. "Your client has been less than forthcoming."

"He's here, isn't he?" the lawyer shot back.

For the next forty-five minutes, Maki made Martin go through the fateful weekend once more, this time, with no hedging or prevarication about the nature of his relationship with Melissa Dunn.

Martin, seeing no new traps, began to relax.

Letting out a loud sigh, the lawyer scowled. "I don't see the point of all this. If you have nothing new—"

"Just trying to make sure we have Mr. Krause's story straight, Counselor." Maki turned and gave Martin a sinister smile. "Mr. Krause, I'm sorry, it's *Doctor*, isn't it? Now, Dr. Krause, has your Mercedes ever been involved in an accident?"

Martin's forehead furrowed. "Accident?"

"I don't see the relevance." The lawyer sounded bored.

"Oh, it's connected." Maki draped one arm over the back of his chair. "For instance, there's the new upholstery and fresh paint job." Maki smiled as he asked, "Would you like to explain this, President Krause?"

"My car is almost a classic." Martin said primly. "With classics, you have to be concerned with esthetic maintenance as well as mechanical."

"Cut the bullshit, Krause," Maki barked. "We already know that your car went off a dirt road in Wisconsin and plowed into a tree."

The lawyer quickly seized Martin's arm to stop him from making any response. He needn't have bothered. Martin was stunned into silence. "May I have a moment to confer with my client?"

Harley pursed his lips, the corners of his mouth upturned. It was obvious that this little tidbit had been news to Martin's lawyer.

"Sure. We'll be back in a few minutes." Maki and Harley got up. The detective made an obvious show of flipping the camera switch as he exited the room.

Upon their return, the lawyer leaned forward. "My client would like to explain about his car."

"Explain away." Maki stretched his legs under the table as Sheriff Harley leaned forward intently.

"Okay, it was in an accident, but I wasn't driving." He spoke passionately, looking directly into their eyes. "I wasn't even there."

Maki grunted. "Let's go back to that Friday evening. You and Melissa Dunn were at the cabin of Ross Johnson, and at some point she got upset. What happened next?"

When Martin spoke, his eyes were downcast as if reciting to a headmaster. "It's like I told you before, I didn't know until later that she'd left the cabin. When I did realize she was gone, I went looking for her, but then the rain got so bad, I went back to the cabin. Somebody else had left and I figured she'd gone with them. But then those people came back and said they'd seen a car in the ditch. That's when I discovered my car keys were missing." He tilted his head back and took in a deep breath.

"Go on." Maki's angular features had softened.

"Ross was already gone in his car. I went on foot and when I got to the road, I saw him on the other side of the road, motioning to me. That's when I saw it. My car had jumped the ditch and hit a tree."

"And Melissa?"

He looked at Maki, tears in his eyes. "She wasn't there," he said, with wonderment in his voice.

"So you weren't with Mr. Johnson when he discovered your car?"

Martin shook his head. "Ross left the cabin before me."

"And when you saw your car, were you concerned about Ms. Dunn's welfare?"

"Of course! But she wasn't there. What could we do?"

When neither Harley nor Maki made any comment, Martin felt compelled to continue. "We thought maybe she'd gotten a ride from someone after all."

Maki's fingers metrically tapped on the table as he stared into Martin's eyes. "Someone from Johnson's party?"

"How should I know?" Martin snapped. "Maybe it was a stranger that came along."

Harley was pleased to see Krause's mask of propriety slipping a bit.

"Was there much damage to the car?" Detective Maki continued to probe.

"Some." Martin shrugged. "It was pretty minor, actually."

"Where did you get it repaired?"

"I don't know," Martin muttered helplessly.

"You don't know?"

"Ross took care of it. He even loaned me a car to drive back to Minneapolis."

Detective Maki blinked in disbelief. "You're telling us you let your friend take your classic Mercedes to be fixed and you didn't ask where?"

Krause attempted a smile. "Surely you can see my predicament."

Just then the door to the interview room opened, causing all four men to fall silent. A uniformed police officer summoned Detective Maki into the hallway.

Within minutes, Maki reopened the door. "Sheriff, could I speak to you for a minute?"

Stepping out of the room, Harley pulled the door shut behind him. "What's up?" He could already tell from the grim expressions that it was bad news.

"Johnson's dead," Maki let out a heavy sigh.

Harley flung his head back. "Aw, damn it all to hell!"

"Drug overdose." Maki ran his fingers through his hair in frustration. "Our men found him next to the crapper with the empty syringe next to him on the floor."

"We've got no time to waste, then," Harley said, jerking his thumb toward the interview room.

Maki slugged a fist into the palm of his left hand. "Okay, here's the way we're gonna play it." He outlined his plan.

Martin and his lawyer looked up expectantly when the two men reentered the interview room.

"Sorry about the interruption." Maki rubbed the back of his neck nonchalantly.

"We're back at the same question, Dr. Krause. Why did you not report this accident and come forward when Melissa Dunn was reported missing?"

"I don't know. I screwed up. I'm a married man, for God's sake." Martin's voice rose with each sentence. "What would you have done?

Maki stared at him for a full twenty seconds before saying, "Explain to us how Ms. Dunn's driver's license ended up in Johnson's fireplace."

"Her license?" Martin's eyes widened. "I . . . I don't know." Covering his face with his hands, Martin remained like this for what seemed like several minutes, then suddenly sitting upright, he looked at them with red eyes. "As God is my witness, I'm telling you the truth. I did not see Melissa after she left the cabin."

"Gentlemen, I think this interview has ended." The attorney slid a hand under his client's elbow and guided him to stand.

Midway to the door, the two men were stopped by Maki's voice. "By the way, President Krause, your friend Johnson is dead." His brutal delivery had the desired effect.

Martin's face froze. "Ross is dead?" His hair was disheveled and his shirt limp from sweat as his attorney tried to physically steer the man through the doorway.

Watching Martin Krause leave the room, Sheriff Harley couldn't tell if Martin's last expression had been one of shock or relief.

CATE HEAVED THE LAST CASE of canned dog food onto the stack and stood back to check the height of their makeshift platform in the east corner of the shelter's storage room. The sunlight flowing in from the west windows had been a consideration in choosing the platform's location, but the deciding factor was that this was the only area not crammed with bags of dog food, cat food, carriers and unassembled kennels. "How's that?"

Robin looked up from her task of affixing her camera onto the tripod. "Perfect."

Crawling onto the platform, Cate stood to straighten the pale blue sheets they had hung for backdrops. "I really appreciate you doing this. So does everyone at the shelter."

"Glad to do it."

"Just from putting photos on our website," Cate said as she billowed a royal blue cloth to cover the platform, "our adoption rate has already improved by a third."

Robin checked her light meter. "It's hard to turn away when you look into their eyes."

Cate put on her most innocent expression. "I knew Grover would get to you! I knew it!"

"*Hard*, I said, not impossible."

"I have to figure out a way to get him a permanent home soon. I promised Erik this was a very short-term situation."

Robin tilted her head toward the door.

"Okay, I'll get the dogs."

After two hours and countless shots of the shelter's newest residents, Robin and Cate relaxed with Diet Pepsis and cheese sandwiches they had put together in the shelter's lunchroom.

"Have you noticed anything different about Grace?" Robin asked before taking a bite.

"She's looking great."

"She does, but does it seem to you she's pulling away from us?"

Cate nodded slowly.

"I know we encouraged her getting reacquainted with Brenda Krause, but lately it seems like it's all Brenda, all the time."

"She's probably offended that we didn't want Brenda to join the No Ordinary Women," Cate said.

"That could be." She picked at the bread crust. "It's probably just Grace being Grace, wanting to fix everyone's problems."

Cate reached into the bakery box, snagged a brownie and munched in silence.

Robin said, "You never told me how Prickly is. Was it epilepsy?"

Cate gave an embarrassed laugh. "It wasn't a convulsion at all. All the foaming at the mouth and jerking legs is just part of what the vet called self-anointing. Prickly was just spreading his spit on his back."

Robin grimaced. "Why?"

"They don't know, but it seems to be a reaction to certain smells."

"How bizarre!"

"Hedgehogs really shouldn't be pets. Of course Prickly was born in captivity so there's no way he could ever be released into the wild now."

"Yeah, I'd hate to think of him falling in with a pack of wild hedgehogs!"

As they packed up to leave, Robin said, "You'll never guess who has experience in wildlife rehabilitation." When Cate shook her head, she announced, with a note of triumph in her voice, "George Wellman."

"George? No way."

Robin nodded. "He raised two orphaned raccoons one summer. When they were big enough, he even bought a kiddie swimming pool and stocked it with minnows so they could learn how to fish."

Cate sat silent, wondering what to make of this new information.

26

With Ross Johnson silenced in the most permanent sense and Martin Krause casting suspicion on his dead friend, the ultimate responsibility for Melissa Dunn's death would most likely be determined by a jury. That didn't keep the Minneapolis newspaper and television stations from conjecturing about the college president's involvement in his mistress's death, and what role the dead millionaire contractor played. It had all the elements of a good news story: sex and betrayal, money and influence. Whether the details of the case had been leaked to the media or merely deduced from the Roseville police captain's terse statements, the talking heads were talking.

A criminal psychologist made an appearance on the evening news extra to do a *post mortem* (not to mention *in absentia*) psychological autopsy on the local contractor. Ross Johnson, who acted alone, suffered from antisocial personality disorder exacerbated by illicit drug use, he concluded. The next night this diagnosis was countered by a criminologist who specialized in body language. She claimed that the college president was hiding something.

The No Ordinary Women, for their part, discussed little else at their next book club meeting, giving short shrift to their July selection, *Their Eyes Were Watching God*, by Zora Neale Hurston. They'd gathered in Foxy's apartment just off Summit Avenue, Saint Paul's architectural showplace of mansions, historic homes, college campuses and churches. In one of the less impressive brick buildings on Summit, F. Scott Fitzgerald had penned *This Side of Paradise*. Cate and Erik's comfortable old Tudor home was not far from there. To the west was the governor's mansion, and to the east, at the crest of the hill and marking the highest point in downtown Saint Paul, stood the magnificent Cathedral of Saint Paul with its copper dome.

While Summit Avenue was still a prestigious address, many old mansions in the surrounding neighborhood had been subdivided into affordable apartments and condos. Foxy's building, once a spacious Victorian home occupied by a childless couple, had been renovated as five apartments that shared a front porch. Foxy's portion was the better part of the second floor. The rent was at her upper limit, but here she was allowed her beloved animal companions: Elvis, aka "the King," a sleek black cat she'd rescued from a dismal alley life in Las Vegas just before rescuing herself from an equally dismal life, plus Jasmine, a haughty Siamese, and Molly Pat.

As honorary book club member and self-appointed greeter, Molly Pat stood at the door to greet each new human with a single yip. When all four guests had arrived, the dog sauntered over to sprawl on her red plaid pillow by the kitchen. From this comfortable vantage point, she could eyeball the women as they lined up to fill their plates at the taco bar Foxy had set up in her small but efficient kitchen. Elvis slunk around, waiting for an opportunity. As soon as Foxy turned her back on him, he leapt gracefully onto the counter for his own chance at the spiced beef.

"Keep doing that and you'll turn into Fat Elvis," Foxy said as she nudged him to the floor. He let out an outraged howl.

The five women ate around a table overlooking the old-fashioned garden in the backyard, making a few stabs at discussing their chosen book, which they all agreed was compelling. Just not more compelling, at the moment, than a real life mystery involving a body that had washed up, quite literally, in Robin's backyard.

Foxy grabbed a magazine off the table and fanned herself with it, then took the rubber band from her wrist and pulled her thick hair into a high ponytail. "It's pretty hot in here. Should I turn on the air?"

"I'm fine," Grace and Louise said together.

Robin, knowing she couldn't count on the accuracy of her internal thermostat, shrugged.

Louise eyed Foxy's shorts and tank top, which definitely won the Least Fabric Contest, and said, "Don't tell me you're having hot flashes."

"I do not have hot flashes." Foxy's exaggerated glare let them know she was only half kidding. It had long been her belief that anyone who kept in good physical shape wouldn't succumb to such things.

None of them dared to crack a smile.

When they'd finished dinner and cleaned up the dishes, they took their decaffeinated coffee and orange flan down to the screened porch, where they settled into a jumble of chairs. Foxy lit candles on a makeshift table before sitting in a rocker. The evening air was heavy with humidity, but a slight breeze wafted through the porch.

From somewhere nearby, they could hear the unmistakable voice of Janis Joplin. Conversations drifted from other porches, open windows and from the sidewalk where people were out for an evening walk. In the only state farther north, the sun would still be shining at midnight. In Minnesota, it wouldn't set until almost ten o'clock, and people who'd been cooped up over the winter were reveling in the extended daylight.

"If Ross Johnson was such a monster, why would Krause hang out with him all those years?" Robin, the only one who'd actually known Ross, expressed her doubt that he could be the sociopath that his old friend Krause was now making him out to be.

"Exactly! And if President Krause is such an upstanding and moral man," Cate asked, "what's he doing with a mistress?"

Louise, spoon poised in front of her lips, pronounced the flan "divine."

Around the room, heads bobbed in agreement.

Foxy's rocking chair creaked with her every movement. "So how should we look at it? Is having a girlfriend on the side just a momentary lapse in judgment?"

"Or a pattern of sleaze!" Louise countered.

"Okay, I admit he's been pretty sleazy, but I still don't think that makes Martin Krause a killer," Grace insisted. Whether it was the fact that she'd met the man years earlier and in his official capacity presiding over the college, or the fact that she and Brenda Krause had become friends, Grace was the only one who believed that Ross had acted alone. "What kind of weasel would blame something like that on his dead friend if it weren't true?"

Foxy rocked forward. "A scared weasel."

Grace said, "Too bad Ross Johnson isn't around to defend himself."

Cate agreed. "It does seem a bit too convenient."

"The whole thing is unthinkable," Louise pronounced.

"Even good people do unthinkable things," Robin said, adding, "if they're scared enough."

They thought about that for a while.

Cate broke the silence, putting to words what, as it turned out, they were all feeling. "I'm a little ashamed to say it, but I'm kind of sorry it's out of our hands now."

Robin agreed. "I know! We had our very own whodunit, starring our five evanescent selves as amateur sleuths, and now it's just turning into a boring old police investigation, to be followed by a tedious courtroom drama."

Heads nodded in agreement.

"We may have found the body," Foxy said dismally, "but after that, what have we really done?"

"Well, I don't know about the rest of you, but I went Dumpster diving!" Grace said.

"You! Who wound up covered in garbage?" Robin wailed, and they all laughed.

Foxy poured a second round of coffee.

"So you think that it has to be either Johnson or Krause or both?" Foxy asked. "Do you think the police have ruled out the possibility of other suspects?"

Grace pointed out that Todd was now completely exonerated. "I liked him," she said. "I hope he can have a normal life again." She collected the plates and spoons and stacked them on the tray.

"I suppose George is off the hook, too." Robin glanced in Cate's direction.

Cate looked dubious. "I don't know about him, but what about that gorgeous creature with the ponytail?"

Louise snapped her fingers. "Oh, right. The one you two saw in the liquor store."

Wiggling her eyebrows, Cate did a Groucho Marx gesture with an imaginary cigar. "I wouldn't mind tailing *him*, if you know what I mean."

Robin just shook her head.

While the others laughed, Cate's mind began sifting through the events of that weekend at the cabin. Naturally it was heavy with significance since that was the weekend Melissa Dunn had died. But she'd been apprehensive even before Melissa Dunn's death. She felt a chill now, recalling her premonition that weekend. She wondered, not for the first time, if she could somehow have prevented it. That was the trouble with her premonitions. They came and went of their own volition. There was no rewind button, no slow motion, no volume control, no zoom focus.

And what to make of her chronic discomfort with George? *Odd little man.* She couldn't think of him without those words following automatically. And yet neither Grover nor Molly Pat had reacted fearfully around him. In her world, that meant something too.

Maybe Robin was right. Odd, even creepy, but not evil. Cate fondled her amulet. Maybe if she went back to Spirit Falls and stood at the bridge, she'd get another psychic clue. With a start, she realized that her thoughts seemed to have merged with the current discussion.

"So I went back to the bridge to get a few shots of the wildflowers. They're pretty spectacular right now." Robin was talking about her most recent trip to Spirit Falls. "And when I got back to the cabin, there was Sheriff Harley at my door. He makes regular stops at the cabin now to check on me. He came in while I got a drink of water, and that's when he got the call on his radio."

Cate hadn't heard this part. She turned her focus to Robin's words.

"It was his deputy calling, and he was having trouble hearing her. So he stepped outside for better reception, and I'm thinking, Damn, now what? But then I found if I stood just inside the door, I could ear hustle pretty well."

"Ear hustle?" Louise asked.

"Sorry. That's what Cass used to call eavesdropping when she was little, and I just adopted it. Anyway, Harley had to talk louder and kept repeating things, so I got the gist of it."

"We're all ears," Foxy said.

A sudden gust caused the candles to gutter.

"From what I gathered," Robin said, "they've determined that Martin's car has recently been repaired, repainted and all the upholstery replaced, so they're pretty sure it was in some kind of accident. And because of the paint on the tree, well, on the log now, they can surmise that the accident occurred at that place."

"And since you reported hearing a crash that night, they can pinpoint the time," Louise said.

Robin sighed, "It's only speculation, and it doesn't mean much unless they can prove Melissa died in his car. The sheriff was saying that the car must have been worked on by professional criminals, or was it criminal professionals? Anyway, I heard him say he'd run out of ideas since they'd checked all the body shops in southwestern Wisconsin looking for a car repair job that matched Martin's car. He also said Minnesota had come up with 'a big zero.'"

Grace hitched up an errant bra strap. "It sounds like they've got a pretty flimsy case for murder."

Cate turned to Robin. "Well, they know Melissa was in the area, I mean, they have your photo to prove it, and you noted the date in your photo log, right?"

Robin nodded.

"You know, what you said, that we haven't done anything? Well, it just isn't true!" Louise's voice rose in indignation. "Just listen to what all y'all are saying."

Robin thought Louise must be plenty agitated. She'd heard her use the occasional y'all, but all y'all, well, that was deep old South.

"Y'all found the body," Louise continued. "Robin, you heard the crash, then we found the tree with paint on it. You took a picture, for God's sake, placing the victim right above where she was found, and because y'all recognized Cate's bracelet in that guy's trailer, and then you went with to console Melissa's mother and Cate remembered the creep buying the bracelet—" She gasped for breath.

"Chicago!" Robin said, clapping her hands together.

They looked blank.

"Chicago," she said again. "What better place to find criminal professionals to strip your car of the evidence?" And then she told them about Lee Ann's account of having to deal with Ross Johnson on the Chicago leg of her flight.

"When was it?" Foxy asked.

"If I remember correctly, it would have been a week or so after our weekend at Spirit Falls."

As she laid out the idea, Grace began to nod.

Foxy leaned forward, suddenly excited. "I think you've got it right. I'll bet anything he was picking up the car for Krause."

Cate screwed up her mouth. "Yeah, he really could have."

"So it was Johnson all along." Grace's expression was smug.

"Maybe," Robin said grudgingly, "but why would he be picking up Krause's car without his knowledge, not to mention his consent?"

"I don't know, but you've gotta call the authorities," Louise said, and Grace agreed.

Cate nodded, a smile starting to grow.

But Foxy's excitement faded. "Are you sure? It's just an idea. It's not like we have proof or anything."

Cate grabbed Robin's arm. "Do you know the sheriff's number?"

Robin shook her head. "Wait, I have it on my cell phone." She sprinted upstairs to get it out of her purse.

THE QUESTION OF MAKING a charge against Krause was being debated by Maki's team and in the offices of the district attorney. They all knew the realities. Smelling a rat was not the same as successfully prosecuting one.

Some of their best stuff might not hold up well in court. First of all, there was the testimony of Candi Damiano. They hadn't been able to corroborate, well, any of it. Johnson himself was certainly in no position to talk. Then there was the supposed friend she claimed had brought her to Johnson's place and had arranged for her to be his "date" for the weekend, a man with the improbable name of José Churchill. Gone. His belongings were still in the apartment, but the absence of money and any form of identification indicated he had disappeared on purpose. Miss Damiano had also named a certain ballplayer who'd attended the weekend party or orgy or whatever. On questioning, he had denied being there, and his wife sewed up his alibi by saying he'd been by her side the entire weekend.

"Fine!" Maki spat the word out. "I want someone on Krause around the clock. That scrote's still lying to us."

Between appointments, Grace called Brenda. "I just wanted to check up on you, see how the two of you are doing," she said.

Brenda laughed brightly. "We're doing fine. In fact, it's been wonderful." She lowered her voice to a near whisper. "He hardly leaves my side. Last night he kept his arms around me as though he was afraid he'd wake up and I'd be gone." She giggled.

This was a side of Brenda that Grace had never seen. "Wow! Maybe now you can get back to rebuilding your lives."

"I'm beginning to believe for the first time that we have a chance—" Brenda's voice caught. ". . . now that Ross Johnson is out of our lives."

Grace wasn't sure why, but she felt obliged to add, "May he rest in peace."

Brenda sighed heavily. "And leave us in peace."

She listened as Brenda, her speech rapid with excitement, talked about the future, using phrases like *put everything behind us* and *a fresh start* and *water under the bridge*. Grace winced at that last one.

"It's hard to believe I have my old Martin back."

Grace found herself wondering if she could be as gracious as Brenda Krause if Fred ever cheated on her. It took a special person to be able to see all the good things in someone when he'd done such a glaringly bad thing. Grace tried to consider it from Brenda's point of view. Maybe she figured he'd been punished enough. And maybe he had. Being handcuffed and brought in for questioning had to have been excruciating, not to mention what all that negative press had done to his career.

Brenda addressed none of this. She was clearly basking in Martin's renewed attention. "It really couldn't have been resolved any better, could it? Oh, that's my other line. Do you mind?"

Grace didn't know if she was supposed to hang up. She was faintly disturbed to hear Ross Johnson's ugly death referred to as a resolution. She checked her watch. Her next client would be in shortly.

Brenda came back on the line. "That was my neighbor, Phyllis. She wants to go out to lunch tomorrow. We're going to eat at the Mall of America and do a little shopping. Want to make it a threesome?"

Grace flipped a page in her appointment book. "I have two clients in the morning, but I could get away by, say, 11:30." She erased her tentative notation: *Lunch @ Galleria w/ Louise?* She would have to call Louise and say that she'd goofed and scheduled clients for the afternoon.

Brenda said, "Great! Phyllis said she'd drive. We can just swing by your office. I think you're going to like her. Besides, Phyllis has an impeccable sense of fashion, and she can smell a bargain a mile away."

THE NEXT MORNING, Grace took extra care choosing her clothing. She wasn't sure what someone with impeccable taste would think of her standard wardrobe. She stepped on the scale and grinned. Thirteen pounds, so far. She decided it was time to try on the black slacks and sapphire top that hadn't fit her in two years. The pants zipped and buttoned with ease. The buttoned top no longer strained across her breasts.

"Diet and exercise. Who knew?" she commented to her reflection. She'd have to thank Brenda. If it hadn't been for her encouragement, she surely would have expended much of her energy, albeit subconsciously, coming up with diversions to avoid the gym.

Grace sat through an interminable session in her Bloomington office with a husband and wife who needed marriage counseling more than financial advice. The wife wanted to set up a trust fund for her children from a first marriage. The husband said her son was a deadbeat. The wife reminded him that neither of his daughters would have anything to do with him. They glowered at each other just long enough to reload. He continued with a terse complaint about the negligible financial contribution she made, and she returned fire, accusing him of taking his higher earning capacity as a male entitlement.

Grace sighed and clicked her fingernails on the arm of her chair, knowing that nothing she said would elicit agreement. "I think we should table this until you've had a chance to discuss a few things in private." She dug in her file drawer and handed them a question-naire. "Use this as a discussion guide, and try to find some common ground."

The husband grunted.

Grace opened her Franklin Planner. "How about two weeks from today?"

From her second floor window, she watched the couple leave, squealing out of the parking lot and almost hitting an entering car, which turned out to be a nondescript black Chevy driven by Brenda's neighbor, Phyllis Carson. Grace hurried outside and slipped into the backseat.

As Brenda predicted, Grace liked Phyllis. She wore her ivory pantsuit loose and her black hair in a swingy bob. She had an easy laugh, even before their second glass of wine at the Napa Valley Grill. When they toasted their new friendship, Grace felt a momentary pang of guilt for lying to Louise. She glanced around, imagining Louise walking up right now. She could only hope Phyllis and Brenda wouldn't blow her cover when she introduced them as "clients."

After lunch, as Phyllis steered them from store to store, Grace seriously regretted her choice of shoes, a pair of low-heeled sandals that looked and felt far better before her feet had puffed like rising dough between the straps. She tried not to hobble as she toted bags from Nordstrom's Rack and Macy's, tried to smile when Brenda suggested getting facials at the spa on the other side of the gargantuan mall.

When they got to the spa, Grace opted for a pedicure. She placed her feet in the whirlpool of hot water, opened a *People* magazine and leaned back in the vibrating chair. Minutes later, she woke from her impromptu nap, wondering if she'd snored, as Fred claimed she'd been doing for the past couple of years. She put fingertips to the corners of her mouth. Thank God she hadn't drooled.

When at last she met up with Brenda and Phyllis, she sported newly painted toenails. "Mata Hari Red," she said. She looked pointedly at her watch.

"Yeah, let's call it a day," Phyllis said, and they gathered up their purchases. Suddenly Phyllis stopped and faced the other two. "Does anyone remember where I parked the car?"

"East side, just to the right of center and three rows back," Brenda said with assurance.

"Okay, but what floor?"

Grace and Brenda looked at each other and shrugged.

"Wait," Grace said, "Didn't we come in on the same floor as Marshall's?"

They found an escalator and went up to the third floor.

Grace, visibly limping now, said, "I can't believe my feet are hurting again. I broke down a couple years ago and admitted I needed to buy a half size larger. But still my shoes don't seem to fit."

Phyllis nodded agreement. "I know what you mean."

More slowly now, they walked through the doors and into the corridor leading to the ramp.

"Ugh!" Brenda said, waving a hand in the air. "Keeping the mall smoke-free just sends all the smokers out here." Her hands went to her neck and she stopped walking. "My silk scarf!"

"Oh, no," Grace commiserated. "And I was thinking earlier how beautiful it was."

Brenda made a face. "I'm sorry, ladies, but I have to go back and look for it. Martin bought it for me in Florence."

Grace looked toward the parking ramp and groaned. "Do you mind—?"

"You two just wait in the car," Brenda said and took off.

Grace eased herself into the front seat and kicked off her sandals. "My husband thinks I should get orthopedic shoes." She made it sound like a profanity. "Granny shoes! I'd rather go barefoot. I'm not vain, but I have my limits."

"I understand." Phyllis smiled. "I sure hope Brenda finds her scarf. She was so lighthearted today. I'd hate for our day to end on a note of disappointment."

Grace shook her head. "I don't know how she keeps her spirits up with all she's been through. I think I'd wind up in a rubber room."

Phyllis expelled a mouthful of air. "I know what you mean. I feel so bad for her."

"It's not fair," Grace said. "She's just one of those people you'd expect to have it all."

"And she did," Phyllis agreed. "When I first met her, I thought they were a little too perfect, you know, the beautiful people—never a hair out of place, and they were always so lovey-dovey together. She looked at him the way Nancy Reagan looked at Ronnie."

Grace could picture it. "I never knew her before the—" She groped for the word. "I never saw them together."

"Well, I guess I'll reserve judgment on *him*, but Brenda really is the perfect neighbor. So thoughtful, too, like this spring when we had that awful storm. Gil and I were down in St. Louis for my nephew's graduation when it happened, and we came back and, well, she'd just cleaned everything up, raked up the branches and debris; she even gathered up all our lawn furniture that had blown all over creation."

"I can believe it."

"And you know Brenda, how she just thinks of every little thing," Phyllis continued. "She said she'd had to borrow my car for some errands while we were gone—I guess hers wouldn't start one day—and she brought it back with a full tank of gas. She'd even had it freshly wa—Ooh, she found it."

Grace saw Brenda coming toward them, waving her scarf triumphantly.

Phyllis tugged at her shoulder harness. It stuck and she tugged again.

"Wait, it's twisted." Grace leaned over, and from her angle, pulled the harness free. "What's this?" She pointed to the dark stain on the inside of the belt.

Phyllis looked. "Soy sauce?" she guessed. "I have no idea."

Brenda threw open the back door and flapped her scarf at them. "Ta-da! It was under the table at the restaurant."

Robin checked all the zippered pockets in her purse before setting it on the foyer table. *Damn and damn again!* She'd already checked pockets, looked under her dresser with a flashlight and crawled under the bed, but her wedding ring was nowhere to be found.

She sat on a hassock and tried to picture where she'd left it this time. She'd been wearing it infrequently, and this was the consequence. Damn it all! She ran her fingers through her hair.

She called Cate.

"I wish you and Brad would get back on track," Cate said. "This is the third time you've mislaid your wedding ring. I think you have to start wondering why."

Robin felt like hanging up. She wanted to remind Cate of all the times Cate had gone looking for her glasses. "Sometimes a cigar is just a cigar," she retorted.

"What?"

"It's what Freud said when, oh, never mind. I keep losing it because my hands are too puffy half the time to wear it."

"I can resize it for you," Cate offered.

"Then half the time it would be too loose and fall off." Robin cradled the phone on her shoulder and twisted her fingers together in her lap. "Dang it all, Cate, I can't remember. I think I had it at the cabin last time, but I just don't trust my memory."

"Maybe it's part of George's collection by now." *Odd little man,* Cate added to herself.

Robin pressed her lips together and shook her head. "Well, I guess I'm headed back to Spirit Falls, but not for a few days. Brad actually said he'd go to church with me Sunday. Can you believe it?"

"Why did he stop going, anyway?"

"He never said, but I think he doesn't like me in the choir because he has to sit by himself, but I've been in some choir or another most of my life."

"Well, I'm glad he's going. So when are you going back to Wisconsin?"

"Tuesday, maybe Wednesday."

There was a long pause. "Grover says he's too confined in our house. Can we come too?"

"Of course."

"Want me to drive?"

"I'd enjoy your company, but I do not need a chaperone."

"Face it, Robin, the police can't say for sure who murdered Melissa Dunn. It's just too easy to say it's the dead guy, but I still think it could be—"

"I know, I know. Poor old George."

Cate sounded miffed. "That's not what I was going to say."

Still on the portable phone, Robin went downstairs to check the workbench in her darkroom. "Sorry I'm puffing," she said to Cate. "I'm just coming up the basement stairs. My ring's not down there either."

"Could the cats have played hockey with it?"

"I checked everywhere I can think of." *Hopeless*, she thought, *absolutely hopeless.* "I can't blame it on chemo-brain anymore, Cate. I know we joke about Alzheimer's, but what if it really is?"

"Then I guess we'll be roomies again. At the home."

28

The next Wednesday, Grace took advantage of a morning cancellation and headed to the club for a lengthy workout. Brenda was already there, doing laps on the track. Grace, still nursing blisters, skipped her warm-up and went directly to the Nautilus machines.

She was grimacing, trying to bring her elbows together on the butterfly machine when Brenda popped up at her side. "Want to grab lunch?"

Grace thought she seemed downright carefree compared to the past weeks. "Sounds good."

"I'm ready for the shower."

Grace nodded and finished her repetitions. "I'm right behind you."

Twenty minutes later, standing next to Brenda in front of the long mirror, Grace squinted, looking back and forth between her own image and that of her friend. "Sometimes I think you're lying to me," she said, her brows pulled together.

Brenda's eyes opened wide.

"About your age, I mean. Look how old and tired I look next to you."

Brenda let out a sigh. Reaching into her Laura Ashley bag, she proffered a small container. "Here, try this undereye gel."

Grace unscrewed it and dabbed some on.

"Now the concealer." She handed a tube to her.

With her fingertip, Grace tapped some onto the bluish crescents under her eyes.

Brenda tilted her head. "Nope, wrong color."

Grace pursed her lips. "It's more than that. You hardly have a wrinkle on your face."

"Oh, trust me, I have wrinkles. But if I refrain from frowning or letting my eyes crinkle when I smile, they're less noticeable. That, and I've found a wonderful cosmetician at the Southdale Dayton's, I mean Marshall Field's, Macy's, whatever they're calling it these days—it will always be Dayton's to me. Tell you what. Let's grab a health drink upstairs and then make a little pilgrimage to Dayton's."

Grace ordered something with pineapple and blueberries. Brenda's drink had peaches, ginseng, and aloe vera in it.

They drove separately to Southdale and met on the second floor of the department store, where they sat on metal stools while Gina, a porcelain-faced youngster in a smock designed to give her the illusion of being a physician, applied various products to Grace's face. Grace, who usually bought her cosmetics at a drugstore, was astonished by the variety of specialized potions, and taken aback by the prices.

Brenda watched with a critical eye. "Doesn't she do wonders?" she asked.

Grace agreed with an enthusiasm she didn't feel. In fact, she was feeling defensive. Had she truly looked dowdy enough to require a complete overhaul?

Perhaps Brenda picked up on her sensitivity, because she abruptly changed the subject. "Do you know of a sewing shop around here?" she asked. She watched Gina apply a liquid eyeliner to Grace's upper lids. "I bought a wonderful sweater in Norway almost ten years ago, and I need to replace a button."

Gina didn't know of any sewing shops.

Grace thought for a moment. "There's a . . . oh, what's the name of that store? It's in the little shopping mall two blocks, no three . . . Oh heck, you turn on . . ." She gestured, unable to come up with the street name. "Oh, great! Now I've lost my nouns!" she said with disgust. "Verbs and adjectives can't be far behind."

"Hold still," Gina said. "I can't put shadow on a moving lid."

"I'll just take you there," Grace said, waiting until Gina was done before turning to Brenda in mock confusion. ". . . whatever your name is." She stuck out her hand to Brenda. "Hi, I don't believe we've met."

Brenda laughed then, showing all of her beautiful wrinkles.

AT THE FABRIC STORE, Grace wandered to the knitting section in back, where she grabbed up an armful of nubbly wool skeins on sale. She had agreed to teach Robin to knit. That had been a couple weeks ago, and she still hadn't called her to set up a knitting lesson.

Brenda showed her sweater to the clerk at the cutting counter, who, after a brief examination, said, "We don't carry anything like this. Have you tried a knit shop or a Scandinavian import shop?"

Grace came up behind her. "Hmm, that's going to be hard to match." She went to the counter with her purchases and paid for them with plastic.

Brenda followed her. "What are you knitting?"

"Prayer shawls for the nursing home," she said, picking up the bag. "The idea is to say prayers for someone as you knit, prayers of health and inner peace, that kind of thing, and all that good intention is supposed to become part of the shawl and give comfort to the recipient."

They headed for the exit.

"What a beautiful idea," Brenda said. "Do you think you could teach me how to knit?"

Grace hooked her arm through Brenda's elbow as they walked to the parking lot. "I'd love to teach you." She thought again of her promise to Robin. Once again, she realized with a sense of unease, she'd set aside plans with one of her old friends from the book club to pursue this new friendship with Brenda.

They both got into Grace's car to drive the five blocks back to Southdale. "Let me look at that again." Grace reached for the bag with Brenda's sweater. "Hmm, I've seen these somewhere," she said, frowning at the silver buttons in the bright sunlight. She put the car in drive and swung out into traffic. "Trouble is, there are three different yarn shops I go to, and I can't remember where I've seen buttons like this." When she pulled up beside Brenda's car, she glanced at the dashboard clock. "I'd better get back to the office. My God, I can't believe the time!"

"I'd better get home, too. I'm planning a special dinner for Martin." Brenda opened the door and began to step out.

Grace said, "Say, if I remember where I saw those buttons, I'll call you."

Standing between the two cars, Brenda used her key's remote control to unlock the door.

"Wait! It wasn't a knitting shop at all!" Grace called out suddenly. "I remember now. It was in Wisconsin."

"Wisconsin?"

Grace's head bobbed excitedly. "On the road right near my friend's cabin. Our book club goes to Spirit Falls every spring. It's a little slice of heaven. Her cabin sits right above a waterfall, I mean *right* above it." Her excitement began to fizzle as she saw the look of what she interpreted as perplexity on Brenda's face. "Sorry for the digression. I found a button on the road and remember sticking it in a sweater pocket. It's probably still there. Maybe I can call Robin and ask her to check next time she goes there."

Brenda's face had become rigid. Only her eyes moved, blinking rapidly as if she were holding back tears.

Don't let your eyes crinkle, Grace wanted to tell her. *Your wrinkles will show.* She mentally kicked herself. Hadn't Robin cautioned her about the awkwardness of mentioning Spirit Falls to Brenda? *Way to go, Gracie,* she remonstrated. *Bring up the painful memory of her husband's mistress. Gracie, you are one sorry excuse for a friend.*

From behind the wheel, she watched helplessly as Brenda turned her back without a word, leaving no doubt in Grace's mind that she'd done something unforgivable.

Grace's eyes widened suddenly, an idea forming in her mind. "Oh!" she said aloud.

Brenda spun to face her. "What?"

But Grace, whose hand now covered her mouth, sat mute, her mind and her heart racing.

"What?" Brenda's eyes were slits.

Grace found her voice. "I just remembered, I, uh," she stammered. "I have to be someplace. With trembling hands, she put the car in gear and left Brenda standing there.

She began racing toward Robin's house, then remembered that Robin had gone to Spirit Falls to look for her wedding ring. She turned toward Interstate 94. Nearing the downtown exits of Saint Paul, she groped in her purse for the cell phone. Her hands wrapped around it. She glanced at it, but in her agitation, could make no sense of the buttons. She pulled off at the next exit to give her full attention to the task.

Squinting at the numbered buttons, she found herself staring at what she now recognized to be the television remote control. "What the hell?" she yelled.

WHAT IDIOCY, CATE WONDERED, had led her to wear a white sundress to walk Grover around the perimeter of Robin's property? At least she'd thought to exchange her sandals for a pair of sneakers. Of course, it had been unplanned. When they were almost to the cabin, she'd had a sudden impulse to go back to the bridge, and suggested that Robin leave her at the end of the driveway to "let the dog stretch his legs" while Robin went into town for groceries.

"If he stretches his legs any more, he'll be a giraffe," Robin had retorted.

Grover galloped ahead of her now, tugging her, not toward the bridge, but to the stump of the tree they had discovered in May, the one with car paint on it. The dog's legs seemed to collapse as he sat suddenly. His whine was eerily familiar.

Cate's fingers began to tingle with a jolt of adrenaline. Crouching, she closed her eyes, and within seconds, an image came to her. It was not, as she'd so often tried to explain, a pure visual image, nor was it, technically, auditory. Appearing suddenly before disappearing was the mental impression of Melissa Dunn's upturned face, mouthing the words Catherine understood, even though she couldn't actually hear them. *Help me*, she pleaded. *Help me.*

Grover whined again.

Cate opened her eyes, and stood slowly to avoid a head rush. She placed a clammy hand on her forehead and listened for Robin's car, but of course, it would be way too early.

"Let's get out of here," she said, tugging on Grover's leash. He didn't need coaxing.

In five minutes, they were standing on the bridge. Once more, she closed her eyes, but no image came to her this time. Instead, she felt a sensation she remembered all too well from childhood—that of going down a roller coaster. She gripped the railing until her fingers ached and the queasiness subsided.

"Are you okay, Miss Wolf?"

Cate gasped and spun around. Grover strained at his leash, almost toppling her as he lunged at George Wellman.

George appeared not to mind the huge dog licking his arms and hands with his huge tongue. "How you doin', boy? Yeah, I love you too." He crouched to pat the big white head. Looking up at Cate, he said, "Sorry, I didn't mean to scare you."

"You scared me half to death." Standing strong, her feet planted wide as she'd learned in a self-defense class, she let anger replace her fear. "You've got no business sneaking up on people."

He looked as contrite as a man whose face is being covered with doggy kisses can look. "I'm really sorry. I just saw you standing there, and—"

"What are you doing here?" she demanded.

He adjusted the glasses Grover had dislodged. "I live here." His eyes cut back toward his trailer, visible in the not-too-distant clearing.

Cate blinked, took a deep breath. She was fascinated, as before, with Grover's unabashed affection for the odd little man. Maybe Grover and Robin were right. He did seem harmless. She nodded, resigned.

"Miss Wolf?" He stood his distance.

"I'm okay now."

He dipped his head, and said, almost timidly, "I was just going to check on the foxes down by the creek."

Cate had thought she heard foxes the last time she was here. "So they've got a den by the creek?" She found herself smiling.

"Yup. Would you like to go with me?"

Tempting as it was, it seemed reckless. Then she saw Grover's tail wagging like a giant metronome. "I'm not really dressed for it."

George grinned, looking like a little boy. "See, every day this week I've been watching the same fox hunting for mice in my compost pile, and I started following her a little more each day. I can be real quiet in the woods, you know."

"Uh-huh."

"Well, yesterday I found her den. She's got two little babies in there."

Cate's face lit up. "Kits?"

"Yup."

To hell with the sundress, Cate decided. Then she remembered Grover. "I can't take him. He'd scare the poor little foxes."

Caught up in his enthusiasm, Cate found herself agreeing to leave the dog in George's trailer.

She and George crossed the bridge and cut through the woods, following the ridge high above the creek. Cate was sure she heard

Grover, protesting his incarceration. With the stifling heat, George had propped the inner door open so Grover had fresh air, at least. But she wasn't altogether sure the screen door would hold him.

Grateful for the soft pine-needle cover, Cate carefully picked her way along the narrow path, avoiding any sounds that would spell alarm to the foxes' discerning ears. She recognized the limestone outcropping ahead as the place where Melissa Dunn had lain, unaware that Robin had captured her on film. Strands of anxiety wove themselves into her thoughts.

George pressed a finger to his lips and gestured to an even narrower trail that led down a slight embankment. He walked with an easy gait, turning occasionally to smile benignly.

Her breathing had become fast and shallow as two ideas fought for dominance.

They stopped upstream of the waterfall and across the creek from Robin's cabin. George seemed to be appraising her. His tongue flicked out to wet his lips.

Cate wondered if Robin had returned yet, but the falls, still running at high volume, smothered all other sounds.

They stood side by side. She caught a sharp smell of sweat, whether it was hers or George's, she wasn't sure. She found herself holding her breath as she scanned the path ahead, trying to judge how much farther ahead they would have to walk to be seen from the cabin.

George smiled. He pointed down below them and slightly downstream from where they stood. "Look," he whispered.

Bracing herself against a tree trunk, she leaned forward to follow his finger. She felt his breath on her neck, the warmth of his hand as it rested on her shoulder.

"No sudden moves, now, " he whispered very close to her ear.

29

By the time Robin nudged her tires against the railroad tie delineating the parking area from the cabin's front yard, the temperature and humidity had risen way past the comfort point. Flinging open her car door, she took a breath of heavy air and called out for Cate, even though she was certain Grover would have galumphed out to meet her if Cate had already returned with him from their romp in the woods. She opened the trunk. Trudging inside with a pair of grocery bags, she set them on the butcher's block table centered on the rectangle of kitchen linoleum. Something clinked on the floor, and she watched the shiny object roll several feet and come to rest in front of the cupboard that held the large serving bowls. With delight, she stooped down and retrieved her wedding ring, putting it on quickly before it could get mislaid again. She looked at it on her finger and realized how much this symbol still meant to her.

Pulling a head of lettuce and a plastic carton of grape tomatoes from the grocery bag, she put them in the refrigerator.

She mopped her wet forehead with the hem of her tee shirt. "I'm sick of hot flashes!" she yelled to no one. Having shoved the glass jar of orange juice and the carton of milk into the fridge, she continued to hang onto the open door, sticking her head as far into the chilled interior as she could, pulling it out only when she thought she heard sounds in the hallway.

"Cate?" she called out again. There was no response.

She shook her head to clear it. "I'm losing it," she said aloud, and unloaded the rest of one bag and folded it. She lined up the paper products on the table—towels, napkins, plates: all had to be stowed in the large metal-lined cupboard to discourage mice from turning them into nesting material. Brad had cautioned her to store matches there as well, lest some misguided rodent strike sparks while munching on them. For all she knew, with this blasted heat, they (the matches, not the mice, she mentally edited) might just spontaneously combust.

As she folded the second bag, the phone rang. Frowning, she tucked the bag under her arm and snatched the receiver from where it hung on the wall next to the refrigerator.

Grace's breathless voice announced, without preamble, "Robin, I'm on my way. I think I figured it out, but first I had to go home and get my damn cell phone. I thought . . ." The phone crackled and several words got lost before anything intelligible came through. ". . . remote control. Anyway, I should be there in half an hour."

Remote control? "What's going on?"

"I found a button—"

"A button?" Robin asked incredulously. "Gracie, are you okay?"

"Yes . . . No! . . . presumed innocent . . ."

"What are you talking about?" She waited for a reply. "Gracie?"

"The book, *Presu*— . . . Remember? It was the . . ." The rest of Grace's answer was incomprehensible.

"What? You're cutting out on me."

". . . when we were . . . pocket of . . ." [another long, crackly passage] ". . . shopping with Brenda . . ."

"Brenda!" *Books, buttons and Brenda: what the hell was Grace babbling about? Not comprehensible, but alliterative, at least.*

More static, followed by, "Hang up . . . get there."

Robin set the phone back and shook her head again. How weird! And then, a more disturbing thought: What if Grace was having a stroke or something!

There was a flutter of motion in her peripheral vision. She swung her head, startled to see the slight figure of a woman at her door. *Exiting* through her door. "Hey!" she yelled.

The instant the woman turned her head Robin recognized her. "Brenda?" *What had Grace been trying to tell her about Brenda?* "What are you—?"

Brenda Krause, momentarily flustered, composed herself. She stepped back inside and eased the screen door shut. "I'm very sorry. I'm afraid I got turned around. I thought this was the Johnson cabin. Ross Johnson's," she explained, since Robin appeared clueless. "I'm Brenda, Dr. Krause's wife. We met at the, uh . . ." Her voice faded.

Robin took the proffered hand. "Yes, I remember." Neither wanted to mention where they'd met. At the funeral of Martin's mistress.

They stood awkwardly until Brenda dropped her hand.

"The Johnson place is across the road, but it's off limits— festooned in police tape, in fact. You did hear—" Robin studied the other woman's face and found it closed to inspection.

Brenda dropped her gaze and nodded. "Yes, he was found dead in his home." She tilted her head, a helpless gesture. "I'm trying to come to terms with—with what the police are saying. I—this probably makes no sense to you, but I don't think I can deal with it until I see the place for myself." She had edged closer. She now stood in the doorway to the kitchen, arms akimbo.

To Robin, it seemed an aggressive stance. She felt suddenly vulnerable. Her eyes shifted to the wall phone.

"Do you suppose I could trouble you for a glass of water before I get on my way?" Brenda had insinuated herself in front of the refrigerator, effectively putting herself between Robin and the phone. "No ice, please."

Cate, come back! Robin sent the telepathic message as she got a glass from the cupboard, filled it from a bottle on the counter. For years, she and Cate had tried various experiments with E.S.P., but it didn't seem to work on demand. Though they could often finish each other's sentences and even read each other's thoughts, it was nothing they could will into happening.

Brenda took the glass and, with a benign smile, said, "I hope Grace got hold of you to tell you I was coming." She took a ladylike sip.

Robin was trying to piece it together: Grace's disjointed words, this woman showing up. Something was off about the whole thing. "But I thought you came here by mis—" She quit when she saw the almost imperceptible shift of Brenda's eyes, but it was too late.

"I'm sorry to have bothered you," Brenda said. She handed the mostly full glass to Robin. "Did Grace have anything else to say?"

Glancing past her through the screen door, Robin looked in vain for Cate and Grover. Her eyes stopped on the lone car in the parking area. Her own. "Where's your car?"

It all happened so quickly. Brenda's hand shot out, snatched the cast iron frying pan and swung it, two-fisted, like a baseball bat, catching Robin a glancing blow to the temple.

Pain blinded her and she had the odd sensation her head was filled with carbonated liquid under pressure. Robin staggered, clawing at the refrigerator door for support before slumping to the floor. The kitchen table shrank to a pinpoint of light before it vanished completely.

SHE WAS CERTAIN SHE'D regained consciousness, had opened her eyes wide, yet the light did not return. Her eyes stung, her head throbbed and she considered that the metallic taste in her mouth was probably blood. She blinked, blinked again, but nothing dispelled the oppressive darkness. How long had she been out? Her fingers tingled painfully.

Don't make a noise now. In her head, the voice was her father's. The darkness, her old nemesis . . . it was happening all over again. And hot! So damned hot!

She tried to stretch her hands to the sides to grope in the darkness, only to discover her wrists were bound in front of her. As were her ankles. She sucked in an audible breath, already beginning to hyperventilate. Soon she was taking huge gulps of air that held, she realized with horror, the sickening and unmistakable smell of kerosene and burning cloth.

Moaning, she allowed herself to fall to one side and roll. One rotation took her to a wall. Stretching her bound and throbbing arms in a limited arc, she began to probe the surface of her dark prison. Something bumped against her head. She stifled a scream. Like a blind person knowing a familiar face by feel, she recognized her spare camera bag. Which meant she was in the storage room at the back of her cabin.

Don't make a sound. I'll let you out just as soon as they leave.

Gasping, she flipped over in the direction she believed was her only exit, felt in the impenetrable dark for the door, and slammed her shoulder against it. It didn't budge. Dread settled on her, immobilizing her. "Help," she sobbed so quietly no one but the darkness could hear. "Oh, God, help."

"See?" George pointed again.

Then Cate saw it—a small vulpine nose poking out from under the rock ledge. Her breath caught. A second nose and furry face appeared. Little yips, happy sounds came from the den. Cate was transfixed. *I could just hug George for bringing me here*, she thought, all caution dispelled.

"Cute little buggers," he murmured.

She didn't know how long they stood there. If it weren't for the shade and a slight breeze, the heat would have been suffocating. Cate passed a hand over her upper lip and savored the moment—the sight of two kits safe in their den, the rushing of the waterfall, the sunlight glinting off the water below, the smell of smoke . . . Why, she wondered idly, would Robin make a fire on a day like this?

She heard him long before Grover bounded toward them, barking insanely.

"Guess I've got a door to repair," George said glumly.

But Cate was alarmed by more than a torn screen. "What is it, Grove?" He danced wildly, his deep bark turning to a growl. Cate looked back at the cabin. "Fire!" she yelled to George.

"THANK GOD FOR AIR CONDITIONING," Sheriff Harley said as pulled his tie to one side, then the other, in an attempt to loosen the sweaty knot.

Deputy Brill jumped up at the sound of his voice in the outer office. When his face came into view, she announced, "Say, 911 Dispatch had a weird one."

Harley tossed his keys on the desk. "Yeah?"

"Yeah, a cell phone call. Not in range, though. All they could hear was a woman's voice. They couldn't trace the location of the phone, but it's a Minneapolis number—name of Fred Samuels."

"Huh!" Harley grunted.

Brill said, "The only word they heard was 'hurry.'"

Harley braced himself, knuckles on the desk, brows furrowed in thought. He stood when he saw Brill's mocking eyes on him. *Lowland gorilla*, that's what she'd said he looked like every time he bent over his desk in that particular posture. His eyes drifted from the phone to the file cabinet to the clock as he conjectured the call's significance. It had the smell of something important.

The telephone's shrill ring got their attention.

Brill snatched it. "Okay . . . okay . . . got it." She hung up. "The mystery woman called back. Still out of range, but they picked up something about Spirit Falls before they lost her completely."

BRENDA'S HEART THRUMMED in her chest. The stench of kerosene clung to her, making her gag as she stumbled down the hallway, propelled by adrenaline alone. She had sloshed so much near the kitchen that the can was empty long before she reached the room where she'd left that stupid woman. Back in the kitchen, she stood as far from the stove as she could and still flip on a burner. The wooden spoon took forever to ignite, but when it did, she set it on top of the folded paper bags on the table and they burst into flame.

Turning toward the front door, she dug in her pants pocket for her car keys. Nothing there but the silver button that had started this whole fiasco. And then it came back to her—the sound of something metallic hitting the floor. Had her keys fallen when she'd tied up the unconscious woman? *No, not then.*

She closed her eyes, calming herself to remember: Tying the woman's hands with a bathrobe sash, wrapping her ankles with the cord of a curling iron, the curling iron almost tripping her as she dragged the dead weight into the closet, feet first. Closing the door, pushing it hard because the body had fallen or rolled against it, then, just to make sure, hauling that enormous trunk in front of it.

Yes, the keys must have fallen then. If she didn't find them soon, her means of escape would be engulfed in flames. The hallway was already filling with black smoke.

What was that infernal wailing? "Shut up!" Brenda screamed in the direction of the blocked storage room. She turned to see flames behind her, licking along the floor between her and the front door. Smoke rolled along the hallway ceiling toward her.

Then she saw them, just a few feet ahead of her on the linoleum running the length of the hall. She dove for her keys, snatched them up, and crawled to the screen door at the side of the cabin.

She raced toward the driveway. The screaming from the storage room sounded louder than ever, unless it was—"No!" Brenda rasped. The sound wasn't human after all. Sirens—closer . . . on the driveway now, she realized, with a clenching feeling in her chest. "No, no, no!"

No, better not risk a return to her car, hidden behind a stand of pine trees near that hillbilly trailer. What if the police had already found it? She looked around wildly, and saw that the cabin roof was sending sparks into nearby trees.

No other choice. She'd have to head to the water. With a quick glance to the driveway, she bolted around the corner of the cabin and toward the back of the property. The sirens were screaming inside her ears, along with the roaring of the fire.

She was scarcely able to make out a narrow path that, if there was a merciful God, would take her to safety. She started down it, going only a few steps when she tripped over a tree root and went sprawling. Pine needles and sand gave way, propelling her forward. When she stopped sliding, she was looking down, a long way down, at a waterfall. She struggled to her feet, gasping to regain control.

Across the creek, high on the other bank, she saw the strangest apparition, a woman in white, dark hair flowing behind her as she seemed to be running down a path parallel to her own. Her mouth was open as if she was screaming, but Brenda heard only the rush of water, the roar of the cabin going up in flames. Bouncing around behind and then beside the dark-haired woman was a shaggy pony. Brenda could not believe her eyes. She blinked to clear the hallucination. The pony threw back its shaggy head as if baying at the moon.

Brenda could hear herself blubbering—praying for mercy, for deliverance. She had to keep moving. Tearing her eyes away from the bizarre apparition, she saw that just ahead a crude handrail sloped downwards. She ran toward it, losing her footing once more. Her right shoe tumbled down the embankment. Lying on her side, she kicked off her remaining shoe, looked over her shoulder and directly into the beet-red face of a man who was rushing at her, arms waving wildly. He wore a tan uniform and his mouth moved as if he was calling out to her.

CATE RUNNING WOLF HAD almost reached the water's edge when Grover, in his exuberance, knocked her down. Her tailbone sent electric shocks down her legs. The dog circled back, tugging at her arm until he had her upright again. "Go, Grover! Swim!" She tried to propel him into the creek where it eddied below the waterfall, but he barked and sat on the sandbank next to her.

"Oh, Lord!" she said, whether as a prayer or a curse, she didn't stop to consider. Together, they waded in. The water was icy and the current strong. She felt her tennis shoes lose their purchase on the algae-covered rocks, felt her elbow scrape over something sharp as she rolled, sank, and then bobbed to the surface, coughing convulsively. Helplessly, she watched the shoreline slide past. Grover, now paddling furiously just downstream of her, bumped his great weight against her, nudging her, keeping her head above water. His shoulders moved powerfully through the water, yet despite his strength and her untidy flailing, Cate and her faithful companion were swept around a bend in the creek. The falls disappeared from view.

IN THAT SPLIT SECOND, Sheriff Harley realized with a start that the woman wasn't Robin Bentley after all. Her face was covered in dark smudges, her hair plastered across her forehead, covering her eyes. Her clothing was torn and she was obviously terrified.

"Where's Mrs. Bentley?" he yelled. "Where's Robin?"

Instead of answering, she extended her arms overhead to grasp the thin railing. As soon as she'd hauled herself up, she went headlong down the uneven steps that ended just below the falls.

Bolting after her, Sheriff Harley was unable to prevent what happened next. He watched helplessly as she again stumbled. It was almost comical the way her feet slewed sideways and in an attempt to catch herself, she spun her arms like propellers, overcorrected, and pitched violently in the other direction. Her mouth opened in an exaggerated O. Her eyes rolled to take in what was her inevitable direction of contact with the handrail. Despite her petite size, despite hour after grueling hour at the gym, her weight, combined with momentum, was enough to bow the wood with a soft cracking sound.

The entire section of railing gave way, then, and she was catapulted over the cliff.

Taking caution not to follow her path, Harley held onto a tree so he could look over the edge. About twenty feet below lay the motionless body on a rocky protuberance just above the waterfall.

INSIDE THE STORAGE ROOM, Robin threw her weight against the door until she was sure she'd broken bones, but it did not budge. When sweat rolled into her eyes, she closed them. She had to get rid of the cloth binding her wrists. Tearing at them with her teeth accomplished little, but did give her time to mentally catalogue the contents of the closet and come up with a better solution. She felt around until she recognized the broken end table, found the protruding nails and scraped her bindings over them until the cloth gave way. Hands freed, she rolled even deeper into the small room, feeling around for something else—anything—that would deliver her. Her hand struck something hard, and vaguely familiar. She slid her fingers up the length of what she recognized as Brad's shotgun.

Don't make a sound.

"Like hell I won't," she said with determination. Sitting, propped against the corner post of the shelves, she fumbled to remove the canvas case. "Please, God, let it be loaded," she prayed, aiming in the dark at what she thought was plasterboard wall just to the right of the blocked door. She grimaced and pulled the trigger. *Blam!* The sound was deafening and her shoulder screamed with pain. Ears still roaring from the first blast, she moved the barrel a few inches to the right and pulled the trigger again.

Dragging her tethered legs behind her, Robin flopped like a seal to the wall, now a mess of shattered plasterboard and wood, and began clawing her way out into the smoke-filled hallway. Each breath brought searing pain to her lungs.

Even after scrabbling through the ragged opening, there was no light to guide her. Robin gasped and coughed, feeling her way toward safety—she could see it now, a narrow band, just a couple of inches of dim light under the billows of black smoke. *Fire doesn't bring light, it brings pure, impenetrable blackness,* she thought idly just before losing consciousness.

CATHERINE LAY ON A SANDBANK, Grover panting beside her. He whined and nosed her. She rolled to her side and vomited water onto the sand before slowly propping herself on hands and knees and standing shakily. "I'm up, I'm up!" she said, sounding like her young self answering her mother's verbal alarm on school mornings. Her eyes lifted to see the sky filled with ominous dark smoke. Maybe it was her overstretched imagination, but she could swear she heard a gunshot blast, followed by another. "Go on! Go get Robin!" She shoved against his haunches.

Grover barked three loud barks.

"Go," she pled. "Please go."

Bracing himself in a wide-legged stance, he took her forearm in his mouth and tugged.

HAVING FORDED THE CREEK upstream in the shallows, George Wellman ran to the uniformed officer, yelling, "She's in there! Mrs. B. is in there!" He gesticulated wildly.

"What?" Brill mouthed, slamming the trunk of the sheriff's car. He saw the double blade of the axe in her hands.

"She's still in the cabin!" he bawled.

Deputy Brill wasn't about to wait for the fire trucks. "I'm going in!"

"I'll go!" George bellowed, grabbing her by her uniform shirt.

She twisted out of his grasp and headed for the side door.

With a mental shrug, he followed.

They'd covered half the distance to the building when they both stopped in mid-stride. An ominous groan was heard through the roar of the fire. The center of the roof sagged, then collapsed. Dark smoke puffed out from the epicenter, and flames flared upward.

"Robin! No!" Cate's shriek cut through the air.

George and the deputy turned to see the dark-haired woman racing toward them, the dog flying along at her side. George hurled himself at her, nabbing her around the middle and throwing her to the ground to keep her from racing into the inferno. Grover, unchecked, sped past them and disappeared around the side of the collapsing building. The entire west side of the building was now engulfed in flames.

One woman on the rocks above the falls, dead or seriously injured. Need rescue equipment. Large hunting lodge on fire. Unsalvageable. The cabin owner missing and presumed to be inside. Danger of fire spreading to trees. Sheriff Harley had just called in the update when he looked up to see the roof cave in. He ran, looking up at the old chimney as he passed it, expecting it to fall any second.

The fire truck screeched toward him, stopped, and four firefighters leapt out. "Get back," one of them yelled.

Deputy Brill, ignoring the order, followed the sound of the barking dog.

Meanwhile, Cate, suffocating under the weight of George Wellman, screamed at him to get off her before heaving him to the side and scrambling to her feet.

A few feet beyond the charred side door stood Grover, his bark deep and rhythmic, his hair singed and blackened. Beneath him on the ground and barely visible through the smoke, Cate now saw, lay Robin. Grover dipped his blackened muzzle, took her leg in his mouth and tugged.

One of the firemen, a young man with a crooked nose, came up behind Cate and knelt over Robin. "She's breathing!" he called out. He did a cursory examination of her as best he could with a 200-pound dog attached to her pants leg. "What the hell?" His fingers slipped between her ankles and seized upon the thing that bound them. "Somebody tied her up."

Cate leaned forward, horrified.

He pulled a knife from his belt and sawed through the electrical cord. "Okay, let's move her." The second fireman came with a stretcher and together they lifted her. Only then did Grover let go.

Brill stooped to pick up the severed cord as evidence.

Well away from the building and beyond the incapacitating smoke, the firemen set Robin's stretcher on the grass.

Her eyes opened. She squinted in the bright sun.

"Ambulance is on the way," the young fireman said as he felt her pulse. "Who did this? Who tied you up?"

Robin opened her mouth but no sound emerged. Her eyes filled with tears.

The others gathered nearby, Cate, Deputy Brill, and George. Grover circled them, woofing. Cate squatted to squeeze Robin's hand.

"Fire." Robin's eyelids fluttered.

Cate, straining to hear Robin's voice, saw her friend's eyes roll back and wondered if she was going to lose her after all.

Robin grimaced, or maybe it was an attempt at a smile. "You and you and you,. . ." she rasped through blackened lips as she looked from one to the next. This time, the smile was unmistakable.

The sheriff's face floated into view behind Cate.

Robin's eyes rolled to take him in. ". . . and you were there," she continued in a voice so weak they had to lean close. "But you couldn't have been, could you?"

"What's she saying?" Brill demanded.

"Oh, Robin, oh God!" Cate covered her mouth.

Harley turned to her.

Shaking her head in disbelief, Cate said, "She's going to be fine. She's quoting from the *Wizard of Oz*!"

30

Up the road, Grace had pulled over for a fire truck, noticing for the first time the column of dark smoke beyond the trees to her left. Driving once more, she felt sick from the increasingly acrid smell, as, once again, she pulled over for an ambulance. Almost immediately, a second one screamed past. She had a terrible feeling she knew where they were headed. *Oh, God, please let everyone be okay. Get there. Get there in time,* she prayed. She coughed and her eyes began to water. Once she'd started down the long driveway, the air was scarcely breathable.

Slamming on her brakes, she was able to stop short of the emergency vehicles. Two paramedics—a man, thirtyish, with close-cropped hair, and a younger woman who wore her hair in stubby pigtails—bent over a figure on the ground.

Coughing and slipping in the sand, Grace rushed to where Cate stood, bedraggled, but thank God, upright, a few feet from Robin. Grabbing Cate's arm with both hands, she could only say, "Is . . . is . . . is she?"

Wet, bedraggled and covered with soot, Cate slumped into Grace's arms, suddenly unable to bear the burden alone. She began sobbing. "She's okay, Gracie. Robin's okay."

Grover lay nearby licking his nearly hairless haunch. He rolled his eyes toward Cate, tried to stand, then, shaking, flopped to the ground with a moan. Cate knelt and ran her fingers the length of his body, checking for injury. Finding none, she buried her face in his wet fur and sobbed.

Grace's lips quivered. She looked back at Robin, frail and motionless. Beyond Robin was the crumbling blackened mess that used to be a glorious hunting lodge. Grace could not hold back her own tears. "Was she the only one in there?"

What?" Cate turned her face to Grace's. She coughed until her eyes streamed with tears.

"You okay?"

Cate nodded and spat in the grass.

"Was there anyone else here?" Grace asked again.

"What do you mean? I don't think so. I was across the creek with George and Grover when I saw the fire." Cate's teeth chattered despite the suffocating heat.

"Anyone else? What about—" Grace shut her eyes and swallowed. "What about Brenda? Did she show up here?"

Cate's eyebrows shot up. "Brenda?"

Sheriff Harley materialized from the woods, talking on his cell phone. He approached them, snapped his phone shut and held out his hand to Grace. "I'm Sheriff Harley."

"Grace Samuels," she said, ignoring his proffered hand and engulfing him in a hug.

Harley held her away from him awkwardly. "Samuels? Husband Fred?"

She nodded.

"Called 911 on your way here?"

She nodded again. "I'm a friend of Robin's."

"You certainly are!" The sheriff smiled broadly.

Behind her, Cate seized her by the shoulders. "You called for help? Gracie, you saved Robin's life!"

Harley nodded. "Yup. Between you and Mrs. Samuels . . . and Grover . . ." He took off his hat, scratched his head and watched the dog with unconcealed admiration. "That's a mighty fine dog you got there."

Grover seemed to know he was being praised. He stopped licking to gaze up at Sheriff Harley. With great effort, he stood and tottered over to lick the man's hand.

The paramedics were still tending to Robin. The side of her head was covered with a white compress held in place by gauze, an oxygen mask covered her nose and mouth. They wheeled her to the ambulance and lifted her in. The female EMT climbed in next to her and pulled the doors shut.

Cate grabbed the arm of the other paramedic and asked, "Is she going to be okay?" Grace loomed over her shoulder.

"The head wound definitely needs attention. I'm sure they'll admit her," the man informed them. "It's really not my place to say," he said with a shake of his head, adding, "But damage from smoke inhalation doesn't always show up right away."

STILL HUDDLED TOGETHER they heard the siren's wail over the fire, announcing the ambulance's departure.

Grace turned and gestured to the other ambulance, still parked and unattended. "Where are they? What are they waiting for?"

Cate shrugged, her brows knit.

"They're with the other woman," Sheriff Harley said.

Grace's mouth fell open.

Harley escorted them around the fire trucks and through the wooded area, giving wide berth to the burning building, to the steps leading to the creek. He stopped, turned to them and said, "There was another woman who fell through the rail. Maybe you can tell us who she is. They're bringing her up right now." Together they watched from a discreet distance as the second EMT crew hauled on a rope that disappeared over the precipice. The other end was tied to a sturdy tree.

Gradually, a contraption came into view, something that looked like a small plastic canoe, a garish green thing suspended from the rope. Strapped to it was a tiny figure of a woman, the side of her face distorted and covered in blood.

Grace audibly sucked in her breath. Her fisted hand flew to her lips. Turning to the sheriff with tears in her eyes, she croaked, "It's her. It's Brenda Krause."

And then, to his bewilderment, she started babbling about a yarn store and a button and a sweater and a remote control. It would take some time to make sense of it all.

ONCE BRILL WAS DONE WRITING down everything Harley elicited from Cate and Grace and George Wellman, the two women followed Harley's directions to the hospital.

"Can this be it?" Cate asked as they approached the two-story brick building. "It looks more like a nursing home than a hospital."

They parked and went inside, where they were told to wait in the spartan lounge. They tried to stay upbeat while waiting for any information about their friend. After an hour or so, Grace went looking for food and a landline.

Cate looked at her watch—it was only 7:34. She rose and went to the window. Looking at the sky, she saw the dark clouds of a developing storm. In the parking lot below, a paper cup skittered out of sight under a parked car. Oblivious to the others in the room, she rested her forehead on the cool glass, thoughts of Robin and the cabin swirling in her head just as wildly as the wind now tossed branches of the willow tree outside the second floor window. A lightning flash illuminated tears slowly rolling down Cate's cheeks.

"Cate?" Grace's hand softly touched her shoulder. "You okay?"

Cate quickly ran her palm across her cheek and forced a smile before turning. "I'm fine."

"Here. I finally tracked down a real coffee pot in this place." Grace handed her a Styrofoam cup. "And two Snickers."

"Super-sleuth to the rescue." Cate gave a crooked smile and took a candy bar.

Grace resettled herself into one of the upholstered chairs lining two walls of the waiting room. A large round table in the corner held a jigsaw puzzle of the Grand Canyon, partially completed. Cate went back to the window. A nurse walked to the bank of light switches and dimmed the florescent lights. She gave them a practiced smile before leaving.

"Come sit." Grace patted the seat of the chair next to her. "There's nothing for us to do now but wait and pray." She reached over and snapped on the large lamp on the end table. Its incandescent light encircled her.

Cate turned. "Okay." Wearily, she sat and quietly sipped her coffee. "Were you able to reach Brad?"

"I got his answering service." Grace tucked an errant peanut back into her mouth. "He was in surgery. They're getting another doc to close for him, so he should be on his way."

"Good." Cate nodded and once again turned her attention to the fat raindrops on the window. "At least the rain will stop any flare-ups at the cabin." She made a hiccupping sound. "The cabin. As if there's anything left."

Just then a loud rhythmic sound caught their attention. "Helicopter," Grace mouthed, her eyes wide.

Outside the window, lights whirled. Through her tears Cate saw that Grace was crying too. Soon the choppety-chop of the blades cut through the rumble of thunder as the helicopter lifted off the hospital roof.

Grace bent to fish her spare reading glasses from her handbag. Shuffling through the stack left on the table, she managed to find a *People* magazine in among the *Parenting, Golf Digest* and *Good*

Housekeeping periodicals. Despite the February publication date, she absently flipped through the pages. "It's all my fault," she announced softly. Tears blurred the magazine photos.

"*Your* fault?"

"I'm the one who tipped Brenda off about the button and the cabin." Grace sniffed. Cate plucked a handful of Kleenex from the box and offered them to her.

Once more, Grace connected the dots between Brenda's missing button and her frantic trip to Spirit Falls today. "If only I hadn't wasted so much time with that stupid remote." Grace lifted her glasses to dab at her eyes. She blew her nose with a distinct honking sound. "Maybe I would've gotten to the cabin in time to warn you and Robin."

"It's not your fault." Cate placed both hands on top of Grace's. "Besides, if I'd gone with Robin to the store, maybe—" Cate shook her head. "No, we can't do this. Second guessing is pointless!"

Both women lapsed back into silence, Grace flipping pages and Cate staring at the carpet pattern while absently fingering her amulet.

Suddenly Cate slammed her palms on the wooden arms of the chair. "What good is my gift if I can't use it to save her?" She made the word *gift* sound like a profanity.

Cate's visions. Though she'd never set much stock by them, Grace had a sudden realization of what they meant to Cate. Blessing, curse . . . or both? *The Dog Whisperer*. Grace had ridiculed Cate with the phrase. Just before she found the button that made Brenda come back here and—"Who said no second guessing?" Grace looked sternly over her glasses.

"I did. But—"

"Cate."

"All right, all right." Cate sighed and ran her hand through her hair. "What's taking so long?" She shot a look down the hallway.

"The sheriff will be here soon," came a voice from across the room. Cate and Grace were startled. Both had forgotten the presence of Deputy Brill, who now sat thumbing through a *Bride* magazine. "His orders are that no one talks to Mrs. Bentley before he does." Brill straightened in her chair, "That's why I'm assigned to babysit you two."

Cate slumped deeper into her chair, her eyes narrowed at the deputy's insinuation. So what if Brill was right on the money?

Within minutes, heavy footsteps announced Sheriff Harley's arrival. "They want to keep Mrs. Bentley here for a day or two," he announced. Turning to Brill, he asked. "Did you notify her husband?"

Brill nodded her head toward Cate, who muttered, "He's on his way."

"Robin's going to be okay, isn't she?" Cate asked.

The sheriff shrugged. "I'm sure she'll be fine."

"What about Bren—Mrs. Krause?" Grace shoved her glasses to the top of her head and looked anxiously at the sheriff. "How bad are her injuries?"

"That one's in bad shape." Harley shook his head. "Broken back, pelvis, shattered leg, and head injuries for starters."

"Oh, my God." Grace covered her mouth with her hand.

"They just air-lifted Mrs. Krause to Eau Claire."

Not Robin. Cate and Grace exchanged a look and relief settled on their features.

"Were you able to talk to her?" Cate sat forward anxiously.

He shook his head, his disappointment apparent.

Grace crumpled forward in her chair, resting her head in her hands "I'll never forgive myself for bringing that psycho bitch into our lives." She started rocking as she sobbed.

The look Harley cast in Cate's direction clearly said, *You handle this. I don't do hysterical women.*

Wordlessly, Cate slid her arm around her friend and let her cry. Harley shuffled uncomfortably.

The nurse entered the room. "Sheriff, we just received a call from Mr. Bentley. He's on his way, but his car skidded off the road just past Menomonie, so he'll be delayed. He's okay, just waiting for a tow." The nurse handed him a piece of paper. "Here's his cell phone number."

He snatched his cell phone from the case snapped to his belt. Quickly he punched in the numbers. "Dr. Bentley? Sheriff Harley here. I'm sending my deputy to bring you to the hospital." He paused to listen. "They want to keep your wife overnight. I was just about to speak with her when I got your message." Again he paused. "That would probably be best. Doctor to doctor." Harley cleared his throat. "Did you notice what mile marker you're at?"

Snapping the phone shut, he turned to Brill and gave her instructions.

"I'm on it." Elbows wide, she set off down the hallway.

"And you two." Harley turned to Cate and Grace with a bemused smile. "Sit and wait."

As soon as he was out of sight, Cate stood abruptly. " Sit and wait, my ass!" she erupted.

A devious smile curled Grace's lips as she stood and motioned for Cate to follow. They moved surreptitiously to the nurses' station, where they found a board listing Bentley, R. in Room 226.

Robin's door was ajar. They stood just outside, scarcely breathing as they strained to hear. Although the sheriff's questions were audible, Robin's responses were muffled.

"What she's saying?" Grace mouthed.

Cate shrugged.

"Why's he yelling anyway?" she whispered.

Cate shushed her with a gesture and repositioned her ear at the narrow opening. "Robin just said something about a gun."

"A gun?" Grace echoed. She leaned closer, steadying herself with a hand on the door. It swung inward. "Oops," she cried as she lost her balance.

Sheriff Harley turned, his eyes widening when the two women literally fell into the room.

"Yow!" Cate yelled from the floor. Her shoulder bag fell next to her, emptying its contents. She rolled to a sitting position and inspected her elbow before grabbing keys, used Puffs, two tubes of lipstick and a dispenser of Tic Tacs.

Grace stood, pulling herself up by the door handle, glaring at the door as if it were the source of the problem.

"Nice of you to drop in." The sides of Harley's mouth twitched. "You might as well stay. Not that you'd follow my orders anyway."

Grace and Cate rushed to opposite sides of the bed. Cate grabbed Robin's hand. "What's this about a gun?"

"What?" Robin croaked and started coughing.

"You'll have to speak louder," Harley said. "Her hearing is messed up from the shotgun blast."

"Permanently?" Cate asked.

"Don't know yet. Other than that, and one whopper of a headache, she's in pretty good shape."

"You got shot?" Grace yelled at her.

"She wasn't shot. She was the shooter," the sheriff explained.

The women looked at her in disbelief.

"Had to get out . . ." Robin's coughing started again.

Harley nodded. "Do you want them to know what you told me?"

"Uh-huh." She coughed again.

He sighed. "She tells me Mrs. Krause was already in the cabin when she got back."

"She hit me from behind," Robin croaked.

"After Mrs. Krause hit her over the head, she tied your friend up and locked her in the closet before setting the fire."

For once in her life, Grace was speechless. A few seconds passed before it hit her full force. "Oh, God, she really was going to kill you."

"Your friend here is mighty lucky her husband left his shotgun in that closet. If she hadn't blasted through that wall . . ."

Both women looked with new respect at Robin, who nodded in confirmation.

"Pretty damn gutsy." Harley slowly shook his head.

"The button!" Grace suddenly exclaimed. "Did Brenda get the button?"

"Matter of fact," the sheriff said, pulling a small plastic bag from his shirt pocket. "They found it in her pants pocket."

"And the sweater, the one with the matching buttons. Did they find Brenda's sweater?"

"Yup. Found her car right where she hid it behind George's trailer. The sweater was in the back seat." Harley smiled.

A soft snuffle came from the bed. Robin's eyes were closed and her mouth hung slack.

Harley motioned them to the door. "Let's let her sleep."

"Besides we still have to rescue Grover from George's trailer," Cate said, adding, "You know, George really isn't a bad sort."

The sheriff looked amused. "George just likes to keep watch over things."

"What do you mean 'watch over things'?" Cate countered.

"How can I put this?" His mouth twisted to one side. "He likes to watch people . . . sometimes through a window."

Grace's mind flashed back on last year's skinny-dipping. "He's a peeping tom?"

"I knew there was something off about him." Cate looked disgusted.

"Ladies, ladies." There was a hint of paternalism in Harley's hand on Grace's shoulder. "Don't worry. It's not your usual voyeur stuff. I've never gotten a report that he's watched through bedroom or bathroom windows."

"Oh, that's comforting." Cate rolled her eyes.

"Way I see it, he's just plain lonely. He watches people watch TV or read. Makes him feel like he's a part of it. He's very protective of Mrs. Bentley, and I guess for that, we should all be grateful."

The women exchanged dubious looks.

"I know it's hard to understand. Took me a while too, but George does seem to have a code of decency.

"Hmmm." Cate was still not totally convinced. "We need to get Grover."

Harley held out his hands. "No need to worry. I had George bring him to the station and give him plenty of food and water. You can pick him up tomorrow." Sheriff Harley started to herd them down the hallway. "You two need to get some sleep. I'd recommend the Super 8 down the road. Place is clean and won't cost an arm and a leg. I need to stick around to talk to Dr. Bentley. And don't worry about the pooch. I'll go and check on him later."

Cate was too tired to object. "Fine, but don't forget to take him for a walk."

"I'll treat him like he's my own."

31

The next morning while Robin slept, Sheriff Harley, wearing a pair of khakis and a yellow golf shirt, strode up to the ICU desk at Eau Claire's trauma center. "How's Brenda Krause this morning?" he asked the stocky charge nurse, flipping her his badge.

"In and out of consciousness." She glanced at a computer screen before slipping off her glasses to let them hang on the beaded chain around her neck. "Her vitals are stable at the moment, but she had a rough night. Her husband had to stay in the lounge most of the time. I don't think he got any sleep at all."

"Is he in with her now?"

With an apologetic smile, she said, "No, the rooms are just too small when the nurses are working with a patient. I told her husband to get some breakfast. I imagine you'll find him in the cafeteria."

"I'd like permission to interview Mrs. Krause. Alone."

She nodded. "I'll detain the husband if he comes back, but please make it brief."

Brenda Krause lay dwarfed by an array of tubes, wires, and beeping machines. Her bruised face peered out of some contraption that looked like a hockey player's shin guard with a cutout. Her eyes were barely visible under heavy lids.

He pulled an armless chair around the equipment, careful not to trip on the electrical cords and hoses. "Brenda, do you recognize me from yesterday?"

She moaned.

"I'm Sheriff Harley. I saw you fall. You're lucky to be alive." He sat on the edge of the chair, leaning forward to rest a hand on her bedrail.

She moaned again. *Mama*, she said. Or was it *Martin?* He couldn't tell.

"I know you've had quite an ordeal, but I need to get a few things straight. Mrs. Krause, can you understand me?"

Her hand fluttered on the sheet. "Uh-huh." Her speech was constrained by the head immobilizer, and probably by pain medication.

Glancing at the morphine drip, he wondered if they could cut back on it long enough to conduct an interview. No time. He plowed on. "Why did you go to the cabin?"

She winced. "'ere was no conf'rence. I had to know. She . . . she . . ." Brenda's eyes filled with water.

He grabbed a tissue to blot her tears. "She what?"

Brenda swallowed, wincing as she did. Her breathing was rapid. "She looked right . . . at me." The next words were unintelligible. Then, ". . . jus' kep' begging me. Over 'n over. Help me, please help me."

He felt like he'd walked into the wrong movie. Who was begging her? Was she talking about Robin?

"Help me."

"You want me to help you?"

"Not me! Her!"

"Who?" he asked, more sharply than he'd intended.

Brenda's eyes rolled wildly before her lids squeezed tight, pulling at the tape holding the nasogastric tube on her nose. "I jus' left her there," she said and licked her lips with a dry tongue.

"Who? Who did you leave?"

Her eyes opened to slits. "Bitch!" She spat the word. "He's *my* husband. She could have anyone. Why'd she have to take mine?"

She began sobbing, huge racking sobs. One of her monitors lit up, its beep loud and insistent. A nurse rushed in and shooed him out the door.

At two that afternoon, Foxy and Louise, summoned by Grace and Cate, met with them in the small conference room behind the sheriff's office. Deputy Brill passed out a round of chewable coffee. Sheriff Harley came in shortly, slid a chair up to the table next to Cate's and slurped the sludge from her untouched cup.

There was a loud clicking in the hallway, the door crashed open and Grover hurtled in. He slid to a stop in front of Cate, who reached down to him.

"Grover, our hero!" She kissed the top of his head.

Grover returned the kiss by slobbering on her jeans, hurriedly purchased that morning at Farm and Fleet.

Grover then swung his head over to lay it on the sheriff's knees. Looking at the man with his big brown eyes, he let a tiny whine escape.

"Brill," Harley said, fluffing the dog's ears, "Can you run out and buy this poor little pooch another bag of dog food? See if they've got it in fifty-pound bags this time."

"Little? Hunh!" She stood. "Should I put him back in the holding cell while I'm gone?" Cate began to object, but Harley grinned. "Not to worry, Ms. Wolf. Our canine friend's been lolling on the cot in there all morning."

As soon as the deputy left, Grover close on her heels, Cate hit Harley with the question they all wanted to ask. "Did Brenda confess?"

He threw a sardonic look in her direction. "You know I can't tell you that."

"Of course not," Foxy said, smoothing a wrinkle on her denim skirt. "But we kind of put together what we think happened. Could we just try it out on you?"

He meant to say something about letting the authorities work things out, but looking at Foxy's hopeful smile, somehow the word that came out was *Okay.*

Grace pulled out her planner, opening it to a list that covered one page. She ignored the sudden slump of his shoulders.

"Go ahead." Staring out the window, he pinched the bridge of his nose.

Grace took a breath and said, "For starters, there was blood in the car."

He sighed. "Actually, we didn't find any blood in Krause's vehicle. It had been thoroughly cleaned and repaired." He sighed again. "And his wife's car was clean."

"Not in Brenda's car, in the neighbor's," she insisted. "Brenda used Phyllis's car the weekend Melissa Dunn went missing, and if you look, I think you'll find blood on the inside of the driver's seatbelt."

"How do you know this?"

"I went shopping with her." Grace sat back with a self-satisfied smile.

Harley swung his hand up to clasp his forehead. "Of course you did," he sighed.

Undeterred, Grace continued. "Phyllis told me about the borrowed car, and I saw the blood. With my own eyes."

"When you went shopping?"

Grace looked at the others. They nodded for her to go on. "Well, since Brenda's car was impounded, and Phyllis is this whiz with finding the right clothes at bargain prices—"

"All right! You were in this Phyllis person's car," he said. "But even if it was blood, which only our lab can verify, what makes you think it belongs to the victim? People bleed in cars, you know . . . paper cuts, bloody noses . . ."

"But it all fits!" Louise exclaimed. "Grace found out that Brenda was house-sitting for the neighbor that weekend. The neighbor comes back and Brenda says, oh, by the way, I borrowed your car while you were gone."

"And had it detailed!" Foxy added.

The sheriff's shift in demeanor was almost imperceptible. He stared at each of them in turn before clicking his pen. "Do you know Phyllis's last name?"

"Carson," Grace told him. "She lives in the house next to the Krause's, to the left of it if you're facing the house.

"And another thing," Foxy said, "Did you ever follow up on Ross Johnson's Chicago connection?"

Harley chewed a hangnail on his thumb. He looked tired and rumpled. "I suppose I owe you that much. Yes, ladies, Ross Johnson did have Krause's Mercedes repaired. At a body shop that has been less than forthcoming. And . . ." He paused. "And all the damage was to the passenger side."

Louise punched the air. "Woo Hoo! So Melissa wasn't driving!"

He shook his head. "Would appear not."

"So who was?" Foxy asked. "Martin?"

"Wouldn't that make him an accessory after the fact?" Grace posed.

Cate threw her hands up. "At the very least, obstruction of justice!"

Harley closed his eyes. He felt a headache coming on. "Look, we don't know who drove the car, but Johnson's the one who had it repaired."

But the women were on a roll. "Leaving the scene of an accident!" Foxy called out.

"Perjury," suggested Grace.

Harley held up his hands. "Ladies. Please!"

"Well, think about it! Let's say Brenda followed her husband when she became suspicious he was having an affair." Grace paused, and the others nodded for her to continue. "The paint on the tree must have gotten there when Martin drove into it."

Foxy interrupted. "Unless Ross Johnson was driving."

"This is how I picture it," Cate said, leaning forward to rest her forearms on the table. Her voice was soft, but her tone commanded attention. "Somebody, either Martin or Ross, drove the car into the tree. He was drunk or high. Definitely scared. He took off, probably to get help." She stared at the tabletop. "Melissa's injured, all alone in the car. There's blood. She's hurting. She sees someone come to the window. The door opens. She tries to turn, but she can't seem to move her legs. So she looks up into the face of the person standing there. Oh, God, not her! But scared as she is, she begs, 'Help me. Please help me!'"

Harley cleared his throat. "Go on."

"And that's when—"

Louise interrupted Cate. "That's when Brenda bashes her head with something—a branch, a tire iron, something like that. Here, take that, you home-wrecker!" She swatted the air with a fist, then sat back smugly.

"A rock," Cate's voice was almost a whisper.

The sheriff turned back to her. "Go on. What do you mean when you say you *picture* it?"

Her eyes slowly lifted to his. "I . . . I don't know how to describe it, but there's something about that spot."

"What spot?"

"By the tree—well, the stump. That's where it happened. Molly Pat picked up on it."

"The dog?"

Cate nodded. "She tried to tell me at the time . . . that first morning. I went back yesterday, and that's when I just . . . I saw it."

A long Grover howl came from down the hall.

Foxy rubbed her bare arms, suddenly chilled.

Harley felt prickles on his neck. "So, are you like a psychic, or what?"

Cate's lids lowered a notch. "Let's just say I'm highly intuitive."
"And accurate," Grace added.

Cate hesitated. "There's something else." All eyes turned to her once more. "Yesterday, after the stump, I felt drawn back to the bridge. When I got to the middle I felt a little sick, so I held onto the railing and looked down. I felt like I was falling." She clung to her amulet, shaking her head. Suddenly, she looked up. "Where, exactly, did George find Melissa's bracelet?"

WHEN SHERIFF HARLEY and his deputy arrived again at the trauma center before dinner, he stopped at the ICU nurses' station for permission to see Brenda Krause once more.

"Her husband's in there now." It was a different charge nurse. This one had the tone and expression of a schoolmarm. "I assume this is of utmost importance."

"Yes, ma'am."

"Five minutes," she said, turning back to her paperwork.

Approaching Brenda's room, they heard Martin's voice. "For God's sake, Bren, why? What were you thinking?"

Harley motioned to Brill with a finger on his lips. They kept their distance.

Martin's voice again: "I know how hard this has been on you, but we can still rebuild our lives, babe."

There was a muffled sob from Brenda.

"My God, Brenda! Why would you throw yourself over the cliff?" Martin seemed to choke on his next question. "Why there, of all places? Why did it have to be the same place where, where . . ."

Her voice was weak, but the words were clear and venomous: "You can't even say it. Why was I there where your precious little whore died?"

His sobs turned to whimpering. "I'm sorry, I'm just so goddamn sorry for all of it. She was nothing to me, I swear."

Harley and Brill edged closer. Through the narrow opening, they could see Martin's shoulders heaving as he sat hunched on the edge of her bed.

The sheriff strode into the room, Brill behind him. He held up his badge. "We need to talk to your wife."

"Now? Can't you see how hard this is on her?" Martin pulled a handkerchief from his pocket and blew his nose. "She's in no shape—"

"Just give us a few minutes. Go down to the cafeteria, get some coffee."

Martin nodded meekly and slunk out of the room.

DESPITE BRENDA'S INTERNAL DAMAGE, including a ruptured spleen, she was fairly lucid. Her head, held in place by the immobilizer, faced straight up, but her eyes followed him. Harley slid a chair close to the head of the bed, perching on the edge of it to reach through the bedrail so he could touch her hand. Standing at attention near the closet door, Sara Brill tried to be inconspicuous.

Harley cleared his throat and plunged in. "Are you up to talking, Mrs. Krause?"

The corners of her mouth tightened, but she didn't answer.

"Brenda?" He had been mulling over how he would conduct this interview, knowing his time was short and the evidence sketchy. The conjectures of the book club ladies did fill in the blanks nicely, he had to admit, and so he decided to use their premise as a starting point. "You started telling me this morning about how you found Melissa Dunn. That must have been quite a shock for you, finding your husband's mistress in his wrecked car. You must have just about snapped when she was begging you—you, of all people—for help."

Brenda's eyes overflowed with tears.

His bluff seemed to be working. "That's when you hit her with a rock." His tone suggested it was a minor detail.

Brenda's lips parted. Her eyes cast about the room before settling on the sheriff's face. "I had to make her shut up." She inhaled deeply, her lip quivering. "And then—" She looked at him, her eyes pleading. "And then . . . after . . . she did."

"She shut up after you hit her with the rock? Was she dead?"

Brenda averted her eyes. With no sound, her lips formed the words: *I don't know.*

"How did you get her to the bridge?" Even as he asked it, he couldn't picture this diminutive woman lugging Melissa's dead weight sixty yards to the bridge, then heaving her over a rail that was almost her height.

Brenda's face contorted in pain. "No! I didn't do that!" She put the emphasis on *that.*

"How did she wind up in the creek?"

She ran her tongue across her bottom lip.

Please implicate those sons of bitches, he willed her.

Brenda appeared to be struggling with a decision.

He let a compassionate tone into his voice. "You must have felt so betrayed when you found out who your husband was with . . . a woman you knew . . . a woman so much younger."

Her lips quivered. "He couldn't deal with it. Too scared. Pathetic! Stumbling around blubbering, calling her 'babe.'" Her face twisted in anger. "'Oh, babe, It's all my fault. I love you so much, babe.'"

Harley patted her hand. "You must have been devastated."

She inhaled in one long shudder.

"When did you find out they were having an affair?"

"I saw them!" she spat. "Standing on the deck all lovey dovey. Never even thought somebody might see them."

"But *you* saw them, didn't you?"

Her anguished expression was answer enough.

He paused, trying to put together a picture in his head. "But how did you know he'd be there? Did you follow him?"

For a moment, she looked almost triumphant. "I figured it out. A couple phone calls. I figured out there was no conference. When the cheating bastard called me, I heard Ross in the background."

"Johnson?"

"Yes, Johnson. So I called Ross's office. Secretary said he was at the cabin."

"You've been to Johnson's cabin before?"

"Not in a while."

"Why did you go this time?"

"I had to know."

"You borrowed your neighbor's car, right?

Her eyes fixed on his for a long, calculating moment. "I parked off the road just past the driveway."

He thought about this. "How did you manage to see them on the deck?"

"I went on foot."

"So you walked up, saw them being all lovey dovey, and then you walked back to the car?

"Uh huh."

He saw her energy waning. "And then?"

"I cried."

"And then?" he prompted again.

"And then the car came."

"Martin's?"

"And she was with him. Waving her arms around just before they hit the tree." Tears oozed from her eyes. He dabbed them with a tissue.

He continued. "Did he know you were there that night?"

Her tone was bitter. "I never crossed his mind."

Stay with me, now. "You never told him, did you?"

Her lips formed a silent *No.*

"And you never confronted him for his part in her death, either, did you?"

He wondered if she'd fallen asleep. He glanced at his deputy, who shrugged and motioned him to continue.

Still holding her hand, he tried another tack. "You must have panicked when Grace Samuels figured it out. And that's when you knew Robin Bentley held something linking you—"

"Who?"

"The woman at the cabin. The one you knocked out and tied up in the closet."

"Robin Bentley," she mused. "Never even knew her name."

"Did you bring the kerosene with you to her cabin?"

She stared hard into his eyes. "Wasn't like that."

He was going with his gut now, aided by information from the Samuels woman and Cate. "But you did set fire to the cabin, right? And then you ran."

Brenda's eyes shifted, staring at nothing. "Did you see her?" she asked. "The woman in a white dress." She blinked rapidly. Her voice was weaker now. "Across the river . . . long dark hair."

Glancing at his deputy, he saw her slap a palm to her forehead. When he looked back, Brenda was clawing at the IV line in the back of her hand.

A buzzer went off on one of the contraptions beside the bed. As before, a nurse bustled in and he jumped up to make room for her.

It wasn't just the shock or the morphine, he thought. He'd seen eyes like that before. There was nothing behind them. She'd lost her will to live.

AT THE SMALLER HOSPITAL forty miles away, Robin Bentley sat on the edge of her bed, alert and animated. Brad had closed the door and sat next to her. Tentatively, he reached for her upturned hand. She let her fingers twine through his and held tightly.

"The girls are on their way, " he said, brushing her hair out of her eyes. "Cass and Maya are stopping at the house to pick up some clothes and things for you."

"Thank you," she whispered.

Avoiding the bandage covering her forehead, he stroked her hair. She kissed him, gently at first.

There was a tap at the door. "You decent?" Cate called.

Brad stood and poked his nose out the door. "Just give us a little while," he said and shut the door again.

"Who all is out there?" Robin asked.

"The whole lot of them." He grinned for a brief moment, then suddenly anxiety changed his features. He ran his fingers through his hair. "I wish—" He stopped and cleared his throat. "I wish I'd been there." Again, he stopped, his voice cracking. "But . . . I'm glad they were." Not meeting her eyes, he tossed his head in the direction of the door.

"You're here now."

"I don't mean just yesterday. I mean this whole last year. God, Robin, I felt so damn useless. I'm a doctor, for God's sake, and I just had to sit there and watch my own wife . . ." His lips quivered. He covered them with a shaking hand.

"Brad, there was nothing you could've done."

"I should have felt the lump. I should have known." He put a fist over his mouth.

She grasped his arm. "No, honey, you couldn't have changed the outcome. You know that, Brad."

At last, he extracted a handkerchief from his back pocket and blew his nose before pulling her into his arms.

"I'll send them in." He rose and went to the door.

32

renda died during the second night. Her deathbed confession, witnessed by two officers of the law, implicated no one but herself in the death of Melissa Dunn and the attempted murder of Robin Bentley.

For the next week, Sheriff Harley obsessed over his investigation. He returned to the tree stump, looking for more clues, wandered down to the bridge, inspecting the area more closely. Positioning himself between the two posts, exactly where Catherine Running Wolf had stood to describe her eerie account, he examined the rail, and tweezed fibers from the roughened wood. He overnighted the evidence envelope to the lab. They didn't match the dress Melissa Dunn wore on the night of her death. At home in the evenings, he pored over articles in two Wisconsin papers and both Twin Cities newspapers, and listened to news on several stations.

"The bastard's going to get off," he fumed to his deputy at least once a day.

Indeed, Martin Krause had not been formally charged. Enjoying a certain amount of public sympathy, the grieving widower had been emboldened to approach the board of regents at Bradford for reinstatement. The talk on campus weighed heavily on the side of overlooking his indiscretion. As one bare-midriffed coed, interviewed and photographed by a salacious magazine, said, "The wife was a nut job. Who wouldn't cheat on her?"

Ten days after the spectacle of Brenda Krause's over-the-top funeral, Harley got a phone call that instantly lifted his spirits.

The male caller spoke with a heavy Hispanic accent. "Hey, Mister Sheriff, I think I got somethin' you want. That college guy, he's a bery bad man. You listenin'?"

He was listening. "What can you tell me?"

A hissing sound distorted the next couple of words. "—there, right where I left it. It's in the—whatchew call it—hayloft." The static returned.

"Hayloft? Where?"

"In the old barn at Ross Johnson's Wisconsin place. I think you'll find all the evidence you need."

For a moment he was confused. Either someone else had gotten on the line, or the man had switched to a British accent. "Who are you? Where are you calling from?" Harley demanded.

He wasn't surprised to hear the dial tone.

Calling out to his deputy, Harley instructed her to come into his office. He was still furious with her for leaking to the local press about "the woman in white" that Brenda Krause had seen running just above the waterfall where Melissa Dunn's body had been found. Thanks to Brill, local teenagers were again trespassing, camping out at night in the hopes of spotting the ghost for which Spirit Falls was named.

Brill walked in, her hair bouncing like copper springs.

Tersely, he told her, "You're in charge. I need to check out a lead." He hurried out the door and into his squad car. Throwing it into reverse, he checked his rear view mirror and saw a car pulling in behind his. Behind the wheel Robin Bentley grinned. From the passenger seat, Cate Running Wolf waved at him. The dog, he saw, occupied the entire back seat.

Harley got out. "You're looking great," he said through Robin's open window. "Cough cleared up?"

"Not entirely. They're keeping an eye on it."

He nodded. "What brings you here this time?"

"We came to see you, of course." Robin looked positively impish.

He tried not to seem impatient. "Shoot! Can it wait? I need to run up to the Johnson place."

"Okay if we follow you?" Robin was pushed aside as Grover thrust his head halfway through her window.

The sheriff made a quick decision. Addressing the dog, he said, "You wanna ride in the squad car again, don't you buddy?"

"Woof," he answered in the affirmative.

Cate laughed merrily as she transferred the dog, not to the back seat, but right up front next to the sheriff. Immediately Grover's entire demeanor changed. He sat at attention, chest thrust forward with pride.

On their way, they passed George, who wandered along the road with a plastic garbage bag in hand, picking up litter. Robin was surprised when Cate grinned at him and waved.

"What?" Cate demanded, reading her silence. "He loves animals."

"Told you."

"Told you," Cate answered in a mocking tone and they both laughed. "I talked to the sheriff about him."

"When was this?"

"When you were in the hospital." Cate crossed her arms and spoke out the window. "Seems I was picking up on something after all. He's a peeping tom, a harmless one. I guess Harley's known about it for years. Thing is, he never looks into bedrooms or bathrooms."

"Oh, that's comforting! How do you know that?" Robin's mind wheeled back to the many times George just seemed to appear. What had he been watching? More importantly, what had she been wearing? And doing?

"That's just what the sheriff told me, and it makes sense. I mean, he's got to be lonely out here in the woods all by himself most of the time. Maybe he just watches people eat and read the way other people watch television."

Robin gripped the steering wheel harder and gave a theatrical shudder. So now Cate was his defender. Well, what could she say to that?

The sheriff parked on the driveway leading to the outbuilding. He got out, opened the passenger door and Grover stepped out sedately, as if born to this position of trust.

Robin parked next to the squad car.

"You two stay here," Harley said through their window. "Grover, sit."

Grover sat. But when the two women, having caught sleuth fever, scurried after Harley, the dog whined, and trotted along with them.

"So what kind of lead are we following?" Cate asked.

He stopped. "You won't give me any peace until I tell you. I got an anonymous tip about some kind of clue hidden in the hayloft."

The side door opened with a groan.

Robin propped her hands on her thighs and coughed, feeling again the smoke damage in her lungs.

"You okay?" Cate put a hand on her shoulder.

"Just gotta get rid of it. It's bound to get better." Lightheaded from the exertion, she stood slowly.

"We'll just wait out here," Cate yelled to Harley

"Damn straight!" Sheriff Harley looked up at the loft. What had they left unexamined? He and Brill had searched the barn from bottom to top, ending by climbing up to the loft. That's when his deputy had begun sneezing so violently that he'd sent her outside. His eyes had itched like crazy, but he'd kept going.

Now, once more, he clambered up the wooden ladder. When he reached the top rung, he shifted his hands to grasp the floorboard. On hands and knees on the loft's floor, he crawled forward. Standing, as he had before, he looked at the assemblage of innocent-looking items—two hanks of rope, a spool of rotting twine, an old window frame, all hanging from the rafters. Hay bales, some still stacked three and four high, reached the back wall. Loose hay lay strewn about amidst the bales he'd flung about during his earlier search.

Had the call been a prank, he wondered, or would this place actually hold the clue that would solve the case that had been plaguing his dreams? With a weary sigh, he nudged a bale and toppled it to one side. By the time he'd reached the third row in, space was getting very limited. He stood, breathing hard.

Sitting on a previously moved bale, he pondered a way to proceed. "Damn it to hell!" he yelled and jammed his foot against the bale in front of him. He pulled his foot back and pushed again. Pulled back. Pushed.

There was definitely something in there, something black protruding between two bales.

"Hah!" he said, wedging his shoe between the bales to widen the space. It looked to be a roll of black plastic. He leapt to his feet and began pitching hay. The item, when he'd finally uncovered it, was a large garbage bag, rolled up. He could feel his pulse throbbing in his throat when he hefted the bag. It was so light.

Coughing, he scrambled down the ladder, the plastic tucked in his armpit.

He saw their faces in the sunlight, questioning him. Grinning, he gave them a thumbs-up.

They crowded him as he laid the unopened bag gently on the hood of his vehicle, not really praying, but anticipating in a pleading sort of way that this was it—whatever *it* was. He was unaware he held his breath as he began to unroll the bag. There was something inside, he realized, wiping a sleeve across his eyes. Peeling off his latex gloves, he pulled a fresh pair from his shirt pocket and pulled them over sweaty hands before carefully opening the bag. A foul smell reached his nostrils and his hopes rose.

Cate and Robin exchanged anxious glances as he reached his hand into the bag.

Just then, all three jerked reflexively as a crow cawed raucously and a flurry of blackbirds lifted into flight overhead. Grover barked until they were out of sight.

Harley's hand wrapped around something cylindrical, and he resumed breathing when he saw what it was—a film case, full, from the feel of it.

He held the bag open and peered inside. Cate and Robin craned their necks. He pulled out a cloth item, its coral color marred by dark smears, splotches and stains. Wordlessly, Harley slipped the wind-breaker into a large evidence bag.

"Whoa," Cate said under her breath.

Robin, afraid they'd be banished if they said anything, gave her a silencing look.

Harley peered once more into the black plastic. There was one more item, small, dark and with. . . feet? A mouse? He poked at it. When it didn't move, he eased it into the light. It took a moment to see that it was actually a shoe tassel, and it appeared to be stained as well.

Grover whined and Cate stroked his ears.

The sheriff looked at the women as if he'd forgotten their presence. "This next part I've got to do solo." Turning to the dog, he said, "Sorry, boy, can't take you with me."

Grover's tail drooped dejectedly as he followed Cate to Robin's car.

BACK AT HOME, PROPPED up by pillows and covered, or so it felt, in cats, Robin tried to nap, but between the coughing spasms, the dead weight of Sampson on her thighs and the constant attention of Delilah licking her on the wrist or nudging her cheek, she was unable to sleep. She stroked Delilah's head, felt the indentations of cheekbone and jaw, ran her fingers to the tips of the ears and along the silky tufts extending from the ears.

She coughed again, her legs convulsing. Sampson rode her legs like a roller coaster, then adjusted himself slightly before lowering his head and returning to sleep. She spat into a tissue and saw pink foam. "Nothing unexpected with smoke inhalation," the hospital doctor had said. But also nothing to ignore for someone who's had breast cancer, she knew. She had not consulted her oncologist, but Brad made her promise to have a chest x-ray if the cough wasn't gone in another week.

She tried her visualization techniques, picturing pink, healthy lung tissue surrounding the gray, damaged cells and squeezing them into the airway, where her lungs, like bellows, would eject the dying cells in a cough where they would be deposited in a Kleenex and thrown into the plastic-lined wicker basket.

Delilah nuzzled into her neck, purring, and they both drifted off to sleep.

CATE WAS DOING HER OWN VISUALIZING. While Grover lapped loudly and with abandon from a bowl at her feet, Cate stared at the newspaper spread out on her kitchen counter, specifically at the photo of a smiling Martin Krause, again seated at his desk, the caption proclaiming him still president of Bradford College. The attractive young woman standing over his shoulder was Melissa Dunn's replacement. Cate pictured taking him by the lapels and demanding to know how he could live with himself after destroying so many lives.

HOVERING OVER THE CRIME LAB TECHNICIAN, Harley watched her dust first the outer film canister and then the inner one for prints. Blood samples from the shoe tassel and windbreaker were already undergoing analysis in the adjoining room.

The tech was short and boyishly thin, with cropped hair showing under a gauze hairnet. "They've been wiped." She shook her head and sighed. "Sorry." Then a smile played across her lips. "But I'll bet you a donut there's a full thumb and index on the film tab."

Harley, realizing he hadn't eaten all day, suggested, "How about donuts either way? My treat."

"Deal." She exposed an inch and a half of film, raised one eyebrow at him, and applied the powder to expose two prints, only slightly smeared, one on either side of the film tab.

They were both grinning when she snipped off the useable portion and handed off the remainder to a waiting tech who would take it to the on-site photo lab.

He had nothing to do but wait. And listen to the growling of his stomach. It was only a few minutes' drive to a hamburger joint, where he downed a double burger with cheese, bacon, and onions, then proceeded to the donut shop known to anyone who carried a badge in Wisconsin. Not knowing the lab tech's preference, he bought a dozen, mixed, from which he extracted a sugared jelly donut.

Back at the lab, he presented the box of donuts to the crew. The tech with short hair smiled and gestured to his face. Sheepishly, Harley brushed sugar from the corners of his mouth.

Out of the corner of his eye, he saw a man in a lab coat coming toward him, holding up a slim handful of photos. "Done!" the man announced. "Only six of 'em. After that, the film was never exposed."

Harley's heart beat with anticipation as his fingers gripped their edges. The first photo, overexposed in the lower corner, perplexed him. Todd Hill, one of the early suspects by virtue of being Melissa's boyfriend, sat in a coffee shop, mugging into the camera. He guessed that someone had gotten hold of Melissa's camera and then hidden the film in the loft.

Harley slipped that to the back and saw a shot, taken from above, of Spirit Falls with the Bentley cabin visible on the far side of the creek. The next, probably taken from the same vantage point, showed the creek directly below the falls, just upstream from where

Melissa's body had been found.

Creepy, he thought. Did she have a premonition about her own death?

Two more photos showed a smiling couple. One had a horizontal orientation, the other vertical. Martin and Melissa posed with their arms around each other in the first. In the second, Melissa held two fingers behind Martin's head in a V, while he positioned a strand of her hair, mustache-like under his nose. Behind them was Ross Johnson's cabin.

In the last photo, leaning against a sunlit rail of the cabin's deck and holding highball glasses, were Martin Krause in a coral nylon windbreaker and Ross Johnson in slacks and a pair of loafers. With tassels. These last three prints were date-stamped for the last Friday anyone had seen Melissa Dunn alive. After that, nothing. These were the last pictures Melissa Dunn would ever take.

Harley's lips curled in a grin. "Gotcha!"

33

Sara Brill smacked her flashlight on her desk with a sharp metallic clap. Her freckles stood out against her pale face, pinched in exasperation as she turned to him. "Stop with the damn pen already."

Harley was taken aback by her strident tone. He clicked his ballpoint pen two more times before slipping it into his pocket. He wasn't about to be ordered around by her, of all people.

She slid a white tube from her purse and inserted it into her left nostril, and blocking her right with a forefinger, she snorted. "Allergies," she explained before turning to him in a confrontational manner. "Why don't you try using that restless energy for good instead of evil."

"I'm still waiting for the lab results." He spread his hands wide. "What do you expect me to do?"

Brill closed her eyes and shook her head. "Do what you tell *me*. Go back over everything you have and see it with new eyes. Talk to the witnesses. Ask new questions. Ask the same questions." Her pager beeped and she looked at the message. "Gotta go."

He waited until he heard her exit the building, then picked up the phone and dialed. He got answering machines at the Bentley residence and again at the Running Wolf residence. Or was it just Wolf? He wasn't sure how that worked. He dialed Foxy Tripp's number.

"I don't have another client for, um, forty-three minutes," she told him.

Harley let out his pent up breath. "Okay, I'm just going over this Dunn case and want to make sure I've got my T's dotted and my, uh, you know what I mean."

"And your eyes crossed?" Foxy's laugh was warm, easy.

Harley indulged in a laugh. "Right. So I'm just wondering if there's anything you can remember, anything you haven't mentioned."

There was a pause. "I think we've told you everything."

"Yeah."

Another awkward silence. "So, do you think your friend Cate is, y'know, clairvoyant?"

She didn't laugh at him. "To a degree, yes. I think her instincts are good. She's very attentive to detail so she picks up on things others might miss. But there's more to it."

"Like?" He shifted in his seat and found himself smiling.

"Well, for one thing, we know people have animal instincts about danger. Take pheromones, for instance. They're secret scents that can warn us about danger or identify someone's identity. They're even part of our sexual attraction to each other."

Harley almost choked.

"Cate isn't always accurate, but it's uncanny how often she is right. If she thinks Melissa was alive when she went over the rail, I tend to believe it." She cleared her throat. "And please don't think I'm all into séances and fortune tellers. I mean, science hasn't even begun to scratch the surface of the paranormal. As a cop, don't you rely on gut feelings?"

Ignoring his demotion, he replied, "All the time."

They both sighed.

"Well, if you think of anything, you just call me, okay?"

"I sure will." She sounded like she meant it.

"I mean anything. I'm just sitting here waiting for lab results that I'm hoping will put that creep Krause away."

"You think he's guilty, then."

"I do. This is the time in any investigation when you've got nothing to do but wait. The tension gets to you, y'know?"

"Tension, huh? I just happen to know a good massage therapist." He thought about her hands on his shoulders. "Yeah, I forgot. You do, uh . . ."

"Massage."

"Right. Say, maybe you could, y'know, do something with the knots in my neck."

"I could. But it would be a long drive for you. I work in Saint Paul." Her laugh was light.

"I'm actually going to Saint Paul this Friday. Say, for this, uh, massage, you keep your clothes on for that, right?

"I always keep my clothes on." She laughed again. "Yours, however, are optional."

The sheriff felt the blood creep up his neck and turn his face glow-in-the-dark red.

THE LAB SHOT BACK RESULTS in record time. Blood found on Martin Krause's nylon windbreaker and Ross Johnson's shoe tassel matched Melissa Dunn's. Fibers tweezed from the bridge railing had been snagged from the front of the very same coral windbreaker, the shredded ends fitting together like a jigsaw puzzle. This placed Martin at a point on the bridge very near the spot, where, according to George Wellman's deposition, he had found Melissa's bracelet.

Martin Krause had no hint of swagger as the news cameras covered his arrest in Minneapolis, his extradition to Wisconsin and his perp walk into the courthouse. In the ensuing interrogation, as evidence against him mounted, his speech became less articulate and at times he referred to his wife as if she were still alive.

When gruesome photos of his dead lover were slapped down on the table in front of him, one after another, he began to crumble. But it was Sheriff Harley who played the winning card—a bluff, perhaps, but well played.

"When you and Ross Johnson picked up Melissa's body and heaved her over the railing into the creek, did you realize she was still alive?"

The prisoner began to raise his eyes, then shut them tightly. "She was—?"

His lawyer clamped a hand on his forearm. "Not another word."

"Did you feel her heart beat against your chest when you held her up, ready to throw her to her death? Did her eyelids flutter? She would probably have survived if you'd gotten her to the hospital." He waited a beat, two beats, three. "Her body was warm in your arms, wasn't it?"

Martin put his head into the crook of his arm where it lay on the table. "Stop!" he sobbed.

The attorney's lips tightened ever so slightly as he fought to conceal his disgust. "May I have a moment with my client?" asked the lawyer.

MARTIN AND MELISSA DUNN HAD, according to his admission statement, been under the influence of alcohol and "an illicit substance" when she left the party and, seeing that she was "wildly emotional," he agreed to drive her home. Distracted by *her* impaired state, *he* hit a tree and though he was unhurt, she was "bleeding from a head wound and barely conscious." He told her to hang on until he could get help. Running back to the cabin in a driving rain, he risked death by "the almost continuous lightning strikes." Once at the cabin, without attracting attention from the others, he told his friend Ross, who informed him that the phone lines were down. Together they drove back to the scene of the accident.

"There I found Melissa Dunn covered in blood and unresponsive. The head wound was more grievous than I'd first thought. After many attempts to revive her, I was desperate and wanted to take her to the nearest hospital, but Ross checked her over and assured me it was too late."

Martin went on to describe his inconsolable grief that ended in the decision to drive her the quarter mile to the bridge and dump her body over the railing. And though he pronounced the act "indefensible," he went on to defend himself on the basis of the "overwhelming influence of alcohol, drugs, and Ross Johnson's unrelenting pressure."

It was never officially concluded whether Melissa was alive or dead when she hit the water. Perhaps none of the participants in her death knew either, but the unofficial conclusion was that all three had caused her death—her secret lover, by not getting her to a hospital immediately, his wife Brenda by bashing her head with a rock, and if poor Melissa had managed to survive that, Ross Johnson and Martin Krause had surely done the deed by pitching her into the creek to be killed either by the impact on the rocks below or by drowning.

Due to overcrowding, President Krause was transported to the minimum-security portion of the prison in Stillwater, Minnesota, and immediately put on suicide watch.

Sheriff Harley called Robin as soon as the deal was finalized. Her husband answered and said she was sleeping. At two in the afternoon.

He dialed Cate's number. "Your hunches paid off!" he said before he realized the voice on the other end was a recording.

THE NEXT MORNING SHERIFF HARLEY decided to catch up on paperwork he'd sidelined in recent weeks. Deputy Brill was packing for a vacation in North Dakota. He figured he could live without her for a week.

He had the place to himself. After a couple hours of filing and returning phone calls, he sat back and put his feet up on a newly vacant corner of his desk. To his growing pleasure, no one was there to criticize him for being unprofessional. As he gazed at his stockinged toes, they moved, just a slight twitch to begin with, then his whole foot began bouncing nervously. Damn, it was quiet! He sat up, feet again on the floor, and thrummed blunt fingertips on the desk. It was just too blasted quiet to think! Something was missing.

Maybe he should just jump in his vehicle and ticket some speeders. He heard a car door. Damn Brill. If she was coming back . . .

From the hallway he could see the door to the parking lot. Suddenly he found himself looking into a pair of black eyes set in a massive face. And below the face, a red tie. No, not a tie, he saw, but a tongue. He grinned back at Grover who gave him a bark in greeting, spattering the bottom half of the door with drool.

At the other end of the leash was Cate Running Wolf.

He rushed to open the door.

Cate held tight to the leash and said, "I know you're eager to see your buddy."

Robin came into view. "Maybe we ought to keep all that energy outside," she said.

Harley laughed and squeezed through the door. "Hey, there, boy." He patted Grover's flank. His voice, still soft, took on a different tone. "Grover, sit." The dog sat.

"I got your message," Cate said, and since Robin was already—"

"I was already coming up because I need to take a few photos to replace the ones that—" Her voice caught. "Anyway, Cate decided to come along."

"Grover was driving me nuts," Cate protested. "I needed to get him out of the house."

Robin stopped her. "So he could drive us all nuts."

Harley enjoyed their easy banter.

"So." Cate looked at him, her eyes shrewd. "You said in the message that my hunches were right."

He raised his wrist to look at his watch. "If you haven't eaten yet, we could all run over to the A & W and I'll fill you in. If we eat outside, this little guy won't have to sit in a hot car."

Robin and Cate looked at each other and said, simultaneously and with the same inflection and tilt of the head, "Okay. Sure."

SITTING AT THE SHADED PICNIC bench behind the drive-in, he told them of Martin Krause's statement of admission. They eagerly listened, protesting only when he said, "They agreed to a term of forty-two months, with ten years' probation."

"But he could be out in less than two years," Cate wailed.

Robin sucked in breath to say something, but instead doubled over in a coughing fit. When she could breathe again, she said. "I'm tired of this nonsense."

Cate looked worried. "Maybe this trip was a bad idea."

Robin shook her head. "I'm fine, really."

"That cough doesn't sound good," said Harley.

"I'm fine," she reiterated. "Anyway, what kind of punishment is that for murder?" Robin demanded.

Harley examined a hangnail. "That's the bugger about it." He gnawed his cuticle and spat something onto the grass. "Truth is, we're lucky to get anything on him at all. And think of it this way: two of the three bad guys are dead, and the other one's in prison, maybe not for long, but he's lost pretty much everything that ever mattered to him."

Cate tossed a chunk of hamburger in Grover's direction. He caught it on the fly. "It just seems to me—" She exhaled in indignation. For the moment she was speechless.

"Yeah, it's frustrating, all right. Believe me, if it were up to me, he'd rot there, but without his confession, this case wouldn't even be about murder. In fact, if it weren't for all of you, I suppose Melissa Dunn would just be another drowning." He hand-fed Grover a french fry.

Robin shifted uncomfortably. "I know we should be celebrating this, but I can't help feeling bad for Melissa's parents. If we hadn't exposed this whole mess, they could just go on believing their daughter died accidentally, rather than having to read in every lousy magazine about her affair with a married man and how she dabbled in drugs."

"At least, they know the truth." Cate's look had grown solemn too. "The truth would've come out eventually. It's better this way."

Grover stood and surveyed the small grassy area behind them. Cate jumped up. "I know that look."

The dog squatted. Robin grabbed her hamburger wrapper and handed it to Cate.

"Got anything about four times that size?" Cate asked with an apologetic grimace.

"Wait a sec. I've got just the thing." Sheriff Harley sprinted to his car and returned with a large evidence bag. He scooped up the mess and deposited it in the covered trash container. "You know, I was thinking," he said as they headed to their respective vehicles, "If you're gonna take pictures, I'd be happy to keep an eye on the dog."

Robin and Cate looked at each other conspiratorially.

"No, really. He enjoys riding shotgun."

They looked at each other again. "Actually—" they began and stopped at the same moment, laughing.

"Actually, we have a proposition for you," Cate said. "How do you feel about adoption?"

He looked bereft.

"Adopting Grover," Robin clarified.

Harley's eyes lit up. "You mean—?"

"Yup," Cate said and Robin nodded, grinning.

Cate shrugged. "I've never seen such a natural with dogs, and Grover—Grover, what's gotten into you?" The dog was pawing deliberately at the door of the squad car.

"Wanna get in, buddy?" Sheriff Harley strode over and opened the door.

Grover understood the opportunity. He jumped in, where he sat, proud as the new deputy he was, in the passenger seat.

EPILOGUE

We gathered for a private memorial service on the concrete patio overlooking Spirit Falls, where we stood looking at the rubble that had once been a magnificent chimney. Three weeks and two rains hadn't removed the stench of fire or the soot covering everything in sight. Louise uncorked a bottle of champagne and Grace provided the stemware. Then, without making a formal toast, we jumped right into telling funny or poignant stories about the deceased.

"It just won't be the same, will it?" Louise said. She didn't bother to wipe away the tears trickling down her cheek.

We shook our heads. More than one of us sniffled.

"I just can't believe she's really gone." Foxy's tone was somber. Heads nodded in assent.

The silence went on until Cate spoke what we were all thinking. "She may be gone. But you can't keep a good woman down." She turned and grabbed the hand at her side. "She can be rebuilt, can't she, Robin?"

Robin squeezed back. Her lips curled in a knowing smile. "I've already done some preliminary drawings. And this time, she won't be decorated with dead animals."

And just like that, the heaviness lifted. We clinked glasses, celebrating the long and rich life of the cabin. It could, we all agreed, be rebuilt, because it was not the wood and stone that had made the cabin extraordinary, but the idyllic setting and the spirited people who gathered there. Nothing like a near-death experience to remember what's important.

We talked about events leading to the fiery death of the cabin, and decided that we made a pretty good detective team. It took all of us working together to make the puzzle pieces fit, but without us, Melissa Dunn's murder may never have been solved. We celebrated our strength in numbers, and admitted that along the way we'd discovered some individual strengths as well, strengths you don't usually associate with youth.

Robin summed it up. "As long as we accept that we've reached the age of character lines and power surges, we might as well claim the wisdom we've accumulated. Right?"

"Right," Cate agreed. "We are, after all, no ordinary women."

Molly Pat just rolled her eyes and yawned.

THE END